# CHOOSE
# YOU
# THIS DAY

# CHOOSE YOU THIS DAY

Walker Buckalew

Fideli Publishing Inc.
WWW.FIDELIPUBLISHING.COM

Library of Congress Control Number:  2011945909

ISBN: 978-1-948638-29-6 (soft cover)
      978-1-60414-516-8 (hardcover)

*Edited by Kelly Bainbridge*
*Cover illustration and design by Jeff Whitlock, Whitlock Graphics.*

This is a work of fiction. Names, characters, places and incidents are products of the author's imagination or are used fictitiously.

Author photo by JOSH NORRIS PHOTOGRAPHY

www.TheRebeccaSeries.com

# Preface

This story can be read by itself, but it is also a sequel to *The Face of the Enemy, By Many or By Few,* and *Such Thy Mercies.* In this episode, as in the others, approximately one year has passed since the previous story ended.

Regular readers of the Rebecca Series are reminded that these stories are set in the late 1970s and early 1980s, and that being the case:

- telephones will have rotary dials;
- long-distance phone calls will usually involve conversations with long-distance operators;
- there will be no cell phones;
- there will be no Internet; and consequently,
- there will be no email.

*And if it seem evil unto you to serve the Lord,*

*choose you this day whom ye will serve...;*

*but as for me and my house, we will serve the Lord.*

Joshua 24:15

# CHAPTER ONE

KORY VAN DIJK EXITED THE CLASSROOM AND TURNED LEFT down the hallway of the nearly empty London city-center junior school in which she had taught for two years. The gentleman with whom she had just been speaking did not turn his head or his eyes to follow her to his classroom door. Still standing beside the chipped wooden desk that served as home base for the math classes he conducted daily, he looked discreetly out the window until he could hear the woman's soft footfall retreating down the hallway.

He looked up at one of the ceiling fans that air conditioned his room and took a deep, audible breath. This was an unsettling time in the gentleman's life.

Kory van Dijk had just stopped by to tell him — no — to *remind* him on this last day of the school year — that Friday, two days hence, would be her twenty-fourth birthday. Did he, in his role as her "best gentleman friend," want to meet her for a midday celebratory dish of strawberries and cream at the nearby inn? After arguing briefly and facetiously in favor of a ploughman's repast of pickles, cheese, chutney, and biscuits, he acknowledged that, indeed, he did. That settled, the rest of their brief conversation had centered on the near-term future of a difficult young student whom they each had taught at times throughout the school year.

A few moments later he heard the heavy front doors close noisily, and knew he and the school's only custodian, busily working the rooms on the other side of the hallway, were alone in the building. He turned, pulled out his creaking swivel chair and sat down at his desk. Luke Manguson, twenty-nine years of age, began absently to finger the dozens of tiny depressions embedded deeply into the flesh of his left cheek and neck.

Relaxing, he began to consider his situation. Yes, one might judge this to be an unsettling time in one's life, provided one wished that sort of dispassionate assessment. But if one preferred a more personal slant, and if that personal slant was Luke Manguson's own personal slant, the only workable assessment would be a *miserable* time in one's life.

For, truth be told, he had begun to fear that he had fallen in love with his young colleague and "best friend," despite his well-developed wariness toward the idea itself. *In love,* indeed! Had not his aversion to the very notion been responsible for his early and easy decision the previous summer to break off a promising relationship with the Italian beauty who had nursed him back to health after  his and his sister's near-fatal, albeit successful, attempt to rescue the Italian and others along the treacherous Amalfi coast? Did the phrase *in love* possess even a particle of real meaning in these days of imported-from-California definitions for all human relationships? He doubted it.

The fingers of his left hand now swung around to the right side of his face, there encountering none of the irregularly distributed pock marks that covered most of the left. What a surprise, he thought, that he should have returned to school that previous fall expecting to find everyone—headmistress, teaching colleagues, students and their parents—recoiling in disgust at their first sight of his still-fresh shotgun blast wounds, only to find that he seemed to be much more an object of clinical interest than of horrified disgust.

In fact, he could give credit to his freshly developed disfigurement, he thought to himself, for his first real conversation with Kory van Dijk the previous September. In their first year as teaching colleagues, the previous one, they had been no more than nodding acquaintances. He was not entirely certain, in fact, that she had even known his name that year. But when the faculty assembled for the pre-term meetings marking their second fall together, "Ms. van Dijk" had immediately sought him out for the plain purpose of learning the facts behind the startling alteration in his appearance.

He had been extraordinarily impressed with her that day. She had seen him from across the room as most of the several dozen junior-school faculty members were still arriving and finding their seats, and, after gaping in undisguised shock, she had moved fast and straight to his side. She had then squared herself directly in front of him and, unflinching, stared up at the ruined left side of his face and neck. Mouth open, eyes continuing to widen, she had then actually gasped aloud, shaking her head in wonderment.

He meanwhile had simply looked bemusedly down at her, waiting, and had found himself laughing aloud at her opening words: "Luke Manguson! What on earth! You look as though you've been hit with a shotgun spray at point-blank range! What on *earth?*"

Her use of the phrase "shotgun spray" had led to a short diversion into a portion of her past that further elicited his attention. She had served, she explained to him, two years in the Royal Navy, toiling as an enlisted communications technician. Although she had never left London during her service, she had been steeped in military terminology and discipline by the time she had reached her twenty-first birthday. Released from her active duty commitment at that time, she had completed her military-interrupted preparation for junior-school teaching in a single academics-packed year.

In any case, her blunt-implement approach to his "new look" had drawn from him his heartiest laughter, a genuine response to her forthright, unabashed concern and curiosity. And from there, the friendship had grown steadily throughout the fall, continued into the winter, and finally bloomed, altogether alarmingly from his perspective, in the spring. They were fast friends now, sitting together often in church, attending the occasional stage play together, and twice visiting the center-city museums. He was even on casual speaking terms with her parents, to whom she had introduced him at the Easter sunrise service.

But when and where, he asked himself, had this friendship begun to deteriorate into "love"?

Rising from his desk and moving to the expanse of windows that ran along one side of his classroom, he stared unseeing toward the playgrounds and parking lots, concentrating fully on his own question. After a moment, he decided to attempt a real answer.

The friendship had begun to turn to romance, he decided, with the arrival of two completely unwelcome but determinedly persistent thoughts. He had no idea if one had preceded the other, or if they had burst into his mind hand-in-hand.

The more startling of the two was that he had found himself beginning mentally to try her on, as it were, as a life companion… as his wife… as a woman eventually to become one flesh with him forever. Each time, as soon as he realized what was happening, he had hastily dismissed the thought and moved on. Yet, time and again, that very idea had returned, resisting expulsion, as though it relished torturing him.

The other was a sudden, explicit consciousness of how she *looked.* Of course, he would have been able to say, even in the early weeks of their having become colleagues almost two years previous, that she was a small woman — not more than five-feet two-inches tall and 110 pounds in weight at the most — and that she was pretty. But he would have been able to say little more than that, even if asked about her appearance after having just passed her in the school's hallways.

Then, suddenly, at Christmastime in this second school year together, he had realized that he knew *exactly* how her eyes looked. Knew that they were a deep, dark brown. Nearly chocolate.

Knew *exactly* how her hair looked. Knew her hair was also brown, though it was quite a different brown from her eyes. Lighter by far. And shoulder length, with subtle waves that changed their shape when she walked or turned her head quickly. He found that he had begun to want to touch that wavy brown hair at times.

This was very bad.

But there was more. He realized that her telephone voice had lodged itself securely in his mind. Her voice played itself over and over again after every conversation, no matter how brief. He might phone her on a Saturday evening to say, "Kory? Luke. Are you going to the 10:30 service tomorrow? Yes? Shall I find you on the right? Good, then."

All she might have said in response was, "Yes," "Yes," and "I'll see you there then." But her voice and those few words would continue to float through and around his mind, making him smile for no reason that he could rationally explain.

She spoke a not-exactly-standard Oxford dialect, one that seemed to him to be tinged with something else. Given her name and its spelling, he was not surprised when, upon asking her finally about the "something else," he had learned that her father had immigrated to England from Holland shortly after the Second World War's conclusion. She was fluent in Dutch, a language used more than English by her parents during their early years in London.

There was more. He suddenly was aware that she disdained cosmetics and jewelry, just as did his twin sister Rebecca. He noticed how her skin seemed to shine simply from what he imagined was plain soap and water. A fresh-scrubbed face. Bright and happy and clean. He knew that her small nose turned up just a little at the end, making her face what people would be inclined to call cute, rather than beautiful. But he had no interest in the labels — cute, beautiful or any other — because what he had come to care about was simply the fact that it was *her* face. It was *Kory's* face.

There was yet more. Also like Luke's own sister, his youthful colleague was a runner. Not the kind of powerful and swift runner, nor all-round athlete, that Rebecca had always been, but a light, almost dainty runner, who seemed to skim the surface of the ground as though she might be floating just above it. Just thirty minutes a day, three days a week, in the mornings in summer and in the evenings during the school year. He had begun occasionally to accompany her on her evening runs.

And finally, he knew more clearly than he had allowed himself to realize previously that this woman was a superb intellect, and that she applied that intellect gracefully in every setting in which she found herself: in Christian dialogue in adult classes they sometimes attended together at their church; in pedagogically oriented discussion with their teaching colleagues in the weekly faculty meetings; in conversations just between the two of them, at which times their discussion might range from the ethical implications of particular New Testament passages to the writings of G. K. Chesterton and George MacDonald to the military/political nuances and ramifications of the Napoleonic wars. At such times Kory van Dijk did not seem to him what she actually was: more than five years his junior.

Luke raised both hands to his face and rested his elbows on his desk. He moaned softly to himself.

This was very, *very* bad.

Kory van Dijk allowed the double doors of the school building to close noisily behind her and began the five-block walk to her small flat. She allowed her mind to play through the conversation she had just completed with Luke Manguson, first thinking of the tentative conclusions they had drawn about the student on whom they had focused, then on the birthday date they had set for Friday and finally to the topic they had *not* discussed: their maturing friendship with each other.

That was, of course, the topic that they had never discussed. Perhaps they never would. And she knew that she could be perfectly accepting of that. Her understanding of her Christian calling was that she was to teach young people at this point in her life, and to continue in that vocation until… well… until she was called, if ever, by the Holy Spirit toward something else that would stand in place of, or in addition to, her calling to teach.

As for this man, Luke Manguson, she recalled that she had noticed him from the first faculty meeting, nearly two years previous, when she had moved to this, her very first teaching post. It would have been hard not to notice him.

Physically, he was an absolutely arresting figure. Ramrod-straight, reflecting his five years' shipboard service as an officer in the Royal Navy, he was perhaps an inch less than six feet in height. But his massive arms and chest were so outsized that one found oneself staring, if for no other reason than to absorb these other-worldly proportions, found as they were in this case in an otherwise seemingly normal-sized human being.

And he was handsome, too, though not exactly in a movie star way. Or maybe he was handsome in a movie star way, just not in a leading man way. Or maybe that was wrong, too.... *Oh, stop it!* she said to herself. It's just that, because he was such a compelling physical presence, she had found herself working especially hard in their first school year together *not* to allow him to think that she noticed. All very absurd and adolescent she knew. But that's how it had been. She had never been very good at this, the purely social aspect of relationship-building, either with men or women.

Then, when she had seen him across the room at the first faculty meeting of their second year, she found that her heart had leaped at the sight of him. And that was *before* she noticed something wrong with the left side of his face and neck. Then she *had* stared, first from across the room and then from a position no more than arm's length, directly in front of him, drawn equally by the desire finally to initiate a real conversation with him and by an overwhelming and perhaps somewhat inappropriate fear that he had been hurt badly.

She had been certain on that day that she was making a complete fool of herself in her open-mouthed, gaping stare and in her blunt, shocked comment on the devastation wreaked by the shotgun's violent, flesh-rending work. And yet he seemed from the first to have delighted in this very foolishness that had so embarrassed her.

Then the year had become, for her, a whirlwind of around-the-clock engagement with students and their parents, with preparation for her classes, with service on her church committees, and… sporadically… with Luke Manguson. And now it was over. The school year was at an end and, following the silly birthday date for strawberries and cream that she had just arranged in her usual clumsy way, she knew that a full three months might pass without more than the incidental and almost unavoidable contact they would have at church.

She looked up. She was at her apartment. She turned onto the short walkway up to her front door, shaking her head at herself. In some ways she was still as much a child as she had been when she was half her current twenty-three years.

Placing her key in the door, she rolled her eyes in frustration. Would she suddenly become an adult on Friday, magically aged by strawberries and cream with Luke Manguson on her twenty-fourth birthday? Hardly.

She closed her front door and called out: "Tiny! I'm home." And her young tabby came running, her high-pitched, squeaky meow gladdening Kory van Dijk's suddenly melancholy heart.

Martha Clark put down the phone, stood, and looked out the side door of her compact home on the outskirts of the town of Oakham, an easy one hundred driving miles north of London. She watched a young brown rabbit roll on its back, right itself, and then scratch its belly, dog-like, in the soft grass she and her husband had cultivated over the twelve months that had passed since they had moved from Birmingham.

After a moment, she spoke.

"Paul," she called out, rather softly and somewhat absently, still watching the rabbit, "Rebecca and Matt just called." She paused. "They want to know if we're coming next weekend."

Hearing no answer from her husband, she peered obliquely toward the backyard and saw him kneeling, just preparing to dig in their ever-expanding flower bed. She smiled.

She liked this pastoral existence, turned upside down in its priorities from the days in which Paul's professional choices determined where they lived and how they organized their lives. This time, once they had reached the decision three years ago not to return from their native England to the New York City life they had known for a quarter century, Paul had placed home before job for the first time in their lives together.

Martha smiled to herself a second time. To be candid, she admitted, *she* had chosen the locations — first, Birmingham as a temporary expedient, then, after two years, Oakham — and then had asked Paul to find teaching posts as near her choices as he could. He had done exactly that, and seemingly happily enough, first accepting temporary posts in two of Birmingham's small-university settings, and then this permanent — in prospect — position in Oakham. It had appeared to her that, from the first day here, the experience of teaching at the Oakham School had surprised her husband. Or perhaps he had surprised himself. He had found that he actually *liked* teaching these young people, though he was not quite certain he knew why.

Martha's own theory was that Paul had never truly enjoyed teaching under-graduate students, either at Cambridge or at Columbia or in the two temporary posts in Birmingham. Rather, he had liked research and writing. He had simply tolerated teaching.

But here, at this midlevel preparatory school, the teenage boys and girls un-der his tutelage had, in the American phrase they had both learned to use during their time in New York, "grown on him." He had grown close to these young-sters in ways that would have been impossible at the prestigious universities in which he had primarily invested himself until now. And so Martha had seen her husband in his fifties expand his capacity to engage and serve others in ways that thrilled and delighted her. She knew he had always felt that the academic life was his Christian calling. Here, with these more malleable youth, she could see him deepen as a servant of Christ. She smiled to herself a third time.

And then she frowned.

And she knew why she frowned, as she allowed herself now to focus on the present. It was the phone call from their son and daughter-in-law. There was nothing ominous or foreboding, exactly, in the words the two had spoken to her in their brief chat this June Friday morning. No, but there had been something unspoken that had begun to trouble her, something just beneath the surface of this seemingly routine telephone exchange among close family members.

Martha walked into the family room and sat down at the small desk that served as her writing table. This desk was the site of her daily morning devotions and now, beginning to concentrate harder on her unsettled response to the ex-change with Matt and Rebecca, she reached for her Bible, situated as always just under the reading lamp at the left rear of the desk's smooth cherry surface. She placed the Bible in front of her, but did not open it.

Both hands resting on its grainy cover, she focused on what had just hap-pened. Matt, her now thirty-year-old only child, had seemed cheery enough. *How had her week gone?* he had asked. *How well had the youth-night service been attended on Tuesday? How had his Dad's community lecture been received the next night?* And then… *Would they, in fact, be coming to London to visit next weekend?*

A simple enough question, she thought to herself, and worded altogether casually. "Mom, will you and Dad be coming to the city to see us and the twins next Saturday?" he had asked lightly.

Rebecca Manguson Clark, her son's wife of nearly two years now, had given birth just four months earlier to Joanna Mason Clark and Samuel Manguson Clark, and Martha had found herself from the start fighting against the impulse to drive to London *every day* to visit the grandchildren. And she had restrained herself nicely enough, she thought. After she and Elisabeth Manguson, Rebecca's mother and one of Martha's oldest and closest friends, had alternated time with the new mother and her tiny brood every few days during the first month, Martha had determined to restrict her visits to one weekend per month, unless specifically invited by the new parents.

She and Paul were, consequently, not preparing to drive to London the next morning, nor had they been there on the two weekends previous. The reasonable expectation in the minds of all concerned, then, would be that they would, as usual, make the two-hour drive on the upcoming weekend, eight days away. And so, it seemed, her son's question should have struck her as unexceptional.

She looked down at her hands as they rested on her still-closed Bible. What *exactly* was troubling her? She concentrated harder.

She focused on the fact that, after she and Matt had spoken for several minutes, Rebecca had come on the line and, after her own pleasantries, had asked the same question: Would they, in fact, be coming the following weekend?

And then Martha knew. There was a certain unmistakable intensity in her daughter-in-law's voice that belied the routine content of her query. Martha's mind instantly moved in a direction that frightened her and sent a chill radiating through her body. And suddenly, helplessly, she found herself caught up in a maelstrom of images: *the cathedral visions… the arena visions… the Amalfi visions. . . .* And now… what? Her mind flew to the grandchildren. She found that placing those vision-dominated images together with that of her twin grandchildren unleashed a flood of fear that washed over and through her. But this was, after all, the month of June. Yes… this was June, the month in which, for three successive years, visions and danger and death had visited this family and had, she hoped and prayed, finally been put to an end the summer before. But was this *ever* truly to be put to an end? Was it reasonable to expect such evil simply to bow out of their earthly experience? To acknowledge final defeat?

Still looking down at her hands, she slowly lifted her Bible and gingerly raised one of the black ribbon markers. She watched the silky pages obediently separate. And then she began to read the words that called out to her from the twenty-fourth chapter of Joshua:

*"And if it seem evil unto you to serve the Lord, choose you this day whom ye will serve…; but as for me and my house, we will serve the Lord."*

She stopped and spoke the phrase aloud: "... *choose you this day....*"

Placing the Bible, still open to Joshua, flat on her desk, she moved her hands to her face. She closed her eyes and prayed: "Dear Father in Heaven, I ask Your presence with this family. Please help us each to know and understand what You now ask of us. Please help us to know Your will for us. Please help us not to flee from our calling... from Your heavenly voice... from the Voice from which no man or woman must ever flee.... In the name of Our Lord and Savior, I pray this now. *Amen.*"

She closed the Bible slowly and thoughtfully, then stood and stepped away from her desk. She padded down the narrow hallway toward the rear of the house. Now striding more quickly as she approached the back door, she opened it and called softly to her husband as he, still on his knees, spaded earth for his new planting: "Paul, dear... please come in when you find a good stopping place. I need you, I'm afraid."

And just as Martha Clark had detected something in the essence of Rebecca Manguson Clark's voice on the telephone, Paul Clark heard the echo of that essence in his wife's soft request. Eyes widening and jaw suddenly tense, he dropped his spade to the ground in midstroke and pushed himself immediately to his feet. He turned his face to his wife's, and their eyes met and locked.

And he knew.

It was starting again.

Two hours later, following a lengthy and prayerful conversation with her husband, Martha Clark stood at the kitchen sink gazing out her east-facing window at the fine chestnut tree they had been able to nurse back to robust health during the fall and spring of this, their first year of residence in their Oakham home. The sun was directly overhead now, the chestnut's shadow folded neatly under its strong arms. Paul was upstairs washing up, and she was just turning to the cupboard to reach for the bread when an odd sensation passed through her mind, a wave of light that seemed to wash her brain clean of all thoughts in preparation for something.

"Oh no!" she exclaimed softly and, incredulous, her left hand gripping the edge of the countertop for support, she sank deliberately, turning her body as she did, onto the floor and into a sitting position, her back resting now against the pantry door she had been reaching to open. She brought her hands purposefully to her face, covering her eyes for what she knew was coming.

And as sure as Heaven it came.

Three years had passed since Martha Clark had last been visited by the eyes-open dreams that had first come to her three decades before, in her early twenties. The visions had in each case been the harbinger of divine dramas that would proceed to play themselves out in day-to-day action in which her role was, in part, to furnish vision-derived "intelligence" — the military term — to her fellow combatants in wars between what could only be described as Good against Evil. Or, more accurately, as God against Evil. For the Forces at work were certainly personal, and they were just as certainly supernatural.

But now, as she sat on the cool floor in her small kitchen, she knew she had not the luxury of time to reminisce about her earlier visionary experiences. She and Paul had just spent the better part of two hours speculating about the possible meanings of Rebecca Manguson Clark's tense voice in her earlier phone call, wondering if their daughter-in-law had herself just experienced a new vision as indeed she had for each of the past three Junes. But the Clarks' speculation had focused exclusively on Rebecca, not on Martha, the *other* dreamer, for it had long since appeared that, once Rebecca became the recipient of supernaturally initiated dreams, Martha was no longer involved in the battles in that way. In fact, for the past two summers, Martha and Paul Clark had been ensnared not at all in the ongoing struggles that had repeatedly threatened their son, Matt; their daughter-in-law, Rebecca; Rebecca's brother, Luke; and the others.

Still leaning against the bread cabinet, her face still in her hands, Martha took a deep breath and prepared herself in the only way she knew: *Father, Thy handmaid awaits: I am ready; do with me as You will. I will do my best. I will do my….*

And then the vision was upon her. Her hands dropped, now clenched, to her lap. As she sat erect, completely motionless, her floor-level view of the kitchen was at first obscured and then obliterated by an image that quickly dominated every aspect of her mind. The image — with sharp, clear borders and bright, bold colors — formed itself directly in front of her wide-open eyes and she stared, focused, prepared to "see" and to remember every aspect of what was about to be given her.

The vision that formed itself placed the dreamer's perspective high above a quiet scene in which she looked down from across a residential street at a series of modest town houses, and upon a woman of perhaps sixty years. The tall woman stood before what the dreamer presumed to be her own town home, with her back to the front door. She appeared to have just retrieved something from the walkway in front of her doorstep, and now she held the parcel — a small, unwrapped, perhaps wooden box — in her hands, looking down at it.

Then the woman made as if to turn to reenter her home, paused, turned back, and looked up and down the street in front of her house. Apparently seeing no one, she then seemed to decide to open the box then and there, in her front yard. She placed her left hand under the box and removed its lid with her right, moving the lid underneath the box so that her right hand could support the thing entire. Her left hand now free to separate the wrapping paper that pushed up from inside the box, she reached into the cavity and lifted an object which was hidden from the dreamer at first by the woman's hand, but then revealed itself as she turned her hand over. There, unmistakably, black against the white of her hand, was an iron cross, each of its arms bent at the right angles necessary to transform cross into swastika.

The woman stood transfixed, holding the monstrous Nazi symbol in her hand. After a moment, she again raised her face so as to look up and down the seemingly deserted street. And as she did, the image began gradually to fade from Martha Clark's visioning mind.

Yet, before the vision withdrew itself completely, the dreamed aspect shifted, raised itself from its downward perspective on the woman and the hideous object she held in her hand, raised itself steadily toward the horizon behind and beyond her small town home, and finally provided a long view in that direction. As the dream faded, the dreamer was presented with a pastoral scene of small homes giving way to rolling fields, giving way in turn, in the distance, to what appeared to be the glistening expanse of a rather dreary seascape, one fronted by a low, possibly grassy ridge that seemed positioned to fight to protect the fields, the homes, the woman and, yes, even the hideous object she held in her hand from the water's otherwise inexorable advance. And as the dreamed images slowly extinguished themselves, the sun dropped rapidly toward the surface of the slate-gray water.

# Chapter Two

AS MARTHA CLARK'S NOONTIME VISION BEGAN TO WITHDRAW from her mind's eye, Kory van Dijk and Luke Manguson, one hundred miles to her south, sat down to enjoy their celebratory strawberries and cream in a modest center-city London inn within easy walk of each one's home and of their school. For the occasion, she was clad in a light yellow sundress and what she considered her "dressy sandals." He wore a short-sleeved burgundy knit shirt with an open collar, and khaki trousers over his everyday brown loafers.

They were a striking pair: she, with her petite stature and proportionately small features, shoulder-length brown waves unencumbered, light brown skin from weekend gardening contrasting nicely with the bright yellow of the dress; he, with his chiseled features, outsized biceps, forearms, shoulders and chest rippling under the lightweight knit shirt. They looked like a couple perfectly matched and happy to be together.

Both, however, were nervous.

"All good wishes on your twenty-fourth, Ms. van Dijk," said Luke playfully, raising his water glass in her direction.

"Why thank you, good sir," she responded with equal playfulness.

"How does it feel to be all of twenty-four years?" he said, continuing the light banter and thoroughly disgusted with himself for doing so.

"Well… it feels about five years younger than twenty-nine," she replied teasingly.

At this Luke did not laugh. His face became stony.

She, instantly misinterpreting his response, blurted quickly, "Luke… I… I don't mean you're really *old*, you know."

Still he did not smile, nor even seem to hear her remark. He placed his spoon on the saucer that supported his small cup of berries and cream, covered his eyes briefly with one hand, and looked up at her, his face expressionless.

Now her eyes widened. Her right hand had stopped halfway to her mouth, a small dollop of the delicate fruit-and-dairy mixture still awaiting her attention. "Luke?" she said, now alarmed. "What's wrong? I don't understand."

He lowered his voice, conscious of others who sat within easy earshot, and, leaning toward her, nearly whispering, said carefully, "Kory... Kory... I *like* you."

Then, miserable, he covered his eyes again with his right hand. After a moment he heard her spoon clink softly into her own saucer. After several more moments he heard her voice, and looked up to find her now leaning toward him, brown hair falling forward dangerously close to the cream that sat atop her strawberries. "Luke," she said softly, "I... I..."

She stopped. To her acute embarrassment and to his complete astonishment, tears welled up swiftly in her eyes and, unchecked, began an immediate procession down each side of her small nose. She looked down, picked up her cloth napkin, and dabbed at her eyes. She shook her head, glanced up at him, smiled briefly, then looked straight down again.

Finally, in that position, she fell silent.

Her companion considered her carefully for perhaps a full half-minute as she sat, eyes downcast, motionless and mute. Then he rose quickly, stepped athletically around their small round table, and stood behind her chair. He leaned down and, his mouth near her ear, whispered, "Kory, let's go outside. It's too crowded."

She nodded, grateful, and stood.

He slid her chair back as she did, took her hand, and placed his massive left arm around her small shoulders — the first such gesture in their nearly two years of increasing closeness as friends — and steered her to the door. Their strawberries and cream largely untouched and now completely forgotten, the two stepped outside, the man's arm still around the woman's shoulders. He moved her purposefully into the shade of the small side courtyard to which the inn's customers often gravitated on spring and fall days. Reaching the shady and, because of the June heat, unoccupied sanctuary, he stepped in front of her, reached down, took both of her hands in his, and lifted them to his chest.

He looked down at her, a magnified intensity emanating from his nearly-always serious face.

"Kory van Dijk," he began, his voice strong, "my sister always used the word 'courtship' to describe how she and Matt thought of their relationship during the first year they knew each other… before they got engaged to be married."

At the phrase "engaged to be married" he found himself blushing bright red, a rare event for Luke Manguson, but one that he, at that moment, accepted as an unavoidable consequence of the action he had prayerfully — early that morning during his regular devotional time — decided that he must undertake. As a Christian man attracted first in plain friendship and now romantically to a Christian woman, he had known by the time he had completed his morning devotional that this would be the day… this, her birthday… that he must disclose to her what he had never before disclosed to any other woman — because it would not have been true — in his nearly three decades of living.

He had earlier in his life, of course, endured the usual spate of adolescent infatuations. This was not that. Almost a decade earlier, both he and his twin had approached the point at which they no longer "needed," if, in fact, they ever had, to search for "love." It had been for both of them an immensely freeing realization.

He took a breath and looked down into the liquid chocolate of her eyes, glistening pools in which he observed for the second time in three minutes the riveting phenomenon of tears materializing, almost instantly overflowing their boundaries and, without further ado, once more starting their twin paths down each side of her upturned nose. "Kory," he said tenderly, still holding her hands against his muscular chest, "I want us… you and me… to be 'in courtship.' I want us to take each other with the complete seriousness of two people who think it possible that God may want them to… to become engaged… to become a couple… eventually to become a family…."

He paused, looked away for a moment, thinking, then continued.

"I want to know your parents, and I want you to know my parents and my sister and her husband and their infant twins, and I want you to know me in ways that no one except my sister knows me or has ever known me… and even beyond that.

"And I want to know you…."

He stopped.

He released her trembling hands, cradled her face delicately in both of his own, moved his lips deliberately to hers, and holding her face lightly so that she could stop his movement if she wished, he kissed her. Lightly and tenderly, and only long enough to convey to her how much he intended this kiss to mean.

It was, he hoped, long enough to make clear to her that this was no perfunctory kiss between good friends. It was long enough to make obvious to her that this was the kiss of a man who intended to court a woman, and to court a woman for the divine purpose of determining whether or not it was the Holy Spirit's intention that this man and this woman be joined as one forever.

And so, under the leafy canopy provided by the little courtyard adjacent the undistinguished inn in the center of the great city, at midday, in full view of anyone who wished to observe, Kory van Dijk and Luke Manguson kissed. To both of them the kiss tasted of strawberries and cream and birthdays and celebration and Christian joy and Christian promise — all of that, miraculously — in one prolonged moment of earthly time.

No more than a half hour after Luke Manguson and Kory van Dijk's first kiss, Rebecca Manguson Clark, unaware of her brother's unprecedented romantic activity and expecting no visitors at that moment, heard a firm triple knock on her front door. "That's Luke," she thought reflexively, standing at that moment in her twins' bedroom watching them sleep. She turned and walked with her silent, cat-like stride toward the sound.

Rebecca was dressed for action, though none was actually on her schedule for the day. She was clad in white tennis shoes and ankle socks, knee-length khaki shorts, and a light blue, sleeveless knit shirt of the type that she often favored for tennis. Her long, thick, jet-black hair was drawn up into a ponytail, secured by a dark red rubber band. She was dressed and coiffed thus because, once she had recovered her strength after the twins' birth, she had learned to go for brisk walks as short as ten minutes in length, a far cry from her three-miles-and-more minimum of the past, but infinitely better than none. On some days she might manage as many as four walks of ten to fifteen minutes each. Any time the twins were sleeping and her husband or one of the grandparents was in the house, she might dash out the door with just such purpose.

She had lived now for four years in the undistinguished flat, first sharing the apartment with her brother, and then, after her wedding nearly two years previous, with her husband. As she extended her hand toward the front doorknob, she stopped herself, withdrew her hand, stood closer to the door and rapped out a specific pattern against it. Immediately a similar, but not identical, pattern was returned from the outside.

She then opened the door to welcome her beloved twin, already spreading her arms for the joyous embrace they always shared. Then she froze, her arms open wide, surprised to see that her brother, always alone when he called upon her and Matt, was accompanied.

Rebecca's penetrating eyes went quickly to the woman's face, then to her brother's, her eyebrows raised quizzically. He responded by blushing again, his second such response within the hour. Rebecca, her hands now on her hips in mock indignation, beamed. "Oh! I see!" she exclaimed mischievously. "This is Kory! This is KORY!"

And Rebecca stepped forward swiftly onto the front stoop and enveloped the smaller woman completely, submerging Kory van Dijk with her six feet of feminine height and her proportionally remarkable length of feline sinew. As a consequence, the diminutive guest disappeared almost entirely from Luke Manguson's view, only her dainty hands visible to him against the small of Rebecca's back, as Luke stood to one side of the pair, grinning and shaking his head at his sister's impetuous and physically overwhelming greeting.

When the embrace ended, Rebecca said simply, "Kory, my brother cannot seem to do a proper introduction, so let me explain that I am his twin sister and that you are most welcome in our home." Whereupon, playfully ignoring her other guest, Rebecca wheeled, took Kory's arm in her own, and escorted her across the threshold. Luke followed, still grinning, knowing with certainty that his companion would be thoroughly enchanted with the effusiveness of this welcome.

Once inside, Rebecca bade the two guests be seated and, leaning down close to Kory, asked how she liked her tea. As the guest responded, Rebecca saw Kory's dark brown eyes flicker away from Rebecca's gray ones, a *faux pas* that both recognized for what it was.

Rebecca refused to allow the tiny mistake to go either unnoticed or unremarked upon. She turned her face to the left, exposing to Kory the fullest possible view of the V-shaped scar that ran across her right cheek nearly from her mouth to her ear.

"I… I didn't mean to be rude," Kory began in some confusion. "Luke had told me about your scar and how it happened and I…."

"Kory, dear," interrupted her host, "I haven't the slightest embarrassment about my disfigurement, and was greatly disappointed last summer when Luke chose to put his face in front of that shotgun blast. I've no doubt he did it because he was terribly jealous of my scar and simply wanted some of his own."

She looked at her twin and nodded her head knowingly. "Yes. Luke wanted some scars of his own, and it was all he could think of doing at the time. Poor man."

At Rebecca's remark, the trio bubbled forth with laughter.

As Rebecca prepared tea for her guests, Luke escorted his companion quietly down the hallway, with Rebecca's permission, to peek in on the sleeping infants. He then provided a tour of the small flat, returning to the sitting room just as Rebecca placed the tea service on the small table around which they were to gather.

Conversation then began in earnest. And as early afternoon became midafternoon, Kory found herself consumed by several aspects of this person named Rebecca Clark, no single one of which came as total surprise, for Luke had prepared her for each, as fully as words can prepare one for some things.

First, there was Rebecca's physical presence. Kory knew that this twenty-nine-year-old was six feet tall, broad of shoulder, and athletic of demeanor, once an internationally ranked tennis player. She knew of the elegant face with its prominent V-shaped scar, of the stunning gray eyes, of the lustrous black hair that fell halfway down her back.

But she was unprepared for the force of the personality behind the remarkable physical appearance. It was not that Rebecca dominated the three-cornered conversation. On the contrary, she asked many questions of them both and listened intently to their answers. Yet, even in her listening posture, she seemed to Kory a force of nature, a human being who dominated a room simply by being present in it. It was impossible to understand, but there it was, and Kory was filled with wonder.

There was even more than this, however, underlying the young guest's sense of being somehow overwhelmed by an ordinary social encounter. She decided after some thought that it must be at least partly attributable to some combination of three *other* elements in the situation.

First, there was the utter magnificence of the closeness between this brother and sister, a closeness that somehow did not exclude the third party, but enveloped the third party in an intangible embrace. Second, there was the sense that no matter what was being said or done in that small sitting room, a quarter part of Rebecca Clark's mind was down the hallway with her children, alert to the slightest auditory indication of a change in the tiny sleepers. And third, there was simply Kory's continual awareness that she was in the presence of someone who, at three distinct points in her recent life — in fact, each June for the past three years — had received supernaturally initiated visions or messages or commands that had led to some of the most extraordinary and consequential interceptions of Evil that one could possibly conceptualize.

And yet, as the conversation took its course over the next hour and a half, Kory could not have pointed to a single word or action from her host that would have suggested in any sense whatever on the part of Rebecca Clark that she thought of herself as anything out of the ordinary. And Luke had indeed been clear on this point: his sister saw herself as a plain Christian woman — a wife and mother and former teacher — who prayed each morning and each evening and catch-as-catch-can during each day, who listened for God's direction in those private devotional settings, and who then took up her cross daily and followed her Lord and Savior. In Rebecca's mind, that was all. And that was enough.

Yes, each June for the last three, certain supernatural events had transpired. Yes, each time, Rebecca had done her best to respond in obedience. And yes, each time, through God's grace she and her brother and her husband and the others had managed to prevail. And they, each one of them, now carried the wounds and scars that had come hand-in-glove with the danger.

But Rebecca was, to herself, nothing more than a Christian wife and mother. And a onetime teacher of children. That was all.

Kory van Dijk was in awe. She very much hoped it did not show.

Afternoon became evening and brought more arrivals. Matthew Clark returned from the errands on which his wife had earlier sent him. Matt's parents, Martha and Paul Clark, having driven down from Oakham and still wearing their gardening clothes, rushed in not long after. And finally, just before the dinner hour, Rebecca and Luke's own parents, Elisabeth and Jason Manguson, arrived from Birmingham, also seeming hurried and tense as they came in.

Kory saw clearly that these family members were delighted to see each other and seemed genuinely pleased to meet "Luke's colleague from school." Further, she saw that although they were appropriately eager to view and hold the now-wakened Joanna and Samuel, there was some sort of agenda — some major issue or concern — completely filling the house and overshadowing all individual transactions. The agenda, whatever it might be, gave a sense of somewhat hurried prelude to everything that was said and done. This, Kory saw from the moment of Matthew Clark's return from his errands, was going to be no casual family gathering.

This was business.

While Rebecca tended to the twins, Matt, his mother and Elisabeth Manguson took the lead in readying a cold supper, arranging the food buffet-style. Kory took brief notice of Matt's dexterity in these routine movements, despite his not having the use of his left arm and hand. Luke had told her that there had been casualties in the past years' events. This, she knew, was one of them.

Once each had a plate and a chair, and once Rebecca had returned to the room and the blessing had been provided by Jason Manguson at his daughter's request, the business meeting began even as the light meal was being consumed.

It took Kory some time to grasp fully the situation into which she and Luke had stumbled. And when she did, it was almost more than she could bear. The very conditions — the supernaturally originated conditions — that had been thrust upon this group each June for the three years previous were now upon them once again.

And this time, "them" included Kory van Dijk, teacher of children, a woman freshly committed to a courtship with one of her teaching colleagues, a Christian servant of the Lord, and, in her own mind, an utterly unequipped ingénue in the face of this colossal confluence. For as the minutes ticked past, she learned that in this very room were four human beings who, at various times over a period of more than three decades, had been chosen to receive the supernatural visions, images, and messages. She had been warned in advance regarding only one of the four, Rebecca Manguson Clark.

But as the meal was consumed and as the interrelated stories were developed fully, Kory learned that both Elisabeth and Jason Manguson, and, Martha Clark as well, had at various times been chosen as recipients for these inconceivable divine initiatives. And finally Kory came to realize that both Rebecca and Martha Clark had received divine visions within the last twenty-four hours. Rebecca's had come to her, as the dreams had most commonly come to her in the past, in the night, awakening her from sleep. Martha's, in contrast, had come to her, as *her* dreams had most commonly arrived heretofore, in the middle of the day, while she was wide awake and engaged in routine household activities.

Kory noted that she was included in everything that transpired just as if she had been part of the family for years. There were no questioning glances exchanged among these people, no comments about the appropriateness of her full participation in what with each passing moment bade fair to become a war counsel.

Luke Manguson had brought a Christian companion into Rebecca and Matt Clark's home. That was obviously enough.

All through this astonishing experience, Kory was struck by the realization that Luke seemed to attend to her almost in the same way that Rebecca tended to her tiny children. He endeavored at all times to satisfy himself that she felt as comfortable as could be expected and that she was, in fact, willing to stay for what was obviously not going to be the drop-in and drop-out affair they had imagined when he had proposed an impromptu visit to his sister's home. She felt deeply cared for by this man who, just hours earlier, had announced that he *liked* her and wanted to enter into a courtship with her. She walked in a new world.

Early in the meal, when all preliminary explanations had been provided, eyes turned to Rebecca as if by prearrangement, indicating even to the new-comer that all was in readiness to hear the data: the reports from the two dream-ers of the divine initiatives. The reports were to be given in the order received: first, Rebecca's, and second, Martha's.

Putting her plate aside, looking down in concentration and at first speaking softly and somewhat tentatively, Rebecca began. Her audience was suddenly tense in a way it had not previously been. Forks and knives rested quietly, no longer in use, on each dinner plate.

"It was, I think, just after three o'clock this morning," she said. "I had gotten up to nurse the twins about an hour before and had just come back to bed."

She looked at her husband for confirmation. Matt nodded.

"I had just fallen asleep when… when it began."

Here Rebecca rose, stepped around behind her chair, and began to pace the confines of the room, striding to and fro and through and around her listeners. Her voice through long habit escalated in volume, unnecessarily in this case, to the level of her "teaching voice." Her hands also came into play, often clasped together in front of her chest, sometimes stabbing the air for emphasis.

Kory noted that she seemed to be the only one in the room turning to keep her eyes on the speaker. Everyone else appeared to be accustomed to this style of presentation from Rebecca, for their eyes focused straight ahead or on the floor. They were listening intently, concentrating on the words, but obviously saw no need to observe their hostess as she circled through and around the room, stopped, reversed direction, and repeated this general pattern of movement.

"I sat straight up," said Rebecca. "I sat absolutely straight up in bed as soon as I realized that I had not been awakened by the children or by Matt's turning over or by some incidental noise from outside. I knew… I knew that I had been lifted from sleep into wakefulness and that my mind was being prepared to receive the visions… again. I knew instantly what was coming. One cannot mistake this sensation for anything else in the world." Here she looked quickly toward Martha Clark and received from her mother-in-law a knowing smile and nod of the head.

"And so I simply adopted an attitude of absolute obedience," Rebecca continued, still pacing, her strong hands pressed forcefully against each other, "and of readiness to concentrate and to attempt to absorb and remember every detail that would be coming.

"And then in seconds it came. Before I had any idea what I was seeing, I could detect the usual bright colors and clear borders of the overall image. But I could not for some time understand what I was being shown. It struck me simply as some sort of veined, wrinkled, dark green art object. Quite puzzling.

"But then the perspective gradually changed… changed as though my mind's eye were a camera lens slowly pulling away from tight focus and beginning to afford a wider angle… and I saw then that the object was simply a leaf… one leaf among many… and, in fact, one leaf occupying its proper niche… nestled in the place from which it had sprouted and grown.

"I was seeing a tree… at first, just one tree. And I think now that the vision's initial focus on a single leaf was to call my attention to the nature of the leaf. I think now that the *type* of leaf must have some importance to the meaning of the vision… must have some importance in leading me… leading us… to an understanding of what I have been shown. This leaf… these leaves… looked like… looked almost like leather. Their leathery appearance, I've no doubt, accounts for the difficulty I had at first in knowing that this was a leaf at all.

"The tree itself was small, and I don't know enough to say whether it was small because it was young or small because… because smallness happens to be the nature of this individual specimen of God's creation."

Rebecca stopped for a moment and seemed to look down at her still-clasped hands, thinking. The room was silent.

Kory realized at that moment, ruefully, that the others were right not to watch Rebecca as she paced and talked. Watching her was distracting. She was so fascinating physically — the height, the eyes, the hair, the obvious strength in her arms and legs, the athleticism evident in her movements, and, yes, even the facial scar — all these aspects of her person made concentration on her words more, not less, difficult.

Kory looked down and resolved to attend better... to stop watching altogether and to fix her mind more carefully on this woman's words.

"And then," Rebecca resumed, again starting to pace, "I saw... I was allowed to see... that at the foot of my tree there was something metal... an object not resting *on* the ground... but implanted *in* the ground. And, after a moment, I realized that this was a plaque... something with words... with words inscribed or engraved... though I was not given to see the words themselves, and cannot even suggest a language."

She paused again in her monologue, though not in her steady, cat-like movements.

"It was then," she continued, "that the dream began to fade from my mind's eye. But, as it did, the angle of view became broader still... very wide... and I grasped finally... finally... that my little tree and its small plaque comprised just one of many, many such little trees and small plaques... all very much the same... all the same *kind* of tree, I am sure... all the plaques the same size and shape, I am equally sure... everything arrayed in fine, orderly fashion... and then it was gone...."

At the word "gone" Rebecca immediately stopped, now standing completely still. The others looked up or around to see her, some twisting in their chairs. Her eyes had closed and she had drawn her clasped hands up under her chin in an attitude of prayer. The others looked away, waiting.

At the conclusion of her silent prayer, Rebecca opened her eyes, turned, walked thoughtfully to her chair, and resumed her seat. Only then did she turn her eyes to the others, looking from one face to the next as if she were still in her junior school classroom, studying the faces of her students to ascertain the extent of their understanding of what she had just explained.

At length, to the surprise of all, Rebecca smiled brilliantly, her scar moving and compressing itself as it always did in response to this bright smile, and said, "Well... dear family.... That would appear to be my June report from the Holy Spirit *this* year. And I know... we all know... we all know that there will be opportunity and danger and terrible risks. But really, the mere *fact* of the thing... of God's *coming* to us like this. Isn't it all just *amazing?* Just completely *stupendous?*"

These words drew smiles and nods all around the room, although from Kory van Dijk the smile was forced. Those were not the words she would have chosen. The words "mystifying" and "terrifying" were, in fact, foremost in her own mind.

But now Rebecca was speaking. Once more serious of demeanor, she asked, "Are there questions, anyone?" again looking slowly around the room.

No one spoke in response. Several heads shook slowly from side to side.

Rebecca spoke again. "Does anyone recognize my description of the tree? I mean, of the *type* of tree? Or the obviously planned and crafted arrangement of the scene? Small plaques in front of little trees… some sort of memorial, perhaps?" Her eyes continued to survey the faces in the room, none of which could provide a response.

And yet, one of the silent participants could have provided an extensive commentary and explanation of the dreamed scene. The newcomer found herself in an agony of indecision as the already prolonged silence continued.

From the instant Rebecca had described the larger scene — not just one leathery-leafed tree with a small plaque underneath, a description which in itself triggered tentative recognition in Kory's mind, but many such trees and plaques, with every aspect of the scene arrayed in orderly fashion — she had, in a flash of complete comprehension, been altogether certain that she knew what had presented itself to Rebecca in this vision. But, at the same time, she found it incomprehensible that she, Kory van Dijk, ordinary Christian, a person who was present in a room filled with out-of-the-ordinary Christians, and, furthermore, present in that room completely by accident, could, in fact, illuminate and explicate for these others the mysteries implicit in this supernaturally charged circumstance into which she had been thrust. It simply defied logic.

It was not *reasonable* that she, an outsider who had been brought to Rebecca and Matt Clark's home simply in order to be introduced to the two of them and to view and perhaps to hold the two infants briefly, and, possibly, to share a cup of tea before her departure, was in fact the only person in that otherworldly room who could identify and explain the nature of the dreamed landscape. It was too fantastic.

She shook her head, looking down, thereby attracting the attention of the man who had brought her into this supernatural maelstrom. Luke reached over and touched her knees lightly with his fingertips, knees covered by the soft fabric of her yellow sundress.

She looked at him. His eyebrows arched, silently inquiring as to her well-being.

And she smiled at him, not because she could provide the slightest reassurance regarding her well-being at that moment, but because his solicitousness toward her was so… she searched her mind for the word… so… *gallant*… she thought to herself. This amazing man was courting her! And this — this! — was how courtship from Luke Manguson was going to feel.

Then Kory noted with some embarrassment that all three women in the room, not just Luke, were smiling in her direction. She blushed and looked down. She was going to have to get accustomed to this… this familial alertness and sweetness that seemed to saturate the Clark and Manguson households.

Then she smiled once more, this time just to herself, still looking down. Getting accustomed to this sort of thing was going to be… well… delightful.

Suddenly she admonished herself harshly at the realization that she had just indulged herself for long moments thinking about perfectly ordinary things… about courtship… about a man's solicitousness toward her… about the nature of Christian family life. How *could* she, when the clear definition of the situation was that the Universe was weighing in on top of her, and that it was she… just *she*… who recognized and understood something that no one else present recognized or understood at all. But before she could respond to her own blandishments, she heard a new voice.

It was Martha Clark's.

As the recipient of the second dream in the new sequence, it was time for her report. And, Kory noted to herself, "report" was the correct word. They were receiving *data* from supernatural sources. These were supernaturally communicated *facts* on the basis of which they would presumably be called upon to formulate plans and then to execute those plans.

She shook her head again in wonderment. But then she turned her eyes to Martha Clark and, as did everyone else, gave full attention to this, the second dreamer in the new crisis.

Unlike Rebecca, Martha spoke from her chair. But exactly like Rebecca, she recounted with care and precision the details of her midday vision, a vision that had led her to telephone her son and daughter-in-law almost the minute the vision withdrew. It had been the combination of the elder and younger Clarks' joint realization that the two women — Martha and Rebecca — had received divine communications within 12 hours, one of the other, that had led Martha and Paul to depart Oakham immediately for London, had led Rebecca to summon her parents from Birmingham, and had caused Rebecca to ask her husband, first, to purchase additional fresh vegetables for the much-expanded evening meal and, more importantly, to find her brother and bring him to their home.

Matt had failed on the second portion of his assignment only because Luke had felt compelled to go to his sister's home for a quite different reason. Or so it had seemed at the time he had asked Kory van Dijk to accompany him there.

Martha Clark spoke for fewer than three minutes, for her dream of the tall woman, the boxed iron swastika and the final long view of fields, distant seascape, setting sun and intervening barrier between water and fields was not descriptively complex. Having reviewed the vision several times with her husband both immediately after the event and during the two-hour drive to London, she was able to report several small details that she had not noticed while actually experiencing the dream. All four dreamers — Elisabeth and Jason Manguson, Martha Clark and finally Rebecca Manguson Clark — over thirty-plus years had experienced this phenomenon. Under questioning from other family members, they had each found themselves invariably able to pull from their minds more detail than they thought initially they had seen and retained.

In this case, under Paul's questioning, Martha had been able to add to her initial recollection several simple facts: first, the dreamed woman's town house had a numbered address posted on its front door.

The number was 9.

Further, the town house numbered 9 was the seventh door from what appeared to the dreamer to be a town square.

And finally, the clear, bold lettering gracing a street sign in the medium dreamed distance announced its name: *Hoofdstraadt*.

In her narration, Martha reported these small details last. She spoke the street name, guessing at the pronunciation but then adding the exact spelling so as to leave no confusion regarding this strange-to-English-ears word. And then she added her reasonable inference from the name and its spelling that this was a scene from a Dutch countryside. With that, she fell silent.

And as she did, Kory van Dijk moaned, leaped from her chair and, holding both hands over her mouth, raced from the room. The others watched astonished and unmoving except for Rebecca and Luke, siblings who had always seemed to others to be programmed from birth by Almighty God never to hesitate when action might be called for. In a flash they were out of their chairs and racing down the hallway on Kory's heels. Rebecca overtook her guest and pulled her into the hall bathroom, the two young women moving through the narrow doorway as if in choreograph.

Luke braked to a halt in the hallway just as the door slammed in his face.

# CHAPTER THREE

REBECCA AND LUKE SAT QUIETLY ON EITHER SIDE OF KORY VAN Dijk, their chairs pulled close to hers. Rebecca held Kory's right hand in both hers, while Luke held her left in his left hand, his right resting lightly on her back.

The newcomer had become physically ill as she listened to Martha Clark's description of her dream of just hours earlier that same day. Kory had run from the room not in terror but in the plain certainty that she was going to be sick. She and Rebecca had remained in the hall bathroom for some time, the birthday celebrant vomiting once into the toilet and then, at Rebecca's insistence, lying prone on the floor, a damp cloth on her forehead, until she began to recover.

Luke had waited patiently just outside the closed bathroom door, confident that his sister understood, if perhaps his companion did not yet, that he would stand guard until he received an explicit verbal indication from Rebecca that his assistance would not be needed. Luke Manguson *never* abandoned a post once taken, even one as simple, unofficial and unmilitary as this one: hovering outside a bathroom in case two women might ask something of him.

Not quite thirty minutes after fleeing the sitting room, the two women had emerged. With Rebecca and Luke supporting her, Kory had returned to the room and resumed her chair.

During the half hour hiatus, almost nothing had been said by the five who had stayed behind. Matt Clark, his parents and the elder Mangusons knew that all parties needed to be present, alert, and undistracted for this conversation to advance properly. And they knew that their ill guest was in good hands.

And so they prayed silently, each in his or her own way asking the Holy Spirit's continued presence and support: for Kory van Dijk, for the two dreamers, Martha and Rebecca, and for all eight of them — all four couples — as they sought to ascertain both the meaning of the new visions and the charge that, they did not doubt, would be forthcoming.

When Kory and her companions reappeared, all stood, Martha and Elisabeth to inquire of Kory whether or not they could bring her something to drink or eat, the three men from simple courtesy. These men always stood when a woman entered a room in which they were seated. It was simply part of who they were as men, and it was of very little interest to them whether a particular woman was offended by the gesture, gratified by it or simply indifferent to it.

The newcomer, who, unlike the other women, had dressed herself that morning for a noonday occasion on which she wanted to look her best, hardly appeared the same person who had left the room thirty minutes earlier. The bright yellow sundress was slightly stained and badly wrinkled. The wavy brown hair was tangled on one side and flattened on the other. The healthy brown of her skin had faded to pasty white. She took her seat shakily.

Once settled, supported physically on each side by Rebecca and Luke, Kory began to speak, as she knew she must. Her voice sounded tremulous and weak, yet eager. She seemed both humiliated by her forced exit and, at the same time, determined to make the contribution that she knew was hers to make. Never mind, she thought to herself, that the situation still seemed impossible: she, an impromptu guest on her birthday, present at the moment of supernatural disclosures the Source of which all understood well, but the nature of which — the scenes depicted and their meanings to the group — none of the principals understood as well as did she… if at all.

"Please forgive me," she began. "I think I was… I am… overwhelmed to be present at such a moment as this…."

She paused, looking down, shaking her head slowly.

"I was overwhelmed from the first, as soon as I realized what was about to happen… and then, when Rebecca spoke, and I saw that seemingly only I recognized the scene… I was… I couldn't… I couldn't *believe* the coincidence… that I should be brought here just to meet Rebecca and Matt and to see the babies… and yet… *this! This* happens while I am here…."

She paused again, still looking down, shaking her head again.

Jason Manguson at that moment leaned forward in his chair, rested his elbows on his knees, and stared intently at his son's companion. "Young lady," he said a little too sternly, thought Luke to himself, "you need to stop this right now."

Kory looked up, wide-eyed at the senior Manguson's tone.

"We…" he continued after a moment, "we — the seven of us in this room who have been through these wars for years — doubt very much that anything of this sort happens by 'coincidence,' as you have chosen to say. No, you were brought here this afternoon because the divine plan required your presence here… now… at this moment. It is of no concern why you and Luke *thought* you were coming here.

"We have seen this numerous times before, young lady. And your professing to be astonished at the Almighty's sense of timing does a disservice both to Him and to yourself, as well as to us.

"Now… gather yourself, Ms. van Dijk. Come directly to the point. We have learned that in these circumstances — when we are called together to analyze data from the supernatural Source and thence to determine what is required of us — there are no minutes to be thrown away. Whatever will be demanded of us… I can assure you that it is being demanded of us *right now.*"

At this, Jason Manguson sat back, his eyes fixed on Kory van Dijk not exactly in an unfriendly manner, but in a manner that suggested strongly that she move immediately to her report. He knew, as did the others, that if she had information to share, they needed to have that information without the slightest further delay.

If Luke Manguson had any concern that his companion might be sent emotionally reeling by this fearsome lecture from his father, he was reassured in seconds. Kory gently but firmly disentangled her hands from Rebecca's and Luke's, attempted unsuccessfully to tidy her sadly marred sundress and sat up as straight as an arrow in her chair, her shoulder blades no longer touching the chair back at all. More than one in the room was reminded of Martha Clark's demeanor when someone or something had made her very, very angry.

And so Kory van Dijk began afresh. "I understood as soon as Rebecca provided her envisioned wide-angle view of trees and markers that I knew that scene, and that no one else in the room seemed to. I was so shocked by that simple fact that I was too dumbfounded to speak. I'm sorry."

Her voice now high, strong and clear, she continued without pause.

"And when Mrs. Clark described the tall woman in front of Number 9 *Hoofdstraadt,* with what I knew to be the North Sea in the distant background, and when I considered the possible meanings of that iron swastika in her hand…

I knew with complete certainty that it was, and is, through God's grace and direction that I am with you this day."

She turned her eyes to those of Jason Manguson, unafraid. "When Mrs. Clark reached the end of her description and at the instant I became ill, Mr. Manguson, I found in that moment that I could no longer think of my presence in your midst as 'coincidence,' though I used that word a moment ago to explain my first reactions. I knew with absolute certainty that your son and I came here — were *sent* here — for reasons completely different from those that we assumed."

He nodded his acceptance of her explanation, obviously no less impatient than before to receive her full report.

She disengaged her eyes from his and looked carefully around the room.

"That woman," she said slowly and deliberately, laying emphasis on each word, "is… my… father's… sister…. Her name is Greta… Greta van Dijk. She is seven years older than my father."

The group received this news in stunned silence.

After a moment, the speaker turned her face to one side in order to look directly into Rebecca's eyes. "Rebecca," she said, her voice now confident and sure, allowing her listeners more readily to imagine the newcomer controlling a classroom of less-than-willing youngsters, "your envisioned scene is of the city of Jerusalem. Specifically, the scene you were given is the national Holocaust place of memory. In Hebrew it is called *Yad Vashem,* from a verse in Isaiah meaning 'place and name.' *Yad Vashem* is set into the slopes of Mount Herzl."

She turned her face back to the group, breathed deeply and resumed immediately. "The leathery leaves are those of the carob tree. Both the tree and its leaves are tough and resilient enough to thrive in the Israeli climate.

"Rebecca's vision is specifically of…" here she paused and lowered her voice, as though about to speak a phrase that demanded reverence from anyone daring to say the words aloud.

"It is specifically of… the Avenue of the Righteous. Yes… the Avenue of the Righteous.

"And each individual carob tree is planted so as to honor the person — almost always a Christian person — whose name appears on the plaque underneath its branches. Each tree… each plaque… honors a person who saved at least one Jew from death at the hands of the Nazis in the Second World War.

"The Nazis made it clear, as each of you must surely know, that any gentile who tried to save a Jew from death would be dealt with, if discovered, in exactly the same manner and with precisely the same ruthlessness as that Jew would be.

The Hebrew name given to each of the gentile rescuers is *Hasidei Ummot ha-Olam* — the 'Righteous Among Nations.'"

At this point the young speaker faltered for the first time since Jason Manguson's stern order that she get immediately to the substance of her report. Her voice caught in her throat and she gasped for breath. Luke and Rebecca simultaneously, from each side, reached gently toward her but she raised both her hands and pushed their hands away roughly.

Fists now clenched over her chest, tears once more coming into, and then flowing from, her deep brown eyes, Kory van Dijk spoke again, her voice filling with emotion and rising with pride. "My aunt… Greta van Dijk… is herself one of the Righteous Among Nations. There is a carob tree at *Yad Vashem* planted in her honor.

"And I was there! I — her only niece — was there just last year when she was invited to plant her tree!

"I was *there!*

"And… and… so… was the Jew… who was saved… by my aunt!

"And so were that Jewish woman's two children… two children who would never have been born except for…."

And Kory van Dijk placed her face in her hands and sobbed, emotions of joy and of pride in her aunt's heroism mixing with the stark recollection, visited anew upon her mind and heart, of the fate of the millions who did *not* find themselves in the hands of a Greta van Dijk. Rebecca Clark, this time ignoring the young woman's halfhearted attempt to fend her off physically, enfolded the disheveled guest in her arms, buried her face in the tangled brown locks, and sobbed as loudly and unashamedly as did Kory herself.

Indeed, in that room at that moment, there were no dry eyes. And that included the eyes of the stern-faced Jason Manguson, who, after observing for a moment, rose and strode across the circle to his sobbing daughter and her guest, dropped to one knee, and, tears now flowing down his own cheeks, encircled both young women in his strong arms.

And together, as one, they wept.

Twenty-four hours after the emotional climax to her unexpectedly eventful twenty-fourth birthday, Kory van Dijk watched as Luke Manguson pulled his parents' right-hand-drive Volvo sedan into a grocery store parking lot in the Dutch city of Leeuwarden. He turned off the ignition and stretched. Then he turned to his left to face his passenger.

"Are you hungry yet, Kory?" he asked. It was a genuine question, for the two had not yet spent sufficient time together that they could reliably anticipate the other's needs.

"Well… no," she said after a moment, "but it seems to me that we really *ought* to eat something, Luke. Once nightfall comes and we finish our drive and sit down with Aunt Greta, I don't know what will happen, then or after. Anything at all could happen. Isn't that right?"

He looked away from her dark brown eyes and stared straight ahead. His jaw tightened, sending such a ripple of muscle across his scarred left cheek that his passenger was actually startled at the physiological display. Her eyes widened as she considered his rugged profile.

After a moment he said simply, "Yes. Anything at all."

She swallowed and turned her face away from him, now staring out the left-side passenger window. As she had turned her head quickly from right to left, her shoulder-length brown waves moved in their own rhythm, finally rearranging themselves around her shoulders to conform to her new position.

Without turning his head, Luke reached over with his left hand, grasped her right, and cupped her small hand in his own. Each was silent.

At first, both were simply recalling the events of the last twenty-four hours. As the minutes ticked by, however, both began to pray, still silent, eyes closed and hands still joined.

Kory's Friday evening revelations — or, more correctly, her translation of others' revelations — had led the group to formulate action plans that of necessity would be launched immediately, before daybreak on Saturday. Absolutely no time could be squandered.

They were on a war footing.

The clear consensus had been that Greta van Dijk was in immediate and mortal danger. The veterans of the June battles among them, which included all but Kory, understood that, while the visions inevitably brought mysteries and dangers and opportunities of potential worldwide consequence, there was often some comparatively small-scale action that must be undertaken first. Such as, in this case, preventing the capture and murder of a single individual.

And they knew from experience, as well, that such conventionally prudent actions as seeking to collect additional information in order to test their inferences, or telephoning and warning the threatened individual, or contacting local law enforcement — in this case Dutch police or Scotland Yard — had no relevance. First, the warnings were divine in origin; consequently, seeking confirmation of their hypotheses was ludicrous to the point of blasphemy. Second, contacting the threatened person, unless such person were already a member of the group and thereby prepared in advance to understand the supernatural nature of the developing events, was simply to invite courteous ridicule.

Aside from the apparent fragility of the claim itself — to have received a detailed, intelligible and meaningful vision from the divine Source — there was the fact that the visions usually depicted a *future* circumstance. In the case of Greta van Dijk, it was entirely possible that, had she been telephoned by her niece Friday evening from London, she might not yet have encountered the dreamed swastika at all, and, even though a family member would be telephoning, could have been expected simply to shake her head in shocked dismay at her niece's irrationality and hysteria.

Finally, the normally reasonable step of contacting law enforcement agencies would carry with it all the same validity problems and questions as would telephoning the threatened person herself, but with the familial connection subtracted from the interaction. The expected result, then, would almost certainly be the same, *sans* the presumed courtesy that one family member might extend the other.

The group had determined swiftly and with almost no debate that it must be Kory and Luke who would travel next day to the farming town of Ferwerd, in extreme northern Holland, to warn Greta van Dijk and to remove her physically from the danger if she would permit it. That might or might not mean bringing her all the way back to London with them. But it had been obvious to the planners that Kory's aunt would have a valid passport and the ability to travel internationally, given her trip to Jerusalem the previous summer for the planting of her tree at *Yad Vashem*.

Kory's presence on the incursion would be necessary both because she provided the family connection and because she spoke Dutch. Luke's presence would be equally necessary because he was the most physically capable: his five years as an officer in the Royal Navy had included extensive training and experience in the specialized techniques required for command of military boarding parties. Leading small groups of superbly prepared combatants onto hostile decks demanded intelligence, creativity, courage, physical strength and agility. The Mangusons and Clarks knew that Luke possessed, perhaps, more capability than any other living person to intervene in the annual June crises both effectively and within the moral constraints implied by the muscular Christianity of which he was the exemplar.

For the Manguson-Clark group had understood always that they could not engage the Enemy physically outside the rule structure implied by their faith: no force if possible, and no lethal force ever, except if unavoidably necessary to prevent the immediate and near-certain death of an innocent. The Enemy might seek to kill Luke Manguson, and, indeed, had sought his death, Rebecca's, and that of the others more than once. That did *not* mean that he could seek theirs in return, and, to this point, neither he nor his colleagues had been required to take a life in order to fulfill any one of their divinely ordained missions.

Deaths there had been on both sides. Woundings there had been on both sides. But neither Luke nor Rebecca nor their comrades had directly caused the death of an adversary.

Thus far.

The planners in London had flatly refused to consider the new parents as members of the rescue contingent, despite their successful experience in the past three years' battles and the grandparents' availability for temporary care of the infant twins. And while the new mother had readily agreed that she could no longer risk her life as she had in the past, her husband had been torn regarding his own involvement.

Matthew Clark had, after all, himself served five years as a United States naval officer, and, though he had not the specialized combat training that had prepared Luke so thoroughly for the earlier battles, he was tall, well-muscled, tough and competent with small arms. And he had learned long before to compensate for the fact of his atrophied left shoulder, arm and hand, one of the outcomes of his, Rebecca's and Luke's original confrontations with supernatural Evil three summers before.

But, while Matt Clark had been divided within himself over the question of whether or not he should accompany Luke and Kory, the others had not been divided in the least. Infants Joanna and Samuel were to be raised by two parents. He could not go. There would be no discussion of the idea.

The vehicle selected for the rescue attempt had been the five-year-old, right-hand-drive Volvo sedan that had been driven to London that afternoon by the senior Mangusons. Their dark blue automobile had low mileage for its age, could easily accommodate a third person and her luggage, and was maintained in excellent mechanical condition by Jason Manguson.

Once the plans had been completed, still very early on Friday evening, Luke, now driving the automobile selected for the trip, had taken Kory to her flat so that she could attend to her young tabby and change out of her soiled sundress and into what Luke and Rebecca liked to call "action clothing." She had needed a mere fifteen minutes in her apartment before she had come trotting out the front door looking much different than when she had entered. She had not only changed her clothes and packed a small case for what she assumed would be two nights away from home, she had actually managed to wash her hair in those few minutes.

She had sat down in the car beside Luke still toweling her brown locks. Clad in white tennis shoes, beige slacks, a white short-sleeved blouse and a lightweight maroon windbreaker against the expected night chill of Friesland — "the Cold Land" of northern Holland — she looked, Luke had thought to himself, just as pretty as she had in the yellow sundress at noon. In fact, she seemed to him more appropriately dressed for another taste of birthday strawberries and cream than for what he knew they might be facing in the next twenty-four hours.

He had decided after a moment's indecision that he should make no comment regarding the extent to which her wardrobe fit his and Rebecca's "action clothing" criteria. Her clothing's lack of fitness-for-action aside, however, he found that her clean, unadorned beauty overwhelmed his natural reluctance to take verbal note of another's appearance.

Steeling himself to make the unfamiliar gesture, he had done what he knew he should, and had said what he knew he felt. Looking at her intently as she sat, towel in hand, looking back at him, he had said quietly, "Kory… Kory, I think you look *very* pretty."

She had frozen, the towel poised in midair. Her eyes had widened. And then, recovering, she had smiled sweetly, having apprehended the depth of feeling underlying his superficially cautious declaration of appreciation.

"Thank you," she had finally said, replying with equal simplicity. "I believe you actually mean that, Lieutenant Manguson."

He had nodded, his face still serious despite the playfulness of her response. "Believe me, Ms. van Dijk… I do…. I mean exactly that. You look *very, very* pretty." And he had leaned across the seat and kissed her lightly on the lips, his hand momentarily framing her face and receiving a swift, cold bath from her dripping wet hair.

Then he had moved back behind the wheel, feeling only moderately embarrassed by these unrehearsed verbal and physical displays of affection. He had then turned the ignition switch, brought the Volvo to life, and had driven away without another word or gesture in her direction, already focused fully on the evening's operation.

For her part, Kory had only smiled happily, emitting as she did the small, high-pitched noise — a private laugh of sorts — that those closest to her knew to be her expression of greatest delight. Then, still smiling to herself, she had resumed her vigorous toweling.

There were two agenda items remaining before they were to leave the great city in the small hours of the next morning.

The first was easy. Luke would stop at his own home to collect both the clothing and the equipment he would require.

The second was expected to be difficult. It was a visit to the home of Kory's parents.

Amelia and Andruw van Dijk knew Luke as their daughter's faculty colleague, as her increasingly frequent companion at church, and as someone whom they admired, especially for his Royal Navy service and for his personal vocation to the Christian education of young people. None of that meant that they would readily understand what Kory was to say to them about her weekend plans.

The twenty-minute conversation had gone as well as could be expected, in Kory and Luke's commonly held view. She could only say to her parents that she would be with him for the full weekend, that they expected to be back in London late Sunday, that the excursion dealt with a family emergency that she could not explain in advance, and that her time with Luke would be completely "proper." This last reassurance was not strictly necessary, given the van Dijk's confidence in the Christian maturity of the two young people sitting in front of them, but it was deeply appreciated nonetheless.

Kory's one request of her parents, other than to reschedule the post-birthday dinner that Amelia had planned for her daughter for Saturday night, had been that they look in on Tiny, the young tabby, several times during the weekend, or even beyond the weekend, if that somehow became necessary. The parents quickly assented.

Kory had been unhappy with having purposely misled her parents — misled them by what she had *not* said — regarding which family had the emergency. She had allowed them to assume that the emergency was lodged in the Manguson or the Clark family, rather than in the van Dijk family.

But Luke had been clear with her that asking these loved ones first to believe that highly explicit divine visions had been given repeatedly to ordinary people, and second to accept the notion that their daughter should risk her life on the basis of such visions was to invite both incredulity and, perhaps, a serious effort to stop her. He had reminded Kory that it had taken her many weeks to gain a certain comfort level with his own history, a history that included grave risks taken in response to the Holy Spirit's dramatic interventions in the Mangusons' and Clarks' lives. Risks that had resulted not only in the shotgun blast to the left side of his face and neck, but, two years before that, a large-caliber bullet's entry and exit track through the muscle of his left thigh, a wound from which he had bled dangerously for hours before it could be dressed by a physician. In the end, it was his emphasis on the possible jeopardy to their mission that could result from her disclosure to her parents of any of the mission's details that settled her mind to do as he urged her to do.

She would, she thought to herself, be able to ask their forgiveness in a mere 48 hours. That would have to do.

The Mangusons' unremarkable dark-blue Volvo sedan had been the first vehicle in line for the Dover-Calais ferry that Saturday morning. The short voyage across the straits had been uneventful.

Once debarked from the ferry in France, and having grown quickly comfortable once more driving the right-hand side of continental roadways, Luke had proceeded north along the coastal highways, passing the outskirts of Dunkirk and crossing the Belgian border near the World War I trench lines. He had turned away from the coast at Ostende, picking up the A14 at Gent, thence to Antwerp. He had then followed the A1 north into Holland.

As morning changed seamlessly into afternoon on this pleasantly warm June Saturday, he had circled the Rotterdam metropolitan area well to the east and then followed the A28 and the A32 northward into Dutch farm country, where the black-and-white Freisian cattle appeared greatly to outnumber the Freisian people. Passing through this picturesque and pastoral land, the two Londoners had understood as they drove why, in the murderous years, the Dutch underground had so often looked north to Freisland when its members had sought sanctuary for Holland's Jews. Not only had the occupying Nazi army there been far fewer in number than in the metropolitan areas to the south, but the ubiquitous Freisian haylofts and cellars had provided nearly unlimited opportunity to sequester and feed this chosen-for-genocide people.

Now, as Saturday evening darkness approached, the young British couple continued to sit in their Leeuwarden parking lot, silent and quietly emotional… praying… thinking… remembering….

The good map of the area they had purchased upon arrival in this provincial capital had confirmed what they knew: that a fifteen-minute drive to the north of where they sat, within a long stone's throw of the grassy dikes that held back the cold waters of the North Sea, would bring them to the deceptively quiet village of Ferwerd. And there, they were confident, their Enemy was present, waiting, as were they, for the night.

Greta van Dijk herself had never lived on a farm. She had spent her entire life residing at 9 Hoofdstraadt, the main street of Ferwerd. During the war years, she had lived there with her father and younger brother Andruw, their mother having died years earlier. Now a vigorous and formidable sixty-plus, a revered elementary school teacher in the village, she occupied the house alone.

She had been in her late twenties when the local physician and the van Dijks' own Lutheran pastor approached the family about the possibility of sheltering a young Jewish woman. Given the location of their town house in the heart of the village and the impossibility of a visitor's going unobserved by the populace or by the occupiers — not usually the case on the surrounding farms — the person selected by the underground for the van Dijk family could not "look Jewish."

She would simply "look Dutch," and she would of necessity possess both the intellect and the self-confidence essential to carry out daily interaction with villagers and with Nazi occupying troops without arousing the suspicions of either. The German border lay but fifty miles to the east of Ferwerd. Some of the villagers could be assumed to be Nazi sympathizers.

But when the van Dijks had been approached, they had not hesitated. "Yes, of course," they had said.

*"Yes…. Of course."*

And so for two full years — from early summer of 1943 until the European war's end in late spring of 1945 — the van Dijk family had harbored, at daily risk to their very lives, a blonde Jewish woman in her early twenties. Using an assumed and "non-Jewish" name, she had been presented to the community as young Andruw and Greta van Dijk's cousin from Amsterdam, and she had participated fully in the van Dijk family's Christian lives.

Greta van Dijk had viewed this as no heroism. She had viewed this as the obvious obligation of any Christian person: willingly and cheerfully to accept the duty of preventing the certain murder of another human being at the hands of an incomprehensible Evil. True, the consequences of fulfilling this Christian duty could be death. So be it, she and her family had said. To a Christian, they understood without elaboration, there are many things worse than mere death.

Greta had been stunned when, almost 35 years after the war, she had been notified, first by the Jewish woman whom she had saved and then by the Jerusalem officials of *Yad Vashem,* that she was to be honored as one of the Righteous Among Nations, as one of the *Hasidei Ummot ha-Olam.* And at first she had been disinclined to accept.

But then she had come to understand the kind of statement that *Yad Vashem* had made and would continue to make to the world by its very existence as a tribute to divinely instilled and inspired Conscience, standing without regard to itself against the face of the Enemy. And so she had accepted the honor with her inbred humility and had traveled to Israel for the ceremonial planting of her carob tree. The now one-year-old photograph of herself and of her Jewish "cousin," both of them seeming to have aged little, their hands gripping the ceremonial shovel, laughing together, had immediately become one of her greatest treasures.

But now this: this inexplicable visitation from the murderous past… this preposterous and disgusting Nazi symbol… placed in her own front yard at 9 Hoofdstraadt… *placed* in her own front yard by someone who had actually walked to her front door in order to lay before her this vile embodiment of iron hatred. And in broad daylight apparently, for she had been out of the house repeatedly on that Saturday and it was only near nightfall when she had gone out one final time with the intention of snipping several flowers for the morrow's Sabbath dining table, that she had nearly stumbled on the box.

Now, two hours later, all lights in the house fully extinguished, she sat in the dark in her small dining room. The vase on the table was empty of the flowers she had intended for it. Her evening meal, untouched, remained on her kitchen counter. The telephone sat mute, its outside line to the street having been cut apparently at the same time the box had been placed at her door. And the box itself, with its horrible iron swastika, sat on the floor just inside the front door. The house was silent.

And then it happened. She heard muffled footsteps crossing her small backyard, treading softly on the walkway from the outbuilding that had served as her father's shop for most of his lifetime.

She put her face in her hands and prayed softly aloud in her native Dutch, "Father of all mercies, I have lived long and You have blessed me far beyond anything I have ever deserved. Please strengthen me to face Your Enemy with forgiveness in my mind and Jesus in my heart. Please. *Amen.*"

She heard the soft knock on the back door. The voice that accompanied the knock was feminine, high and young, though not the voice of a child. *"Aunt Greta! It's Kory!"* it called softly in Dutch. *"Aunt Greta! It's Kory! Aunt Greta, let us in, please!"*

Greta van Dijk sat perfectly still for a long moment, weighing the likelihood that this voice might actually be that of her beloved niece. Then she heard the same voice, still more urgent. *"Gretee… Gretee… please!"*

At the purposeful mispronunciation of her name, the lovely mispronunciation from more than two decades past when the child Kory van Dijk was still learning to speak, Greta sprang from her chair at the dining table. She strode through the darkened kitchen with the confidence of one who had lived sixty years in one home, and quickly unlatched her back door.

Swinging the door open and stepping to one side, she immediately glimpsed Kory's small shape as it glided past her. And then she tensed at what followed on her niece's heels.

The shape that followed the young woman into her aunt's house was frightening even in the half-light that spilled through the door as it stood partway open for perhaps three seconds. It was the shape of a man of near-impossible proportions — barrel-chested, huge of bicep and forearm — and not only dressed entirely in black, but with blackened face and dark knit cap pulled down low over his eyes.

As soon as the man cleared the threshold he spun, closed the door swiftly but quietly, and motioned in the semi-darkness for the two women to move away from the door. Kory grasped her aunt's hand and pulled her back toward the dining room.

As she moved past the looming masculine figure, Greta van Dijk saw, or thought she saw, what appeared to be an array of terrifyingly huge knife blades slung across the man's chest in some sort of shoulder holster. She tightened her grip on her niece's small hand as it tugged her toward the dining table, held fast, and followed.

A scant 45 minutes following the Saturday night arrival of her niece and of the apparition that accompanied her, Greta van Dijk no longer sat huddled at her dining room table, fretting alone in her darkened town house. Her home was now lighted fully and the front curtains were thrown wide open, long the custom in the village of Ferwerd. From time to time, she strode back and forth in front of those same wide-open curtains, doing her best to carry out her normal evening routine.

After each circuit through and around the ground floor of her home, she returned to sit on the fourth step of the staircase that led upward to the bedrooms above, there to crouch in complete darkness, praying for the strength to do what she knew she must. This position near the foot of the stairs provided quick access to her back door. Its deadbolt was in place, as was the case with the front door.

Suddenly and without the slightest warning a tremendous, thudding crash seemed to shake the entire house. Her heart flew to her throat as the terrifying concussions continued… twice… three times… four times… now five times.

Although she had never before experienced this terror, she recognized it at once from her "cousin's" graphic depictions in the long ago of the sound of German jackboots thudding into the front doors of Jewish residences throughout Amsterdam. This time, instead of the shouted demand to open the door, there came the shouted slogan, found posted in the murder years on the front doors of hotels, restaurants and other establishments throughout Nazi-occupied Europe: *"VOOR HONDEN EN JODEN VERBODEN! VOOR HONDEN EN JODEN VERBODEN! VOOR HONDEN EN JODEN VERBODEN!"* The menacing translation: *"Dogs and Jews Forbidden."*

Greta van Dijk — vigorous, agile and strong at sixty —— leaped from the steps on which she sat, flew to her back door, wrestled the deadbolt, jerked the door noisily open, and raced into her backyard. In her fifth running stride, cruelly strong hands seized her arms roughly from each side, wrestling her abruptly to a stop.

If the two muscular and well-armed assailants thought this sixty-year-old schoolteacher would offer them no resistance, they were disabused of that fantasy in the first instant. She fought them like a wildcat — scratching, kicking, biting — thereby so fully occupying each attacker that neither was remotely aware of what approached from behind.

For once the intended victim had fully engaged her two antagonists, Luke Manguson emerged from Greta van Dijk's back door, running. He charged the assailants in his combat attack crouch, the largest of his several knife blades inserted in its universal handle and upraised in front of his blackened face. He raced straight for the attacker on the right, and, knife in his left hand, reached down to the huge man's exposed left Achilles tendon and severed the cable-like anatomical feature with a deft, slicing right-to-left stroke. The burly combatant collapsed instantaneously, screaming German obscenities at the top of his lungs.

Confused by his comrade's screams and still absorbed fully with the task of securing the victim while trying to keep her nails and teeth away from his hands, the other German turned his head to the right. As rehearsed repeatedly in her small kitchen, the Dutch woman dropped to the ground almost as rapidly as did the wounded combatant on her right, leaving the bewildered attacker on her left fully exposed to what was already rising to meet him.

The knife still held in his left hand, Luke Manguson's open right palm rose to strike his remaining adversary with the explosive force of a battering ram. Making contact just under the attacker's nose, the rock-hard base of Luke's hand drove upward with all the force of his muscular body under and behind it. The blow snapped the German's head back, shattered his nose, buckled his knees and rendered him unconscious in a fraction of a single second.

This second target was still toppling to the ground when Luke wheeled back to his first, pushed the screaming assailant onto his face, pulled both his hands behind him and, using the coil of coated wire at his belt, trussed the man into a writhing, moaning, yet helplessly immobile mountain of pain. Just as swiftly, as Luke completed his truss, Kory van Dijk, having followed on her companion's heels as he arrowed into the fray, wrapped three loops of strapping tape around the large gauze pad that she held against the German's bleeding heel, while her aunt at the same time affixed two strips of the same tape tightly over his eyes and around his head.

As these coordinated binding, bandaging and blindfolding actions were being completed, the Germans at the front of the town house ceased their jackbooted assault on the front door and stopped shouting the disgusting Nazi slogan, finally becoming aware of their comrade's screams from the back of the row of town houses. Their first response was to attempt to force the front door.

But the Dutch door was not only sturdy of construction and locked by a well-engineered deadbolt, it was further secured by one of Luke Manguson's specially designed rubber-and-metal door stops, just one component in the vast array of accoutrement — varying sized knife blades among them — that he carried within the recesses of his leather shoulder-holster-and-belt combination.

Realizing at length that the front door could not be forced no matter how they attacked it, the three Germans turned and ran toward the near end of the long row of town houses, eventually to wend their way around, over and through a series of backyards filled with natural and man-made obstacles. Finally reaching their disabled comrades-in-arms, they found one still screaming and babbling uncontrollably and the other completely unconscious.

The former, with his eyes and ears taped tightly shut, was unable to tell them anything about which direction "they" had gone. Without pausing to understand what their comrade might mean by "they," two of the attackers ran north toward the fields and the protective dikes, while the third remained with the two survivors of the short-lived assault on Greta van Dijk.

As the front-of-the-house jackbooted thunder had fallen silent and the shouted slogan had ceased its assault on her ears, the *Righteous Among Nations* honoree herself, together with her London-born niece and the former Royal Navy boarding-party officer, having disposed in mere seconds of both their initial attackers, quietly reentered the still-open back door. They left the door standing wide open, as though they had fled northward toward the sea in great haste, and proceeded deliberately through the kitchen and dining room toward the front of the town house.

Finding that the German threesome assaulting the front door had long since begun a lengthy, running encirclement of the town house row, Luke stooped and removed his special-design doorstop device while Kory unfastened the deadbolt and pulled the front door cautiously open. Her aunt then picked up her small night case containing personal items, all hastily packed shortly after Kory and Luke's arrival less than an hour earlier.

As Greta van Dijk stepped through the front door, Kory van Dijk knelt to lift the small wooden box containing its iron monstrosity. She lifted the box to her waist and found herself unwillingly twisting her face in disgust at the thought of holding the despised symbol of hatred and genocide in her hands. Then the three, closing the front door of town house number nine softly behind them, strode rapidly across *Hoofdstraadt,* passed down the nearest alley, and disappeared into the Friesland night.

# Chapter Four

TWO MORNINGS AFTER SATURDAY-NIGHT VIOLENCE IN A SMALL Dutch village, and six time zones to the west, Solomon Rosenthal smiled with warm pleasure at the sight of his two guests as they approached the main doorway of the Jewish Theological Seminary at 120th and Broadway. It was midmorning on this June Monday in New York City.

Rosenthal, the Jewish seminary's Associate Director of Finance, had made himself immediately available that morning when telephoned by Union Theological Seminary's Eleanor Mason Chapel. Aside from her immense stature as the Christian world's preeminent Old Testament authority, her long-standing and highly successful efforts to link the two seminaries' libraries and other resources — making each one's holdings readily available to the students and faculty members of the other — had made her a valued member of the larger community. When she had asked Rosenthal for an audience as soon as he could possibly grant it, he had not hesitated.

"Please, Dr. Chapel," he had said in his heavily accented English. "Come right now. I will clear my morning calendar immediately. Please. Come."

Eleanor Chapel had not mentioned, in her haste, that she would be accompanied, but Rosenthal was not surprised to see, as he watched her approach the main doorway of the seminary after the short, one-block walk from her office on 121st Street and Broadway, the wizened, rumpled figure limping energetically alongside her. Rosenthal had never met this man, but he knew exactly who this was. It could only be private detective and former senior NYPD Detective Sidney Belton, the Roman Catholic husband of Southern Baptist Eleanor Mason Chapel.

Solomon Rosenthal, like many others in this academia-laced Manhattan neighborhood, even knew a few of the details of the couple's short history together. He knew they had met two years earlier, had fallen rather quickly in love, and had married not long after. This, despite their divergent Christian perspectives and backgrounds, and despite Eleanor Chapel's being fifteen years Sid Belton's senior. Rosenthal smiled again to himself as he watched them passing through beyond-state-of-the-art security at the JTS entrance. One would never guess from their appearance and movements that it was she who was in her mid-sixties and he who was but fifty.

For the erect, four-foot-ten-inch and eighty-five-pound Eleanor Chapel was as graceful and unencumbered in her quick, dainty movements as her husband was stooped, awkward and physically impaired in his. Aside from various wounds received in the line of duty over the years, including shrapnel from an explosive device that sent him into early retirement from the NYPD, there had been a vicious and very nearly fatal beating at exactly the point two years earlier when he had met Eleanor Chapel. Rosenthal knew nothing about the details of those circumstances, but he had been told that the now-private detective's right arm was frozen at the elbow, that that same arm and hand had been burned by torture and that the beating with blunt implements had left him with considerable internal damage and scarring not only on his face but on his torso, as well.

Rosenthal winced at these thoughts, but consciously let go of them as the two cleared the substantial network of JTS security personnel and advanced to meet him, the detective clutching the curved handle of a highly polished walking cane in his undamaged left hand. Rosenthal extended his hand first to Eleanor Chapel, who grasped his hand in both her own.

"Mr. Rosenthal," she said in her high, child's-register voice, "I do so appreciate your seeing us on no notice whatever. Thank you."

As he nodded his head graciously in return, bowing slightly at the waist, she continued, gesturing to the man at her side and saying, "Mr. Rosenthal, may I present my husband, Sidney Belton. I hope you don't mind that I have dragged him along with me."

Although Rosenthal had been in numerous meetings with Eleanor Chapel, this was, he realized, the first time he had stood directly in front of her at close range, and he was struck by the bright, blue-green eyes and by the iridescent red scarf she wore around her neck. These two patches of bright color stood out dramatically against the nearly uninterrupted gray of everything else about her: gray hair pulled into a tight bun, two-piece gray suit, off-white blouse under the gray suit jacket and, unmistakably, the famous and faded white tennis shoes, themselves graying with age.

Rosenthal was struck equally in this brief, welcoming exchange by her husband's deep-set black eyes, extraordinarily penetrating gaze, and surprising strength in his handshake, a gesture that Belton accomplished somehow without bending or straightening his right elbow. And the voice and dialect were all of a piece: deep-throated, scratchy Brooklynese.

"How y'doin' Mr. Rosenthal?" he had said as they shook hands. "I gotta tell ya', you're a smart guy to see my wife when she says she's gotta see ya' *now*. If y'say no to her, she'll just show up in y'r office anyway. An' she'll hang out right there all day and all night until y'either let 'r in or throw 'r out. Might as well *pretend* y'got some control of her. Know what I mean, Mr. Rosenthal? Know what I mean?"

Laughing appreciatively, their host nodded and gestured for the couple to precede him to the elevators. Moments later Rosenthal faced the twosome from across his ample desk.

"I am sorry we have this desk between us," he said politely, aware of the thickness of his accented English and, through long habit, enunciating carefully. "You can see my office is too filled with books, manuals, files and Hebrew artifacts to allow any other arrangement."

Solomon Rosenthal himself was the same age as Eleanor Chapel, sixty-five, and a trim, compact five-foot-ten-inches, a man who on this Monday morning wore a modest brown suit, blue-black patterned tie against a long-sleeved white shirt, and ever-present yarmulke on the back of his blond-fading-to-gray head of hair. He was clean shaven.

Eleanor Chapel leaned forward, a small notepad in her hand, prepared to explain without further courtesies the nature of the urgency underlying her request, when her husband interrupted before she mouthed the first syllable.

"Mr. Rosenthal," he said, his crooked smile displaying itself incongruously, "I know Eleanor's got a lotta stuff she wants to ask, but I just gotta get this out first."

His wife turned her head and fixed him with a look designed to freeze him into silent inaction. Their host, noting this, smiled and spoke quickly.

"Dr. Chapel," Rosenthal said lightly, "do not be concerned. Your husband is a *detective*, you know. Detectives must ask their questions before they can attend fully to anything else."

Turning his eyes to Belton, he continued, still smiling, "I imagine you cannot wait another moment to ask about my eyes and hair, detective? and, perhaps, about the origin of my accent? and, perhaps again, about the bandage that covers the back of my hand?"

Belton's quirky grin extended itself further, making his scarred, gnome-like face even more lopsided than before.

"Well, yeah, Mr. Rosenthal," he admitted in his deep, raspy voice, "I gotta know how come you got eyes that are bluer than Eleanor's. And I gotta know why your hair is — or was — just plain blond. And I gotta know what's that dialect you got. And, yeah, I gotta know what's under that big square bandage. I gotta know those things, just like y'said, before I can pay much attention to anythin' else, and, y'know, I do wanna pay attention to Eleanor's stuff...."

"Sidney Belton!" his wife interrupted. "Are you out of your *mind?* Do you actually think you can accompany me to *my* meeting and just walk in, sit down, and begin some silly interrogation regarding the *appearance* and *speech* of a man who has been so gracious as to open his calendar for us? Are you just out of your *mind?*"

Rosenthal was interested to observe Sid Belton's response to this forthright reprimand. He seemed genuinely embarrassed, almost like a small child. He sat back in his chair, hung his head, and mumbled, "Sorry, Eleanor. Didn't mean to be rude. Sorry, Mr. Rosenthal. Didn't mean to be rude. Really... didn't mean to be rude... sorry... sorry...."

Rosenthal was touched. He looked at the Old Testament scholar. "Dr. Chapel," he said, "do you mind if I go ahead and answer the detective's questions? The ones he did not actually put into words until I did? I really don't mind. I get these questions frequently. Then the detective can stop... well... obsessing... and you can get on with your agenda."

At his use of the word "obsessing" all three smiled broadly. Eleanor Chapel sat back, rolled her eyes in an exaggerated *what-can-I-do-with-this-man* gesture, and nodded.

"I was not born Jewish, detective," said Rosenthal comfortably, obviously accustomed to relating his story. "Some years after the war, in 1952, I converted to Judaism and changed my name at the same time. I had been a foot soldier in the Austrian army and had been able to get work in a state-run bank after the war. I converted to Judaism just before I came to the U.S., and have worked in New York ever since, first in local banks and, for almost ten years now, in the seminary's finance office. The accent you hear is my schoolboy English, learned in Austrian classrooms from my earliest years."

The small room was silent for several moments, the two visitors thoughtfully digesting this information. The professor glanced at her husband, obviously hoping that Belton would quickly thank their host and end this unfortunate diversion, but she found him nodding his head appreciatively, still embarrassed, but nonetheless clearly looking forward to hearing something regarding his remaining question.

Rosenthal then raised his right hand, turned his wrist so that the back of the hand faced the detective, and peeled back the large, square bandage. A dark blue tattoo — a clear and geometrically perfect image of the Star of David — made its appearance. Rosenthal exposed the tattoo only for a moment, then replaced the covering carefully. "I cover my Star of David simply because here at the Jewish Theological Seminary, we're not… ah… as the young people say… not very 'big' on tattoos. It's a little embarrassing here at the JTS to display such a thing, so I cover it up. Maybe I shouldn't, because the bandage generates as many questions as the exposed tattoo probably would, but it's a longstanding habit now."

Another silence followed.

Rosenthal turned his eyes to the professor. "There," he said to her. "That's out of the way, Dr. Chapel. Quite painless."

Belton's lopsided smile returned. "Thanks, Mr. Rosenthal," he said gratefully. "That was good of ya' to tell me all that. I'll stay outta th' way now."

Rosenthal nodded good-naturedly and again looked at Eleanor Chapel.

"Dr. Chapel?"

"I understand, Mr. Rosenthal," said Eleanor Chapel, "that you serve as the seminary's liaison to the committee that oversees *Yad Vashem,* including selection of all those chosen to be honored as *Hasidei Ummot ha-Olam.*"

She spoke the Hebrew phrases expertly, confident in her use of the language after decades of immersion in all things Old-Testament pertinent. She paused, eyebrows lifted in request for confirmation.

Rosenthal nodded immediately. "Yes, Dr. Chapel. It has been my privilege to serve the seminary as official liaison to the committee for more than five years now. I may be, in all the world, the only converted Jew serving in such a role. That was the impression I was given at the time I was selected."

The professor nodded, then continued. "Saturday evening, in a village in an extreme northern province of Holland, a member of the Righteous Among

Nations was attacked by, we believe, five men — apparently Germans — who either were neo-Nazis or were posing as such."

Rosenthal's jaw sagged. His eyes widened in disbelief. *"What? What?"* He looked from one face to the other. *"What? How on earth? Why on earth?"*

Eleanor Chapel replied immediately. "We have several very dear friends in the UK, Mr. Rosenthal. The woman who was attacked is a close relative of one of those friends… um… his girlfriend's aunt. She — the Dutch woman — was in Jerusalem just last summer for her induction ceremony and for the planting of her carob tree."

Rosenthal struggled to collect himself, took a deep breath, and turned in his swivel chair to a set of file drawers within easy reach. He selected one and pulled it open. Turning his face back to his guests, he said quietly, "This file drawer contains my records of last year's honorees. The woman's name?"

"Greta van Dijk," the professor replied. She then spelled the last name.

Rosenthal slid his hand back over the files and quickly found the name. He lifted the file, slid the drawer closed, and turned again to face the visitors. Placing the thick file on the desk, he opened it to the covering page. "Greta van Dijk," he said aloud. "Ferwerd, the province of Friesland, Holland. Yes… I recall her nomination papers. A wonderful story… hid a young Jewish woman in plain sight, right in the center of the village, for two years…. Yes….

"But what has happened? Tell me what you know… please."

"We know," replied the professor immediately, "that an iron swastika was placed on her doorstep Saturday afternoon, that her telephone wires were cut about that same time, and that sometime that night men came to her door and kicked repeatedly at it, shouting that sickening slogan from the war years — *Voor Honden en Joden Verboden* — and then, when she attempted to flee out her back door, she was physically attacked by two gunmen who were stationed at the rear."

Rosenthal's eyes bulged. "Is she…"

"She is fine, sir," said the professor. "The assailants were, in turn, attacked and… ah… rather violently disabled… by one of those close friends of ours from the UK, assisted by the twenty-four-year-old niece of Ms. van Dijk, and, as well, by Greta van Dijk herself."

Rosenthal shook his head in confusion. "But…"

"These friends of ours in England, Mr. Rosenthal, have… well… special… ah…." She stopped and turned to her husband.

Belton leaned forward. "These people in the UK, sir, got special connections. They sometimes learn about things that nobody else knows about. In this case, they got messages that let them know this attack was gonna happen. And… well… y'don't wanna fool around with 'em when they get goin' on this kind of thing." His lopsided grin emerged.

Rosenthal was no less confused. Shaking his head, he began again. "But…"

"See," the detective continued, "some of these people… well… they receive… they get sent…."

"Mr. Rosenthal," interrupted the professor, "it's all right out of your scriptures… and ours. The scriptures we call the Old Testament? It's all right there, sir: visions… divine visions… sent by the Almighty to those chosen as adequate receivers of such. It's right out of the Bible itself, Mr. Rosenthal. And, with these people to whom we are referring, this has been going on for more than three decades.

"In this case," she continued, "they received the pertinent visions last Friday, assembled immediately, and commissioned one of their number, a former Royal Navy boarding party commander, to rescue Ms. van Dijk. And he did."

She paused while her host attempted to absorb what he had just been told. After several moments of silence, she continued.

"Once Luke Manguson — that's the young man who disabled Ms. van Dijk's assailants — returned to London with the Dutch woman and her niece, the whole group, which now includes eight adults and a set of infant twins, plus, for the moment, Greta van Dijk, decided to sequester themselves in their fortress mansion back in Birmingham. That's where they are now."

She went on to explain to her astonished host that the "visioners" had been in battles with various "opponents of the Lord," as she put it to Rosenthal, for many years. Partially in response to this ongoing war, Luke Manguson's parents — his father having been the original visioner — had purchased years ago a Birmingham-area mansion, converted the structure and its walled grounds into an inn, and made their living by taking in guests.

However, she explained further, when they went on a war footing, as now, guests were sent to other accommodations, security was employed beyond the perimeter of the walls, and a state of high alert was maintained until the crisis was resolved in one way or the other. The mansion had originally been selected by Jason and Elisabeth Manguson in part because it included a large, Second-World-War-era underground bomb shelter, situated just outside the foundation of the main structure. The senior Mangusons had improved and modified the shelter as soon as they had taken occupancy decades ago, so that they could on a moment's notice cut off all dependency on the outside world.

"So, Mr. Rosenthal," the professor concluded, "I asked you for this session in order to find out, first, if you were aware of this assault in Holland. And I see that you were not. And so I ask now if you are aware of any similar assaults, recent or not recent, upon any member of the Righteous Among Nations."

Rosenthal shook his head. "I am… I am horrified. It has never crossed my mind that Nazis… or neo-Nazis… or Nazi sympathizers… would shift their hatred and aggression from us… from the Jewish people themselves… to those who sheltered us…."

"And yet," he continued, "why do I find myself so astonished at this? The Nazis themselves made everything so clear, did they not? They said so very clearly in the horror years that anyone sheltering a Jew would be dealt with exactly as though that person were herself or himself a Jew."

Silence again enveloped the small office.

"And so," Eleanor Chapel at length resumed, "I am brought to my other question, Mr. Rosenthal. It seems, to say the least, highly unlikely that this one member of the Righteous Among Nations — Ms. van Dijk — would be singled out from among the many. We — our UK friends, my husband and I — have adopted the working hypothesis that she was but the first, so far as any of us knows, in what may quickly become a systematic attempt on the lives of the surviving Righteous Among Nations. We are operating under the plausible assumption that these neo-Nazis, if that is what they should be called, seek now to *exterminate* the Righteous, to visit upon them the total destruction that they once visited upon your people.

"And so I ask you, Mr. Rosenthal: Can you be of assistance to us now? Can you help us in considering what kind of action to take? Is there any sort of protective or policing function that exists within the Committee on the Righteous? Does the committee have any sort of official connection to Mossad?"

At this last, a reference to the State of Israel's widely respected — and, to some, widely feared — intelligence agency, Rosenthal's hands came up from Greta van Dijk's file folder, palms facing Eleanor Chapel. "Oh, no, professor," he said quickly. "The committee is simply an overseer of *Yad Vashem*, and, of course, a screening-and-judging body that determines which ones of those nominated should, in fact, be honored as Righteous Among Nations. There is no protection or policing function, and surely no connection to Mossad.

"However," he continued, "that most emphatically does *not* mean that the committee — and I — have no interest in this report from Holland, nor does it mean that there are not some on the committee with… ah… *informal* connections to individuals within Mossad.

"There is hardly any subject you could name that would or could be of greater concern." He glanced at his watch. "It is early evening now in Israel, but that does not mean that I cannot… cannot 'do business'… with some of my colleagues on the Committee on the Righteous… and do so right now… in the next several hours. And I fully intend to do exactly that."

He nodded to himself, staring down at Greta van Dijk's still-open file. "As soon as our discussion here is finished," he continued, "I will clear my calendar for the rest of the day. There are a number of our committee members who will be especially concerned with what you have reported. I will start with them."

He paused for a moment, looking uncomfortable, and added, "I will… ah… omit the… ah… the references to the… ah… to the visions… to the… ah… to the supernatural aspects of your report. It will be enough to communicate the facts of the attack itself. That is all the committee members will need to understand."

Rosenthal stated this as a simple fact, not seeking the permission of his visitors to omit their explanations of the group's prescience, nor offering them some perspective on how he would explain to committee members the stunning failure of an armed, five-man Nazi attack on an unarmed, sixty-year-old Dutch woman. He left his guests to conclude that his Israeli counterparts would simply assume law enforcement's intervention as the obvious explanation.

"These Nazi atrocities *will not* resurrect themselves," he concluded forcefully, fists striking his desk lightly but emphatically. "They… absolutely… will… *not!*"

Fewer than 18 hours after the conclusion of the brief meeting in Solomon Rosenthal's office in New York, Luke Manguson was awarded the final standby seat available on the Tuesday morning British Airways flight from Heathrow to JFK. The transatlantic phone lines between the Manguson-Clark group, first in London and then in Birmingham after their wholesale move to the lodge, and Eleanor Chapel and Sidney Belton in New York, had buzzed almost continually since the Sunday afternoon return to London of Luke, Kory van Dijk and the newly rescued member of the Righteous Among Nations.

Knowing something about the connections that Eleanor Chapel had established and nurtured between the Jewish seminary and her own, Rebecca had placed the first call to the group's esteemed colleagues in New York. These two were veterans: in the detective's case, of three summers of warfare side-by-side with the British contingent; and in his wife's case, of the last two. Rebecca had reasoned that the Jewish seminary would surely have formulated some sort of institutional connection with *Yad Vashem,* and that Eleanor Chapel would know, and would be known by, the JTS institutional coordinator of those efforts.

She had been correct, and, following the Chapel-Belton-Rosenthal meeting and Rosenthal's reportedly "productive and promising" conversations with nearly a third of the 35-member Committee on the Righteous on that Monday evening in Israel, Rosenthal had placed a midafternoon call to the professor in her Manhattan office one block away. She, having then conversed with her husband at some length, had placed a late-afternoon-in-New-York transoceanic call to the lodge in Birmingham, where the time was nearly 11:00 p.m. Monday.

By midnight in Britain, the group had reached prayerful consensus that Luke Manguson should go forthwith to New York to meet face-to-face with Solomon Rosenthal, Eleanor Chapel and Sidney Belton on Tuesday. If he could succeed in getting a standby seat on the British Airways flight out of Heathrow next morning, and with the five-hour time change, he could be in Rosenthal's office by midafternoon. If he failed to get on the flight, he could, as an active Royal Navy reservist, contact the Royal Air Force and seek a space-available flight to the East Coast of the U.S. sometime that night. He would not, certainly, in that case be in New York on Tuesday afternoon, but there was every chance he could be there and ready for a Wednesday morning conference at the JTS.

All of those at the lodge had been in agreement on two things: first, that Luke and only Luke should undertake this part of the mission; and second, that, although they knew of no actual threat to the global membership of the Righteous Among Nations, urgency should be assumed as a matter of course. The first conclusion was reached simply because, with Matt Clark committed to staying "home" — that is, at the lodge in Birmingham — with Rebecca and the twins, that left only Luke with the military reservist connection allowing the likelihood of air force transportation, if needed, and other possible military assistance, as well. The second conclusion was simply an extension of the urgency that had led the group to send Kory and Luke to the Dover-Calais ferry within hours of their first meeting.

The two rescuers had, after all, arrived at 9 Hoofdstraadt in Ferwerd less than one hour before the Nazis' would-be assault on Greta van Dijk. And this had been characteristic of the group's experiences from the first: that divine intervention, once received, left absolutely no time for human hesitation.

And so Luke had departed the lodge's fortress-like perimeter at first light, the full assemblage having gathered in the side yard to pray together and to bid him Godspeed. The final and most heartfelt embraces had been reserved for, first, his mother, next, his sister, and finally, though she hung back shyly, Kory van Dijk.

As he took his seat on the British Airways Boeing 747 — an interior aisle seat near the tail — Luke closed his eyes and gave prayerful thanksgiving. He gave thanks for his family's love and support. He gave thanks for the blessings that he had already experienced in his first real courtship. He gave thanks for the successful rescue of Greta van Dijk just three nights earlier.

He prayed for the recovery and well-being of the two gunmen whom he had cut, smashed and trussed. And he prayed God's forgiveness for his sins, calling to mind singly his most recent missteps, lapses, angers, fears, selfish acts, prideful thoughts....

And he prayed for the Holy Spirit's gifts of clarity, readiness and strength to face what inevitably lay ahead.

His prayer completed, he turned his attention immediately and fully to the upcoming session with the professor, the detective and Solomon Rosenthal. His expectation was that Rosenthal's telephone conversations with members of the Committee on the Righteous — those hoped-for "productive and promising" conversations — would provide him and his two colleagues with sufficient perspective to allow them to formulate at least the outline of a plan to stop the impending violence toward the Righteous Among Nations, violence that, they each knew, was just now at its starting point.

Luke tossed his bright red gym bag — the only piece of luggage he had brought on the trip — onto the seat of the cab at JFK's teeming taxi stand and gave the driver the Manhattan street address of the Jewish Theological Seminary. He had stopped in the men's room of the terminal just long enough to wash his face and to change into a fresh shirt. He felt reasonably refreshed.

He had no way of knowing in advance of the meeting whether he would be returning to London that same evening on another standby, whether he would be staying in New York several days, or whether his subsequent destination would be somewhere in the world other than the UK. Rather than attempting to bring clothing suitable for the myriad possibilities, he had brought an absolute minimum, knowing that he could shop effectively in New York City for anything that he might need, and for whatever mission might be forthcoming.

The meeting was itself "productive and promising," as, reportedly, had been Solomon Rosenthal's long-distance conversations. And Rosenthal had been genuinely pleased early that morning to receive Eleanor Chapel's call, informing him that Luke Manguson was by then at 39,000 feet over the Atlantic, and requesting permission to bring the Londoner with them to their scheduled meeting later that day at the JTS. Rosenthal had replied that not only would Mr. Manguson be most welcome at the meeting, but that he, Rosenthal, would look very much forward to hearing a first-hand account of the *contretemps* in northern Holland Saturday night. Ever the efficient organizer, he had then reserved a conference room large enough to accommodate the now-expanded number of participants in the upcoming session.

In the meeting, after listening intently to Luke's account of the assault in Ferwerd, Rosenthal reported that several of the committee members with whom he had spoken the previous evening in Jerusalem had heard "rumors" of an organized assault on the surviving members of the Righteous Among Nations. The rumored centerpiece of the clandestine activity was a neo-Nazi group of West Germans whose shadowy existence was, as Rosenthal had guessed from the start, being tracked by Mossad. Not just one, but four different committee members, Rosenthal reported, had said that they "understood" that Mossad had been monitoring such a group.

While none had specifics, each of the four members promised to pursue his own, individual contact within Mossad and to learn as much as possible, as quickly as possible. Finally, each of the four had assured Rosenthal that he would telephone with information as soon as there was anything useful to report. Rosenthal had asked each to phone him by Wednesday, late afternoon, in Israel, whether there was anything "useful" or not, thereby giving each man almost two full days to work on the question.

Accordingly, calculating the seven-hour time difference, he had asked the threesome in the conference room with him to return next morning for an 11:00 a.m. meeting at which time he expected to have all four reports in hand. They each agreed to return at that time.

Solomon Rosenthal escorted his guests to the main doorway of the seminary, bade good-bye to each, and, after watching them exit, returned quickly and eagerly to his office and his telephone. Outside, the professor and the detective asked the Londoner if they could take him to an "early" dinner, knowing that his body clock understood the time to be approaching midnight. Luke declined, listened carefully to Eleanor Chapel's directions to the guest room she had arranged for him at her seminary, and turned to cross Broadway while the couple proceeded east on 120th toward their parked automobile.

Luke waited for the signal, crossed the wide thoroughfare and continued west on 120th, toward the Hudson River, for another block. He walked rapidly, fighting the fatigue that sought to overtake him. Aside from his small gym bag, its long strap slung over his right shoulder, he carried nothing.

Unlike the professor and the detective, he had taken no notes during the meeting with Solomon Rosenthal. A fundamental component in his Royal Navy training had been to develop a high capacity to retain, memorize and prioritize, as needed, large and complex units of information without committing anything to paper. This had stood him in good stead on many occasions, some military and some not.

He turned north on Claremont Avenue, as the professor had instructed. Tired though he was, he strode along the sidewalk with all senses on absolute highest alert. He, like his family in England and his companions in New York, was on a war footing. Danger could be found — and often, in fact, actually was — anywhere and everywhere.

Halfway along the north-south block, he heard a sharp squeal of tires, very close behind him. In one movement, he wheeled to his left, allowed the gym bag to slip from his shoulder and, as it fell, pulled from it the heavy universal knife handle that was housed in a specially tailored pocket along the side of the bag.

The handle itself, *sans* knife blade, looked innocuous. Wielded by Luke Manguson, it was a formidable blunt instrument.

He saw that two very large men had already exited the right-side doors of a glistening black Lincoln Town Car, and that each was showing him the handle of a large-caliber pistol, the muzzle of each gun partially concealed in each man's clothing, but ready for instantaneous use. While walking, first on 120th and now on Claremont, Luke, his eyes scanning continuously for threat from any quarter, had already taken note of the fact that the sidewalks were nearly empty of pedestrians, despite the crush of rush-hour vehicular traffic on both streets. Alone on the long sidewalk, he faced the two gunmen.

The men came at him running, one on each side. Their approach conformed almost exactly to one of the training scenarios he had many times practiced and, upon occasion, executed on hostile decks during his years as boarding-party leader. He stood relaxed, the knife handle cupped in his right hand so that its shaft was hidden from his attackers' eyes behind his massive forearm.

As they drew abreast and closed on him in their well-rehearsed, two-man pincer movement, Luke suddenly became a blur of purposeful, physically devastating action. In a single, fluid maneuver, he crouched and strode laterally to his left in a lightning-like thrust that took him well away from the gunman on the right. As part of the same movement, he reached with his left hand for the assailant's pistol as it was being withdrawn, too late, from its housing. He seized the barrel in his iron grip and held the shaft immobile in a downward-facing position while the attacker struggled vainly, now with both hands, to extricate the weapon.

The attacker on Luke's right, having continued to lean in toward him in a fruitless attempt to grasp his near arm, extended his reach still further as his would-be captive took the long lateral stride in the direction opposite. He was then utterly helpless a millisecond later when Luke, the gun barrel secured in his left hand, pivoted to his right and in a movement too quick to follow with the eye drove the heavy steel knife handle up and under the assailant's jaw.

The stroke was similar to the one he had delivered with an empty right hand in a Dutch village several nights earlier, and the results were nearly identical. The assailant's jawbone was shattered by metal-on-bone impact, his head snapped back violently, his vertebral column bent impossibly backward and his knees buckled fully under him. Unconscious, he fell uncontrolled onto the sidewalk, his weapon clattering to the concrete beside him.

Luke, still holding the other gunman's weapon by the barrel, turned his head back to the left to find the unfortunate man swinging his left leg and foot upward in an unskillful attempt to deliver a blow to his would-be victim's torso. Luke blocked the clumsy effort with his right bicep and forearm, and, still holding the gun barrel's shaft in its original position, drove the knife handle directly into the attacker's throat. The gunman dropped as though shot through the heart, grasping his neck and making gurgling, choking sounds as his weapon, too, released by Luke at the moment of impact, fell harmlessly to the sidewalk.

Luke kicked the two handguns away from his incapacitated assailants, then spun around to see the Lincoln pulling away from the curb, its engine roaring. The muscular automobile fought its way into the Claremont Avenue traffic, its driver blowing the horn continuously and, at length, successfully bullying his way forward.

The attackers' intended victim, now in complete command of the field, stood relaxed and still, hands at his side, knife handle still at the ready, and watched the Town Car's noisy, halting departure for a long moment. He then stooped, sheathed the knife handle in its tailored pocket along the side of his gym bag, hoisted the lightweight bag onto his shoulder and resumed the short walk to his assigned guest room at the seminary.

He looked very much forward to getting to his room and to his bed. Luke Manguson was tired.

Most men, after a day like the one Luke had just completed — that day coming on the heels of a violent incursion into Holland just three days before — would have lain awake in their beds, their minds racing through the chaotic scenes just completed or the chaotic ones upcoming. And Luke was indeed lying awake, despite the lateness of the hour in the UK where his day had begun.

His thoughts were, however, not on chaos or violence at all. They were on Kory van Dijk. He found to his private embarrassment that he missed her terribly. He wanted to be able to *talk* to her, and right now, this minute. He wanted to talk to her about what had happened every second since he had embraced her at his departure from the lodge so many hours before.

He wanted to tell her about the uneventful drive to Heathrow, the success at the airport in getting the hoped-for flight, the transatlantic flight itself, his arrival at JFK, the long taxi ride from the airport to the seminary, the meeting with Solomon Rosenthal and its anticipated fruits in next morning's scheduled meeting and finally the mysterious and failed assault on Claremont Avenue. He wanted to tell her everything, and he wanted to hear her questions and responses and reactions.

He wanted to ask her about her own day. He wanted to hear her voice, see her brown eyes, study her expressive face. He wanted to hold her hand.

He shook his head in the darkened room, staring toward the ceiling. "So, this is how grown-up love feels," he mused to himself.

Then he smiled and closed his eyes. He was very tired indeed.

At almost the same moment that her brother, five time zones away, was so violently parrying, disarming and defeating two gunmen on the streets of Manhattan, Rebecca Clark was tapping softly on the door of the guest room occupied by Kory van Dijk. Hearing no response, she determined to tap just once more, but before her hand reached the dark wood of the door, it opened tentatively.

"Kory?" whispered Rebecca, "were you asleep? I saw the light under your door and thought you might still be reading."

Kory swung the door open and smiled. "I was reading," she whispered, "but I wasn't sure that little tapping noise was on my door or my aunt's."

Rebecca turned her head and looked behind her at the door across the hallway, then back at Kory. "Her light seems to be off. She must be exhausted."

Kory nodded, opening the door still further and stepping to one side. "Do you want to come in, Rebecca?" she asked, still whispering.

Rebecca nodded and entered. There were only two chairs in this guest room, as was the case with most of the single-occupancy rooms in the lodge. One was upholstered and was positioned under an antique floor lamp. The other was a straight-backed wooden chair situated at the small writing desk.

Kory walked to the desk, pulled the straight-backed chair out and turned it to face the other. She gestured for Rebecca to sit in the larger chair.

Both women were dressed for bed, each wearing a light summer robe over nightclothes. Rebecca's hair was disorganized, some of the long, thick strands falling forward haphazardly, framing her high cheekbones, while the rest trailed down her back and out of sight. Kory's brown locks were lustrous, looking much as they had when she had arrived at the Clarks' home in her yellow sundress. Her hair had just received its nightly brushing: one hundred strokes, administered every evening before bed, without fail.

Rebecca saw the guest room's Bible open on the bed. "Were you doing your evening prayers, Kory?" she asked.

"Yes, I had just finished with my hair, and had just begun my reading," she said, nodding her head. "I'm in First John, a favorite!"

Rebecca smiled in recognition. "Isn't it just *wonderful?*" she asked, but then, without waiting for Kory's response, continued.

"Kory, I'm so sorry to interrupt you," she said. "I did my devotions earlier, and just finished feeding the twins. I watched them until they fell asleep, and then found I wasn't sleepy anymore. When I came in the hallway, I saw your light still on. And I realized I wanted to speak to you.

"And now I realize how selfish I'm being. You're in First John and here I am keeping you from him and from your prayers. I'm *quite* embarrassed."

"Oh, no, Rebecca," said Kory, "I'm so glad you've come. I'd *so* much like to know you better than I do. I know you only through Luke's stories about you. I think it's amazing how close the two of you are, Rebecca. I've never seen anything like it, and it just seems to me that… well… this is how brothers and sisters *always* ought to be with each other."

Rebecca smiled and nodded. "It *is* extraordinary. We're very blessed, and we know we owe so much of it to our parents. But we also know that we owe a great deal to… well… to the Holy Spirit's demands… as they have been pressed upon us over these last three years. We were close before, but we have become comrades-in-arms, and that adds quite an unusual ingredient to a brother-sister relationship, as you might imagine."

Kory nodded, but then frowned ever so slightly. Rebecca's reference to the last three years' battles had sent a disturbing shaft through her mind, and that shaft had then registered fleetingly across her expressive face. She looked down and shook her head.

"What is it, Kory?" asked Rebecca, concern reflected in her near-whispered question.

Still looking down, Kory blushed. "It's… your brother, Rebecca. Luke has been gone only one day, and… and… I miss him terribly. I know he's only gone to New York for a meeting, or maybe more than one meeting, and he may be back soon… but… I just *miss* him.

"Isn't that just so silly, Rebecca?"

In response, Rebecca smiled her brilliant smile. She nodded. "Yes, Kory," she said softly. "It is terribly, terribly silly.

"And it is also absolutely wonderful… absolutely *wonderful* beyond any words I can bring to mind."

After a moment, she continued. "You know, Kory, I've never seen my brother like this before. I've never seen him so… well… *absorbed* by someone like he so obviously is with you. I had begun to imagine that that sort of thing was just not part of his make-up, and that the Lord had simply put him together without that particular component part.

"But, Kory, I see that it is… it *is* part of my brother's make-up. He *does* have that component part. And I want you to know that I could not *possibly* be happier than I am to see him like this. I didn't know if God would grant him this kind of blessing at all, Kory.

"And now I do. Now I know.

"And I am just so very grateful."

# CHAPTER FIVE

HOURS AFTER HER LATE-NIGHT CONVERSATION WITH KORY VAN Dijk, yet well before sunrise on Wednesday morning, Rebecca sat bolt upright in bed. Her and her husband's bedroom on the lodge's second floor was semi-dark, a small nightlight illuminating the area near the corner where the cribs nestled.

She had returned to bed just fifteen minutes earlier, having fed, changed and quieted the children again, and had fallen immediately asleep.

She knew instantly why she had wakened. Sitting bolt upright she breathed deeply and prepared her mind. *Father, help me to receive that which….*

But the vision was upon her before she could complete even the opening sentence of her prayer. As always, the center of her field of vision was, first, obscured and then filled completely by an image with sharp outlines and clear contrasts. She concentrated fully, her gray eyes wide in the darkness.

And swiftly — very swiftly — the vision materialized.

It seemed to begin exactly where her first vision had ended, with a wide-angle view of what she now knew was *Yad Vashem*, the rows upon rows of carob trees stretching before her mind's eye, the tiny plaques under each providing mute testimony to the courage and godly obedience of the Righteous Among Nations. Although she watched the shifting scene as intently as she could, she found herself afterward unable to describe the stages by which the envisioned rows of trees and plaques translated themselves into something altogether different, and yet the same.

She simply knew that somehow, before her dreaming eyes, *Yad Vashem* had slowly been transformed into the interior of an elongated vault, several times deeper than it was wide, and that the exquisitely ordered columns of trees and plaques had become, instead, row upon row of sinister, gunmetal-gray filing cabinets.

The vision communicated the essence of the Righteous Among Nations to her mind, just as before, but no longer did the vision feature an arboreal tribute to these gentile heroes. The vision now comprised — and comprised ominously — what Rebecca was given to understand to be these heroes' identities, histories and locations. She knew and understood immediately — for she found that this knowledge and these understandings were fed directly into her mind — that she was being presented with an image of the records of those who, in repayment for their courage in hiding the Jewish remnant, were now earmarked for extermination by a new generation of Nazis.

The orderly, metallic images remained before Rebecca's mind's eye for long moments, stationary and stark, while the accompanying knowledge and understandings were implanted systematically into her alert, receptive, capacious mind. And finally, as the vision began to fade, her dreamed origin-of-perspective began to recede from the morbid chamber, the lens through which she observed retreating slowly back and back until, still retreating, it passed through heavy metal doors and out of the vault entirely.

Continuing without pause, the lens moved, still facing the vault from which it had withdrawn, through a second padlocked steel doorway, this one with wide, hinged metal doors secured both by the padlock on the doors themselves and by a crossbar that was itself separately padlocked. And as this final image faded and the dream drew to its close, Rebecca knew that she had just been shown the tomb of the Righteous Among Nations, as their tomb existed at that moment — in the form of records and plans and histories — prior to the actual, murderous onslaught that was to come.

And, although there had been provided to her dreaming mind no external landmarks or visual clues of any kind, she was given by the Source of All Visions to know and understand that this vault — this tomb — was situated within the Promised Land itself.

This was Israel.

Eleanor Chapel and Sidney Belton were early risers. When their oversized, wind-up alarm clock began its clattering proclamation of morning at exactly five o'clock, the detective rolled into a sitting position on his side of the bed, moved the small lever on the side of the clock to the *off* position, and rubbed his eyes sleepily. Then he turned his head to call his wife's name.

Before he could utter a syllable, he heard her calling his.

"Sidney," she said in her high, soft voice, "I've been thinking."

He turned his head all the way around and looked at her.

She had been sitting up in their bed, obviously for some time, pillows fluffed behind her back. Her gray hair fell loosely onto the front of her treasured, decades-old, cream-colored nightgown, framing her small face and leading her husband to smile his lopsided smile in the simple joy of seeing his beloved like this, the Eleanor Chapel that only he was ever allowed to see.

"How secure," she said immediately, "do you think the *Yad Vashem* records are? How hard do you suppose it would be for someone to duplicate those records and export them somewhere? The Righteous Among Nations are publicly honored, you know. Each name is right there under each little tree, there for all to see. What's to keep someone from organizing an entire locator system?

"Why, Solomon Rosenthal appeared to have in his own files, right here in Manhattan, a dossier of some sort on every single honoree. There could be dozens of such files in offices around the world, couldn't there, Sidney?

"Well? Couldn't there?"

The small bedroom was silent for a long moment. Then Sid Belton spoke.

"Eleanor," he said, his early-morning waking-up voice even deeper and scratchier than at other times, "it's too early to think this hard. It's too early even to *listen* to somebody who's thinkin' this hard. You're givin' me a headache."

He paused. And then, with his natural comedic understatement, he added, "Eleanor, I think I'm gonna knock you out."

Her tinkling laughter filled the room and filled his heart. She laughed and giggled delightedly, alternating between covering her mouth demurely and holding her aching sides. Finally she moved her index fingers to her face and wiped away the pooled tears that had risen in response to her miniature bout of hysteria.

Her laughter subsiding, she took a deep, happy breath, kissed the tips of the fingers of her own hand and reached over to her husband to deliver a light, second-hand kiss to his stubbly cheek. Fastening her bright eyes upon him once again, she arched her eyebrows.

"Okay, okay, Eleanor," he said, affecting a stylized grumpiness that transparently was anything but that, "here's an answer for ya'.

"Just havin' a Righteous member's name and general location isn't enough to get a serious campaign of terror underway, if that's what we're really lookin' at here. See, the master files for an operation like that, if there's any such thing somewhere in th' world, are gonna need a lot more than just a name and a country-of-residence, Eleanor. And that's all y'got on those little plaques.

"They're gonna need exact addresses. And they're gonna need all kinds of stuff about each person's routines, y'know what I mean?

"If you're gonna go after a lotta people in th' way these dirt bags seem to have in mind, you'd wanna know *how* they live their lives, see, not just where. You'd wanna know how y'get to their house, see, and how many people live with each one of em, and how young and strong *those* people are, and… well… you'd wanna know if there's a dog in th' house, and how big it is, and what kind it is.

"See what I mean, Eleanor? See what I mean? Y'do?

"So," he continued without pause, warming to his task, "if there is any such thing as an organized set of files that's bein' put together by some modern-day Nazi group of some kind, it would hafta be the work of a pretty good network of *clever* dirt bags, not just a bunch of hoodlums, see, and they'd hafta work on gettin' regular updates and doin' regular upkeep of each one of those files….

"Know what I mean, Eleanor? Know what I mean?"

Sidney Belton's concluding question was followed almost instantly by the jarring, jangling punctuation of the nightstand telephone at Eleanor Chapel's elbow. She looked across the bed at the alarm clock which now suggested ten minutes after five o'clock, frowned, and turned away from her husband to lift the receiver.

"Yes?" she said inquisitively.

Five minutes later, having returned the telephone to its cradle, Eleanor Chapel turned to face her husband, who remained sitting on the opposite side of the bed, his head still turned fully in his wife's direction.

"It was Rebecca, dear," she said.

The identifying remark was courteous but unnecessary. Sid Belton, in the early morning stillness of their bedroom, had heard faintly but distinctly the musical Oxford dialect with its unmistakable inflections, and, as well, had attended to his wife's quick series of opening questions: How were the twins doing? How was Matt getting along? How were Elisabeth and Jason?

"Rebecca dreamed last night, Sidney," she continued finally. "She waited until ten o'clock in England to call us, sweetheart that she always is, knowing we would arise at five here in New York."

She paused, thinking, then continued.

"Sidney, Rebecca's vision slips right in to the conversation you and I were just having, as though Shakespeare were writing the scene and we were acting it out, right here in this bedroom. Doesn't it just make your spine tingle when the Holy Spirit reaches down and *choreographs* an entire scene like this?"

She then summarized for him Rebecca's complete dream, emphasizing, as had Rebecca herself, the certainty that these sequestered files contained the exact kind of data that Sidney Belton had just described as absolutely necessary for the plot's furtherance. She concluded with the words, "And Sidney, would you believe it? Rebecca's mind was given the *full* certainty that this dossier-packed tomb of the Righteous Among Nations was right in the middle of the Holy Land. Sidney, it's in Israel!"

As Eleanor Chapel spoke her exclamation point, the telephone rang again.

Incredulous, she turned her head away from her husband and actually looked down at the offending instrument, feeling as she did that she was acting out some ridiculously implausible movie scene.

"Oh, for pity's sake!" she exclaimed, reaching again for the clamoring device.

"Yes?" she inquired once more.

"Why, Luke!" she said with genuine surprise in her voice, her face brightening. "I just got off the phone with your twin, dear. Can you imagine? Just that very moment!"

In response to the caller's question, she then proceeded to summarize Rebecca's report of her dream, just as she had for her husband moments earlier. The caller asked several more questions, then fell silent.

After a moment, she spoke again. "Luke? Why did you call, dear? Surely you didn't know that Rebecca...."

She then listened intently while Luke Manguson provided a detailed account of the Claremont Avenue assault that he had, the afternoon previous, successfully withstood. As he spoke, Eleanor Chapel's face changed, suggesting to her watching husband equal parts astonishment, confusion, and anger. When the conversation ended, she turned thoughtfully to face the detective once more.

"Luke was *attacked* on Claremont, just after we said good-bye to him yesterday, Sidney! Gunmen! Right there on the sidewalk! In broad daylight!

"What? Oh, no, no, he's not injured, he claims. Minimizes the whole thing, as usual. Just wanted us to know.

"Said he wanted to ask us to give the *fact* of the attack 'a little thought' before our eleven o'clock session this morning with Mr. Rosenthal. Said it seemed to him that there must be — um… what phrase did he use? — oh, yes… that there must be 'a touch of treason' within the ranks of that committee over in Israel… the people that Mr. Rosenthal had gotten in touch with to find out if they knew anything about some sort of plot against the Righteous."

She stopped and looked at her husband. He had turned his head away from her as she spoke this last, and was now looking down at his feet, continuing to sit on the edge of the bed, still unmoving since he had rolled into a sitting position fewer than twenty minutes before.

His wife knew that he was by now deep in thought, and so she remained silent, allowing him to process the avalanche of unsettling information that had been transmitted to them, first by Rebecca and then by Luke, and all within moments of the little alarm clock's announcement that 5:00 a.m. had arrived in New York City.

Hours later, three grim New Yorkers and one equally grim Londoner settled themselves in the small Jewish Theological Seminary conference room that Solomon Rosenthal had again reserved for their use. It was not quite 11:00 a.m., but each had wanted to be early, visitors and host alike.

Recognizing anew, after the Claremont Avenue attack, the danger faced by each of them just in moving from their own places of residence to the JTS, the couple and the Londoner had been escorted from their overnight locations — the professor and the detective from their third-floor Washington Heights apartment, and Luke from the seminary's guest room — by uniformed NYPD officers. The escort had been arranged as a no-questions-asked courtesy by the precinct captain in response to Sidney Belton's early-morning request. Both police units waited outside the JTS for further escort duty, if asked.

Rosenthal began the session unceremoniously, shaking his head as he spoke and, thought Eleanor Chapel, with more than a touch of embarrassment.

"I am *so* furious… I am… I am humiliated… I am… I am disbelieving, Lieutenant Manguson," he said haltingly in his heavy Eastern European accent. "I simply cannot… ah… cannot even *imagine* this action… this trespass… this… this criminal assault that… that was done to you just as you departed from us yesterday. And *here!* Such a short way from our seminary… I cannot…."

His voice trailed off.

Eleanor Chapel leaned forward quickly, shifting in her chair. "No, no, Mr. Rosenthal," she said softly, "really, you mustn't. You mustn't think that somehow this is an accident of *your* doing. Really…."

She stopped, thinking, and began again.

"You know, the possibility that someone on the committee… the Committee on the Righteous… actually engineered yesterday's assault on Luke is just one of so very many possibilities. What happened to him was probably not related in any fashion at all to your having contacted your colleagues in Israel. You mustn't assume that it was, Mr. Rosenthal. Please.

"The truth is that we just don't know. We can't know. New York can be a most violent city, after all. In fact, the whole thing could, you know, have been just a random attack on a pedestrian walking alone on a sidewalk."

She sat back and turned to her husband. "Talk to him, Sidney," she said insistently, her face earnest.

Sid Belton responded to her request immediately. But his tone and his words were altogether different from those of his wife's. She had been solicitous, reassuring, comforting, hopeful. Her husband was not.

Before addressing Rosenthal, he returned his wife's gaze and shook his head slowly. Then he reached over and patted her hand softly. Murmuring a single word — "no" — to her, he turned his face to their host.

"Eleanor's not exactly wrong, Mr. Rosenthal," he said brusquely, glancing quickly once more at his wife. "But you… and we… we all gotta take a real good look at the possibility that you've got… well… that you've got bad guys right there in your own organization, sir.

"Sure… there are some other possibilities, like Eleanor said. But not one of 'em is anywhere near as good as the possibility that you got problems… big problems… right there in your own ranks… right there within the Committee on the Righteous itself. And that's just a fact, sir. Y'know what I mean? Hm? Know what I mean?"

Sid Belton's perfunctory, rapid-fire manner of making and ending his statements, practiced and honed over decades of service in the NYPD, elicited a reluctant nod of the head from Solomon Rosenthal. But, seeing that the detective had finished his statement and that he would await an answer, Rosenthal cleared his throat and spoke again.

"What… what exactly *are* the… as you said… the 'other possibilities,' Detective Belton? I don't think I follow you. I'd *like* to believe that…."

Once more his voice trailed off without completing his sentence.

"Well," responded Belton immediately, "you've been the seminary's liaison to the Committee on the Righteous for a while now, sir, and that's no secret from anybody. If there is a plot out there to *get* these people… well… you, yourself, would be a very likely target. Y'know what I mean?"

Seeing only a puzzled expression move cross Rosenthal's face, Belton continued.

"If there is an organized effort here, Mr. Rosenthal, then these tacklin' dummies are gonna be smart enough to understand that puttin' some sort of listenin' device in your telephones, here at work *and* in your home, would be a basic step that they oughta take. And, now that somethin' has happened… y'know… this attack that Luke beat back yesterday… somethin' that would… y'know… get you thinkin' that your phones might be tapped… well… those listenin' devices, if they were there, might've already been taken outta your phones. Y'know what I mean? All of that would, y'know, be pretty easy for a bunch that's as organized as these baseball bats have gotta be. Y'know what I mean, Mr. Rosenthal? Um? Know what I mean, sir?

"Y'gotta understand," continued the detective without pause, "that just because you've got above-average security down there at the main doors to the JTS, that doesn't mean *anything* about the chances of somebody gettin' to the phones in your office and your apartment. And not just your phones. Y'can put a 'bug' in a lamp, in a TV, in one of those little mementos y'got all over your office….

"There are air-conditioning guys and plumbers and electricians and all kinds of people goin' through these buildings every day. It's not just your own JTS personnel. And these people — the bad guys, I mean — are major league, Mr. Rosenthal. First-class and major league."

Eleanor Chapel rolled her eyes at her husband's unique way of referencing his suspects. But she knew from experience that his apparently artless form of making his points and asking his questions, whether he considered an interviewee to be among the good or the bad, was both carefully crafted and extremely effective.

Solomon Rosenthal, after a moment, nodded his head thoughtfully. Then he inquired again, "What else, Detective Belton? What other possibilities are there, in your mind? How else, other than by subversion within our committee or by my telephones or office or apartment being… ah… 'bugged'… how else could this attack on Lieutenant Manguson have developed? I *want* to believe there are other possibilities. But…."

Belton, rare in his ability to communicate reassurance in the large context and urgency in the small, continued for some time, opening up avenue after avenue for his tiny audience, painting an elaborate picture of the means by which interested parties could have become aware of Luke Manguson's presence in New York City: penetration of Union Seminary's faculty, listening devices in his wife's desk telephone or elsewhere in her office, stake-outs of the Heathrow-to-JFK gates both in London and in New York, stake-outs of the baggage claim areas at JFK, and, among the simplest tactics of all, a stake-out of the main doors of the Jewish Theological Seminary, doors through which Luke would have entered and out of which he would have exited immediately prior to the assault. A prudent enemy would set up close observation of the JTS whether it had any foreknowledge of Luke Manguson's arrival from the UK or not. And that same prudent enemy could be expected, in point of fact, to be waiting outside right now, alert for the departure of any of the three.

None of this would necessarily have required collusion among the members of the Committee on the Righteous, Belton explained further. And, beyond all this, it would be naïve, he continued, to assume that some of the enemies who had fought Rebecca, Luke, Matt and their allies for three years had actually disappeared from the face of the earth, or that *those* enemies — the original enemies — had established no connections to the neo-Nazis who were mounting their attacks on the surviving members of the Righteous Among Nations.

True, the human head of the snake had been cut off one year ago by Luke Manguson's twin sister in actual physical combat of the most extraordinary kind. But this snake's body could, perhaps, regenerate in ways beyond the reach of the ordinary imagination.

When the detective had finished, Solomon Rosenthal smiled wanly and said quietly, "All of those possibilities, Mr. Belton, and yet… and yet… none of them strikes me as being quite as probable as the one I most fear: that there is subversion within the Committee on the Righteous itself. And, if I understand you fully, you tend to agree with me. Yes?"

Belton's lopsided grin emerged. "Well, Mr. Rosenthal," he said slowly, "I think I'd hafta put it a little stronger than that. I'd hafta say that all those other possibilities added together and stacked on top of each other wouldn't equal even *half* the likelihood that you got a rat inside that committee of yours.

"Know what I mean, sir? Y'know what I mean?"

Rosenthal looked down at his hands and nodded. Then he raised his hands to his face and slumped in his chair. A low, soft groan came from behind the hands, filling the small room with an exquisite sadness.

After a pause, he placed his hands flat on his desk and, speaking in a low, mournful voice, said quietly, "I must go there now."

Another pause, and then, "I must go to Jerusalem… now."

The room was silent. The guests waited.

Finally, Rosenthal brought his conclusion. "I must go to Jerusalem now. I must meet with members of the Committee on the Righteous with whom I have served for years, those whom I trust with my life. I must seek assistance from Israeli law enforcement. I must seek assistance from Mossad….

"I must go to Jerusalem… now."

At one o'clock, following a sixty-block trip down Central Park West in one of the NYPD mobile units — the other unit following at a discreet distance — Eleanor Chapel, Sid Belton and Luke Manguson were escorted to a corner table near the back wall of The Conservatory, the Mayflower Hotel's bustling coffee shop and restaurant. This had been the site of the professor and the detective's first conversation exactly two years earlier, and they smiled at each other as they took their seats, each joyfully recalling the encounter that had eventually changed their lives in so many and in such unexpected ways.

Resisting the temptation to reminisce at length, they simply acknowledged the fact of the anniversary to Luke, expressed good-natured regret that this could not be a more romantic occasion, and turned to business. Their lunch orders placed and a lyrical blessing offered by Eleanor Chapel, they plunged in to the topic at hand. The detective began with obvious reluctance, his dark, childlike eyes boring into the small floral centerpiece.

"We gotta go, y'know," he said cryptically.

His wife reached over and covered his hand gently, thereby drawing his eyes to hers. She knew that at times he could speak in a stream of consciousness that ignored the fact that there were listeners who needed fuller, more coherent declarations in order to stay abreast of him.

"We 'gotta go' where, Sidney?" she said, dropping her high, girlish voice to a lower register, mimicking joyfully both her husband's dialect and his guttural growl. "We 'gotta go' where?"

Belton cackled delightedly, provoking a broad smile from Luke at the byplay from this always-affectionate Christian couple. Luke realized that, from the moment he had joined the two the previous afternoon for their first session with Solomon Rosenthal, he had begun intuitively to study this marvelous relationship in hopes of deriving lessons he might apply to his and Kory's burgeoning romance. But quickly he forced himself away from the distraction and moved his eyes from the professor to the detective.

"We gotta go," repeated Belton, "with Mr. Rosenthal to Israel… to the Holy Land… that's where." His eyes moved alternately from his wife's to Luke's and back.

"Rosenthal says he's gotta go right now, y'know, and that he's gotta get Israeli law enforcement involved in this, y'know, and that he even wants to get Mossad in on the thing, if they're not already. Well, he may be right about both things, but I don't think he knows how t'go about doin' any of that. It sure doesn't *sound* like he knows how t'go about doin' any of that, anyway."

"Oh… and you *do*, Sidney Belton?" said his wife brightly.

"Oh, yes ma'am," he said, nodding his head, unsmiling. "Yes ma'am," he repeated. "I absolutely do. I *absolutely* do.

"And so… I gotta be there… and I gotta be there at least as fast as Mr. Solomon Rosenthal… maybe faster.

"And you two gotta come, too, y'know."

He stated this as a simple fact, not as a question or even as a proposition.

"You two gotta come, too, because you, Ms. Very-Smart-Old-Testament-Professor, are the one who is gonna be able to translate young Mrs. Clark's Israel visions — I figure there's gotta be more of those comin' any time, don't you? — into somethin' we can take action on.

"And you," Belton continued, turning to Luke Manguson, "*you* gotta come, Mr. Big-Shot-Royal-Navy-Boarding-Party-Officer, because you're the only warrior we got on our team, what with Mrs. Clark and Lieutenant Clark tied up at home in London with those two babies of theirs.

"It'll be pretty dangerous, I'd guess," he continued thoughtfully, "but I'm thinkin' that if I can get the arrangements I want with the Israelis, we'll actually be safer there than we are here. I mean, just *look* at us! We're actually ridin' around in NYPD police units! And we don't even know who that was tryin' to get at Luke yesterday, and so we don't even know how to protect ourselves, other than gettin' the police to escort us around as a favor to an old NYPD guy....

"And... y'know... when all's said and done... we'll only be safe... *after*... *we... win.*"

He looked again from one somber face to the other. "Y'know what I mean? Hm? Know what I mean?"

He paused, now returning his gaze to the table's small centerpiece. Then he nodded his head at his own conclusions and repeated thoughtfully, "So... we gotta go. And we gotta go right now."

There was a short silence. It became longer, and, before conversation could resume, the waiter arrived with their sandwiches, chatted briefly with the detective, and departed. Moments later, their first hungry bites having been taken, conversation resumed. Luke Manguson spoke first.

"Detective?" he inquired, "do you think that Israeli law enforcement will really have any interest in this? And Mossad, too?

"I'm more accustomed to going on the assumption that there is little to be gained going to the police — or, in Mossad's case, a government intelligence agency — with information that is derived even in part from our 'visioners,' as we're starting to call them now. How would we — how would you, detective, or Mr. Rosenthal or anyone — broach the subject without referencing my sister's... and Martha Clark's... divine images? As we've agreed so many times, we cannot realistically expect law enforcement to take action predicated on supernaturally initiated-and-received reports."

Belton nodded. "Right, Luke. But there's a difference here... a difference from what we've been faced with before.

"This time, there's at least some kind of rumor... some kind of whisperin'... somethin' that has started to float around... and it has to do with a physical threat to a whole bunch of people. And the sources for the rumors... whatever those are... are *not* our visions.

"Mr. Rosenthal told us that committee members had heard rumors of an organized assault on the Righteous. He told us that the center of the action — accordin' to the rumor — was a neo-Nazi group of West Germans. He told us that these West Germans were — also accordin' to the rumor — bein' tracked by Mossad. He told us that four different committee members had said that they 'understood' that Mossad had been watchin' such a group.

"And Ms. van Dijk, one of those, it seems, who's marked for extermination, was assaulted in Holland last Saturday. That's a plain fact. And you, Luke, the guy who ruined that attack, got assaulted right here on the Manhattan streets, just yesterday. That's a plain fact, too. We can present those facts… and the rumors that go along with 'em… without talkin' about visions at all."

"But…" said Luke.

The detective stopped him with an upraised hand and continued, now speaking with real urgency in his voice. "Even with all that, I don't think Solomon Rosenthal will get to first base with Israeli law enforcement, Luke. But if he knew how to work with Mossad… and if there's any substance to this report that Mossad is *already* trackin' and monitorin' this thing… that's a different story.

"And since Mr. Rosenthal does *not* have any idea, I'd say, how to work with Mossad… I gotta get there now, folks. And you, too.

"Know what I mean? Hm? Y'know what I mean?"

"But, detective…." said Luke.

The detective again raised his palm toward Luke Manguson and the torrent of words resumed. "I figure Mr. Rosenthal is gonna be scared now of talkin' with these particular committee members, given his suspicions about how word of your trip to New York got out in time to try and snatch ya off the streets. I figure he'll try Israeli — probably Jerusalem — law enforcement himself and get laughed outta the precinct, and then he'll probably go to Tel Aviv and try to walk right into Mossad headquarters. Now, you know *that's* gonna go over big.

"I'd like to stop him before he does too much damage, Luke. That'd allow me to move into my Mossad circles and get — and give — some credible information….

"Know what I mean? Hm? Y'know what I mean?"

This time, as the detective paused for breath, Luke did not attempt to speak, having learned better on his two previous attempts. And, after several moments of concentrated silence, Sid Belton nodded at the younger man.

"Detective," said Luke quietly, having finally been given the floor, "am I not correct in saying that *eventually* Mossad — or any other agency, or anybody at all who seeks to assist us — would be compelled to act, or not, on the basis of data that would have come from one of our visioners?

"If this adventure is anything like our others, at some point our only actionable clue… our only means of understanding what is required of us… will be obviously supernatural in origin….

"And what then?"

There was a very long pause.

Finally, the detective smiled his lopsided smile and shook his head, still looking at the centerpiece. "I guess we'll hafta find out, Luke. I guess we'll just hafta find out."

Again silence descended on the small table, each member of the threesome now lost in thought. Then Luke spoke once more.

"But Mossad, Mr. Belton?" he said softly. "Do you actually have contacts within Mossad? I'm under the impression that no one really knows who is Mossad and who's not, any more than anyone knows who is with MI6 in the UK or with CIA in the U.S."

"Well, Luke," replied the detective immediately, "I really can't comment on that one way or the other.

"Know what I mean, pal? Y'know what I mean?"

# Chapter Six

JAAKOV ADELMAN FOLDED HIS LANKY, SIX-FOOT-FIVE-INCH FRAME into a chair that he found, like all such upright, wooden chairs, thoroughly uncomfortable. The chair was situated at one of the small window tables at a coffee shop he had never before visited. To those diners who may casually have glanced his way, Adelman gave the impression of a man preoccupied with the news magazine that he held open in his right hand. But any who held him in their gaze for seconds longer would perhaps have seen that he did not look exactly in the direction of his magazine. Instead, his bright, almost black eyes looked just above the printed page, roaming the sidewalk on which Manhattan pedestrians bustled past just on the other side of the spotless plate-glass window.

In fact, however, Adelman studied neither the periodical nor the pedestrians. He had selected this seat because of its geometric relationship to the restaurant's interior. From his seated position, he could now study in the window's ghostly reflected image a threesome that he had shadowed into the bustling coffee shop, having first followed them in his automobile as they were driven in an NYPD police van on a lengthy, halting journey south from the Jewish Theological Seminary to the Columbus Circle area.

Jaakov Adelman was a highly skilled shadow. For him and for all of his kind, following a marked police unit for sixty New York City blocks, in this case a journey with hardly a single turn, was child's play.

Now, appearing to gaze vacantly out the window, he stared thoughtfully at his three targets. Relaxed and unhurried, secure in the impenetrable veil of deception he had arranged for himself, Adelman considered his quarry: an Old Testament professor at Union Theological Seminary; her husband, a private detective of impressive renown both domestically and internationally; and, finally, a Londoner, a former Royal Navy lieutenant whose arrival in the city the previous day had attracted immediate and aggressively hostile attention from an organization that Adelman was coming to know better each day.

For Jaakov Adelman was a *katsa* — a Mossad field agent — and during his ten years of service in Israel's elite intelligence organization he had distinguished himself consistently, so much so that his colleagues and superiors in Tel Aviv viewed him now as a true master of his craft. He was, in fact, sufficiently valued within Mossad to have been apprised immediately of the failure of a Mossad-predicted assault on a Dutch woman in extreme northern Holland less than a week earlier. And he had actually witnessed firsthand another fully anticipated-by-Mossad attack just twenty hours before, this one professionally conducted — though no less emphatically defeated — against Lieutenant Luke Manguson himself on the streets of Manhattan.

Agent Adelman would not have been in the least embarrassed had he been charged by, say, detective Sidney Belton with dereliction or with cowardice at having made not the slightest effort to intervene in the previous day's assault. And, truth be told, Belton would not have lodged such an accusation in the first place.

For Belton understood Mossad, its nature and its purposes, just as he understood MI6 and CIA. No intelligence agency — Israeli, British, American or other— was in the business of rescuing individual citizens simply because it might be religiously, ethically or morally the right thing to do. All such agencies were in the business of spying, of knowing secrets that no one else knew, and of using those secrets in support of national agendas that were nearly always themselves secret. And, beyond this, all such agencies were in the business of killing, or — to use the more precise parlance — in the business of assassination, where assassination was deemed to be in the national interest and where no other solution was readily obtainable or likely to be equally effective. Within Mossad, the operative euphemisms were: to send someone "on vacation" or to the "better world."

Mossad agent Jaakov Adelman had long ago reconciled the world of deception and violence within which he moved as a member of perhaps the world's most feared intelligence agency with the world of purity and service to Jehovah within which he moved as an orthodox Jew. The inherent conflict between the two, as he understood that conflict, was not, at its core, between violence and nonviolence, but between the use of falsehood and deception as necessary tactics in reaching national goals versus obedience to Almighty God, regardless of circumstances or consequences, in service to all that that necessarily implied: truth, integrity, honor. Yes, a Jew might be violent when necessary. A Jew could *not* be false to others, to himself and to Jehovah as a basic way of relating to the world.

But Adelman was Mossad. And so he consciously subordinated his orthodoxy to his secret, danger-ridden and sometimes murderous allegiance to his country. He appeared to the few New York City residents who knew him as nothing more than an ordinary citizen of the State of Israel, in the United States on long-term business.

And that meant that he did not wear the garb of the Orthodox Jew. That meant that he did not hold membership in an Orthodox congregation. And that also meant that he would always pose, in the U.S., as a nonreligious Jew, casually acknowledging his Jewish cultural history and behaving true to his strictly observant beliefs only in the privacy of his shabby, obscure and minimalist apartment in Morningside Heights.

Jaakov Adelman was, then, to all appearances a Jewish-American businessman working for an Israeli financial services company. As such, he needed no office in New York, and simply worked out of his apartment, located several blocks from the institutional cluster formed by the Jewish Theological Seminary, Union Theological Seminary and Columbia University.

Remarkably, Adelman had come to understand, and even to understand well, something of the nature of the "special connections" possessed by the Christian threesome that he continued to observe confidently, dividing his attention between the thoroughly non-kosher club sandwich on his plate and the reflective window at his side. Through highly sophisticated espionage techniques and, equally, through simple due diligence, Mossad agents in the UK and in the U.S. had collected data for three years on the group they termed the *Rebekka Yahalomin* — the "Rebecca Special Communications Unit" — their coded means of referencing the Manguson-Clark group.

This, they understood, comprised a small body of Christians who had apparently been granted some form of divine access to events — events that lay in the future — that posed threats directly or indirectly to traditional Christianity. Adelman, having no doubt of the supernatural authenticity of the group's connections, would have said "the group was *obviously* granted divine access." His colleagues would have said "the group was *apparently* granted divine access." And each of them would have, and, in fact, had, drawn that "divine access" conclusion simply because no alternative explanations could realistically be formulated. If they had been questioned, Adelman's colleagues, ultimately pragmatic like nearly all in the intelligence services, would have displayed little intellectual, philosophical or theological interest in the whole subject. By whatever means, the *Rebekka Yahalomin* "knew things." How they knew them was of much less interest than the fact itself.

And as an organization, Mossad had passed no judgment on the mysterious nature of these divinely-accessed warnings, foretellings, and commands. The agents involved had simply concluded that certain events that they — Israel's master spies — continued to observe at approximately one-year intervals could be accounted for in no other manner. They viewed the issue as one of unexplainable and unknowable Cause resulting in unexplainable but knowable effect. And that meant that the members of the *Rebekka Yahalomin* were periodically tracked as "special resources" that could conceivably, at some point in an uncertain but forever-threatened Israeli future, be used to the State of Israel's advantage.

As an Orthodox Jew whose belief in Jehovah and in a divinely ordered universe was absolute, Jaakov Adelman believed as surely in the authenticity of the Manguson-Clark visions as did the Christians directly involved in receiving, interpreting and acting on them. That did not make Adelman a Christian. That made him an Orthodox Jew who believed that Jehovah could act in any way He chose, at any time, using any method and any "good" human being convenient and suitable to His purposes.

Like all veteran *katsas*, Adelman operated independently and with almost complete authority to decide how to conduct himself within the broad framework of the assignments he was given. Indeed, as an experienced and extraordinarily successful agent, he was authorized to craft any highly imaginative course of action he thought necessary and expedient to reach a "solution" to the problems layered within each of his assignments.

When he had witnessed the attack on Luke Manguson on Claremont Avenue the previous afternoon, he was, first, surprised at the brazenness of the attack, one which, in his assessment, clearly had kidnapping, not murder, as its immediate goal. He had been certain that if the assailants had simply wanted Manguson dead, they would have gunned him down from their Lincoln Town Car's open windows without ever slowing the vehicle.

Adelman had been genuinely astonished at the outcome of the fracas. Never had he seen an apparently unsuspecting civilian disarm and devastate well-trained, carefully prepared gunmen with such dispatch. Yes, he knew that he himself would have handled the attack with equal skill, but only because, unlike Luke Manguson, he carried concealed firearms and they were always at the ready. Attacked in the same manner, Jaakov Adelman would simply have shot the two gunmen before they had taken a second step from the Lincoln.

He also knew, however, that he was Mossad, and that as an intelligence agent his primary currency was secrecy. No one would be likely to attack him on the street, because no one would identify him as an espionage agent or, indeed, a target of any kind.

Of that he was sure.

And yet, he knew, he was just moments away from compromising his greatest asset: his professional anonymity.

Jaakov Adelman called for his bill and paid for his lunch as soon as he saw the threesome begin to look for a waiter. His own transaction completed, he lifted his half-full coffee cup and saucer from the table, rose from his chair, and strode casually back through the coffee shop's interior, meandering slowly toward the rear wall where his targets remained seated, still fully engaged in their conversation. Moving to a position behind the empty fourth chair and seeing three sets of eyes move guardedly to his, he addressed himself to the detective.

"Detective Belton," he said quietly, "my name is Jaakov Adelman. I am with a federal agency. Do you mind if I join the three of you for a moment before you go?"

Having asked the question, Adelman now stood relaxed, coffee cup and saucer in hand, towering over the seated threesome from his six-foot-five-inch height. He looked down impassively at Sid Belton, awaiting the detective's response, which, he knew, could as easily be No as Yes. After a moment, Belton, his face equally impassive, nodded once.

Adelman bent gracefully at the waist, placed his coffee carefully on the table, pulled out the empty chair, and, as he seated himself, looked left to Eleanor Chapel. "Dr. Chapel," he said softly, "this is an honor for me. As a Jew, I'm deeply appreciative of your efforts to establish mutually beneficial policies for the students at our respective seminaries, yours and mine."

At this, she smiled uncertainly, but his eyes did not linger on her. He turned his head to the right and eyed Luke Manguson.

"Lieutenant," he said simply, nodding once to the Londoner.

Adelman then turned his face immediately to the detective. He drew in his breath to speak, but was interrupted before the first syllable could be formed.

"I wondered," said Sidney Belton, his crooked smile just beginning to appear, "whether you were just gonna stare at us in that window pane for an hour and then follow us outta the restaurant, or whether y'might come over and introduce yr'self, Mr. Adelman. And I won't bother askin' to see your identification. I know you don't carry any."

Adelman's lean, angular face froze. His eyes widened in obvious surprise, a condition almost entirely foreign to him.

Meanwhile, Eleanor Chapel smiled brightly at this man whose entire self-explanation to that moment had been that he was "with a federal agency." Luke, glancing at her across the table, sensed a kind of triumph in this particular smile. She seemed, he thought to himself, delighted that her husband had stunned the mysterious interloper with his powers of observation.

At length, Adelman recovered and started again. "Very good, detective. Very good," he began.

"Your reputation in the world of law enforcement is impressive, detective, and I am certain that you understand that federal agents with any government rarely identify themselves as such, and that my introducing myself in this way might well be frowned upon by my superiors."

Neither Belton nor his companions made any response, and so Adelman continued. "I will not say with which federal agency I am associated, nor with which nation. I have said that I am a Jew, but that narrows the range of possibilities only slightly, does it not?"

Again neither the detective nor the others responded, and so the agent continued with his prepared remarks.

"We know about the neo-Nazi plot against the Righteous Among Nations. We knew there was to be an attack on the Dutch woman. We know how that attack was defeated." At this he looked briefly to his right, at Luke, then turned his face back to Belton.

"We expected some kind of attack on Lieutenant Manguson, though we did not know when or how."

He looked at Luke again. "I observed the attack yesterday, and saw you defeat the gunmen with your hands… and with the blunt instrument you so swiftly produced."

Adelman, at his own words, nodded his head at Luke in appreciation. "Very impressive," he said simply.

"Detective," he continued, facing Belton again, "we have tracked what we refer to as *'Rebekka Yahalomin'* — the Rebecca Special Communications Unit — for about three years now. When we use the term, we refer not primarily to you, although all three of you at this table are included in the reference, but to those in England who make the visions… who *receive* the visions. We at times refer to them as 'the visioners.'"

He turned his face again to Luke. "Your sister, Lieutenant… and your parents… and your sister's mother-in-law… 'the visioners.'"

Still there was no visible or audible response from the three, and Jaakov Adelman, undeterred and unsurprised by this, drove on with his presentation. Now facing the detective again, he began to make his case. "You have access, through these visioners, to data which we very much would like to access ourselves. These criminals — these neo-Nazis — are well-led and well-financed and their systems are advanced. We cannot locate the nerve center of the insanity. We knew of the plan to kidnap and kill the Dutch woman only because of the amateurish *bravado* that led the gunmen to brag in advance to their families and their peers. And we expected the assault on Lieutenant Manguson because we are not so foolish as to think that he would be allowed to stop an assault, as he did in Holland on Saturday night, there to wound two of the attackers, and then to be allowed to continue his work unpunished.

"If you'll consider the assailants' approach against Lieutenant Manguson yesterday, detective, you'll agree that the obvious fact that they intended kidnapping rather than simple murder means that they wanted to use him. He was going to be tortured. And the goal of the interrogation would have been to extract from him something that only the *Rebekka Yahalomin* would know: the details of the visions, as provided to your visioners to date and reported by them to the rest of you.

"We doubt that the small handful of people with whom you work will have the resources to defeat this large-scale and well-organized neo-Nazi assault upon the Righteous Among Nations.

"I… my organization and related organizations… we… have the resources." He paused, then continued. "You can assist us in the quick defeat of these criminals by providing us with data received by your visioners. There is no need for a single member of the Righteous to be kidnapped, tortured, and murdered by these people. With your assistance, we can stop them before they move again. Right now.

"It is a fair bargain."

Agent Adelman paused. He saw that there was still no reaction from any of the three. He understood that both the professor and the Londoner were unresponsive simply because they grasped the fact that it was Sidney Belton who was being addressed and that it was he, and he alone, who was being asked to make a decision.

After another moment, the detective spoke. "How, exactly, is this a 'bargain'?"

"You are being 'protected' by two NYPD units," replied Adelman immediately, "neither of which can actually protect any of the three of you for a single moment, should your adversaries decide they would like you dead right now. Your police escort can, at least theoretically, assist in preventing your kidnapping, but, as with Mr. Manguson on Claremont Avenue yesterday, if they decide simply to kill you with automatic weapons fire, then they will succeed. You will be dead.

"And that may be exactly what you should expect right now if you walk through the front door of this coffee shop in the next five minutes."

He turned his face to Eleanor Chapel, then back to Sid Belton. "Your wife, detective, is not safe. But we can protect her. We can indeed protect each one of you. The New York Police Department cannot. They may be able to make an arrest after the fact. But they can *prevent* nothing. Not this. Not now.

"We can. And, since we can… I offer to you… this 'bargain.'"

At that, Adelman stopped. He was finished.

He sat back slowly in his chair until his elongated frame was tenuously supported by the chair back. Then he folded his long arms across his chest and waited, his eyes on Sidney Belton.

At length he was rewarded.

"You're Mossad," the detective said simply.

He paused to let this assertion settle into the minds of his companions at the table. Knowing there would be no response from Jaakov Adelman, he did not pause for long.

"Tell me two things, agent Adelman. First, how does this threat to the surviving members of the Righteous Among Nations qualify as a threat to the State of Israel? Why should Mossad have more than a passing interest?

"And second… you, like all agents, use falsehood and deception as the most basic tools of your trade. Why should we take seriously anything you say to us, including your claim that you — your organization — can and will protect us?"

Now it was Sidney Belton's turn to sit back and fold his arms across his chest. And he did, mirroring Adelman's posture exactly and comically, the tall, long-limbed agent folded into his chair like some unwieldy, collapsible agricultural implement, and the compact, physically impaired detective tucked into the confines of his chair like a child's bedraggled teddy bear.

Now Adelman slowly reorganized his complex frame, leaned forward again and placed his elbows on the table. "I will answer your first question from the point of view of the State of Israel and of Mossad without for a moment suggesting that I have anything to do with either one. I will, in fact, answer just as I would if I were MI6 or CIA, both of which employ Jews like me in considerable numbers."

Adelman paused to organize his thoughts, then continued.

"It is true, detective," he said, "that a plot to exterminate the Righteous could have nothing directly to do with Israel's security. But this plot is so saturated with the Nazi imprint of Jewish-focused hatred and Jewish-focused genocide that Israel — and Mossad, I should think — could not possibly ignore it as simply another crackpot movement which will find itself thwarted by local or national law enforcement, case-by-case. And it stands to reason that Israel — and Mossad — would enlist the aid of other countries and other intelligence services in bringing action against this threat to these innocents… to these heroes.

"No group that seeks to harm those people who risked their lives to protect Jews from the medical experiments and the gas chambers and the ovens — the death camps — can be allowed to execute its program with impunity. This is not something that can be tolerated. This is an obscenity that must be met with force as ruthless as that which it seeks to bring against the Christians and others who took the ultimate risk on behalf of the Jewish people."

Jaakov Adelman's thin, pale face had become flushed during this softly spoken — nearly whispered — outburst. He caught himself, paused, consciously relaxed the muscles in his shoulders and prepared to begin again.

Belton interrupted. "If I had a film of that little speech, agent Adelman, and if I showed it to ya' so you could get a look at yr'self… if I let ya' see how y'looked just now… you'd see not just a Jew… but a Zionist… and a *katsa*…."

The two men stared at each other, unblinking, across the table, both now leaning toward the other, two pairs of deep-set black eyes boring into the other's.

"If y'want me to even *think* about this 'bargain,' Mr. Adelman, you're gonna hafta drop the pretense.

"And you're gonna hafta drop it now."

Silence fell again on the small table. The detective and the Israeli continued to stare into each other's eyes.

Seconds ticked past.

At length Adelman began slowly to nod his head. "Yes," he whispered. "Yes… Jew… Zionist… Mossad."

Belton rose quickly from his chair and, struggling, began to try to reach across the table to grasp the agent's hand. Adelman, clearly aware of the detective's array of physical disabilities, reacted gracefully and athletically, his hand meeting the detective's well to Belton's side of the floral centerpiece. Their handshake was firm and lingering, a gesture of deep respect, each for the other's professionalism and expertise.

The two then resumed their seats, the agent courteously remaining on his feet until the older man, again struggling, had settled himself.

Then Belton spoke, the unique grin emerging as he did. "Now I'll tell ya' somethin' y'need to know, Mr. Adelman."

The agent's eyebrows lifted.

"I got contacts inside your organization," said Belton. "I knew ya' by sight, as soon as y'came in th' door of th' coffee shop. That's all I can tell ya'. But I wanted y'to know."

Jaakov Adelman considered this bit of information long and hard, now looking down at his hands as they absently cradled his half-filled coffee cup. As improbable as this assertion was to him, it was, he knew immediately, far more probable than the alternative: that this particular detective — Sidney Belton — would put forth a gratuitous falsehood under any circumstances whatever. Adelman knew that Belton, as one of the *Rebekka Yahalomin*, maintained at all times a theological True North, and that his ethical compass, derived therefrom, pointed always toward The One known to Adelman himself as Jehovah. Belton, unlike Adelman in his role as Mossad *katsa*, could not and would not adjust his ethical stance to conform to the pragmatic demands of the moment. Adelman knew this, and knew this absolutely.

If Sidney Belton said he had contacts inside Mossad, then he did.

If Sidney Belton said he knew Jaakov Adelman on sight, then he did.

Adelman looked up from his hands and nodded.

Belton returned the nod, then said, "Mr. Adelman, you've addressed that first question I asked ya'. Now, what about the second?"

"The second has no answer, detective," said Adelman quickly. "As it turns out, you already knew my professional identity. And so, having known that, you also know that I lie whenever I need to lie, as do all in my trade. And so you know I could be lying when I say that my organization can and will protect you, and that we offer you our protection in exchange for access, through you, detective, to your visioners' data: these warnings, foretellings, and commands that they are repeatedly given.

"Promised access to the data, we can accomplish what you cannot: first, provide safety for the *Rebekka Yahalomin,* and second, wipe out the neo-Nazi criminals before they murder a single member of the Righteous Among Nations.

"I could, right now, ask Mr. Manguson to take the interior exit from the coffee shop into the hotel lobby, and from that concealed vantage point to scrutinize each parked vehicle and pedestrian in sight, all those in position to see you exit the front door of the restaurant. And he would come back in five minutes and report that there are obviously at least two and possibly three sets of individuals — not counting the two NYPD units — ready for action.

"But that would prove nothing, would it, detective? Mr. Manguson would have no way to know whether those were the Nazis themselves, or, more likely, hired guns on contract with the Nazis, or our own agents, or someone else's agents or even NYPD plainclothes personnel.

"So... in the end, Mr. Belton, you're simply faced with the proverbial 'leap of faith,' are you not? I'm either telling the truth or lying. And my truth is that those people outside the restaurant are either the Nazis or their hirelings. It doesn't matter which. I'm not certain if they are going to gun you down right now or follow you for minutes, hours or days awaiting the chance to snatch you off the streets... or something else entirely. But they *are* going to murder all three of you, most probably after having tortured you to their satisfaction.

"My truth also includes the fact that we have a small bread truck backed up to the loading dock in back of this coffee shop. The four of us can go back through the kitchen, get in the truck, and go straight to the airport at White Plains. We have a Lear jet sitting on the runway, engines running, waiting for us. The crew is El Al."

He glanced at his wrist watch. "Right now it is a little after 9:00 p.m. in Tel Aviv. With two stops for fuel and crew change, first in Dublin and then in Naples, we'll be in Israel by midafternoon tomorrow, Thursday.

"Once we are there, in our headquarters, we can put you into secure communication with the visioners of *Rebekka Yahalomin.* And then, maybe... just maybe... within twenty-four hours of *that* time, we can move on the criminals and it is over and done."

Adelman stopped. He knew it was time for him to be silent and to allow the threesome to process what he had just said. He was also certain that they would want to pray before coming to a final decision. "Are there questions I can answer before I leave you alone for a few minutes?"

"Just one," said the detective. "When you said that with access to the visioners' data you would be in position to 'wipe out' the Nazis... and, just now, when

you said you would 'move on the criminals' and it would be 'over and done'…
what should I picture, agent Adelman? In the end, are the perpetrators dead?
Or are they in prison?"

Adelman smiled. "*We* will decide whether or not to employ our *kidon*, detective. Circumstances will dictate our approach: the enemy's numbers, dispositions, firepower, the element of surprise. You know that, sir."

The detective turned to his wife. "The *kidon* are the Mossad assassination units, Eleanor."

She blanched and looked away.

Belton turned back to Adelman.

"I know *this*, sir. Our group has never yet gone into combat with anything more than a hunting rifle and Luke's array of knives. If we make our information available to you, there will be plenty of restrictions on how we go after these dirt bags, Mr. Adelman. Y'can count on that."

"Restrictions imposed by whom, detective?"

"By Almighty God, Mr. Adelman."

The agent smiled in response, but saw only deadly seriousness in the detective's face. Then he nodded. "Perhaps some negotiation on this point will be permitted?"

"Probably not, Mr. Adelman."

"But there are times when casualties are not avoidable."

"And there are times when they are."

Silence fell on the table, all four playing the implied sequence of events forward in their minds. At length the agent spoke.

"Detective, your bread truck… and your Lear jet… await your decision."

"Dr. Chapel is going to lead us in prayer, Mr. Adelman."

The agent gathered himself, but the professor stopped him, her small hand on his arm.

"We are going to *wrap you up in this prayer*, Mr. Adelman," she said in her high, soft voice. "Do *not* think you can get away from us. You are officially, as of now, part of… um… *Rebekka Yahalomin*…."

She smiled brilliantly at him, eliciting a broad smile in return.

She bowed her head, and the men followed suit.

# Chapter Seven

AT THE SOUND OF THE WHISPERED "AMEN," KORY VAN DIJK LIFTED
her head and reluctantly opened her eyes. Jason Manguson had just begun their
evening session with a lengthy, impassioned prayer for the Holy Spirit's continued
engagement and guidance as they sought to understand and act upon His communications and directives to them. The prayer had been so emotionally captivating
that Kory had resisted its conclusion.

Her eyes, adjusting to the soft light from two floor lamps placed in opposite
corners of the room, fell on Max and Margaret, both curled near the feet of their
master and mistress. Margaret, the lithe 45-pound border collie and successor
to the beloved Mildred with whom Rebecca and Luke had grown up, actually
rested her chin on Elisabeth's foot. Max, the muscular 115-pound German shepherd, lay on his side with his nose between Jason's feet. Kory had already learned
that, although both animals seemed pleased to relax under circumstances such
as these, the two were supremely athletic and superbly trained working dogs
skilled in adding their own, unique level of protection for this resort-and-fortress
and its extensive grounds.

Kory smiled down at the two creatures. She missed her Tiny, and tried to
imagine the little tabby, racing under full steam through her parents' London
home, her temporary quarters during the emergency. She hoped the reunion
with Tiny would come soon… and she hoped even more for a different reunion,
sooner still.

The group was assembled in the underground meeting room of the miniature mansion that the elder Mangusons had purchased and developed decades
earlier, laboring for two years not only to convert the house proper into a suitable

lodge, but to transform its primitive bomb shelter into something much more so-phisticated than the World War Two original. The subterranean complex, com-plete with conference room, chapel and two dormitory spaces, could be made completely self-sufficient — powered independently of the house by battery or generator — with the flip of a master switch.

Further, within the meeting room, an elaborate control panel permitted the Mangusons to detect penetration of the perimeter wall, to direct remote cam-eras to exact penetration points and to follow the progress of intruders across the ample grounds up to the point at which they might attempt to enter the lodge itself.

Jason Manguson's prayer concluded at 8:35 p.m.

It was then 3:35 p.m. at the White Plains airport near New York City. There, at that moment, Eleanor Chapel, Sid Belton, Luke Manguson, Jaakov Adelman, and a two-man El Al flight crew hurtled down the runway in their sleek, twin-engine Lear for the first leg of their flight to Israel. The Baptist-Catholic couple's prayers, the Anglican's prayers and the Orthodox Jew's prayers mixed together with Jason Manguson's in Great Britain in a divinely sanctioned preparation that ultimately would await the Master's definitive response. Now, Jason's prayer hav-ing freshly infused the minds of Rebecca and Matt, of Martha and Paul and of Kory and Greta with purpose and clarity, all eyes turned to those of their hostess.

"Thank you, dear, for the lovely prayer," began Elisabeth Manguson, touch-ing her husband's arm with her fingertips. The couple exchanged an expressive look as the husband returned his wife's touch. The warmth of the brief exchange was noted appreciatively by all in the room.

Elisabeth turned her face to the group.

"It seems to me," she said, looking around the circle, her eyes stopping mo-mentarily to rest on the two infants held close to the chests of their parents, "that we should go forward now on the assumption that Luke and the Chapel-Beltons are by now on their way to Israel. Rebecca explained her dream fully to Eleanor and Sidney early today, placing the vault of the Righteous somewhere in the Holy Land. I can think of no other explanation for the absence of phone contact from them since the scheduled end of their meeting with Solomon Rosenthal. That would certainly have been more than two hours ago… probably three."

Her husband had begun to nod his head before his wife completed her state-ment. "I agree, Elisabeth," he said immediately. "We know the agenda for that meeting: first, Mr. Rosenthal's reports from the committee members in Israel; then, discussion of an action-response to Rebecca's vision of last night; and, finally, discussion of the implications of the attack on Luke in New York yesterday. Luke made clear in his call to us early today that the latter two subjects would necessarily comprise the agenda-behind-the-agenda, and that the last item was likely to derail whatever Mr. Rosenthal might have imagined the full agenda was going to be.

"Treasonous conduct within his committee, as suggested by the attack on Luke… the existence of an entire locator system for the Righteous Among Nations, to be found somewhere within the boundaries of the State of Israel, as shown by the vision… I can only imagine that Mr. Rosenthal, hearing those reports, immediately demanded that the seminary call upon all its resources — institutional, financial, governmental — to provide transport to Jerusalem, both for himself and for the others.

"And it may well be, also," he added quickly, "that he has attempted to make a case with Luke that you, Rebecca, and, perhaps, you, too, Martha, should join them there. As crucial as it will obviously be to Mr. Rosenthal that Luke, Eleanor and Sidney join him in Israel, he will see immediately that having one or both of the current visioners there, at the same time and in the same place, would bring access to the data Source directly under his hand… not to imply *control* of the data Source, it goes without saying, but instantaneous *access* to the communications initiated by the Source.

"He may or may not take seriously the purported Source of the visions, but he certainly understands that some system for the use of back channels for communications and information exists, and that those back channels extend well beyond anything he can personally access."

Rebecca and Matt's faces, both inclined downward toward the nuzzling infants whom they each held, looked up quickly. Rebecca's gray eyes widened; her husband's became slits. Martha Clark, unencumbered, nearly jumped from her chair, turning her face to Rebecca. Paul Clark, in contrast to his wife, slumped forward, his hands rising to his face.

A deliberate pause ensued, while Kory van Dijk whispered her translation of these words to her aunt. As soon as she had finished, Greta's eyebrows lifting at her niece's concluding words, Jason Manguson spoke again.

"I said it may be that Mr. Rosenthal has *attempted* to make that case with Luke." He paused, looking from one couple to the other. "I think we can readily predict how far he is likely to get with such an argument. Can we not?"

Matt smiled at the thought and continued to cradle young Samuel tight to his chest with his one good arm and hand. His wife looked back down tenderly to Joanna's tiny face. Paul Clark remained slumped in his chair miserably, his hands still covering his face.

But Martha quickly stood, a movement that startled and alerted the border collie, the German shepherd and their human colleagues, as well. A bright fierceness shown in her face and eyes. "I'll go!" she said, her voice sure and strong. "Rebecca cannot. I can. I'll *go!*"

In the silence that followed this pronouncement, there was a soft rustling as Rebecca, stirring carefully so as to disturb Joanna as little as possible, rose slowly to her feet. She crossed the small circle to her mother and there stooped to deposit the child in her grandmother's welcoming arms.

Rebecca then turned to face her mother-in-law, extended her left hand to grasp Martha's right, and turned her toward the only door of the meeting room. Without a word they quietly exited, turned left, strode hand-in-hand down the hall to the doorway to the underground chapel, and entered the carefully appointed worship center. Rebecca turned and closed the door behind them.

Still holding hands, they advanced worshipfully to the altar rail. There they knelt together and silently entered the supernaturally charged world of prayer, that world which, available to all people at all times and in all places, awaits continually the adoration, thanksgiving, confession and petition of the faithful.

The two women, related by the marriage of one's son to the other, but, before that event, by their shared genealogy as visioners, prepared to begin their individually crafted prayers. They did so knowing that before this night ended they would receive from the Presence a set of images and messages that would leave them each in a state of utter and absolute exhaustion. Nevertheless, embracing the holy fear that even now began swiftly to encompass them, they bowed their heads and began.

For perhaps a full half hour, their individual silent prayers ran in thematic parallel: acknowledgment of the fact of God as Creator of all things, of all moments, of this moment, and expressive adoration both for His everlasting judgment and for His everlasting redeeming activity; thanksgiving to Him for the ultimate gift, that of His crucified and eternally triumphant Son; confession of personal failure, of frailty, of pridefulness; and, finally, at length and in detail, petition. Each in her own way and in her own words, the women asked God for His direction in the face of the immediate question: the movement forthwith of one or both of them to join the others in Israel, and, in Rebecca's case, the weighing of that newly suggested responsibility against the opportunities, demands and obligations of motherhood to the infant children whom she had so recently birthed.

But well beyond this foreground issue, they addressed in their prayers all that lay behind and beyond in the larger crisis: the imminent extermination of the living members of the Righteous Among Nations; their group's proper involvement, or not, in a preemptive counterattack against neo-Nazi forces, once those had been identified and isolated; the appropriate levels of involvement of Solomon Rosenthal or even Greta van Dijk, individuals who stood outside the nuclear family of visioners. These themes played steadily through the silent prayers of the two as they continued to kneel, side by side, at the small altar rail.

Just over three-quarters of an hour after beginning their prayers, Martha sensed rustling movements beside her, opened her eyes, and looked toward her daughter-in-law. Rebecca had risen and, padding softly across the carpet, was just reaching for copies of both Bible and prayer book from the shelf that ran the length of the left-hand wall of the chapel. Martha, still kneeling, turned her head to watch Rebecca as she sat down on one of the four folding chairs that formed the front row of the diminutive sanctuary, placing one copy of each volume on the chair next to her, now beginning to read to herself. Martha turned back, brought her prayer to a close, then rose, retreated to the chair on which the books had been placed, and sat down, cradling both in her lap.

Rebecca immediately reached over and held the small blue Church of England prayer book open for Martha, so that she could view the page number. With her eyes, Rebecca indicated her wish that they read that prayer aloud together.

And so, after Martha found her place, they began, softly, to read aloud, under their breaths, not addressing each other, but the Father whose guidance they sought.

> *Almighty God, Father of all mercies, we thine unworthy servants do give thee most humble and hearty thanks for all thy goodness and loving-kindness.... We bless thee for our creation, preservation, and all the blessings of this life; but above all for thine inestimable love in the redemption of the world by our Lord Jesus Christ, for the means of grace, and for the hope of glory. And we beseech thee, give us that due sense of all thy mercies, that our hearts may be unfeignedly thankful, and that we shew forth thy praise, not only with our lips, but in our lives; by giving up*

*ourselves to thy service, and by walking before thee in holiness and righteousness all our days; through Jesus Christ our Lord, to whom with thee and the Holy Ghost be all honour and glory, world without end. Amen.*

And so the extemporaneous, two-person worship service continued, quarter-hour after quarter-hour, the women alternating readings systematically between scripture and prayer. Two of the scripture passages, in particular, evoked lengthy silent-prayer responses from each supplicant.

From Isaiah 40, they had read:

> *Comfort ye, comfort ye my people, saith your God. Speak ye comfortably to Jerusalem, and cry unto her, that her warfare is accomplished, that her iniquity is pardoned: for she hath received of the Lord's hand double for all her sins. The voice of him that crieth in the wilderness, Prepare ye the way of the Lord, make straight in the desert a highway for our God. Every valley shall be exalted, and every mountain and hill shall be made low, and the crooked shall be made straight, and the rough places plain. And the glory of the Lord shall be revealed, and all flesh shall see it together: for the mouth of the Lord hath spoken it…. Behold, the Lord God will come with strong hand, and his arm shall rule for him…. He shall feed his flock like a shepherd; he shall gather the lambs with his arm, and carry them in his bosom, and shall gently lead those that are with young.*

Much later, from Matthew 2, they had read:

> *… Behold, the angel of the Lord appeareth to Joseph in a dream, saying, Arise, and take the young child and his mother, and flee into Egypt, and be thou there until I bring thee word: for Herod will seek the young child to destroy him.*
>
> *When he arose, he took the young child and his mother by night, and departed into Egypt….*
>
> *Then Herod… was exceeding wroth, and sent forth, and slew all the children that were in Bethlehem, and in all the coasts thereof, from two years old and under….*
>
> *In Rama was there a voice heard, lamentation, and weeping, and great mourning. Rachel weeping for her children, and would not be comforted, because they are not.*

And midnight came eventually. And midnight passed them by. And in the dormitory rooms across the hallway all slept: adults, infants and guard dogs alike.

And suddenly the Holy Spirit descended in all His naked force upon the two worshippers in the tiny chapel. At the moment of His arrival both women had, moments earlier, put their Bibles and prayer books aside and had returned to the altar rail, there to kneel and to continue their silent prayers.

The customary visual opening — clear images with sharp outlines and bright contrasts — was this time accompanied for both of them, as they were later to explain to each other, by an auditory phenomenon described by each as "a symphonic, multi-octave major chord" that played overpoweringly throughout the paired, but differing, sets of visions. The chord, like the visions, was, they knew, *implanted* in their minds and nervous systems, not projected or transmitted from some point outside their minds but inside the chapel. The beauty and volume of the chord would, they agreed, have driven them to their knees whether it had attended their visions or had come independently.

The Holy Spirit thus entered their minds primarily as He had entered in the past: by placing forcefully before their minds' eyes both images and messages. And, in this instance, He chose symphonic accompaniment as a form of secondary communication. At no point during the supernatural intrusion was either woman aware of the other's presence, nor, indeed, of any other presence in the universe. Neither could have said in the end whether their separate visitations transpired over the course of sixty seconds, sixty minutes, or some other earthly time-measure between the extremes of one minute and one hour. They simply knew that they were themselves consumed by their separate visions.

When the Visitor had finished His work in the chapel, in whatever length of earthly time might actually have transpired, He departed. And when He had gone and they became once more aware of themselves, both women found that they were prostrate, face down on the thick carpet, their clothing and hair drenched with perspiration.

In Rebecca's case, as her mind cleared, her thoughts flew to the children. What time was it now? What *day* was it now? Where were the infants? Had they been adequately cared for in her absence?

She struggled to her hands and knees, then, still unsteady, sat back slowly on her haunches, pulling her long, wet, tangled hair away from her face with both hands. Her head continuing to clear, now holding her hair back with one hand, she leaned forward and stretched to reach her companion's shoulder.

"Mum?" she said softly, and then again, "Mum?"

Seeing no response, she shook her mother-in-law's shoulder gently. "Martha?... Martha?" she said more insistently, "Wake up, dear... wake up."

Martha Clark stirred.

"We must wake the others, Mum," Rebecca continued. "We must give our reports. We must tell them everything… all that we have seen… and right now, dear… right now."

She paused as Martha struggled to rise to hands and knees.

"And I *must* have my children," Rebecca added.

As though given fresh strength by these final words, Rebecca bolted to her feet, turned and stooped low to assist her fellow visioner to her own. Then, supporting the older woman with a strong arm around her shoulders, she moved determinedly toward the chapel door, her jaw set, the V-shaped scar on her right cheek moving with the ripple of jaw muscles clenching and relaxing.

For Rebecca Manguson Clark knew, and knew well: the battle was about to be joined.

The adults remaining in the meeting room at 8:45 p.m. — when Rebecca and Martha Clark had wordlessly left them — had understood immediately what Rebecca sought, and, without discussion, had followed her lead, each seated with eyes once again closed, Elisabeth and Matt continuing to cradle still-quiescent Joanna and Samuel. The veteran participants in the room were strongly conscious of the fact that, unlike their situation three years previous when so much had transpired in these very subterranean rooms, there was no divinely appointed leader in the new crisis.

Then it had been Elisabeth Manguson; years earlier it had been Jason Manguson. Now there were simply the elder Mangusons who served as hosts… and there was the Holy Spirit. Prayer was, then, this time, implicitly demanded of each one, and of each one equally.

By 9:30 the infants were sleeping soundly in the portable cribs that had been placed in the women's dormitory room across the hallway from the meeting room. By 10:00 the adults who had remained there after Rebecca and Martha's departure, having at length completed their private prayers, had followed suit: Kory, Greta, and Elisabeth now bedding down in the sleeping room with the children; Matt, Paul, and Jason in the dormitory room adjoining.

The door to the chapel remained fast closed.

At 1:30 in the morning, nearly five hours after the two women had entered, the door opened. Rebecca and Martha Clark, each saturated in perspiration, emerged slowly, Rebecca both supporting her mother-in-law and warming her against the chill.

Quietly they roused the five sleepers — not six, for Matt Clark's eyes had never closed — and the meeting resumed after an interval sufficient to allow the two visioners to discard their damp garments, change into their pajamas, and wrap themselves in spare blankets from the dorm rooms' shelves and closets. Rebecca, satisfied that the twins slumbered comfortably and leaving the meeting room door and the children's door open wide, looked to her parents — their hosts — for permission to begin. Together, they nodded to their daughter.

Rebecca rose from her chair and began immediately to pace the outside of the circled chairs, both hands holding the blanket closed in front of her chest, her words stabbing the air in place of the gestures she habitually used for emphasis when speaking. Without conscious plan, she repeatedly circled the group as she spoke, wheeling to reverse direction each time she reached her own empty chair, circling the group again in the new direction, and, again and again, retracing her orbit. She was barefoot on the thin carpet of the meeting room. Her hair, still unattended since the mental and physical stress brought to her by the vision, remained wet and disorganized, moving only when she wheeled with each reversal of direction.

None of the seated participants attempted to maintain eye contact with the speaker. Each had learned that, during Rebecca's monologues, the best plan was simply to look at nothing and to maintain absolute concentration on her words and their implications.

"I want to say this first," she began, already pacing. "Before our visions resumed tonight, Martha and I spent hours and hours in prayer and in the scriptures. And I came to this certainty during those hours: Neither I nor the children are allowed to leave the property until the crisis ends. Not for a moment. Nothing was given me on this question regarding anyone else here. I don't know about Martha's going to Israel… or Matt's… or anyone else's. But not Joanna. Not Samuel. And not me. My place is with the children each moment, and their place is in the most protected environment we can provide. And that is here, on this property. Nowhere else."

At these words, Matt Clark nodded with deep satisfaction, as did his mother.

Rebecca, still pacing, continued after a brief pause.

"My vision's perspective was, from start to end, from what seemed to be a mountaintop. At first I looked far into a distance and saw a long, curving coastline, one that I did not recognize either from experience or from photographs. As the vision continued, my attention was drawn gradually closer to my point-of-perspective, and I saw nearer to me a vast harbor, filled with ships of all descriptions.

"And then, still nearer, I saw below me a great city, a city that filled all the space between the harbor and the foot of the mountain on which I stood. And finally, my attention was drawn to the slopes of the mountain itself, rising up almost under my feet. And as the slopes moved from the edge of the city up to the point on which I stood, the incline became steeper and steeper, actually approaching the vertical as it rose up and up to meet me."

She paused in her monologue, still pacing. The room was silent except for her soft footfall. She resumed.

"I was shown this same developing aspect three times, something I've not experienced before when in vision. Repeatedly the perspective rose to the distant, curving shoreline, then gradually withdrew toward the harbor, then to the city itself, then to the slopes of the mountain.

"But the second and third times, as the perspective passed from distant shoreline through the harbor and to the city, something happened within the harbor itself. And I don't know exactly what it was, or how to tell you....

"I just know that, as my view passed over and through the shipping, whether the ships were anchored, arriving, departing or moored to the piers... there was something about the ships themselves... or about one of the ships, perhaps... that connected to my previous dream... that connected to the vault... to the files... to the records that will doom the Righteous....

"But I don't know how that connection was given me in my mind, and I don't know how to say more about that...."

She stopped and looked across the small circle of chairs to her husband. Matt's eyes rose from the floor to meet his wife's. "I'm sorry, Matt," she said. "I know this is crucial, but I don't know how to explain...."

Matt Clark nodded and looked down again. He knew from experience, as did most of the others, that Rebecca would invite questions as soon as she had finished completely, and that she was not yet to that point.

She resumed her movements and, within seconds, her monologue. "I think the only portion remaining is this.... I was given the strong sense that action is imminent... that whatever is happening... and wherever it is happening... the battle is *now*...."

She stopped again, looking down at her feet. Then she nodded her head and repeated her conclusion. "Yes... action is imminent. There is *no* time to lose. We must draw the right conclusions and move into battle *now*.

"And," she added, now looking up and toward her parents, "without me. This time… this battle… all to be done without me."

She said this without embarrassment, regret or relief. She was stating a fact, one that was divinely given. There was no need for her or for anyone else to have feelings or opinions about the fact. Divinely communicated facts are, they all understood, simply to be acknowledged and accepted.

Rebecca then moved inside the circle of chairs, stepped softly to her own and, gathering her blanket securely around her, sat. After a moment, she looked up, lifting her eyebrows inquisitively.

Matt spoke immediately. "Rebecca," he said, "this shipping you've seen in the vision. Can you describe any of the ships by type? Are these all commercial vessels? Are there military vessels? Can you say?"

Rebecca looked down, thinking. Then she nodded her head. "Yes, Matt," she said, pleased.

And she looked up. "There were both. Thank you!

"There were freighters… there were tankers… there were container ships… there were tugs, of course… there were all kinds of commercial vessels… but there were also naval vessels, further from me in the distance, but definitely there."

She thought for a moment. "I'm afraid I can't distinguish one from the other," she added, "except to say there was nothing that was perfectly huge like… say… a battleship or an aircraft carrier.

"But yes, Matt. Warships were present. I can't say how many."

She stopped and looked around the circle, asking with her expression for other queries. Her father spoke.

"Was it Israel again, Rebecca? Were you given that?"

She looked away, thinking.

"I'm not quite certain," she said. "I think I've been assuming that it was, simply because of the connection that I perceived… somehow… between the ships… and the vault of the Righteous… and because I was given so clearly to understand from the previous dream that the vault was, in fact, in the Holy Land.

"But in this dream… I don't know. There was nothing so explicit, I'm afraid," she concluded, shaking her head slowly.

Silence resumed. After perhaps a full half-minute, Kory moved her hand, attracting Rebecca's attention. "Should I explain to my aunt?" she asked quietly.

"Oh, Greta!" said Rebecca quickly, looking at the older woman. "I'm so sorry!

"Yes… please, Kory," she said. "Please go ahead."

And so the Dutch translation began and continued for some time. Twice during her interpretation Kory stopped, uncertain, and asked Rebecca in English to repeat a particular portion of her narrative. And twice Greta stopped her niece to ask for clarification in Dutch. Eventually both were satisfied and turned their faces back to Rebecca, who then turned her eyes to Martha Clark.

"Mum?" said Rebecca.

Martha sat up straighter in her chair and began immediately, pulling her own blanket carefully up around her shoulders. Her brown eyes gleamed with excitement despite her obvious fatigue.

"This is *so* incredible," she began.

"I am nearly certain that my point-of-perspective is from the same mountaintop as Rebecca's! Can you just *imagine* this!

"But my view does not duplicate hers. I think her view — Rebecca's view — is to my left, although I was never actually shown that aspect directly. The direction of my vision was angled away from Rebecca's, and, so it seemed to me, gave me a view right along a ridge of which our mountaintop was, perhaps, an end-point. The ridge was very, very lengthy… many miles, I think…. My sense is that, perhaps, this ridge rises from some place in the interior and ends where Rebecca and I 'stood' in our dreams."

Martha Clark continued for five minutes with a detailed description of her ridge. She explained that it fell off to her left — the side facing the harbor — precipitously, but, on her right, much more gradually. In consequence, the right-hand slope was much more settled than the other, with residential areas, commercial areas, synagogues, mosques and churches. She also noted structures that appeared to be monastic, both  nearby and at a middle distance. Her final comments concerned what she portrayed as a "gorgeous and expansive" valley fronting the left-hand ridge in the mid-to-far distance.

There were but two questions of Martha when she had finished, one from Paul and one from Matt, as both her husband and her son sought a clearer sense of the fit of her vision — the physical congruence of valley and ridge and city and harbor — to Rebecca's. And this led in turn to discussion of the one component in the two visions that had to do with an action… a forecast… a warning… a prophecy. As Rebecca had related that component, something had happened as her perspective had passed from the distant, curving shoreline through the harbor and to the city… something had happened within the harbor… and that something pertained in some fashion to the ships themselves… and, moreover, that something was connected to her previous dream… to the vault… to the files… to the records that collectively pointed to the doom of all still-living members of the Righteous Among Nations.

The other components of both visions, all agreed, were simply descriptive. They appeared to describe a particular port city, one that was located presumably in the State of Israel. And they appeared to focus upon a particular mountain-and-ridge that ran from that harbor and that city into a distant valley.

As for the implications, they were elusive. And yet Rebecca's clear sense had been that action was imminent. The battle was at hand.

But so was exhaustion.

It was now just minutes before 3:00 a.m. in the UK. Two-hundred fifty miles to the west of the Birmingham lodge-and-fortress, a twin-engine Lear jet lifted gracefully into the darkness from a Dublin-area airstrip. On board, Eleanor Chapel, Sid Belton, Luke Manguson, Jaakov Adelman and a fresh two-man El Al air crew climbed out over the Irish Sea, then set a southeasterly course toward a distant Italian airfield that would provide their final rest-and-refueling stop.

From there they would set a direct course for the Holy Land of Israel.

Rebecca exited the meeting room first and went straight to the children who, not unexpectedly, were beginning to call for her attention. Matt went immediately to assist.

Though some, having slept several hours while Rebecca and Martha had passed through utterly enervating experiences in the chapel, still felt not only alert but highly energized, all were conscious of the obviously weakened condition of their two visioners. And all were conscious, as well, of the demands upon the young mother. Regardless of the urgency in the overall situation, they could go no further that night. This they knew.

The last person to exit the meeting room was Kory van Dijk. As the others filed out, their backs to her, she glided swiftly over to the master control panel, reached for one of the three master keys to all doors on the property, lifted it from its hook, and slipped it into one of her skirt pockets.

As all except Rebecca, Matt and the infants filed out of the subterranean fortress and into the basement proper, thence upstairs to the lodge's array of bedrooms, Kory, wide awake, bid good-night to her aunt and the others, saying she was going to read for a while. Having said so, she went to the east library on the first floor, lifted a Bible from the shelf, sat down at the reading table, and turned to the Epistle to the Ephesians.

She read the book entire.

She then closed the Bible and prayed. She prayed for strength to act in obedience to what she had become convinced was her charge.

Then she returned the Bible to its shelf, picked up paper and pen, wrote a short note in Dutch to her aunt, and tiptoed upstairs to Greta's room. She slipped the note under the door, went into her own room long enough to collect her purse, toiletries, change of clothes and a wrap, and padded softly down the main stairs, overnight bag in hand. She exited at the side of the lodge, using the master key to secure the door from the outside, and walked to the main pedestrian gate in the perimeter wall.

There, she used the same master key to unlock the gate, knowing that the alarm system would not react to use of a proper key in a proper lock. She struggled to open the heavy, little-used gate, closed and locked it with the same master key, and walked briskly downhill along the driveway to the guardhouse at the foot of the heavily forested knoll on which the house had been originally constructed more than two centuries earlier.

The time was 4:45 a.m. when, as she approached, she called out to the guards, "Hello? Hello? Anyone awake?"

Three uniformed security men immediately scrambled from the small structure, all of them obviously awake indeed. She saw that the first guard out the door had his hand on his sidearm, though it remained holstered.

Kory then identified herself, explained that she needed to get to London right away despite the hour, and asked for their assistance. The men, relaxed and pleasant to her once they understood who she was and after they had found her name and photo in the guest registry, telephoned for an intercity cab. They then accepted the return of the master key from her, and ten minutes later, helped her into the clean, compact limousine.

The driver turned his head to look at his passenger. "G'mornin', ma'am," he said pleasantly. "And where can I take you this early mornin'?"

She looked back at him and took a slow, deep breath. Her small hands tightened into fists, fingernails digging into her palms.

"Ma'am?" said the driver again. "Your destination?"

She turned her head away from him and looked out the car window. After another moment, she gave her reply.

Though small and soft, her voice did not waver.

# Chapter Eight

AS THE ON-BOARD HOURS DRAGGED BY, FIRST ON THE NEW YORK-to-Dublin leg of their flight, then the Dublin-to-Naples portion, and, now, finally, the Naples-to-Tel Aviv conclusion, Luke agonized at the absence of opportunity to communicate with his sister or his parents at the Birmingham lodge. He knew that they would speculate — with their habitual attention to all realistic probabilities — about his non-communication with them. He assumed correctly that they would, after prayerful discussion, conclude that he and the Chapel-Beltons were on their way to the Middle East, and that the arrangements had been made so quickly that no chance of telephoning — at least, none affording a sufficiently secure arrangement — had materialized.

He also knew that they could not possibly guess correctly at the actual cause of the effect. They would, he decided, focus on Solomon Rosenthal's presumed response to, first, Rebecca's reported dream of a secret vault located in Israel, and, second, Luke's having been assaulted in New York. They would guess that these reports, coupled with whatever details Solomon Rosenthal might have gleaned from his contacts with the Committee, would lead Rosenthal to arrange transportation for the threesome to Israel, and, further, perhaps to try to persuade Luke to induce one or both visioners to join them there.

They would have no way to know that Rosenthal had, in fact, seemed to profess an interest only in getting himself to Israel straightway, apparently in hopes of spearheading an investigation of the threat to the Righteous and of the traitor or traitors within the Committee. Nor could they know that it was Sid Belton, not Solomon Rosenthal, who argued that they must go to Israel themselves. And, Luke knew with certainty, they would have no possible way to guess that it was, in the event, Jaakov Adelman and Mossad, not Solomon Rosenthal and the JTS, that had whisked them away to the Middle East.

Luke found it impossible to relax under the circumstances, regardless of what his sister, their parents and the others might have surmised. And at some point early in the first leg of the trip he forced himself to address the question, "How much of your misery in these circumstances is a function of noncommunication with your sister and your parents, and how much is the result of your ridiculous, lovesick urgency to hear a certain young woman's voice and to reassure her of your own safety and of your consuming thoughts of her?" At that point and at all subsequent points when the same question arose, he dismissed the question as absurd in its formulation and as without meaning in its answer.

That did not prevent the question's return.

Now, as their nimble craft began its descent into Tel Aviv airspace, Luke found himself looking forward eagerly to getting inside the Mossad headquarters building. Jaakov Adelman had assured them that, once there, he would arrange a secure line for them to use in speaking with their family and colleagues in the UK. Luke and, he thought, Eleanor Chapel had decided to believe the *katsa* in this assurance. She had, after all, informed Adelman that she had "wrapped him up" in her New York City prayer and that he was henceforth to be considered, by Eleanor Chapel, at least, as part of the *Rebekka Yahalomin*.

Luke did not try to guess whether or not Sid Belton's reaction to agent Adelman's assurances of a secure communications line was the same as his. Luke understood that the detective's grasp of the workings of Mossad, MI6 and CIA passed through layer after layer of mystery. And he knew that Belton's inferences and conclusions about anything whatever related to government intelligence agencies could not profitably be anticipated by him or by anyone else. His mind worked like no other. Luke simply knew that he was, as always, grateful to be in the detective's company.

Two hours following the Lear's precision landing at the Tel Aviv airport, its four passengers stood inside the lobby of the Mossad headquarters building. They looked and felt tired.

A full hour between the plane's landing and their arrival at the unimposing building on King Saul Boulevard had been consumed in a comical attempt to purchase clothing, toiletries and other necessities for Eleanor Chapel and Sid Belton. While Luke had kept his small red bag with him at all times in New York, and thus was able to take it with him on board the plane, the couple had gone to the JTS meeting with Solomon Rosenthal, and then to lunch at the Mayflower Hotel, with only their thin briefcases in hand. This meant that, while they had with them their passports, credit cards and the like, they had nothing to sustain themselves during what would clearly become a multi-day excursion.

The diminutive professor, despite the sameness of her everyday clothing — scuffed, graying tennis shoes, gray skirt, white blouse, gray suit jacket, red scarf — was not an easy shopper, for herself or for anyone else. Her size and her adherence to the singular gray-white-red color pattern limited choices dramatically for her own wardrobe; her strong opinions about function-over-style introduced similar limitations when she chose for, or advised, someone else.

As for the detective, his absolute disregard for his own appearance made him as difficult to clothe as his wife. His refusal to take an interest in the process led her at length to threaten him: "Sidney Belton, if you don't come over here and pick out three shirts — at Israeli government expense, you know — I'm going to throw *all* your clothes away tonight after you go to sleep."

He believed her.

Finally, the shopping excursion — during which the threesome had been watched over by no fewer than four Mossad agents, not counting Jaakov Adelman — had ended, and they had resumed their automobile trip to headquarters. When they had exited their armored vehicle, their *katsa* had led them immediately through an impressive phalanx of security personnel and detection devices and into the lobby.

Yaakov Adelman's guests were uniformly surprised at the unprepossessing, even shabby, interior. To one side of the threadbare lobby was a branch of the Bank of Israel, several business offices and a small café. The only people in the lobby with them were bank tellers and a handful of individuals and couples, presumably employed by or associated with Mossad, seated on the cheap plastic-covered chairs arrayed in and around the café.

Sid Belton was the first of the threesome to notice a closed, unmarked door in the far corner of the lobby. He inquired of Jaakov Adelman, "Is that headquarters' entrance over there?"

The *katsa* nodded. "Yes. That door is keyed, of course. Behind the door are banks of elevators, also keyed for security.

"Mossad HQ covers eight floors, as you'll see later. Nothing here on the main floor except that doorway. HQ comprises a building-within-the-building: power, water, sanitation… all separate from everything else. The lower floor houses the listening and communications center. The next floor up holds the offices of junior staff. Upper floors are for analysts, planners and operations people. R & D has its own floor. The Mossad director and senior aides are on the top floor. All very serviceable."

"Well, Mr. Adelman," said the detective, "I need you to tell y'r boys to give us some room here for a few minutes. Tell 'em to give us some room."

The agents quickly acceded to the request. Three *katsas* remained with them in the lobby, stationed in a loose, thirty-foot circle around the foursome, facing away from them.

Belton addressed himself again to Jaakov Adelman. "Here's what you gotta understand right now, son," he said brusquely. "The three of us haven't been able to say anything to each other outside your presence for a couple of lifetimes now. Once we go up in th' HQ part of th' buildin', everything we say can be picked up with y'r listenin' devices. *Everything*.

"We gotta work through a few things right now, and we gotta do it in private, and that means here, by ourselves, in the lobby, and it means without you, too."

He paused to let this last sink in.

"Eleanor has decided to trust you, I think," Belton continued. "I don't. It's nothin' personal, son. It's just that I understand who you work for. I think you might guarantee us a secure phone line to the UK… and you have. And I think you might believe you can give us one. I just don't believe that your people are gonna allow it, Mr. Adelman. You might trust your own people in somethin' like this, but I don't."

The detective's wife eyed him with annoyance. "Sidney," she began, "I really don't think…"

"Eleanor," he said abruptly, cutting her off, "we're on my playin' field right now. This is not somethin' you know… really…. It's just not. You cannot even *imagine* what Mossad — and CIA and MI6 and all the others — have t'do every day just to protect the citizens of their own countries. You can decide to trust this fella all you want… and I can, too… but I'm here to tell ya' that not only will his superiors assure him of one thing and then do another… I'm here to tell ya' that they would *throw his life away in a minute* if they decided it was in their country's best interests to do it.

"And they're not exactly wrong, Eleanor… they're not *exactly* wrong. It's a set of ideas that's got nothin' to do with anything you've ever seen before. That's why I'm a detective, Eleanor, and that's why, before that, I served in the plain ol' United States military. That's why I do what I do, and not what Mr. Adelman does. I can't put my Christianity over on one side just because that might help me get t'some criminal faster and better.

"Now, Mr. Adelman here… he has decided he *can* put his Jewish beliefs and understandings over on one side… can separate 'em, y'know, from what he's doin' from minute-to-minute as an intelligence agent. He can do that. I can't.

"And I'm tellin' ya', Eleanor, that's how it is."

She had rarely seen her husband like this, and understood well before he had completed his diatribe that this was a nonnegotiable matter. When he was finished, she simply nodded to him, expressionless, and turned her eyes to Jaakov Adelman.

He met her eyes with a smile. "It's all right, Dr. Chapel," he said quickly. "Your husband is both correct and incorrect. He is correct in obvious ways. He is incorrect as follows: separating my Jewish… ah… beliefs and understandings… as he says… from my… ah… my work… is a little more complex than he assumes. You see, if one believes that this land — the very land itself — has been *given by the Almighty* to one's own people… well… you can immediately see how that actually is, *in itself*, a 'belief and understanding,' is it not?"

The Old Testament master nodded her head quickly. The agent's words were precisely the ones she herself would have spoken to her husband, had she chosen to engage him on the question.

"But," Adelman continued, "he means it when he says that this is not about me. It's about government agencies like mine. You *cannot* trust them, and that means you *cannot* trust me, either, even though you have made me an official, first-class member of *Rebekka Yahalomin*."

He smiled at her again.

"In any case, Dr. Chapel, I'm going to step outside the building and wait for you there. Several of my colleagues will remain here inside the lobby, facing away from you, as they are now. They are out of earshot, and they are simply on guard. When you complete your conversation, let one of them know, and he will come out front and get me. I'll be waiting.

"Take your time, detective," he said, smiling again and looking back at Sid Belton. And then he was gone.

The detective looked down at his feet, thinking. He had acceded to the *kat-sa's* insistent proposal in the Manhattan coffee shop primarily because he came to believe Adelman's contention that they could not escape otherwise. But now his conundrum was obvious: he needed to communicate with his colleagues in Birmingham, needed to hear anything the visioners might have to report, yet he had no obvious way to accomplish this without opening up every word, every inflection, every nuance of every communication to this alien world of clandestine intelligence that completely surrounded them at that moment, a sordid world in which every value he held was, or could be, turned on its head in a moment.

Belton studied his feet at length, thinking. He stood with his back to the lobby's main entrance and its labyrinthine security systems, his wife and his colleague facing him, waiting patiently. He seemed finally to reach a decision and looked up to speak to his companions. As he did so, he saw their eyes widen in surprise at something behind him. He turned toward the security system's innermost aperture.

Belton saw that Jaakov Adelman was walking toward them. He saw as well that Adelman was accompanied, one on each side, by a man whom the detective recognized and by a woman whom he did not.

The man appeared to be mid-sixties, a compact five-foot ten-inches. He was clad in brown suit, dark tie and plain, long-sleeved white shirt. He wore a yarmulke on the back of his graying head.

The woman was just over five feet in height, weighed perhaps 110 pounds, and appeared to be in her early twenties. Her hair was shoulder-length and light brown; her eyes a very dark brown, almost chocolate. She had a fresh-scrubbed appearance, a woman who was pretty, Belton noted, *because* of the absence of cosmetics on her face. She wore a simple, off-white, long-sleeved blouse and a blue denim skirt with pockets on each side. She carried a wrap in one hand and a small overnight bag in the other.

The professor and the detective, having never seen the young woman before, were then astonished to witness Luke Manguson, after several moments of outright gaping in her direction, bursting from their small huddle to race directly toward the woman. Reaching her, he seemed to consume her small frame within his massive chest and arms. She simply disappeared from their view, her overnight bag and wrap falling to the floor unceremoniously. They turned and looked at each other in wonderment.

The two men with whom the young woman had been walking paused briefly, smiling at the emotional scene next to them, and then turned and continued toward the professor and the detective. Upon reaching them, the shorter, older man extended his hand toward Eleanor Chapel.

"Dr. Chapel," said Solomon Rosenthal in his heavily accented English, "I'm delighted you have come."

He turned to the detective and grasped the hand that was extended in its physically limited fashion, adding, "Mr. Belton, it is good to see you here. Who would have thought that our next meeting would be held on schedule, but halfway around the world? It never occurred to me that you would be either willing or able to make such a trip, and so I never asked."

Explanations and introductions followed.

Only then did the Chapel-Belton couple come to understand two things. First, they learned the identity of the mysterious young woman. Second, they learned that there had been no apparent connection between her arrival and that of Solomon Rosenthal, other than providential timing.

Throughout all this explaining and introducing, the young woman and the young man stood arm-in-arm, looking more at each other than at the others, plainly and simply enraptured. When it came her turn to speak, Kory van Dijk's explanation of her presence in Tel Aviv was highly efficient, she having taken some pains to rehearse during her direct, El Al 747 flight from London to Israel that same morning. She made her points quickly.

First, she had fresh information from the visioners, information that included Rebecca's certainty that the battle was at hand. The information needed to be transmitted immediately.

Second, Rebecca could not travel, and, although Martha Clark could, Kory was less encumbered, and, to be candid, younger and stronger. Communication of the new information from the visioners could best be accomplished by her getting a seat on the first available flight, London-to-Tel Aviv. And no, she acknowledged, she had asked no one's permission to take this action. She had left a note for her aunt. That was all.

Third, the involvement of Mossad, as suggested by Solomon Rosenthal's conversations with "four different committee members" in Israel and as relayed by Luke to the family in Birmingham, meant to Kory that everything — all investigations of the neo-Nazi plot, all coordination of all counterterrorist activity, all surveillance of all participants — would be channeled through Israeli intelligence. And that, given the Birmingham group's surmise that the New York contingent must be on its way to Israel, meant to her that Mossad, not Rosenthal and his Jewish Theological Seminary, would be the vehicle for their conveyance.

That also meant to Kory that she needed to get to the Mossad headquarters building, the location of which on King Saul Boulevard in Tel Aviv, she knew, was no more secret than the location of CIA or MI6, and that her information would need to be transmitted face-to-face. She knew enough about intelligence agencies, she said with a smile and a quick "no offense to you, sir" in the direction of Jaakov Adelman, to know that no telephone call could be regarded as secure.

This lengthy, extended third point, which astonished Sid Belton and Luke Manguson in both its reach and in its accuracy, reminded Luke that Kory had herself served in the Royal Navy, and that, although her military role had been only midlevel and highly technical, it would reasonably have included the need to come to certain understandings about intelligence agency operations in the UK and elsewhere. Nonetheless, her independently derived conclusions filled both men with awe.

The professor, much less in position to grasp the brilliance and sophistication of the newcomer's analysis of the situation, understood clearly what she read on the faces of the two men. And she beamed both with this understanding and at what she saw passing between the young woman and the young man who clung so happily to each other an arm's length from her.

Finally, there was a pause, and Jaakov Adelman seized the chance to move in the direction he thought essential. "Well, everyone, I suggest we go up to one of the conference rooms. There is a great deal to review, and there are plans that need to be developed right away. Shall we?"

At this, he turned and gestured gracefully toward the inconspicuous door in the far corner of the lobby.

No one moved.

Seeing this reluctance, Adelman, just as gracefully, withdrew his gesture and turned back to the group.

"I understand perfectly," he said. "But think about this. You need me. You need us. You need Mossad, and you may need police and you may even, in the end, need either *kidon* or the Israeli military… or both. The chances of your cutting off this extermination effort by yourselves are nil. You can't do it. You'll have to come to some sort of accommodation between your need to maintain your own True North in all that you do and in the practical matter of engagement in large-scale action against large-scale villainy."

He paused, then continued.

"I suggest this. Mr. Rosenthal and I need to have a conversation between ourselves. We'll go up to a conference room and begin. You four stand right here and continue what you began before Mr. Rosenthal and Miss van Dijk arrived. When you are finished, tell one of the agents and he'll escort you up to us.

"Fair enough?"

"Well, son," replied the detective after a moment, his lopsided grin emerging, "I'd say that anybody who can use a word like 'villainy' without fallin' all over himself can't be all bad.

"So… sure. You two go ahead. We'll talk here."

The sun dropped steadily toward the blue-green curvature of liquid that formed the Mediterranean horizon. The watery glare stretching toward him from the great sea caused Jaakov Adelman repeatedly to adjust his position on a hillock a quarter-mile distant from the outdoor café near the waterfront where the British-American foursome hungrily consumed their first unpackaged meal in a very long night and day.

Through his government-issue binoculars, Adelman watched unhappily, acutely disappointed that he had failed to lure them to a Mossad conference room two hours earlier. He was not angry. He genuinely understood why they wanted an extensive private conversation with each other. They did not trust the intelligence agency –never mind that Eleanor Chapel seemed to trust Adelman himself — and the three understandably deferred to Sidney Belton when he insisted that they be allowed to have a meal outdoors, alone, watched over from a suitable distance by Adelman and other *katsas* of his choosing.

His respect for the detective continued to rise. Not only did Belton clearly bear no animosity toward him, he had been wholly affable in each interchange they had shared, and, to Adelman's mild chagrin, had even waved cheerily to him almost immediately after the *katsa* had — stealthily, he had imagined — taken his position more than 400 meters from the small café. Adelman had assumed the detective would be at that moment focused only on the conversation that had been urging itself upon them since they had left the Mayflower Hotel's coffee shop the previous day, and especially since the surprise arrival of young Kory van Dijk just three hours previous. Adelman was wrong; the detective seemed to see everything. Seemed, in fact, to anticipate everything. Adelman was genuinely impressed, something he did not often experience in his professional encounters and relationships.

Adelman leaned back uncomfortably against the uneven, rocky surface of the low wall at his back. He adjusted his sunglasses and sighed deeply. This was going to be more complicated than he had imagined.

At that moment, Kory van Dijk was just drawing to conclusion her summaries of the two visioners' reports, delivered at the mansion-fortress what seemed to her eons ago and yet, she knew, actually the early morning of this same day. Luke had watched Eleanor Chapel begin to edge forward in her chair from the moment Kory had begun to describe the scenes depicted by Rebecca and

Martha Clark. At the young woman's final words, the professor fairly leaped into the sliver of silence.

"Oh, my Goodness! Oh, my Goodness!" she exclaimed. "It's all so utterly clear! Oh, my! Oh, my! I always get chills when I hear these people — our visioners! — describing something they have never seen or forewarning us about something they have no knowledge of. It's all so *perfectly* miraculous."

She shook her head in wonder.

And then she began excitedly. "Mount Carmel… the Jezreel Valley… Nazareth… Tel Megiddo… Haifa…."

As she paused to gather herself after this introductory recitation, Luke said quietly, "Haifa?… the Israeli port of Haifa?… there'd be ships from the United States Sixth Fleet in that port… and, probably, elements of the Royal Navy…."

He stopped as soon as she resumed. She did not appear to have noticed the interruption. "Mount Carmel rises from the interior in northern Israel," she explained thoughtfully, "and extends northwest all the way to the coast. It may run for… oh… perhaps twenty-five miles altogether, if you count its foothills, as most do. It is a high ridge, in other words, rather than just a peak… almost a mountain range in itself… surging to the Mediterranean and then suddenly plunging to the water from more than 1,700 feet at its extreme northwest point… sloping on both sides right into the middle of the city of Haifa… and dropping off steeply, just as our visioners explained, all along its northeast edge but only gradually along the southwest edge…."

"And Tel Megiddo! Tel Megiddo! My Goodness! The history!"

She shook her head in wonder, smiling to herself, then continued. "The great fortress is positioned just alongside the only real passage through the Carmel ridge, maybe fifteen miles from Haifa and the coast… looking directly across the magnificently verdant Jezreel Valley toward Nazareth, and, beyond Nazareth, toward ancient Magdala — the Magdalene's home town — on the waters of the Sea of Galilee, and, beyond those historic points, north to Caesarea Philippi and to Saul's road to Damascus… my Goodness! My Goodness!"

She continued, almost gasping for breath in her excitement, the blue-green eyes blazing with a kind of inspired joy that filled her husband with both admiration and happiness. His eyes misted as he watched and listened.

"And the battles at Tel Megiddo!" she cried. "Why, they have raged century after century after century, from Old Testament times right on up to the First World War! And you see why, of course. Tel Megiddo is sited astride the passage through which any army or large migration of people would need to travel when moving from Egypt and other points far to the south, northward and eastward, away from the sea and on toward Damascus, and even beyond that great city…."

She paused, her mind far away in both time and space. She breathed in the faint scent of salt Mediterranean air, smiled afresh, and continued.

"Tel Megiddo at its peak had enormous barracks for the soldiers… extensive stables… amazing equine-supply capacity… and, if you can even *imagine* such a thing, a stupendously deep shaft straight down through the rock, connecting with an impossibly long and straight subterranean passage to an underground water source….

"Why, do you know? You can walk through that passage even today!"

Luke, slowly becoming almost as excited as the professor, again interjected quietly as she paused for breath, "Yes! Of course! That would remove a besieging army's easiest and most obvious means to victory… a simple blockade designed to cut off all water to men and beasts!"

"Exactly!" she continued, more and more animated. "And… you know… this is the very site of Armageddon, as we have that reported to us in Revelation…. You hear the similarity in the sound of the words? In the sound of our English, 'Megiddo,' and in the Hebrew, 'Har Mageddon,' and a slight corruption of 'Har Mageddon' back into the English 'Armageddon'? Oh, my Goodness! My Goodness!

"*And,*" she continued, this time not even pausing to breathe, "the Carmel mountain ridge itself… its own history!… just filled, on the precipitous northeast side, with caves of all sorts… caves that have been used for millennia for every imaginable purpose… by criminals to hide from the law… by Elisha, we are told, to attempt to hide from the Almighty Himself, poor man… and by Elijah, as well, whose very cave — Elijah's cave! — is positioned at the extreme seaward tip of the range, the headland, and at its very highest point…."

Suddenly she stopped, breathed deeply once more, and turned her glistening eyes toward her husband. And suddenly she seemed actually to blush. Her small hands went to her elfin face and she covered her eyes for a moment.

Then she dropped her hands and looked again at Sidney Belton. "Oh dear," she said contritely, her voice now at its usual girlishly high pitch and womanly softness. "I've done it again, haven't I? I've sailed right into our Old Testament world… the world that I love so dearly… without giving a moment's thought to our greater purposes here, Sidney. I'm so sorry. I'm just so sorry.

"Let me go back… let me go back to Haifa itself, where our visioners were positioned, to the port and the shipping and the navies…."

Her husband displayed his trademark lopsided grin and shook his head, reaching for her near hand. "No, Eleanor," he said in his rumbling Brooklynese, "no apologies….

"Actually, we needed all of that… and more…."

"I mean, we do know from young Ms. van Dijk's report of the visions that somethin' has happened… or is gonna happen… within the port somewhere… or maybe in its sea lanes and channels… but we also gotta assume that Martha Clark's long-range view from the Mediterranean end of th' range, toward the southeast, where, you're sayin', this Megiddo fortress has always been, has gotta have importance, too, or it wouldn't have been given to her at all. No, you're not makin' a mistake, Eleanor. Not at all. You're doin' great, in fact. Don't stop. Keep goin'. Really… just keep goin'."

She turned her eyes to Luke for evidence of support for her husband's statement, and found him nodding vigorously in agreement with Belton's commentary. "Yes, ma'am," he said simply. "Just *go,* Dr. Chapel."

Then she looked to Kory van Dijk.

Kory, instead of giving the quick assent that Luke expected, looked down, thought for a moment, and shook her head. "I think, Dr. Chapel, Rebecca's vision means we can't spend another minute here. Really, I don't. You've given us Mount Carmel and Haifa."

"And, now, that having been established, I believe we are to get in a vehicle — *right now* — and just go straight there! I've said to you each what Rebecca reported to us… that three times her vision carried her from distant shoreline narrowing to the far harbor, to the near harbor, and across the city to her ridge. And, she reported, she was given something troubling out there in the harbor itself. Each time something happened within the harbor. She could not say exactly what. She just knew that as her view passed over and through the shipping there was something about the ships… or about one of them… that connected to her previous dream… that connected to the vault… to the files… to the records that will doom the Righteous.

"That's what Rebecca said: it all connected to the vault that will doom the Righteous. Oh!" she exclaimed to her own surprise. "Oh, please! Please, Luke! We must go there *now!*"

"Luke," said Kory quietly as the rising Middle East sun played across the vastness of the harbor before them, "look at the last set of ships in the southernmost anchorage line.…"

She handed the Israeli-Army-issue binoculars to him and turned back to the panorama of shipping 1700 feet below them and stretching nearly fifteen miles into the blue Mediterranean distance. Jaakov Adelman stood near the young couple, clearly uncomfortable.

The Mossad agent had argued as vigorously as he dared the previous evening, when, their café dinner and planning session at an end, Sidney Belton and his companions summoned him from his observation station to their side. They needed to go to Haifa immediately, they had told him, despite the fact that evening was upon them and they had had almost no rest since the previous day. They had given the agent no reason. They had simply asked for a car and a Mossad escort to the port city 80 miles to the north of Tel Aviv.

Adelman had come quickly to understand that they were going to Haifa with or without his assistance. The detective had put it to him concisely.

"So, Mr. Adelman," he had finally said in his rumbling Brooklynese, "y'can throw us in jail, y'can get outta th' way, or y'can help us get there. What'll it be?"

Adelman had arranged for cars, drivers and lodging in Haifa. They had made the 90-minute drive northward along the coast without incident, had been in their hotel rooms well before midnight: Kory and Eleanor in one room, the three men in the other. Then Kory, Luke and Jaakov Adelman had been up and out well before first light, positioned high above the harbor on Mount Carmel. Eleanor Chapel and Sidney Belton, exhausted, had remained in the hotel, *katsas* on guard outside their rooms.

Now, taking the binoculars from Kory, Luke rested his elbows on the ancient stone wall that separated them from the steep northeast face of the mountain. The binoculars thus steadied, he scrutinized the ships at the far end of the southern anchorage, as she had asked.

"You're right, Kory," he said quietly. "Royal Navy. Ulster-class destroyers. I think the near one may be *Ulysses*. We operated with her for an entire cruise one spring. Tip-top ship and crew.

"In fact, I'm almost certain that one of my shipmates on that cruise became the engineering officer on *Ulysses*. I would think he'd still be with her. I wonder...."

"Displaces 1,710 tons," mused Kory softly.

Luke took his eyes from the binoculars and stared at her.

She turned her head and smiled at him. "Three-hundred and sixty-two feet, bow to stern... four 4.7-inch guns, paired and mounted in two forward turrets...

four 40-millimeter AA guns… eight 21-inch torpedo tubes… 34 knots at flank speed… full complement of 337 in wartime."

Still smiling, she turned her eyes back to the harbor. "A magnificent warship."

Luke, continuing to stare at her, finally spoke. "It's ridiculous that you have all that in your head, Kory. What was there about your Navy post in London that made it necessary to commit all that to memory? And how many ships' data points are filed away somewhere in your brain?"

She laughed, turning her chocolate eyes back to his. "There was really nothing in my Navy job that required me to learn any of that, Luke. I just like ships. No, I *love* ships. I think they are amazing. I just wish I had served on one, instead of having a desk job for my whole tour."

He shook his head in fresh wonderment at his companion, and turned back to peer through the glasses at the two ships. After a moment he said, his voice rising slightly with excitement. "Kory! It looks like the two ships' boats are starting a shuttle run to the military docks."

He turned his head away from his companion to address the agent. "Jaakov," he said quickly, "will you take us down to the military docks? It's going to take those two small craft about fifteen minutes, I'd say, to cover the distance. Can you get us down there that fast?"

Ten minutes later, as the early morning sun rose higher over Nazareth and the Jezreel Valley to the east of Haifa and the mountain ridge, the three stood at the gate to the military port installation toward which, Luke had guessed, the two ships' boats were headed. And ten minutes after that, the young couple stepped gingerly onto the gunwale of the motor whaleboat from Her Majesty's Ship *Ulysses*.

Their Royal Navy reserve identification cards had gotten them past the guards at the gate to the installation, and their persuasiveness with the young lieutenant in command of the small craft had gotten them on board the whaleboat. Luke, after showing his ID, had explained to the junior officer that he had served with Tom O'Malley for two years aboard the HMS *Zealous,* and that he understood that now-Lieutenant Commander O'Malley was the engineering officer for *Ulysses*. The young boat officer had confirmed this, and readily acceded to the reservist couple's request to accompany him on his return run to the ship.

The officer had loaded the boat with sailors returning from overnight leave in Haifa, and, within five minutes, had cast off and was underway to the mother ship. Jaakov Adelman, again frustrated in his efforts to gain control of — or, if not, at least to participate in — this secretive foray from Tel Aviv to Mount Carmel and beyond, watched the small craft depart from his position in the military port's civilian parking lot.

Adelman shook his head. He felt certain that neither this young couple nor the detective and his wife, still resting back at the hotel, fully understood the nature of the enemy that they were facing. And he was becoming increasingly sure that he did.

# Chapter Nine

AS HER BROTHER AND HIS COMPANION MOVED AWAY IN THE *Ulysses'* personnel boat from the military dock in Haifa, Rebecca Clark rose from her knees at the completion of her morning devotions. It was just after six o'clock on this Friday morning in England, two hours earlier than in Israel.

Having first completed her Bible selections, then her prayer book's scripture readings with their familiar situational prayers, she had spent more time than usual — nearly thirty minutes — with her extemporaneous prayers, many of them focused upon Luke, Kory, Eleanor, and Sidney. Now Rebecca moved to the window of the second-floor guest room and looked across the breadth of the east yard and its ever-expanding gardens, toward the tree line in medium distance. Her husband and their infant twins still slept soundly, the sounds of their soft breathing coming to her across the early morning stillness of the room.

The rising sun climbed to meet her, warming her face. She closed her eyes, delighting in the sun's radiant energy as it tingled the soft skin of her cheeks, and she tried to imagine where her brother might be… tried to picture his actions… tried to reach for his thoughts.

But Rebecca, her gray eyes still closed against the sunshine, found that her mind soon began an irresistible progression down a disturbing avenue. She found her thoughts gravitating toward the unsettling fact that, unlike the three previous summers' supernaturally orchestrated dreams, neither she nor her visioning partner, Martha Clark, had as yet been provided with an image of the enemy. No sinister emanations from the telegenic face of a Meredith Lancaster. No satanic transformations of the handsome countenance of a Cameron Stafford. No furious feminine eyes rising above a dreamed field of vision to forecast the cool, ruthless destructiveness of a Helene Jamieson.

No… this time… thus far… there was just the stately Greta van Dijk and the disgusting Swastika… the broad, green expanse of Jerusalem's *Yad Vashem*… the mysterious, sterile vault of the Righteous… the conjoined vistas from the crest of an Israeli mountain ridge… an unclear yet disturbing action in an unidentified Israeli harbor… and a dreamed, suggested connection between the vault of the Righteous and the harbor's indistinctly perceived shipping….

Where, exactly, was the enemy in all this? Who, exactly, was the enemy? What authority, precisely, lay behind the brute-force attackers in Holland and the pistol-wielding assailants in Manhattan?

Always before, Rebecca and the other visioners had by this stage in their annual June crisis been given some indication of what manner of horror they were ultimately to face. But this time, thus far, they could only speculate. Surely, despite the absence of specific divine communication on the point, there was supernatural evil above, behind and below what they had thus far been given. But where? Who? What form would this summer's horror choose to take? How would it materialize and when? And what sort of counteraction would Luke and the others be able to take without specific forewarning from the visioners? Could they possibly survive under the circumstances? Would they be able to make any sort of effective response? Could they manage to save themselves, to say nothing of saving the Righteous?

It seemed overwhelming.

And, now, where, exactly, was Luke? And Kory? And Eleanor and Sidney? And their shadowy ally Solomon Rosenthal?

Rebecca had fully agreed with the family's conclusion that the five were together, and that Luke, the Chapel-Beltons, and their Jewish liaison had flown in haste to Israel with no secure means of communicating with their Birmingham family and colleagues. And Rebecca was confident, too, that Kory had left them only to find Luke and the others and to relay the freshly minted visions face-to-face.

Yes. Kory van Dijk, Rebecca was absolutely certain, could be relied upon. Luke had chosen well.

But even if all that were true, and even if no hitches or surprises had developed, how were any of them to recognize the threat they would face when neither Martha's nor Rebecca's visions had provided so much as a hint of *this* evil's identity for those who were enmeshed in the danger? Still standing at the window, Rebecca opened her eyes guardedly and, squinting now against the sun's early strength, looked once more across the east yard and gardens.

She shook her head. This was far, far more difficult than she would have imagined… this not knowing… this not being at the site of the action… this being on the safe side of a distant danger….

She turned and looked to the far corner of the room where the twins still slept soundly. Rebecca sighed deeply and nodded her head. She would not give way to the temptation. Almighty God had given her this family — this husband and these infants — and here, and only here, would she continue to be.

And then an ominous thought passed swiftly through her mind and sought lodging there. Was this place, in very fact, "the safe side of a distant danger" ? Or could the tentacles of the unknown creature or creatures reach for the first time even into this sanctuary? Her gray eyes widened as she stared, unblinking, at her little family.

And suddenly she felt cold.

The *Ulysses* swung gracefully at anchor, its high prow on a westerly heading, its stern angling toward the Haifa airport, the field just inland and to the east of center-city. Also at anchor, alongside and to the immediate south, lay HMS *Undaunted,* sister ship to *Ulysses.* The two Royal Navy destroyers, in perfect fighting trim despite their more than three decades of wartime and peacetime service, lay near the center of the north-to-south anchor line. They were the only warships awaiting their turn at dockside. The other ships in the anchorage, perhaps a dozen in all, were commercial vessels of various purpose and size: freighters, tankers and container ships, flying a wide variety of national flags.

Kory van Dijk, standing on the destroyer's forecastle on the starboard side, trained her binoculars on the container ship to their immediate north in the anchor line. The rusting ship flew a Greek flag.

Luke, stationed on the port side just across the forecastle from her, examined the Turkish-flagged freighter to the south, just on the other side of *Undaunted.* Lieutenant Commander Tom O'Malley stood just aft of his two visitors and near the centerline, curious about their mission but respectful of their obvious need to maintain a level of secrecy. As long as he and *Ulysses* were not requested by these two reservists to take action of any kind, he was perfectly willing to accommodate their need to use the ship as an observation platform. He knew Luke well and, as with all in the Royal Navy who were familiar with Lieutenant Manguson's accomplishments during his five years of active service, was highly respectful both of his judgment and of his bravery.

Suddenly the engineering officer's ruminations were interrupted by an unexpected movement from the young woman. She quickly lowered her binoculars, turned, crossed the forecastle in front of O'Malley, touched her colleague on the shoulder, and motioned for him to follow her aft. The two of them were, after ten steps, squarely abreast the number one gun turret, on the port side, the gun turret now solidly between the two and the container ship to their north. LCDR O'Malley followed them, inquiring with a raised eyebrow.

"Luke," said the diminutive reservist breathlessly, her shoulder-length brown hair shimmering in response to the quick movement of her head as she turned to face him, "I don't quite believe what I think I just saw on that container ship. And I know I could be wrong.

"But… really…," she continued eagerly, "I'm almost certain I saw that man that arrived in Tel Aviv yesterday at the same time I did… that man that entered Mossad headquarters alongside me… the financial officer from the Jewish seminary in New York…."

Luke's eyes grew wide. "What? You saw Solomon Rosenthal on the ship at the next anchorage? *What?*"

LCDR O'Malley, understanding nothing of this, nonetheless quickly grasped two facts: first, these two civilians had been inside Mossad headquarters within the last twenty-four hours, and, second, the woman had seen someone on the neighboring container ship that was obviously of great interest to them both.

"Come with me," he said to them without hesitation. "Let's go up to the bridge. You'll have a better look from that height, and you can stay hidden from view in the bargain. Since we're at anchor, there'll be no one on the bridge except the petty officer on duty. It'll be nearly as private as we are right here."

The four huddled together in the men's hotel suite, chairs drawn close. Jaakov Adelman, his patience visibly nearing its limits, stood outside with two other *katsas*. The atmosphere in the room was tense.

Kory and Luke presented their facts to the detective and his wife, leaving out no detail. They explained that they had watched a man who was — they were as certain as they could possibly be from a distance of one-quarter mile, viewed through high-powered military instruments including the telescopic sight of the *Ulysses'* boarding party's sniper rifle — none other than Solomon Rosenthal. He and two other men had moved repeatedly in and out of a particular container on the port side of the Greek-flagged ship, near the bow. The two observers had concluded almost immediately that the container's dimensions could readily conform to Rebecca's dreamed vault of the Righteous… the vault in which the envisioned files of the Righteous were secreted and organized for the speedy liquidation of the still-living members.

The young couple, well-organized through long military habit and practiced in presentation as educators, completed their statements of observations and findings in fewer than ten minutes. They then fell silent while the detective considered the implications of what he had heard from them. He considered for a very long time.

He then gave a long, deep, rattling sound that could only be described as a prolonged grumble, reached for his walking cane, rose with its assistance and hobbled to the door of the hotel room. He stuck his head out the door only long enough to mutter, "Agent Adelman, I need ya' now."

Adelman entered swiftly and gracefully, drew up the remaining chair in the small suite and listened with increasing agitation to Sidney Belton's summary, a summary occasionally embellished either by Kory or Luke, the actual observers, and, in Kory's case, the actual hearer of the visioners' most recent reports. The detective focused his summary carefully on Solomon Rosenthal, knowing that Adelman had met privately with Rosenthal the afternoon previous in Tel Aviv, and had doubtless formed his own views of the man.

At the detective's final words, the *katsa* turned immediately to Eleanor Chapel and, to the delighted surprise of all, asked her to pray for them. It was obvious that the request was genuine. The professor responded gratefully.

She prayed for the *Rebekka Yahalomin*, each one by name, specifically including Jaakov Adelman. She prayed for the wisdom and understanding necessary to make correct decisions, including decisions regarding the use of force. She prayed for God's help in deciding how to ask for help beyond the *Rebekka Yahalomin's* own ranks, and from whom. She prayed for God's hands to rest upon them each.

And she prayed using memorized phrases from Rebecca's own prayer book, phrases purposefully deposited in her private memory bank two years earlier, when she first had been introduced to them:

> *We make our address to thy Divine Majesty in this our necessity, that thou wouldest take the cause into thine own hand, and judge between us and our enemies. Stir up thy strength, O Lord, and come and help us; for thou givest not alway the battle to the strong, but canst save by many or by few…. [H]ear us thy poor servants begging mercy, and imploring thy help, and that thou wouldest be a defence unto us against the face of the enemy….*

When she finished her prayer, silence fell. All five participants remained still, eyes closed. And for the first time but not the last, Kory van Dijk understood in her bones the consequences of her personal involvement with the visioners. She understood in a deeply felt wave of emotion that surprised her to such an extent that a small sound — a short, high-pitched, barely audible moan — escaped her as she was led to confront the likelihood of crippling injury and death.

She thought of Rebecca's vicious facial scar. She thought of Matt Clark's atrophied left shoulder, arm, and hand and the near-lethal head injury that had accompanied those lesser-but-permanent wounds. She thought of the entry and exit scars from the bullet that had passed through Luke's thigh three years before, and of the pocked expanse of face and neck scarring from the previous summer's shotgun blast. She thought of the detective's battered, bruised, and very nearly destroyed torso and of his shuffling, cane-assisted gait. And she thought of her colleagues' descriptions of their ally from two years previous, the reporter from the Christian news-and-perspective journal, whose broken and shredded remains still lay scattered upon the floor of the Chesapeake Bay in the United States.

And she now understood — truly understood — that violent injury and death might well await her, Luke, and the others, within mere hours. Eyes still closed, she suddenly sat up straight, rigid in her chair. And mentally she added, obedience flooding her body and mind, her own silent prayer to Eleanor Chapel's eloquent spoken one: "Father… Heavenly Father… my life for theirs… my life for the Righteous… if it must be, then let it so be… my life for theirs… Thy will be done…."

Her emotion-laden silent prayer was at that instant interrupted by the sound of the detective's voice as he cleared his throat to speak. Slowly… very slowly… Kory opened her eyes and looked up at him.

His deep-set black eyes bored into Jaakov Adelman's similarly dark orbs. "Agent Adelman," said the detective, "if our full complement could've been here with us… I think I might decide somethin' different. But we don't have Matt. We don't have Rebecca. We're not really… ah… complete without 'em.

"We basically have an attack force of one… no offense intended, ma'am," he added unnecessarily, glancing toward Kory, "…and I just can't see how we'd be sendin' Luke to anything but his own capture, torture, and murder….

"These two young people havin' seen this Rosenthal guy on that ship this mornin' changes everything…. It explains everything and it changes everything, see….

"If I thought this Rosenthal guy was operatin' on his own, or just with a couple of other dirtbags, I wouldn't have called ya' in here. But I'm thinkin' Rosenthal has got a lot more people he's workin' with than just a couple. I mean… I figure he was probably in on plannin' the attack in Holland on Miss van Dijk's aunt… and I figure he was the one who sent those thugs after Luke right after we met with him in his office in New York… and I figure if he can reach all the way to Europe and the Middle East as easily as he can reach around a New York corner, he's got a lot more help than that… help, maybe, all around the world…."

Belton paused, looking down at his shoes and shaking his head.

"We're supposed to be careful, y'know. Yeah… we're supposed to take risks, and plenty of 'em. But we're not supposed to send our young people straight to their deaths, Mr. Adelman. Y'know what I mean? Hm? Y'know what I mean?

"And so…" he continued, without pausing for a response, "like my wife just said in her prayer… we're supposed to use enough good sense to call for help when we need it, even from an outfit that looks at things in ways that don't fit the way our outfit looks at things. Y'know?

"Because, in this case, Mr. Adelman… the direction where our team's compass points, and the direction where your team's compass points have got enough overlap to bring us around… I *think*… to the same actions, our team and yours. And anyway, all said and done, you're right. You're right, when you say we can't get this done by ourselves. I'm guessin' we're facin' a bunch that's big enough to fan out all over th' world to exterminate these Righteous people… and that's a lotta people to contend with. Y'know what I mean? Hm? Y'know what I mean?

"I mean… when it comes down to it… we got Luke. And that's it."

Sid Belton stopped, his eyes again cast down at his shoes. An oppressive silence returned to the room.

Finally Adelman prepared to speak, convinced that Belton had finally completed his statement, the longest by far the agent had ever heard the detective make. But he first unzipped a leather document case that he had held in his lap. He removed a set of papers, including a thin, plastic spiral-bound document, and leafed quickly and surely through them.

"Thank you, detective," he began. "I have some sense of how difficult this must be for you… for all of you… this needing to go outside the *Rebekka Yahalomin* itself. For what it's worth… it makes me uncomfortable, too. I feel like something of an interloper on sacred ground. I just don't see an alternative, whether I look through your eyes or mine."

He paused, opened the bound document and brought it closer to his face.

"I was careful not to say anything to you about Solomon Rosenthal after I met with him in Tel Aviv yesterday," said the *katsa*, glancing up at Sidney Belton, then looking down again. "He and I spent some time in a Mossad conference room, as you know. It's not that I then suspected him of anything. I really did not. And it's not that this cursory report on him and his background reveals anything of real interest.

"I just didn't like him, detective." Adelman looked up again, meeting Belton's gaze. "He came across to me as an amateur who wanted to engage in sleuthing not so much for the obvious reason… the noble reason… the holy reason… the need to intercept this grotesque assault on the Righteous Among Nations… but because he was offended at the purported 'leak' in his communications network.

"Of course, now… with this totally unexpected — by me, that is — report of Rosenthal's sighting on board the container ship, and the intriguing likelihood of connection between one or more of those containers and your visioners' own reports… I now see that Rosenthal himself is almost certainly the 'leak.'

"But even before I heard… just now… this report of Kory and Luke's sighting of this… ah… this *dirt bag*…."

He smiled, nodding, at Belton.

"The truth is," continued Adelman, "… the truth is… the more I questioned him at Mossad headquarters yesterday, the less I considered him a worthwhile interview for us… and I sent him packing, detective. Told him to stay out of our way… and told my colleagues to keep *him* away from *you*, too."

At this, he saw surprise on all four faces.

"Yes, I know," Adelman said, a trifle sheepishly. "I should have told you that. I'm not sure why I didn't, except that I knew that that part of my distrust of him was grounded simply in the fact that I didn't *like* him."

He smiled. "Not very Mossad-like, is it, detective? We're supposed to draw our conclusions from evidence. Well, it's true that I didn't like my sense of the 'evidence' he claimed to have, but I'm admitting… beyond that… that I just didn't like the guy. I mean… really… what is this thing on his hand? I asked him about that bandage and he showed me the tattoo… the Star of David…. I mean… really… what kind of Jew would do that?

"That's just stupid." He spat the words, contemptuous.

The detective's lop-sided grin emerged at this, and he nodded his head at Adelman. He then exchanged glances with his wife.

Eleanor Chapel's blue-green eyes were wide, confused. She *had* trusted Solomon Rosenthal, just as she continued to trust Jaakov Adelman.

The couple returned their eyes to the agent's as he prepared to continue.

"I think this sighting of Rosenthal on the container ship, going in and out of a vault that conforms to your visioners' images of the files and other records, may give us the last piece of this puzzle. We already have quite a few of the puzzle pieces, and I'll need to share some of that with you later. For now, though, I want to say how grateful I am to you… to each one. You have no idea what this means to me as an Israeli… but, also, personally… as a Jew.

"And, without waiting even to fill you in on the scattered pieces of evidence we have on this plot… evidence we've been pulling together for months without seeing how to fit it into something coherent… until now… I'm going to start a priority history on Solomon Rosenthal right this minute."

He glanced at his watch.

"New York City is just waking up about this time, detective," he said excitedly. "Let's get on this telephone and get things moving right now, and on all fronts: NYPD investigative units and Mossad agents in New York, and, as well, Mossad units throughout Europe, the Middle East and North Africa. Maybe South America, as well. Let's get a lot of people focused over the next several hours on Rosenthal's deep background. Let's get a reading on this guy's real history today… this very day… and let's have it completed by nightfall here in Haifa."

# CHAPTER TEN

AS THE SUN DROPPED TOWARD ITS INTERSECTION WITH THE Mediterranean horizon, preparation was well underway in every observant Haifa household for the start of the Jewish Sabbath. But for the *Rebekka Yahalomin*, the late Friday afternoon hour meant, above all, that it was time to awaken from opportunistically seized catnaps in order to convene once more in the men's hotel room: now to plan for specific action on behalf of the Jewish people and those who had risked their lives to save them.

Sipping gratefully at the coffee his wife had prepared for the two of them — the only coffee drinkers in the group — the detective nodded at Jaakov Adelman to begin. The agent's demeanor was grave.

"I'll go to the heart of what we've learned in the hours since this morning's session, then I'll review briefly the main facts we'd put together before today, then I'll cover the observed activities of the enemy this afternoon."

He lifted a spiral-bound document nearer his thin face. This was not the similarly bound document he had referenced in the earlier meeting. This one appeared new, its covers stiff and unscuffed. His brow furrowed and his jaw clenched in anger.

"This was delivered to us within the last half hour." Adelman turned several pages in the small document. "It's the urgent report I ordered on Solomon Rosenthal. My emergency inquiry went to Mossad agents around the world, within minutes of our finishing our morning meeting here, and all communications related to the inquiry were coordinated by our headquarters unit in Tel Aviv....

"Are you ready to hear this?"

His listeners nodded in unison, bursting with a curiosity that was nine-tenths apprehension.

"Solomon Rosenthal was until shortly after World War II… Adolfus Rademacher." Adelman looked at the startled faces before him, nodded to confirm the accuracy of his own announcement, and continued. "Rademacher was a Berliner. Served with the *Wehrmacht* as a midlevel officer.

"During the Nazis' western European occupation from 1942 until 1944, he was with occupation forces stationed in northern Holland — in Friesland — the farming area visited by the two of you…" (here he nodded to Kory and Luke) "just last Saturday night… impossible to realize… less than a week ago….

"I suspect, Miss van Dijk, though I can't know with certainty, that Rademacher knew your aunt personally. He may have admired her romantically, from a distance… an educated, unmarried woman not then thirty years of age….

"Or he may have just come to hate her later when he learned that she had successfully sheltered one of us — a young blonde Jewess — right under his nose. I don't know. But I'm guessing it was one, or maybe both, of those, and that that explains why he targeted her for the first of what he intends to be many hundreds of murders of Christians like your aunt Greta."

A thick silence enveloped the room as the listeners turned this revelation over in their minds. After several moments, a high, soft voice filled equally with incredulity, dismay and disgust dropped into the silence.

"Do you mean…" said Eleanor Chapel, "… do you *mean*… that Mr. Solomon Rosenthal… the Jewish Theological Seminary's Solomon Rosenthal… is the individual behind this *unspeakable* plan?"

Adelman nodded again. "Yes," he said simply.

He paused. "But, if you'll forgive me, ma'am, I'd suggest that among ourselves we begin to use his real name… Adolfus Rademacher… as a reminder of his actual origins and his true background…. This man is *not* a Jew.

"But yes…" he said again, "yes… Adolfus Rademacher is indeed, I am convinced to my own satisfaction, the leader of the extermination plot… or, if not the formal leader of the operation… the principal instigator and planner."

He looked down again at his document, breathed deeply, and resumed.

"It looks as if Rademacher staged a *faux* suicide in Vienna, in 1952, which is the year after Mossad was formed in Israel. He then assumed the identity of an obscure Austrian Jew — a real Solomon Rosenthal — who had been among those killed during round-the-clock Red Army artillery shelling as the Germans' eastern front collapsed in 1944 and 1945. Rademacher took on a Jewish identity as the best, if most brazen, way to disguise his past, moved to the United States, secured productive work on Wall Street, and moved on from there."

Adelman paused and looked into the faces of his four listeners. "I know you'd like to discuss this man and his history and his life of deception in the United States, but there is much more I must share with you," he continued. "As gripping as the details of Rademacher's story would be to you… you who were getting to know him and beginning to view him as your ally and colleague… it's the rest of the picture that I need to make clear to you. And right now."

The *katsa* adjusted his elongated frame in the straight-backed chair, looked down again at his document and went on. "We've been getting hints of this extermination plot for some time, as you know, but we'd only been able to collect random, unconnected bits and pieces until now, when, thanks to the… to your visioners… the picture has suddenly come together for us.

"I think we're going to find that this container — the vault which you, only this morning, observed this man entering and exiting — has been moved systematically during the last year to and from ports in Morocco, southern France, Greece, and now, Haifa. And I think we're going to find that the documentation on individual members of the Righteous Among Nations has been developed, collected, systematized and stored in that one vault… that very container… all by hand… by members of an unholy alliance of neo-Nazis and Islamic terrorists based in north-African countries, in Europe, in Greece and throughout the Middle East. Possibly three hundred trained Nazi and Islamic terrorists altogether."

Adelman's listeners emitted a collective gasp.

*"Three hundred!"* exclaimed Luke.

Adelman nodded grimly.

"Yes, lieutenant," said Adelman. "Three hundred. Possibly more than that, in fact. Almost certainly not less. And *that* is what we're facing here. I'm guessing they are going to assemble somewhere in Israel, quite possibly nearby… all of them together… all in one place… there to divide those files among themselves… and then to fan out throughout continental Europe and beyond — certainly to the United Kingdom and the United States — killing systematically until either the Righteous are all murdered, or the conspirators themselves are all killed or captured by law enforcement or the various militaries who may ultimately become involved. I'm think that's probably the plan.

"And I'm guessing that the reason we have gathered such sketchy, unconnected information up to now is that they have been too disciplined for our networks to succeed… too disciplined to communicate in any fashion except face-to-face. They transmit nothing by telephone or by radiotelephone… or even through the mails. It has to be incredibly inefficient and cumbersome to restrict communications to such an extreme… and yet… the wisdom of the approach is evident. I mean… just *look* at this….

"They have reached this point of readiness… possibly prepared to set out from this area within twenty-four hours from now to do their murderous work around the globe… and yet… without the data supplied by the *Rebekka Yahalomin,* and without your astonishing surveillance success this morning, Seaman van Dijk and Lieutenant Manguson, we would still have absolutely nothing other than isolated, indecipherable pieces of this plan….

"I'm betting that they — all three hundred of these neo-Nazis and Islamic terrorists — are going to assemble together, all in one place, all right here in the Haifa area… right now….

"This very evening… or later tonight… or early tomorrow. I don't know exactly. But *now.*

"And we need to stop them before they have their marching orders — the documents, the files, the records — in their hands and before they disperse. Once they fan out across Europe and around the world we'll have the devil of a time. After all, *they* will know exactly where the Righteous are *and how to get to them* as soon as they have the materials in their hands….

"Certainly," he continued without pause, "we can get 'last known address' from the Committee on the Righteous, but those are nothing but outdated mailing addresses. Compared with what they've assembled, it's nothing."

Adelman stopped. He knew his listeners were stunned. He knew that they wanted to think… to pray… to ask questions of him and of each other….

And Jaakov Adelman was both a thoughtful and a perceptive man.

"I know you want to take time to absorb all this, my friends," he said kindly. "I know. But, you must understand, we cannot take the time, because that is exactly what we do not have.

"I must continue."

He looked at them, and they nodded at him, each in turn.

"Midafternoon," he continued, "the tugs moved out to the container ship and helped it move into one of the city piers. The whole maneuver took less than two hours. The ship has been tied up at the dock for about an hour now. The cranes are at the ready. The floodlights and spotlights have already been turned on, even though we still have daylight. It looks as though they'll go ahead and unload right away, even with the sun's setting and the Sabbath nearly underway.

"There appear to be at least four flatbed trucks in position, each of them capable of carrying the largest of the ship's containers. We've already ordered three dozen *katsas* to Haifa this afternoon, and we have alerted two teams of *kidon* to be here by nightfall. We need to be fully ready within hours."

"Ready for what?" asked the detective immediately.

"Ready, first, to follow the flatbed truck... or trucks... to wherever they are headed, and, once we have followed them to their destination... ready to attack."

Again there was a pause.

Adelman prepared to resume, but this time he was stopped.

"That doesn't make sense to me," grumbled the detective.

"Nor to me," added Luke quickly and emphatically.

"What do you mean?" asked the agent.

"Well," responded Belton, "what *I* mean is that, if the objective is to save the Righteous Among Nations from murder, y'need to grab that container — the vault that's got all th' files — right now, before it gets loaded on anything. The thing is... y'know... what y'wanna have in your hands *right now* is all these records Rebecca has dreamed for us. We wanna have those records in our hands, son. Right now, like I said. Know what I mean? Hm? Know what I mean?

"Sounds to me..." the detective continued, "sounds to me like you got somethin' else in mind, agent Adelman. You got somethin' else in mind entirely. That right, son?"

Without waiting for a response from Adelman, Luke nodded and added quickly and with some vigor, "Yes, and beyond that, Mr. Adelman, if you allow the trucks to leave this immediate area, you introduce the difficulties of trying to follow vehicles in the dark and into areas that surely have been set up to foil exactly that kind of thing. And beyond even that, sir, your three dozen agents and another handful of assassins could be outnumbered by... what?... five-to-one? Even ten-to-one?

"I agree with Mr. Belton, sir," Luke concluded. "I don't follow your thinking here. We need to seize that container before it even leaves the deck of the ship. I led boarding parties in the Royal Navy, sir. Give me a half-dozen armed agents — and no assassins — and we'll control that ship within fifteen minutes."

Luke was leaning forward, his massive forearm muscles visibly rippling as his body tensed for action that he assumed was imminent.

Kory stared at him, her eyes wide.

But Jaakov Adelman shook his head. "No, my friends. No... we must accomplish *two* objectives, not just one. We must seize the files, certainly, but we must also seize the Nazis and the terrorists. To miss an opportunity to eliminate *three-hundred* trained murderers would be unconscionable, gentlemen… and ladies. We must follow the vehicle or vehicles to their destination and then seize *everything:* the records and the murderers."

"How?" said Kory van Dijk, suddenly on the edge of her chair.

"What do you mean, ma'am?" responded Adelman.

"How, *exactly,* will you 'seize' three hundred fully armed terrorists, sir?"

Adelman shifted in his chair, for the first time appearing uncomfortable under this sudden flurry of challenges. But his face remained expressionless.

"Well…" he said after a moment, "I admit that my use of the word *seize* was a trifle euphemistic."

"Yes?" answered Kory, obviously not surprised by his acknowledgement.

"Well…" Adelman repeated, "the fact is… once we have the terrorists… once we have the terrorists… ah… cornered… so to speak… once we have them pinned down somewhere… well… we will… well… we will…."

He stopped and sighed deeply, dropping his eyes in embarrassment. "Once we have them pinned down… we will just… we will just… we will just bring in the Cobras."

Seeing that the others appeared to comprehend this last, the Old Testament professor interjected after a moment, "The Cobras? What?"

"Helicopter gunships, Dr. Chapel," responded Kory immediately. "The AH-1(G) is used both by the U.S. Army and the Israeli Army. It is basically a gun platform mounted in a helicopter. A crew of two… pilot seated behind and above a gunner… a 20mm Gatling gun in a steerable gun pod just under the nose of the aircraft. It's an M197 three-barrel Gatling that rotates the barrels for maximum rate of fire… which is roughly 700 rounds-per-minute. Cobras can also fire wire-guided missiles when that's called for….

"The Cobra has a very narrow profile from head-on… very difficult to detect… it can hide… that is, it can hover… quite effectively either in trees or in ravines… waiting for the right moment to lift up and swoop in…. If you have a flight of, say, a dozen Cobras, Dr. Chapel, then you've got the flat-trajectory firepower of a small army."

She felt silent, suddenly aware of the incredulous stares from her colleagues. And then she actually blushed, looking down much as she had under the gaze of Luke Manguson in a London ice cream parlor just over one week — and seemingly an eternity — before.

"I'm sorry," she said in genuine embarrassment, her chocolate eyes still down, soft brown hair falling forward and partially covering her face. "I like helicopters, too, Luke, not just ships," she added, now peeping up at him through a curtain of hair, a small, shy smile on her lips. "I just like *data.*"

Then the professor smiled, too, as, indeed, after a moment, did they all, marveling at this young gem of an intellect that they were just getting to know.

"So…" Eleanor Chapel said finally, turning her face back to the agent, her smile fading as she did, "you're saying in answer to Kory's question regarding the 'how' of this operation that you'll bring in helicopter gunships… presumably from the Israeli Army… and simply blast these people into Kingdom Come?

"Is that it, Mr. Adelman? You'll just kill them all?"

Jaakov Adelman almost responded to the professor's near-rhetorical question with the obvious — "They will certainly be pleased to kill *us* all" — but held his tongue, something he had learned to do well in his years as Mossad *katsa.* He saw immediately that the group was not going to allow him to go forward without discussing the issue of how the terrorists were going to be confronted, or, prior to that, whether or not the container — Rebecca's dreamed vault of the Righteous — was going to be permitted to leave not only the ship's deck, but the Haifa area itself. And so he sat back in his straight-backed chair, folded his long-fingered, sinewy hands in his lap, and waited.

He knew that he could force the issue now, and that he and his organization could simply set out to execute the counteraction he had just outlined, with or without *Rebekka Yahalomin,* but he was loathe to do so. He wanted this foursome solidly with him and fully committed to his solution. He wanted their determined and even, if possible, their enthusiastic assistance not simply because they were, each in his or her own way, supremely gifted as analysts and planners, but, in the case of Luke Manguson, an indispensable combat tactician.

And there was another reason, as well.

He knew that the four had contacted their colleagues in the UK by telephone, and with his blessing, as soon as their morning session had ended, Belton having finally decided that Mossad involvement could no longer be postponed, and, thus, that maintaining secrecy from Adelman and his colleagues was immaterial. And the agent knew, too, that they would contact their British colleagues yet again at the end of this meeting. He knew that more visioner-derived messages could well be forthcoming during any such long-distance exchange.

The agent desperately wanted any such supernaturally originated informa-tion relayed to him the moment it was in hand. He was, after all, in regard to the visioners and their received messages, fully a believer. God was, he was certain, active with these people in ways that gave them insights that no strictly human "special intelligence" could equal. The proof was all around him in that room. The proof had preceded, accompanied and followed these people for at least the last three years.

And so he sat still: relaxed, alert, and fighting his impatience to swing into action. He needed these extraordinary people, and he would wait for them… within limits.

He sensed that Luke Manguson and the two women were now, as before, prepared to defer to the detective. And Belton was, as usual, studying his shoes, holding his head in his hands, immersed in concentration.

Finally he spoke, but without looking up.

"Well… let's say we let these scumbags hole up somewhere tonight, Mr. Adelman," he said, his low rumble of a voice barely audible to his listeners. "Let's say we let 'em all climb into their hole-in-th'-ground and we manage to follow 'em and we know they're all in there together. You gonna try to capture *any* of 'em? Or do y' really just want 'em all dead?"

Adelman hesitated only a moment before replying softly, "We really just want them all dead, detective. If they are all dead, then not only are the Righteous saved from their executioners, but so are countless other innocents in my coun-try and around the world. These people's *raison d'etre*, after all, is clear. They are murderers, sworn to kill Jews, to kill those who help Jews, to kill even those who *allow* Jews to live." He nodded his head soberly and then repeated, "We really just want them all dead, detective."

Belton, still staring at his shoes, shook his head slowly. After a moment, he spoke, his voice still barely audible, "Well… we can't, son. We… y'know… we… the… ah…." He stopped and looked up at his wife.

"The *Rebekka Yahalomin,* dear," she said quickly in response to her hus-band's unasked question.

"Yeah," he continued, "right… us *Yahalomin*…" — here he grinned at his own effort to pronounce the Hebrew term — "us *Yahalomin* aren't allowed… as Rebecca herself has said to us more than once… to use *their* methods to serve *our* ends, Mr. Adelman.

"We've been lookin' this kind of thing in the face every summer for four years now, son. Every summer at some point I think to m'self, 'We oughta just give Luke, here, a couple of automatic weapons and a half-dozen grenades and send him after these people. Tell him to just… y'know… just wipe 'em out.'

"And every summer, as soon as I hear m'self think that thought, I come right back and say, 'You've lost your mind, Sidney Belton…. You've lost your Christian mind….' Sure, it's always possible we might have to take somebody's life at some point in order to save somebody else's life… but y'don't just send your best warrior out to slay every single bad guy when it might be at least *possible* to take the bad guys outta th' game without killin' em.

"In fact," he continued, "even if there's the chance y'might save just *one* of th' bad guys… well… then that's what y'try to do.

"Know what I mean, son? Hm? Know what I mean?"

Belton paused, looking up now at the agent.

The agent looked back unmoving, seemingly bemused.

"Like… well…" added Belton, "like what Luke and Kory pulled off up there in northern Holland last Saturday night, Mr. Adelman. Like that. Y'know… nobody killed. Just taken outta th' game.

"Or like what Luke did to those two guys that came at him in New York just… what?… three or four days ago…" he continued, still looking at the agent. "Like that… y'know what I mean?"

Jaakov Adelman nodded his head. "Yes, detective," he said softly, "I do. I certainly do.

"But…" Adelman continued, "those men that Luke defeated are still out there, detective. All those men are quite likely to be among those assembling right here in Israel this afternoon… tonight… right here.

"They did not surrender. They were not converted to the Good. They are still as devoted as ever to the Evil.

"And beyond that… there is the obvious practical question, Mr. Belton," said the agent. "Given the fact — and it is simply a fact — that these men are all terrorists… each one of them prepared to die rather than give in or give up… each one of them prepared to fight to the death… each one of them absolutely unwilling to surrender, regardless of the circumstances….

"How, Mr. Belton, can you see an alternative to bringing in the gunships? To unleashing the Cobras as soon as the terrorists have all assembled in one place? To killing them all before they kill all of the Righteous?

"This is not some small, manageable number of somewhat civilized, strategic evildoers, my friends. This is a mobile army of *terrorists*. What alternative is there to the Cobras? I can imagine none at all."

There was a brief pause, and then Kory answered.

"Load the Cobras with non-lethal ammunition, sir," she said quietly.

Adelman looked at her.

She looked back.

"You mean like rubber bullets in the Gatling guns?" he said, smiling indulgently at the naiveté of the suggestion.

"No, sir," she replied, "like a wire-guided missile filled with some form of nonlethal toxin."

Adelman turned his eyes first to Luke Manguson, then to Sid Belton, both of whom were now looking at the young woman. Then the three men shook their heads slowly at each other. Finally all three turned back to this, their living, breathing in-house encyclopedia.

"I'm no expert, you understand, on this kind of weaponry," said Kory, realizing she still had the floor and was expected to continue, "but I do know that the nitrates… or phenyl hydride… or cyclohexatriene… can be used in this way…. I know that benzene, for example, can be converted from a liquid at high temperature to a vapor at about 26 degrees centigrade… and I know that inhaling these types of vapors will cause instantaneous central nervous system distress… weakness, dizziness, nausea, vomiting, blurred vision, tremors… and if the exposure continues, unconsciousness… eventually, perhaps, death….

"But my point is simply that a wire-guided missile from a Cobra, fired directly into the terrorists' building or cave, could incapacitate most or all of them in seconds and allow your people, Mr. Adelman, to go in and get them all in handcuffs. And I'm quite sure of another thing… I'm quite sure that if someone like me… someone who spent a fairly short time in the Royal Navy working in a London office… if someone like me can know this much about nonlethal toxins… you're certain to have people in your organization, sir, that will know one hundred times more… people who will also know of other not-necessarily-lethal substances that can be packed into a missile or a shell and delivered into the midst of these…" — and here she smiled teasingly at the detective — "into the midst of these *dirtbags*… if I understand your technical term for these gentlemen, Mr. Belton."

She stopped and turned her eyes to Luke. He smiled, then reached out and covered her small left hand with his thickly muscled right. He shook his head at her in amazement, and finally said quietly, "I'm certainly glad I took you to Rebecca and Matt's place last week as part of your birthday celebration, Kory van Dijk."

Then he rose from his chair, stepped behind hers, and bent over her. He embraced her from above and behind with his massive forearms and, squeezing her gently in a playful bear hug, delivered a light kiss to the top of her head.

Without changing his position, he looked up at the others, smiled broadly, and added, "You'll have to forgive me, everyone. I just can't help myself."

This brought forth the tinkling laughter of Eleanor Chapel, the rumbling chuckle of Sidney Belton, and, heard for the first time by the others, a high-pitched, cackling sound that they identified as Jaakov Adelman's version of laughter. Adelman actually seemed surprised at himself. He covered his mouth in feigned embarrassment and said, "Excuse me, please, I've never really learned how to laugh, and when I do, it seems to distress people rather than make them happy. I just don't do it very well."

Kory, still buried under Luke's avalanche of an embrace, looked up at the *katsa* and smiled brilliantly at him. "Oh, you're not distressing us, Mr. Adelman," she said happily. "I'm just pleased to see that you can appreciate the humor in what I am forced to endure from my… ah…."

Her voice tailed off.

"From your *boyfriend*, Kory," said Eleanor Chapel quickly. "That's the only word that can possibly fit the context, my dear. That's your *boyfriend* who has you in the vicious stranglehold from which you'll be fortunate to escape with your very life."

Elisabeth Manguson and Martha Clark had refused to take "no" for an answer. Rebecca *would* attempt an afternoon nap, and that was that. The twins were well in hand, they would be attended by an entire house full of loving and competent adults, and their mother was exhausted. To this Rebecca had not put up serious resistance.

She had been asleep — deeply asleep — in the darkened bedroom for just over two hours when the Divine Interrupter had again brought her to full wakefulness. Pushing herself, at first groggily, into a sitting position, Rebecca now pulled her confused hair back from her face and steadied herself for what she knew was quickly to be upon her.

She found immediately, as she alerted herself to commit each expected detail to memory, that she welcomed the visitation. She desperately wanted to be shown the face of *this* enemy. She wanted to be able to alert her brother and the others to the look and nature of their adversary.

The gray eyes opened wide. She sat erect in her bed. And she waited.

And swiftly the vision came upon her… sharp colors and clear borders… and yet, this time, she found she saw but dimly… so dimly that she could make little of the scene at first. Then it became apparent to her that she was being shown a night scene, and that the dimness of the perceived vision was simply a faithful representation of how the envisioned setting would look to someone actually face-to-face with it, with only the night sky and the three-quarter moon to provide illumination.

She was shown, first, a torch… not a battery-driven lamp of some kind, but an actual, burning torch, fueled apparently by its own flammable liquid. Its base was planted in sandy, rocky ground. The flame appeared to announce the start of a broad path… a path that would mark a traveler's departure from an ancient, earthen roadway that continued straight before her, and onto something less like a roadway than a recently machined cut through the desert terrain… a graded, freshly graveled driveway branching from the ancient road… a drive that extended through the semidarkness and straight up toward, and apparently *into*, the rocky face of a hillock marking the onset of a more serious geological feature… a massive ridge disappearing into the more distant darkness.

And as she perceived that the rough, dirt-and-gravel drive seemed somehow to enter the side of the hill itself, the visioner was then permitted by the Giver of All Visions to understand that this drive curved sharply back upon itself, finally to end in an abrupt, vertical face… perhaps an entrance, she thought immediately, to an underground complex, one sealed fast shut by a hinged and camouflaged vehicular doorway… a doorway large enough, Rebecca saw instantly, to accept something as large as a flatbed truck — perhaps several such trucks — and any bulky cargo such vehicles might carry.

This image, darkened and yet altogether clear to her, lingered before her mind's eye for some time, forcing its detail into her receptive consciousness.

And then, as the vision began incrementally to fade from her view, the dreamer was taken higher along the hillock to a point seemingly above whatever might be lodged underground, finally to a lone tree, also perceived dimly in the darkness… a tree she recognized immediately as a carob… leathery leaves, tough and resilient… the same tree that, by the hundreds, had marked the Avenue of the Righteous — *Yad Vashem* — in her Jerusalem vision of one week earlier, as earthly time measures itself.

And, just behind and slightly above the diminutive, solitary tree, Rebecca was shown finally something she recognized after a moment as a kind of vent… a wide, metallic pipe protruding vertically from the earth… its opening covered by a tent-like device obviously intended to keep out both rain and desert animals… and to permit fresh air to move down and into the interior of whatever lay beneath.

And as the last features of the vision disappeared from her mind's eye, Rebecca realized that there was, as well, machinery connected to the ventilation device… something mechanical that could perhaps provide for a forced-air exchange with all that lay hidden under the natural surface of the hilltop.

And then the vision was gone… gone as swiftly as it had come.

The visioner lay down heavily, her breathing rapid. She put her hands to her face, felt the perspiration, and moved her fingers through the dampness of her hair. Exhausted from the visitation, but knowing from long experience that immediate recall and review of the events was crucial, she called out to her husband through the darkness of her bedroom. "Matt!" she cried, urgency in her strong voice. "Matt! I need you!"

# Chapter Eleven

LUKE PRESSED THE SMALL BUTTON THAT ILLUMINATED THE FACE of his digital wristwatch. "Okay," he said softly, more to himself than to his four companions as they crouched, scarcely breathing, high on the Mount Carmel ridge. "Not quite 0200 and we're in position. Excellent."

Events had unfolded rapidly that night. Luke had made the prearranged telephone call to his sister at exactly 10:00 p.m. in Israel — 8:00 p.m. in the UK — and had received her detailed report firsthand. Rebecca's careful description of her early evening vision had been tape recorded, also by prearrangement, in order that the *Rebekka Yahalomin* in Haifa, Mossad agents already involved in the case and, newly engaged, a small cadre of Israeli Army forces and helicopter gunship pilots could listen repeatedly to her words.

When, near the end of the call, Rebecca had expressed regret that she could not provide a physical description of the enemy, Luke had informed her that the enemy — or, if not *the* enemy, the primary instigator — had been revealed not by supernatural, but by natural means. Luke had then summarized for Rebecca the sordid biography of one Adolfus Rademacher.

Not all of the Mossad operatives and Army officers now assigned to the case had attended to this tape-recorded account of a secret mountain hideaway with the faith in the report's accuracy that was so evident in the response of Jaakov Adelman. Some had been openly skeptical. But all — *katsas* and Army personnel alike — had understood that in this operation Adelman had been given tactical command. And that fact, coupled with the outstanding reputation he had earned during his time with the agency, had been enough. Dutifully, his *katsa* associates and his military comrades-in-arms had begun to prepare themselves for a night action planned almost entirely around the presumed accuracy of a supernaturally originated report by a young woman who had never set foot on the terrain she had described.

It was extraordinary. But so was Jaakov Adelman's testimony to the record of reliability established in past episodes by the *Rebekka Yahalomin.*

Some of the Israeli listeners to the tape were lifelong believers in the living God and had themselves experienced divine influences and interventions, if less spectacular than this, in their own lives. Others were formerly observant Jews whose hearts and minds had been strangely moved by Rebecca's words and by Adelman's testimony to the authenticity of all such *Yahalomin* reports. And still others were non-religious Jews whose assumptions about the universe permitted no acknowledgement, even provisionally, of the possibility that the report had been supernatural in origin. Even these, however, were willing to grant the Mossad leader the benefit of the doubt: the report could not be supernatural, they had told themselves and each other, but it had come from a source in which, for reasons of his own, a no-nonsense *katsa* of high accomplishment had placed his confidence. If he wanted to hide the actual source from the others involved in the operation, that was his business. As professionals, they would do their part, and do it well.

Just after 11:00 p.m. in Haifa, one half hour after Rebecca's description of the target had been circulated among all engaged Mossad and Army units, four fully loaded flatbed trucks had pulled away from the container ship that had provided their cargo. The trucks, followed at discreet distances by a small fleet of Mossad-owned vehicles of various makes, models, colors and ages, had made their clumsy way, first, from the harbor to the nearest entrance ramp to Route 4. From there they had continued southeast at good speed along the east face of the Mount Carmel ridge to Route 70, and thence, more slowly, onto the older, less traveled Route 66.

Only two Mossad vehicles — one battered sedan and one late-model pickup truck — had been ordered to follow the four trucks onto the smaller roadway, but all other pursuit vehicles had remained in the chase, peeling off both to north and south with the purpose of picking up the scent again, should the flatbeds abandon their southeasterly course. Four Israeli Army Cobras — each chopper's Gatling guns fully armed with live, lethal ammunition — had hovered over strategic sites in the area, ready to move immediately if so requested by Mossad.

Forty-five minutes after leaving Haifa's docks, the trucks had slowed to turn sharp right at the intersection of Route 66 with Route 65. With this turn, they were now headed southwest over Mount Carmel itself, each vehicle a modern, mechanical beast of burden seeking to cross the millennia-honored pass that led from the storied Jezreel Valley back toward the coast and then south toward far-distant Egypt.

As hundreds of thousands of soldiers, settlers, nomads, camels, horses and donkeys had done before them, they passed under the brow of the ancient structure that had guarded this, the only pass on the entire length of the Mount Carmel ridge, century after long century: the *Tel Megiddo* fortress itself. At midnight, the mighty redoubt had hovered menacingly in the moonlight, less than one-half mile from the laboring engines of the flatbeds as they had begun their climb to the pass.

Only one Mossad unit — the late-model pick-up — had been permitted to make the turn onto Route 65 with the flatbeds. Following instructions, its driver had paused for minutes before actually proceeding to the intersection itself so as to allow an almost three-quarter-mile gap to develop between the followed and the follower. Then, having made the turn, the driver had taken further care so as not to narrow the gap between himself and the slow-moving flatbeds as they struggled up Mount Carmel and, gaining the crest, geared down for the delicate descent of the southwest slope.

So it was that the pickup's two *katsas* had been screened both by distance and by the mountain itself from the flatbeds' careful but efficient turn off of Highway 65 and onto the unnumbered and unmarked secondary road that lay near the foot of the southwest slope. This primitive, ancient thoroughfare had carried the four heavy trucks immediately out of sight of the main highway and, circuitously, back toward the rear of *Tel Megiddo* itself.

As they had crested Carmel ridge and looked down the slope in the moonlight, the pick-up's agents saw immediately that their prey had vanished. Without delay, the two agents had notified the tactical commander of the fact by radiotelephone. Jaakov Adelman had then promptly requested the nearest Cobra to take position near the intersection of Routes 66 and 65, and to hover there, running lights extinguished, at high altitude, from which position systematically to search the slope and its immediate environs for anything that could be interpreted as torchlight.

Within five minutes of receiving this message, the Cobra's pilots contacted Adelman to report a tiny pinprick of flickering light, its coordinates placing it a scant three-quarter-mile west-by-southwest of the fortress, easily within the Carmel foothills themselves. Satisfied, Adelman had thanked the Army commander, requested that the helicopters return to base, and asked the commander to have the Cobras refueled and ready to return at first light.

Now, less than two hours later, Luke and his companions looked down upon the area designated by the coordinates as the mountain hideaway of the terrorists. The torch had long since been extinguished, and so, as they peered down from the western edge of the *Tel Megiddo* complex, they could as yet, even in the ample moonlight and with high-powered binoculars, see nothing.

In hushed voices, they discussed their next steps.

"Let me go down alone," said Luke quietly to Jaakov Adelman. "That's our best chance to remain undetected and to locate the air vent. With this much moonlight and with Rebecca's description of carob tree, vent, and machinery, I should be able to find the site quickly."

"No," replied the tactical commander immediately. "Pairs. Four eyes, not two. You go, Luke, but with Saul Coen here. He speaks every Middle Eastern language. If you find the vent guarded, it will probably be guarded by several sentries, and, if they're like sentries around the world, they'll either be talking or sleeping. If they're talking, I want you to be able to hear the language they're using and to try to talk your way into close range. Pretend to be late arrivals to their terrorist party. Greet them as friends. Get close. No gunshots. Fists and knives only."

Luke nodded. "Right then," he said. "Saul and I go down. We'll take one radiotelephone. When we've found the vent and secured the area, we'll let you know and you can bring the toxin reservoir and generator."

At this mention of the noxious agent, all glanced down at the portable unit. They knew that the reservoir's contents could be anything at all. They had been assured by the unit's suppliers — one of the Israeli Army's anti-terrorist units — that the gaseous agent could be forced into any air vent by its attached generator, and that the toxin was nonlethal in moderate dosage, but beyond that they knew nothing. They had been further assured that the toxin would incapacitate instantly. Luke and Kory trusted that all of this was true. They had no means of gaining independent verification.

There was a pause. Then a woman's voice slipped softly into and through the darkness. "And what if the guards are German, Mr. Adelman? Does Mr. Coen speak that language, too?"

Faces turned to Coen.

Saul Coen shook his head.

Faces turned back to Adelman.

Adelman turned back to the woman and sighed.

"It's true that the sentries, if there are any, are as likely to be German as anything else. And I suppose you're going to tell me that you speak fluent German as well as English and Dutch, Ms. van Dijk?" queried Adelman, a mischievous smile on his angular face.

From the young woman came the equally mischievous reply: *"Jawohl, Herr Adelman!"*

They crouched just fifty feet from Jaakov Adelman and the other two agents, and looked into each other's faces at close range. Luke had asked Adelman for five minutes of privacy with his companion, and Adelman had acceded to the request. "But just five, Luke," he had added unnecessarily. "We need to get moving. If we're going to have any realistic chance to incapacitate these people successfully, we've got to do it well before first light, or the Army Cobras — and maybe the Air Force Phantoms, too — are going to blow this mountain apart."

Now, facing the woman, his hands covering hers, Luke whispered, "Kory, I just wanted you to hear me say that… well… I don't *like* you anymore."

She giggled at this.

Then, embarrassed, she looked down and murmured, "I know, Luke. I know you don't *like* me now. You *liked* me a week ago in London, and we've lived half a lifetime since then. So… I know…."

"I love you, Kory van Dijk," he whispered softly, squeezing her hands.

"And it's not, you know," he added, still whispering, "that I've come to love you in the week or so since I said I *liked* you. I've *been* loving you, Kory, for months… or is it years…."

He shook his head in the moonlight.

"I don't know," he continued quietly. "I think I've loved you forever, but I've reached the point now where I can — where I must — actually say it, Kory. And so I'm saying it to you now…. I love you, Kory van Dijk."

Still she looked down, silent. But after what seemed to him a very long time, she looked up.

"I know you love me, Luke," she replied finally, her chocolate eyes bright in the shimmering moonlight. "You've been telling me that and you've been showing me that in so many ways, and for such a long time. I've never felt… cherished… until you, Luke. Now I do.

"And… and… I love you…. I love you, Luke."

Each released the other's hands as if by signal.

Now, hands gently cupping the other's face, the man and the woman leaned slowly to each other and, hesitating briefly, kissed softly, lingering. Then, slowly, reluctantly, they sat back, joined hands once more, and smiled into the other's eyes.

Kory broke the silence.

"Luke… are we… are we going to die in a few minutes?"

He smiled at the question, not in amusement, but in appreciation.

"Well… I try to remind myself every day, Kory, of our Lord's words: 'This very night your life will be demanded of you.' I try to live every day on that assumption. That way, if it happens…."

"I know, Luke," she said quickly. "I use that verse just that way, too. But I was just asking, you know…."

"Yes, my love," he said, surprised at the ease with which the endearment came from his lips, "I know what you're asking.

"And my only answer is that we — you and I — are tonight enacting what my family calls the blueprint of the universe: *my life for yours.*

"We are doing what we were placed here on earth to do… every day… in large ways or small… in heroic acts, if needed, or in small courtesies: *My life for yours….*

"Luke's life for Kory's. Kory's life for Luke's. Luke and Kory's lives for the Righteous Among Nations. This is Christianity. We live and die in service to one another, in any possible way we may be called upon. And… when you think about it, Kory… the blueprint of the universe is really nothing other than obedience, isn't it? Just simple obedience to the God who made us all…."

She nodded and murmured a softly whispered, "Yes."

"But Kory… each June… in the crisis… my sister and I — and the detective — have always reminded ourselves that Almighty God has chosen to be involved *directly* in what we are called upon to do. It is unlikely, given the force of His involvement, that He will allow our defeat.

"But that's not quite the same as saying that you and I shall both live to see His victory. I think we will. And I think your moment of real decision took place back in England… at the lodge… when you took the master key, read your Bible, said your prayers, and left the safety of that sanctuary… when you came to us.

"This is the path on which God set you that night.

"And I expect that you… and I… will live to see the morning, Kory.

"But if not… then something better. Something eternal and much, much, much better, my love."

She beamed at him, radiant in the moonlight. And he gazed enraptured at her, filled with wonder that God had brought to him such a woman. The seconds ticked past, each lost in the other and in the holiness of the moment.

Finally, she said simply, "Prayers."

He nodded.

Without need to speak further, they bowed their heads and prayed silently for perhaps a full minute. Then Luke whispered the now-familiar phrases, used so often by his sister, taken from memory from her prayer book, "Stir up thy strength, O Lord… for thou… canst save by many or by few…."

And she replied in her soft whisper, "… Hear us thy poor servants begging mercy, and imploring thy help… that thou wouldest be a defence unto us against the face of the enemy…."

It was 0245 Saturday.

After fewer than twenty-five minutes of silent, careful descent, Luke, Kory, and Saul Coen stopped for the third time to reconnoiter their approach to the enemy lair. As soon as the glasses were at his eyes, Luke whispered, "There! Two-hundred yards. Maybe 150. The carob tree… the air vent and its compressor… and one… no, two… two sentries."

He passed the binoculars first to the *katsa* and then to Kory. Then he took the field glasses again and scrutinized everything about the moonlit scene: the sentries, their apparent firepower, the terrain, the vegetation, the opportunity to move to very close range without detection.

The obvious route required them to backtrack briefly and to approach the sentries from behind a spur that ran at right angles to the axis of the main ridge, at which point to take advantage of a cluster of bushes and small trees near the very end of the spur. Accordingly, the threesome proceeded without delay, their soft footfall carried away from the sentries' ears by a rising southwesterly night wind. After fifteen minutes of maneuver, they were able to look down upon the two solitary watchmen from very close range, perhaps thirty yards.

After a moment, Kory leaned close to Luke's ear and whispered, "Luke, I think one of those people is a child."

He looked more closely at the smaller sentry. The boy held a rifle across his lap, his back to a rocky outcropping, his head drooping. The other sat across from the boy, his back against an oversized knapsack, rifle propped against the compressor itself. He appeared to be sleeping, his forehead resting on his crossed forearms, which in turn rested on his knees.

"I think you're right, Kory," whispered Luke. "That's just a boy sitting on the right."

After a moment, Kory spoke again. "No," she said. "That's not a boy, Luke. That's a girl. Look at her head covering. She can't be ten years old."

Luke nodded grimly. After another moment he leaned over and put his head near both his companions' faces. "Saul," he said to the agent, "they're asleep or nearly so. I think we try to get within fifteen yards — cover half the distance between here and there without alerting them — and then rush them.

"What do you think?"

Coen said nothing. His mouth hung open stupidly. He gaped vacantly at the scene in front of them.

"Saul?" repeated Luke.

After a moment, the *katsa* shook his head in wonder. "I can't believe it," he said in a low whisper. "I *don't* believe it…. This looks *exactly* as your sister said on the recorded message from England. What is *happening?*"

Luke nodded at the agent. "Yes," he whispered. "I understand. When you see our visioners' actual scenes for the first time, right in front of you… it takes your breath away, doesn't it?"

Coen shook his head, trying to clear the stunned confusion from his mind. "All right," he whispered at last. "All right. I'm ready, Luke. What did you say?"

"I'll go straight for the man. Kory, you go straight for his rifle. Try to get it in your hands before he can realize what's happening. Saul, you go for the child. Seize her rifle first, then cover her mouth so she can't alert the people underground here."

Coen shook his head immediately. "No. Adelman was clear with me, Luke. If things work out so that we actually capture any of these people rather than kill them… okay. But, really, that's *your* objective… the *Rebekka Yahalomin* objective. The Mossad objective is to kill every last one of them.

"Adelman has made this bargain with you in order to gain your cooperation… your sharing of the… the divine reports… and we will honor the terms of the bargain… but if at any moment your objective is compromised, *our* objective comes into play."

"And so?" whispered Luke after a moment's pause.

"And so I will remain in this position with my rifle lined up with the adult terrorist's forehead. If he gets his hands on his rifle, I will kill him. And if the child picks up her rifle, I will kill her, as well.

"And, yes," he continued, whispering rapidly, "gunshots will alert the Nazis and the other terrorists underground. They may attempt, each one singly, to grab one or more files of the Righteous and, as your movies say, 'make a run for it.' That is why eight teams of *kidon* have formed a perimeter. Not one terrorist will make it out of here alive.

"And if any of them choose to stay in their underground… well… then the Army will go in after them.

"And so, one way or another… unless your plan to incapacitate and capture these people somehow manages to succeed… we will kill them all.

"And for each one it will be exactly the death he has earned for himself."

# Chapter Twelve

ON THIS NIGHT, LUKE MANGUSON AND KORY VAN DIJK HAD dressed for action.

In her case, this meant that she had accepted Mossad's offer to provide her with dark-colored exercise togs, lightweight hiking boots, and a black, billed cap. In his case, it meant that he had donned his own, but it meant one thing more.

It meant that he wore his treasured shoulder holster, a device replete with notches and pouches and pockets into which an expansive array of weapons, tools and related accoutrement could be housed. The array included knife blades of five different sizes, any of which could be accommodated by the heavy universal handle that was itself an effective blunt instrument. Also included were such items as small wrenches, wire cutters, coils of rope in several lengths and diameters, duct tape in three widths, eye black and a great deal more.

As always, he carried no firearm.

At this moment, on the darkened slopes of Mount Carmel, the largest and most menacing of the five knives was upraised in his left hand. He glanced to his right at his female comrade-in-arms, nodded once, and exploded forward in his patented half-crouch.

Neither of them had needed to say a word to the other regarding their approaches to the two sentries. With a look, they had communicated the tactical maneuver of choice: Luke would run straight for the adult sentry, placing himself purposely on a line between the muzzle of Saul Coen's automatic weapon and the sentry. His companion would do the same, positioning her body between Coen and the child.

They were certain that Coen would do as he said, if given the opportunity: he would shoot to kill either sentry or both, should they make a move toward their weapons. And they were equally certain that Coen would not risk a shot that might strike either of the *Rebekka Yahalomin* as they sprinted toward the enemy, their backs to him. A Mossad agent's moral compass might point in a direction different from that of a Christian's — or a Jew's — but that did not mean there was no compass at all.

Luke and Kory, in fact, held complete trust in Jaakov Adelman, Saul Coen and the other *katsas* involved in the operation. It was a limited, narrowly circumscribed kind of trust. But it was trust nonetheless. Coen would not pull the trigger so long as his round was as likely to strike Luke Manguson or Kory van Dijk as one of the sentries. This they knew.

Luke was upon the adult sentry before the man understood what was happening. He looked up, sleep transforming itself into confusion and then to terror in a mere second of earthly time. Luke drove the blunt end of the universal knife handle into the sentry's temple at exactly the spot at which the least force would produce the most certain loss of consciousness. The sentry toppled sideways to the ground, his rifle still leaning, untouched, against the compressor.

Luke wheeled to his right, searching in the semi-darkness for Kory.

Her sentry had not been sleeping, but merely nodding. The child had looked up to see, first, a large, dark shape closing on her sleeping partner, and then, to her left, a smaller person running straight for her. There was no time for her to bring her rifle into play.

But her knife was a different matter.

As Kory, still sprinting, reached down toward the child's mouth to prevent the scream she assumed would be forthcoming, the knife came up from inside the child's loose-fitting garment and was thrust directly toward the onrushing assailant's face. Kory simultaneously deflected the blade with her bare hands and turned her head violently to the left as she fell upon the little girl. The razor-sharp knife sheared the fingers of Kory's right hand, cutting to the bone. The knife thrust, thus deflected, failed to make contact with the woman's face but readily found the exposed right side of her neck.

Kory, now fully on top of the child, seized the girl's knife-wielding right wrist with her uninjured left hand and at the same time tried to place her bleeding right fingers over the girl's mouth. But Kory saw in a flash of understanding that the child was making no effort to scream, but to bite. Kory withdrew her hand, concentrated on the knife, and forced its point into the sand.

And suddenly it was over.

Luke Manguson hurled himself into the midst of the furiously grappling combatants, the impact of his arrival launching his companion headlong into the rocky outcropping at the child's back. Kory threw up her arms to protect her head and thudded roughly into the stony surface, her forearms and rib cage taking the brunt of the impact. She fell back to the ground, stunned.

Ignoring his comrade for the moment, Luke slapped a wide strip of heavyweight duct tape over the child's mouth, ripped the knife away from her small hand, and, without pause, lifted her bodily from the ground. Carrying the child as though she were a lightweight sack of potatoes, he swiftly removed her from the immediate area of the air vent, deposited her gently on her stomach 35 yards away and bound her wrists behind her back, then her feet, using one of the coils of clothesline wire from his shoulder holster.

He then rose and raced back to his dazed and bleeding companion.

Kory lay on her side, woozy from the accidental impact of the 200-pound, rock-hard man who had arrowed to her aid. Her uninjured left hand felt absently for the right side of her neck. Her cruelly gashed right hand lay uselessly on the ground. The sand darkened under her as blood coursed from the wounds.

Luke and Saul Coen arrived at her side simultaneously, but Luke gestured toward the unconscious adult sentry. "Bind him," Luke said simply, tossing the small roll of duct tape and a short coil of clothesline wire on the ground. Luke struggled to avoid uttering a malediction in Coen's direction, even mentally. But he knew, as did Coen himself, that a trained combatant should have been rushing the child sentry, not a diminutive elementary teacher whose military experience had been restricted to desk work in a London office.

Forcibly, he thrust the thought aside.

He spun around, dropped to his knees and reached for his beloved. He pushed her hair away from her neck, removed her covering hand and studied the wound in the moonlight. Blood ran freely from the gash, but it did not pulse. Luke removed gauze pads from one pocket and a small roll of sanitary adhesive tape from another. He covered the wound with two pads, taped them firmly into place, and then gently examined the ruined fingers of Kory's right hand. Although this wound was not the life-threatening one that the neck wound could easily have been, it was more difficult to treat.

The knife had cut most deeply her small finger, then, progressively less severely, the third, second, and index fingers. Luke set to work, first wrapping the four individual wounds with gauze strips and tape, then securing the whole with wider strips. But he knew stitches were essential, both on the gash at her neck and on at least two of her fingers.

During this flurry of emergency activity, the two of them had not spoken. Both knew words would prove a distraction under circumstances in which the nature of the required action was obvious. But now, Kory's knife wounds having been temporarily dressed, Luke spoke, his mouth near her ear as she continued to lie where she had fallen, "Kory, are you cut anywhere else?"

She shook her head.

"Are you hurt anywhere else?"

She smiled. "I think you may have broken a few dozen bones when you flew into our midst, Luke," she whispered, "but no worries there."

"Do you feel as though you're losing consciousness, Kory?"

She paused. "I do feel faint. Yes."

He nodded. "Okay. Enough talking."

He then carefully placed one arm under her shoulders and the other under her knees, lifted her easily from the ground, and cradled her high against his chest, high enough so that her head could rest against his shoulder as he carried her. He strode quickly toward Saul Coen.

Coen had just completed his work with the adult sentry, having bound the man's wrists and ankles, covered his mouth with the tape, and dragged him some distance from the vent. Coen stood up quickly as Luke approached.

"How is she?" he asked anxiously.

"She needs stitches, Saul. Now."

Coen nodded and pulled his small radiotelephone from a belt loop.

"Adelman! Adelman! Come in!"

"Adelman here."

"Mission one accomplished. Sentries down, bound, gagged. No shots fired. Bring toxin unit to the scene immediately."

"Roger."

"Need medical team. Here. Now."

"Nature of injuries."

"Knife wounds."

"Roger. Toxin equipment ETA two-zero minutes. Medical team ETA half that."

It was 0400.

Kory van Dijk lay on her back on the lightweight stretcher on which she had been placed by the Mossad medical team. They had moved her no more than fifty yards from the site of the skirmish, had set up their field generator and lights, and had worked over her for nearly half an hour.

"All right," said the Mossad surgeon to Luke, rising to his feet as he spoke. "She's set. The blade did not get *quite* deep enough to reach the carotid artery or the jugular vein. And that's why she's alive, of course. I've got fourteen stitches in the neck. No problem there.

"I've got seven stitches in the small finger, four in the third, four in the second, and two in the index. I don't much like the look of the little finger and the third finger. Pretty sure we've got muscle or ligament involvement. Not sure about the use of those two digits, long-term. She'll need operating-room-level attention on those two fingers.

"Otherwise, ship-shape."

Luke nodded. "Thank you, sir. We're very grateful."

As the Mossad medical team moved off, Kory, smiling, said softly, "Luke, why did he talk to you is if I weren't here?"

Luke, smiling back, said simply, "Longstanding habit, I'm sure. These field medical teams aren't accustomed to working with patients who can actually converse with them — before or after their emergency treatment — and so that just doesn't occur to them, I'd imagine."

She nodded. Then, after a moment, "Luke, where is the child?"

He turned his head in the direction in which he had carried her forty-five minutes previous. Then he looked back down at his companion. "Kory," he said sheepishly, "I'd forgotten completely about her until this very moment. My attention has been… ah… diverted…."

"Luke!" she said, much too loudly, urgency in her voice. "No!"

She struggled to sit up.

He reached down, placed his arm around and under her waist, and lifted her to her feet with one arm. Half-supporting and half-carrying his wounded companion, he strode rapidly through the moonlight in the direction in which he had carried the girl. Kory's feet barely skimmed the ground.

After less than a minute of this odd but swift means of travel, they saw the small shape of the girl, unmoving in the moonlit distance. The child looked even smaller than before, her slight form face-down and completely still.

Together, the two *Rebekka Yahalomin* dropped to their knees on each side of their enemy. Luke frisked her efficiently and then rolled the child over on her back. He placed his hand on the duct tape covering her mouth.

Knowing the chances of the girl speaking English were small, he nevertheless said to her before he ripped the tape from her lips, "Tighten your lips, child. This will hurt less."

To his surprise, she nodded immediately and appeared to do as he had suggested. Then he ripped the tape away.

The child neither made a sound nor flinched.

It was 0500.

Jaakov Adelman huddled in the chill of the June pre-dawn with his small "toxin team." Three of his four followers were present: Kory van Dijk, Luke Manguson, and Saul Coen.

Before Adelman could begin, Luke spoke, the tension that he felt apparent in his voice. "The boarding party is in place, then?" he asked.

Adelman smiled. "Well, Lieutenant, that's not the term we land-lubbers use, but… yes… the hand-to-hand combat and rescue team is ready to blow the garage door with explosive charges and rush any conscious enemy they find. The gas has been forced into the air vent for a full twenty minutes now. That may prove to be too long for some of them. There may be fatalities. But we deemed it better to err on that side than the other."

"Is the combat team Army or Mossad?" said Luke.

"Army," Adelman replied. "We wanted a forty-man unit that had trained together for sustained periods. Mossad has no units of that size."

Adelman glanced at his watch.

"They attached the explosive charges to the garage door a few minutes ago. They'll blow the door at 0510. Just over five minutes now."

Luke nodded.

"Lieutenant Manguson," Adelman continued after a moment, "I'd like you and Seaman van Dijk to enter the cave within fifteen minutes of the combat team's deployment, assuming the fight, if there is one, is over by then. I'd like the two of you to help me identify Adolfus Rademacher. The three of us are the only ones here who have actually been with him, though others have seen photographs. He's the only leader in this group whose name and appearance we actually know with certainty. And, of course, he may, in fact, be the group's actual and only leader. We don't know."

The two *Yahalomin* nodded.

Adelman glanced at his watch, then looked to the woman.

"How is the child?" he said.

"Well… she appears unhurt, Mr. Adelman. And she says so."

"She *says* so?" the agent asked in surprise. "She does speak German then?"

"Actually, I didn't think to ask her that," replied Kory. "She speaks English! She speaks English with a Middle Eastern accent and not with perfect fluency, but she seems to understand without difficulty. She says her nationality is Saudi."

"Hmm," Adelman mused, then glanced again at his watch.

Kory then continued, ignoring the fact that Adelman's attention had moved immediately back to the impending attack on the terrorists. "The child's name is Sari," she said, her brown eyes welling in the soft moonlight. "She thinks she may be nine years old, but she is certain of nothing: neither her birth date nor her birth year.

"And she has never known her parents. She seems actually to be very… well… very sweet."

"*Sweet?*" said Adelman incredulously, his focus brought back momentarily to Kory's report. "She's *sweet?* You're speaking of the child whose knife nearly ended your life not two hours ago? You're telling us she is *sweet?*"

Kory smiled. "She thought I was rushing to kill her, sir. She had been taught to defend herself with the knife, if that seemed the only way to survive. She is desperately embarrassed to have hurt me."

Adelman stared. Then he shook his head in open disbelief.

And at that instant they heard and felt the detonation.

It was 0525.

Kory and Luke crouched near the ruins of the truck-sized door that led to the interior of the mountain. The Israeli combat and rescue team had been inside for exactly fifteen minutes. The two *Yahalomin* had heard no gunfire.

The eastern sky was beginning to lighten with the first suggestion of sunrise, though darkness still prevailed on the ancient mountain. Luke felt the woman's fingertips on his arm.

"You know what I always think about when I am out and about just before sunrise, Luke?" she whispered. "I always think of Mary Magdalene. Always.

"I think of the Fourth Gospel. I think of the twentieth chapter's opening, which I do so love in the King James: 'The first day of the week cometh Mary Magdalene early, when it was yet dark, unto the sepulchre, and seeth the stone taken away from the sepulchre.'

"It gives me chills. Always. It just gives me chills."

She took his hand and squeezed. "Do you ever think of her… how she was… and what she saw… at that moment, Luke? I mean, do you think of her other than at Easter? At times like now… you know… 'when it is yet dark'?"

He turned his face to hers and nodded. "Yes," he said quietly. "Yes, as a matter of fact I do. I'm so grateful to her. You know? She stayed… she stayed there by herself….

"I'm very appreciative."

She nodded and squeezed his hand again. "I know! I know! It's just so wonderful!

"And then," she continued, still whispering, "my very favorite sentence…."

"You mean verse sixteen?" he said immediately.

Her eyes widened. "Luke! Yours, too?"

He nodded and smiled lovingly at her. "Of course," he said. "It's so perfect. It's exactly what any of us would say when someone we know well, for any sort of reason, just doesn't yet realize who's speaking to them. We would just say the person's name."

"I know, I know," she said happily. And then she murmured the beloved phrase. "'Jesus saith unto her, Mary.' It's *so* perfect… *so* perfect."

And together, filled with the shared memory, they relived in their minds the scene in that other early morning, two millennia before, just miles to the south of where they now crouched on the slopes of Mount Carmel. And then he, careful not to touch her wounded and bandaged right hand, enfolded her left in both his own, leaned down to her, and kissed her brown hair.

Then he looked up quickly in response to a new sound.

They began faintly to hear soft footfalls and, now peering through the fading moonlight toward the cave entrance, they saw members of the Army combat team beginning to emerge from the depths of the hideout toward the cavernous opening. Each soldier looked massive in his protective body armor, yet oddly insect-like with his gas mask's strange protuberances and elongated snout.

Kory and Luke found themselves touching their own gas masks, preparing to don them as soon as Jaakov Adelman arrived to escort them forward.

"I see," she said softly, "how my idea of packing the toxin into one of the Cobra's wire-guided missiles couldn't have worked here, Luke. The way this driveway curls round on itself, the gunner would have had no possible shot, even if somehow the door could have been blown in advance."

Luke nodded. "That's true, but it's also true that your idea gave substance to the detective's insistence that Mossad develop an alternative to the simple execution of all three hundred of these people. Without your suggestion, I don't know what would have happened. It seemed to me that Jaakov and Mr. Belton were coming to an impasse.

"I mean… if even one of the terrorists is simply captured and taken prisoner, rather than killed outright, your suggestion will have had lifesaving effect, Kory.

"And besides," he continued after a moment, "we already know that two of these people have been spared, and that one of them is an innocent."

She brightened at the thought of the little girl. "Yes," she whispered. "Yes, Sari lives. I know."

And then, as one, they tensed.

One of the masked figures was motioning them forward. They pulled on their gas masks and rose to enter the cave.

Inside, they knew, Adolfus Rademacher awaited them, dead or alive.

# CHAPTER THIRTEEN

It was 0630.

Kory, Luke and Jaakov Adelman stood still, deep in the terrorists' underground hideaway. They had just removed their gas masks in response to the "all clear" signal given by one of the Israeli Army officers, he having completed his sweep of the cavern with an instrument designed to detect airborne toxins. At their backs stood three large fans carried in with a second wave of two dozen additional Army troops, the fans connected to a portable generator and running full force now for more than a half hour.

During their 45 minutes in the cave, the threesome had first walked past the flatbed trucks and their detritus: scattered files and papers strewn haphazardly about the cave floor. The lead truck, they saw, had carried the primary container from the ship — the data-laden vault of Rebecca's vision — and its contents had actually been fought over by many of the three hundred neo-Nazis and their Middle Eastern counterparts. The men had bloodily contested with each other to snatch as many files of the Righteous Among Nations as they could cram into their standardized document carriers, each one with its own ingeniously designed secret compartment.

The threesome had also come to understand why the terrorists had wanted more than the single, data-filled vault carried by the leading flatbed. They had discovered that each of the three secondary trucks had served as a small-arms weapons transporter. And this, in turn, told them that at least some of the newly heavily armed terrorists' exits from the nation of Israel would of necessity have been clandestine, doubtless under cover of darkness and concentrated along those borders which the country shared with overtly terrorism-supporting governments.

Kory, Luke and their Mossad comrade-in-arms had then looked closely and systematically into the faces of the more than three hundred men. Most of the men, still only dimly conscious, had sat stoically and stupidly for this inspection, their faces and bodies still showing the powerful effects of phenyl hydride poisoning: stupor, muscular lassitude, disorientation. They had sat with their backs to the cavern walls, their hands and feet secured. A few of them, just beginning to regain normal alertness, had eyed their three inspectors with unconcealed malevolence.

Several appeared to be unconscious. Several more were actively ill.

All three examiners had noted that fewer than one in three of the terrorists appeared to be European by heritage, with the remaining two-thirds appearing to be Middle Eastern. All had been carried or dragged by Israeli Army combat personnel into orderly groupings for the dual purposes of first, disarming each of them systematically, and, second, wherever necessary, administering antidotes to the toxin.

Although she was thrilled to see that she walked among the living, Kory had found the scene — macabre in its pervasive and sinister silence — eerily suggestive of death: theirs, hers, that of the Righteous. But to the two men, each more accustomed than she to the aftermath of violence, the conditions were exhilarating. They had from time to time glanced at each other through the encumbrance of their gas masks, amazed at the uniform success of the operation, one that had produced no casualties among the Israelis and that had resulted in the swift and stunningly humane capture of more than three hundred determined and superbly trained killers.

There was, however, a substantial difference in how Jaakov Adelman and Luke Manguson thought about the new captives. To the former, the prisoners comprised a treasure trove of interviewees, potentially useful to Mossad, to Israel and to their allies around the globe. In contrast, to Luke the prisoners were, above all, simply alive — each living person newly given a chance to rethink his life and his purposes on earth — and, even more important to Luke, no longer a threat to the Righteous Among Nations. Where his Mossad colleague saw nationalistic opportunity, Luke saw second chances for the prisoners and safety for the Righteous.

Now, gas masks in hand, the three of them stood in the welcome draft of the portable fans, looking back through the dimly lit cave. Adelman, still fully in his role as designated leader, spoke first.

"Well," he said thoughtfully, "while I'm absolutely delighted with this outcome and grateful to you, Ms. van Dijk, for giving us the idea for a non-lethal approach in the first place, I certainly don't like the fact that Rademacher is not present. Why have we not come upon him? We've looked carefully at them all… every one of them."

The two *Yahalomin* were silent, thinking.

After a moment, Luke replied, not with an answer but with a suggestion.

"What would you think," he said tentatively, addressing them both, "of showing our Rademacher photograph to the child — to Sari — and asking her if she knows where he is? She might be forthcoming in ways that none of the adults is likely to be at the moment… or ever. And, unlike all these here in the cave, she has not been impaired by the toxin."

Adelman frowned. "I don't follow, Luke. Why would she — a girl who introduced herself to Kory by attempting to stab her — have any interest in assisting us? I know you referred to her as 'sweet,' Kory, but surely you can mean only that her post-attack demeanor seemed benign in comparison?"

Kory started to reply, but Luke interrupted. "Jaakov," he said, warming to his own idea, "you would need to have seen this little girl talking to Kory in order to understand why I'm suggesting this. As soon as Sari saw that she was speaking with a woman, she changed completely from a guarded, sullen child into an open, engaging youngster. Not talkative, you understand. I don't mean that. I mean… I mean that she seemed to relax… to *like* being talked to by Kory. It was astonishing, really.

"At least, that's how it seemed to me. It made me wonder, in fact, if the child had ever been around a woman at all, within her memory.

"In all seriousness, Jaakov… it was miraculous, the transformation."

Adelman looked to Kory and found her nodding at Luke's words.

"Yes," she said immediately, "he's right, sir. And the change in her did not seem to have anything to do with the things that I said. The change in her face as soon as she heard my voice — a woman's voice — was instantaneous. It was as though she suddenly realized that she was with one of her own… well… with one of her own kind… and maybe… as Luke just said… with one of her own kind for the first time in her memory….

"In any case, I agree with Luke, sir. It can't hurt to ask her. I actually enjoyed speaking with her… and the longer we spoke, the more I liked it."

"And it was clearly the same for the child," added Luke. "The more Kory engaged her, the happier and more relaxed she seemed."

Adelman's brow was still furrowed. But finally he looked up, fixed his dark eyes on Kory and said, a hint of humor in his tone, "All right… all right… but only if you, ma'am, will stop calling me 'sir.'"

"It's terribly irritating, you know… I think you've made me twenty years older than I was last week in New York."

It was 0710.

Jaakov Adelman stood at a distance and watched as the child and the two *Yahalomin*, having walked slowly to the rear of the cave, came to a stop. They stood, silent, as the girl visually inspected the cavern wall. She and the youthful school teacher had held hands as they traversed the length of the cavern, walking past hundreds of incapacitated and bound prisoners. They continued to hold hands as they now stood motionless.

Adelman quietly moved close enough to hear the conversation he assumed would be forthcoming.

"It's just there," said the child, ending the long silence, pointing one small index finger in the direction of what appeared to Kory and Luke to be solid rock wall.

Letting go of the girl's hand, Kory took several steps in the direction indicated. After a moment, she turned her head back to the child. "I don't see a thing, Sari," she said softly, speaking just as she would to one of her students back in London, using a practiced tone that communicated both respect for the child and an honest need for further explanation.

Sari, in response, took five child-sized steps forward, and placed her small hand on the solid vertical surface. Kory reached out and placed her own hand near the child's.

Only in that position, less than arm's length from the face of the wall and at a specific point along an eight-foot indentation, did she notice the fissure that ran irregularly from ceiling to floor, just to the left of Sari's hand. Slowly, the girl moved her hand to the fissure and indicated a nearly invisible, darkly metallic plate, perhaps three by five inches, imbedded within the fissure itself and at the child's eye level. The girl stepped back and looked up at Kory expectantly, suggesting with her eyes that the plate should be manipulated.

"Stop!" said Luke suddenly, not loudly but insistently.

He strode to the spot and looked intently at the metallic plate, his hands in and around the fissure but not yet touching the metal device. Then he turned to the two and said softly, "Please step back, ladies." Taking each other's hand once more, they did as he ordered.

Luke then turned to Adelman. "Jaakov," he said, "can you get the dogs back here double-time?"

Adelman nodded, turned quickly and spoke an order to one of the Israeli Army couriers who stood nearby. In seconds, two Belgian Malinois arrived with their Unit Oketz handlers, all four at the run. Luke indicated the area of interest and then stepped away while the handlers and their canine sleuths did their swift work. After just under sixty seconds of determined sniffing in and around the fissure and at the plate itself, the two Malinois turned almost in tandem, walked several steps, turned again to face the wall and their handlers, and sat, satisfied that no explosives were present. The senior handler then nodded to Adelman, and the Oketz unit moved away.

Luke quickly returned to the fissure, placed his left hand in position, averted his face against the possibility of the presence of an eye-searing flash device, and depressed the plate.

The three immediately heard a quiet, mechanically refined sound, a gentle humming noise from the wall itself. As they watched, the fissure gradually became a perceptibly widening crack in the vertical rock surface, increasing in size as the seconds passed until the opening was fully shoulder width for a man even as broad as Luke Manguson. Peering toward the aperture, they could see only darkness within.

After a moment, Kory reached into a pocket in her Mossad-supplied athletic outfit and pulled something out. She leaned over, lowering her face to the child's level. She again placed the photograph of Adolfus Rademacher under the child's eyes. "Sari," she said softly, "do you really think he is in there?"

The child shuddered involuntarily, nodded once, and shrank back from the photo. Kory stood and looked searchingly at Luke, who, having peered for a long moment inside the opening, had moved to join them.

Luke waved for Adelman to come to their side. When the agent arrived, Luke said quietly, "Sari has just indicated that she thinks Rademacher could be in there, Jaakov. And I think I've got to go in and have a look. This mission — the *Yahalomin* mission — can't be regarded as complete until the leader is apprehended. If he entered this passage as soon as he saw some of his colleagues reacting to the toxin, he's got a substantial head start on us. And he may have taken others in his Nazi entourage with him. There's no way to guess on the numbers.

"But I think I've got to give it a go."

Kory's eyes widened in horror at the thought. Involuntarily she mouthed the word, "No!"

As she did, she felt the girl tugging at her hand. She looked down, then bent down, placing her ear near the child's moving lips.

Kory stood. "Sari wants to talk to me alone, gentlemen. We'll be just over there." She started to turn, then stopped.

"Luke," she said softly, "please, please don't go through that opening until we have talked about this more."

Having said this, she stood looking up at him, her hand in the child's. He saw she meant to have a response.

He nodded to her. "Yes, Ms. van Dijk," he said softly, not smiling in acknowledgement of the seriousness of her request. "I'll stay on this spot until you return."

As the two walked away to conduct their tete-a-tete, Adelman spoke. "What did you see when you looked in there, Luke? Could you see whether or not this is actually a passageway?"

"Yes," he replied. "Just from the indirect light supplied from the main cavern, I could see the head of what is obviously a corridor. It's not just a room. It's a freshly chiseled passageway, Jaakov.

"And by 'freshly' I mean that it's not ancient. It's obviously cut with machinery.

"And as soon as I looked, I was put in mind of the information Dr. Chapel supplied us when Kory first reported my sister's most recent vision.

"Dr. Chapel described *Megiddo* at its peak — in the old times — as a fortress with enormous barracks, extensive stables, and a one-hundred-foot-deep shaft straight down through the rock. The vertical shaft, she said, connected the surface of the fort's interior with a horizontal, subterranean passage stretching more than two hundred feet, all the way to the outside of the fortress perimeter and linking to an underground water source. She said that this entire underground arrangement is still intact today.

"That, of course, is how the fortress protected itself from siege. The water source allowed them to supply men and horses indefinitely."

Adelman looked down, thoughtfully processing this information, his face impassive. After several moments, he looked up. "So, you're suggesting that as part of this campaign against the Righteous, Rademacher and his troops have been establishing an underground connector from this cave to *Megiddo's* ancient subterranean network?"

"Exactly," said Luke. "One or more tunnels from here to the area under the fortress would not need to be exceptionally long. If Rademacher has been preparing his campaign even for, let's say, three years, he and his people would have had plenty of time to get the right men and equipment in here to make those digs."

The two men fell silent, thinking. After a moment, the woman and the child returned. The men looked up expectantly.

"Sir… I mean, Mr. Adelman…" said Kory, smiling at the agent, "Sari has explained to me that she has spent many hours in the passage that runs toward the fortress from that opening. One of her jobs was to take water and messages back and forth from the cavern to the men who were digging. She learned to navigate the tunnel even in semi-darkness. There is, she said, a network of low-power lights illuminating the tunnel floors, somewhat like theater lighting, I gather.

"But Luke," she continued, her eyes moving to his face and fear creeping into her voice, "Sari says you'd be unable to find your way, even if you take electric torches with you. The tunnel lights are too widely spaced and too weak to serve as guides. She says she will go and guide you. She says a spur of the tunnel leads all the way to the ancient water source, and another leads to a small opening that allows egress from the fortress walls, on the near side… on the western side… of *Megiddo* itself.

"And she says that 'he' — by whom she clearly means Adolfus Rademacher — will be impossible to find, if he does not want to be found."

She looked down at the girl, who looked up from under her dark, plain head scarf and nodded somberly.

"And Luke," Kory added, "she tells me that she has never seen 'him' without four armed men in tow. He apparently comes only intermittently, which would fit his role back in New York with the seminary. I'm sure faculty and staff members make regular trips to Israel… so his periodic absence from the seminary to journey to Israel would have aroused no suspicion.

"She suggests that he comes, inspects work in progress, and goes away… but always with four bodyguards alongside."

Another thoughtful silence ensued, broken at length by the agent.

"I think," said Adelman, "that Rademacher's only objective at this point would be escape. He can't know with certainty that he has been exposed, but he may guess that he has. And, either way, I'm thinking that by now he has used the outside exit the child describes to put as much distance between himself and these Israeli Army units as possible.

"I'm going to request that an Army patrol begin a search of the area to the immediate west of *Megiddo,* looking for one man or five, and in any combination. And I'm going to alert Israeli commercial airports of the situation, as well as law enforcement and the military."

"Good," responded Luke immediately. "And while you do that, I'll check on these passageways leading toward the *Megiddo* underground. If we're correct, Rademacher and his gang will have left the cavern when the toxin first entered and he saw others falling ill. That means he would have exited… oh… about two hours ago. He would certainly have reached that surface exit on the west side of the fortress long before now, unless he plans some sort of counterattack from his underground net and is, for tactical purposes, staying in the *souterrain* in anticipation of further devilment.

"But if you're right, Jaakov, that he is simply trying to get away, I doubt the Army will have any luck with a surface search of the area."

He paused, then continued.

"But… the fact is that I'm just not convinced that this man has escape as his only objective. He's too invested in this, Jaakov. With the weapons that were brought in here by the other three flatbeds — the ones not carrying the files — he could have enough firepower and enough men with him to retake this cave at any moment he chose. This forty-man Israeli Army unit is lightly armed. Rademacher and his troops may be heavily armed. They could initiate a fight that could go on a long time, using the ancient water source and the underground networks they've built to their advantage.

"He will eventually want to get away, of course, but he may want to do it on his own terms, rather than running like a rabbit. I'm going in to reconnoiter."

He looked at Kory. She was shaking her head in urgent protest.

"I'm not going to take these people on in a fight, Kory," he said, trying to be reassuring. "I'm just going to find out if they are still on the premises, so to speak."

He tried to give a jocular twist to this last comment. With her the effort failed utterly.

"No," she said simply. "No."

"Kory," he said gently, "if Jaakov is right, they're gone. If they weren't quick enough in leaving, the Army patrol may find them on the surface.

"If Jaakov is wrong, then they're still in there. I can't just go back to England without finding out. Our charge is to save the Righteous. We don't know how many of those files he has with him. It could be one file. It could be a dozen. It could be ten times a dozen. We must find Rademacher himself, Kory. Until we do, we have not done what we have been commissioned to do."

"But Luke," she said plaintively, trying not to allow her voice to get so high that it would become a child's piping whine, "the Army people can send a patrol into these passageways just as easily as they can send one above ground. Why should you — and you *alone,* with none of the soldiers or *katsas* with you — try to track these people down in nearly complete darkness, under conditions that they know perfectly and which you'll know only from some little map that we can draw from Sari's directions?

"You remember what the detective told us, Luke?" she continued. "He told us we can't just send our people — the *Yahalomin* — to their deaths. We always, he said, have to balance the divine charge against some sort of prudence. This is *not* prudent."

Luke opened his mouth to respond, but the *katsa* spoke first. "Kory," he said carefully, "I understand your position on this. And I do think you would argue against Luke's solo reconnaissance even if you did not… ah… care about him as much as I know you do."

At this she did not blush. She simply stared at him, wide-eyed, scarcely able to comprehend the fact that he was going to support Luke's proposal which, to her mind, was suicidal.

"In something like this," Adelman continued, "a single, highly trained and highly skilled individual is actually more likely to succeed than a patrol of any size, small or large. He's not going to fight them. He's going to determine their presence… or not.

"That's one reason Mossad operatives work alone. And it's one of the reasons that 'special ops' military personnel, whether Israeli or UK or U.S. or something else, are so often alone.

"Luke's ability to enter these passageways, to move undetected, and to come back out this very opening in less than, say, ninety minutes, having learned whether or not Rademacher and his troops are in there, is simply not rivaled by any other option we have at hand. He has the ears, the eyes, the background, the craft, and the equipment to do this.

"And he's right. We *all* need to know if Rademacher is still in the area. It's not just the *Yahalomin* that need to know. So does Mossad. We, just as much as you, need to know if he has departed with even a single file from the vault of the Righteous. And, beyond that, we simply need to bring him to justice, Kory.

"The surest way to find out is to send a single operative… not to fight them… but to find out if they are there. And Luke Manguson ranks at the very top of those who can do this.

"It's just the truth, Kory."

She looked away, fighting tears.

Her face still averted, she finally asked, "What 'equipment,' Mr. Adelman? You said he would have the ears, the eyes, the background, the craft, and the equipment to do this. What 'equipment' are you talking about?"

Adelman hesitated. "The Army has a… ah… a top secret… ah… telescope, of sorts, Kory. That's all I can tell you. Luke will have something that will… um… enhance his vision, let's say, as he moves through these passageways in semi-darkness. It's very effective in the hands of the right person."

Still struggling to hold back the tears that begged to escape from the deep brown of her eyes, Kory turned her face back to the agent. "Are you making reference to an NVD, Mr. Adelman?" she asked, her voice tremulous.

He stared blankly into her upturned face.

"A Night Vision Device?" she said softly.

He shrugged.

"Is this an NVD," she continued, "attached by a Weaver rail to a standard-issue Israeli Army rifle? Is the rifle an automatic rifle? And is it 'top secret,' as you said, because it is next-generation NVD technology?"

Adelman looked down.

"Please answer me, Mr. Adelman," she said, her voice growing stronger.

He looked up at her.

Then he turned to an Army corporal who stood nearby, ready, at the *katsa's* service. "Corporal," said the agent, "please ask the colonel for five minutes."

The corporal disappeared forthwith and another long silence followed. Both men knew better than to attempt to speak to the young woman in this situation. She needed not the false comfort of empty reassurances.

Kory van Dijk required data.

They turned at the sound of the Israeli unit commander's arrival, he and the corporal moving at the double-quick. "Sir?" the colonel said to Adelman, choosing to speak English in courteous acknowledgement of the others present.

The agent handled introductions and then added, "Sir, Miss van Dijk is a Royal Navy reservist and has several technical questions about the device Lieutenant Manguson will carry. I need very much for you to provide answers, if you are willing, despite the obvious clearance issue.

"Will you consider a limited battlefield clearance for her, sir?"

The colonel stared hard at the *katsa*. He then turned to the young woman. "What are your questions, ma'am?" he asked, his voice guarded but not hostile.

Her questions flew at the officer. She asked but one at a time, then stopped to listen intently. He absorbed each question, seemed to pause to process the underlying question — could he provide 'limited battlefield clearance' for this young British reservist under these extraordinary circumstances — and then answered quickly, concisely, respectfully.

*Yes,* this was indeed next-generation NVD technology.

*Yes,* it could operate with even less external light than, say, starlight… or theater lighting.

*No,* the rifle to be used by Lieutenant Manguson did not use a Weaver rail.

*Yes,* the firearm was among the standard types used by the Israeli Army.

*Yes,* the firearm was, to be specific, the M16A3 automatic rifle.

*Yes,* it had the new multipurpose accessory rail — not technically the Weaver — which meant it did not have the carrying handle that was standard.

*Yes,* it was fitted with the M203 40mm under-barrel grenade launcher.

And *yes,* the grenade itself was armed with the newest 'optical disruption' explosive designed not to kill or wound the enemy, but to blind him temporarily.

There was a pause while the young woman concentrated, her eyes on the ground. Finally she looked up. "Thank you, Colonel," she said, her voice strong and sure. "I'm very grateful."

The colonel nodded once to the woman, turned his eyes to the *katsa,* nodded once to Adelman, and said to the corporal, "Bring the rifle to the Lieutenant."

The three adults and the child watched the two soldiers depart, then turned again to each other.

Finally Kory took a long, deep breath, turned her face back to the child, and leaned down. "Sari," she said softly, "do you think you could help me draw some maps for my friend Luke?"

The child nodded her assent.

After a moment, Kory and Luke, the Saudi child between them, knelt exactly where they stood on the rocky surface. The girl and the agent, as soon as they saw the Britishers' intent, knelt with them, eyes closed.

Quietly, in full view of soldiers and captives lined against the walls of the long cavern, the two Londoners alternately spoke their prayers. Luke's focused on thanksgiving for the bloodless assault on the terrorists and for the recovery of the files of the Righteous. Kory's prayers concentrated upon Luke himself and on his probe into subterranean terrors that, she feared, most surely awaited him.

Finally, echoing her soft "… in the name of Our Lord and Risen Savior Jesus Christ… Amen," came Luke's own strong *Amen*.

And then, after several seconds of meditative silence, the three adults heard a small, almost whispered voice at their side, barely audible. And all three of them thrilled to the sound of the child's tiny benediction: *Amen, please… Please, Amen.*

# Chapter Fourteen

It was 0735.

Adolfus Rademacher crouched alone in the darkness. His right hand rested lightly on a valve that, at a turn, could rapidly flood large portions of the *Megiddo* underground, the ancient water source newly harnessed for a quite different purpose than its original one.

This water could indeed still save. But now, this water could destroy.

Rademacher turned his head slightly in the dark silence, straining to hear the smallest sound that might suggest a pursuer.

There.

For the second time in less than a minute, he did, in fact, hear something faintly in the underground distance. His hand tightened on the valve.

Small animals — rodents, usually — did at times make their way into the underground complex. The sound he detected did not suggest that kind of animal. It was a clumsy sound, one made by something not indigenous to subterranean living.

He shifted his position in the crouch that he had maintained for nearly thirty minutes. As he did, his right hand, the hand resting on the valve, raked against the sharp metal base of a small pressure gauge that extended out over the valve some four inches above it.

He withdrew the hand briefly and lodged a violent mental protest in the direction of the valve's designer, the system's installer, and anyone else associated with the cumbersome physical arrangement. With the fingers of his left hand, he rubbed the back of his right, attempting thereby to dampen the lingering pain from the accidental impact. In so doing, he drew his own attention to the covering bandage that hid the Star of David tattoo.

He thought for a moment. Then, having reached a decision, he grasped the large, square bandage and peeled it abruptly from his hand.

He tossed the bandage aside in the darkness and moved his left-hand fingers back to the same surface, the back of his right hand. But this time he felt carefully and for several seconds in the blackness, searching with his fingertips for the edge of another and much more subtle covering.

Finally he succeeded in locating a corner of this second adhesive. Carefully he dug into and under its edge with his left index fingernail. The adhesive resisted for long moments, then yielded with reluctance.

Rademacher peeled the covering slowly in the darkness, imagining what gradually was becoming visible there, had there been light to see it. Now, with the exquisitely rendered Star of David completely separated from the skin surface to which it had adhered for so long and with so much effect, he flung it away from him and smiled his tight smile. For he knew that now his core identity would once more announce itself boldly on the back of his right hand, and that the stark, jet-black swastika stenciled indelibly into his skin would soon celebrate by its conspicuous existence his hatred-inspired reemergence onto the surface of the earth.

And he knew, too, that Solomon Rosenthal was now — as once before — merely the name of an old Austrian Jew, an insignificant human being who became collateral damage during the Red Army's march toward Berlin thirty-five years before. And he knew as well that that Jew would once more rest in peace while Adolfus Rademacher, newly emergent, would live once more in war.

More than two hours before this private, signal moment, Rademacher had been busy making certain that he and his four bodyguards — European Nazis each — had prepared themselves for an instantaneous exit from the main cavern into the tunnels leading to *Megiddo's* ancient underground. Of the more than three hundred combatants who had assembled in the cavern that night, no more than a dozen were aware of the hidden passageways.

For those who had labored to dig the modern-day tunnels over a three-year period were not those who had gathered to receive their data packets identifying the Righteous Among Nations. They had been, instead, laborers from the West Bank who, in exchange for their work on what was obviously, to them, an archaeological project of interest to a handful of religious scholars and historians, had asked for nothing more than a paycheck and a weekly day off.

The little girl who had become their primary water-and-message carrier during the last ten months of the dig had come with a vanguard of Saudis who comprised the spearhead for three Middle Eastern terrorist organizations invited by Rademacher and his neo-Nazis to join in the operation against the Righteous. She had appeared on arrival to belong to no one and to everyone. She simply did her work and kept to her childish thoughts, earning and retaining Rademacher's confidence almost from her first day on site.

He had on this Friday night assigned Sari to join one of the Saudi men on sentry duty, knowing that she could be depended upon to remain faithfully at whatever post she took. He wanted every one of his nearly one hundred Nazis around him closely for self-protection and was unwilling to part even with one of them for sentry duty. He knew that the Middle Easterners were more than twice the Europeans in numerical strength, and trusted none of them except the child. He had not come this far in order to be murdered by those who, he knew, would almost as gladly kill him and his Europeans as they would kill the Righteous Among Nations.

So it was that as the time for Saturday's sunrise drew inexorably near, Rademacher and his four personal protectors had positioned themselves closer and closer to the secret doorway in the rear of the cavern wall. This they did not in anticipation of a gaseous toxin forced into their underground from the outside ventilating system — the sentries had been placed to guard against the plain sabotage of the air-exchange machinery — but in the knowledge that, should the Middle Easterners turn on the outnumbered Nazis, escape would be possible. For once the terrorists had in hand their data packets and weaponry, anything could happen, as, in fact, it had done in small scale while the first flatbed's files were being distributed earlier that night.

From his position at the extreme rear of the cavern, Rademacher had been perfectly situated to see what was happening, and to see it in plenty of time to take the requisite action to save himself. The cavern's air-exchange outlets from the surface vent were positioned midway along the length of the cave, allowing him to see immediately the effects of the gas as it began its odorless and devastating work. Initially incredulous — the introduction of a gaseous toxin never having occurred to any of them, given the utter obscurity and isolation of the ground-level vent — he had recovered from his shock and, with his four henchmen, had glided swiftly to the secret aperture and had disappeared, the hidden doorway returning to its closed position before anyone else in that part of the cave — Middle Eastern or European — had so much as sensed anything was wrong.

Rademacher's mind had then raced through a half dozen well-researched alternatives as he retreated through the tunnels at the head of the small column of men. Within thirty seconds of his quick and efficient exit from the cave, he had selected one of those alternatives. Accordingly, he had led his four bodyguards to the virtually undetectable surface exit just to the west side of *Megiddo* itself, sending them off in the pre-dawn darkness to recover their vehicle. He had instructed them to wait there with the small van until 0900 — more than three hours away — and then to rendezvous with him, as previously detailed, at the small loading dock situated at the *east*, or opposite, side of the fortress complex.

He had then moved back through the tunnel network, using his hooded flashlight and his excellent spatial memory to navigate the passageways leading to the water source and its control mechanisms. And there he had waited.

He had expected the Israeli military, or, perhaps, Mossad *katsas* or *kidon*, to storm the cave itself, once the toxin had dissipated. He had not known whether they would be able to identify the hidden doorway, but he knew it was possible. Even though a mere handful of those remaining in the cave knew of the doorway's existence and of the passageways to which it led, just one such would be enough. In the hands of Israeli interrogators — military or Mossad — any such captive would quickly reveal the doorway's location and its operating mechanism. Middle Eastern terrorists might resist Israeli interrogation to the death, but his neo-Nazis had not the religiously grounded motivation to do anything of the sort. All they had was bigotry and hatred, and, under torture, that would not be nearly enough.

Now, crouching in the darkness next to the water release mechanism, Rademacher began to concentrate hard on the broader ramifications of this colossal disappointment. He had little doubt but that the responsibility for the disaster lay ultimately with the *Rebekka Yahalomin*, the Hebrew label that, he had only lately learned, was used by Mossad to reference the visioners: those miserable, meddling Christian seers who had sent Eleanor Chapel, Sidney Belton, and Luke Manguson into his office in New York just days before.

Like Jaakov Adelman, Adolfus Rademacher was a supernaturalist, and so he did not seriously doubt the authenticity of the phenomenon that, he knew, sought to destroy him. Unlike Adelman's, however, Rademacher's belief system was rooted in the otherworldly power of Evil. He felt that he fully understood this power, and, as well, its origins in his own being.

For he had both experienced this power and followed after this power. He had first come to embrace what he conceived as supernatural Evil during the World War, as a young German Army officer, when he came to comprehend deeply the meaning of his authority over the Jewish population of northernmost Holland, an unlimited authority to find and destroy these imposters who claimed for themselves the status as Chosen People.

As he had begun to experience the thrill of finding and destroying systematically an entire population of human beings, he had come to understand what he felt was his true purpose on earth: to embrace and harness the Evil that he had come to know, and then to wield this authority as completely as possible, with the ultimate goal of absolute extermination of all who called themselves Jews. He knew in his heart, he had felt, who the actual Chosen People were, and those people were his own, those who strode up and down the streets of Europe's cities, towns, villages, and farms wearing the Nazi uniform and ferreting out the imposters — the false Chosen — in order to apply the final solution that was so apparent and so within his grasp.

Still crouching in the darkness next to the control valve for the underground water flow, Rademacher suddenly frowned. His mind had found itself confronting for the thousandth time his failure to identify Greta van Dijk as one of the Christian vermin: one of the protectors of the Jews... of *his* Jews.

Greta van Dijk, a churchgoing, unmarried school teacher in her late twenties, harboring a young, blonde Jewess in her own home, calling the Jew "a relative from Amsterdam," and hiding her right in the center of one of the towns under his immediate jurisdiction. And now, not only did that failure from decades past fasten its weight afresh to his Nazi body and soul, but the incomprehensible defeat of five of his handpicked troops at the van Dijk home, just one week earlier, multiplied that increasingly intolerable weight a thousand times over.

*How could they possibly have failed to capture and kill this aging Dutch woman?* he asked himself once again. But he knew the answer. He knew the answer with the absolute certainty of one who grasps the fact of supernatural activity in the universe, even while choosing to respond only to one side of that activity. And so he once more acknowledged internally the answer to his own question: it was the *Rebekka Yahalomin.* It was they who were responsible for the fiasco in Holland, and now for the debacle under Mount Carmel's western ridge line.

And now the cauldron in Rademacher's brain began to boil with a renewed fury, his hatred for the Righteous as a group mixing with his old antipathy toward Greta van Dijk, and then those mental eruptions mixing in turn with his newly conceived bitterness toward the *Rebekka Yahalomin*. This highly unstable mixture began rapidly to coagulate and harden, seemingly without his direction, into an emotional mountain that he could hardly recognize in himself.

And in this supernaturally inspired state of pure malevolence, Adolfus Rademacher consciously forced himself back into his role as mastermind on behalf of the Real Chosen: the Nazi Chosen. With supreme effort, he redirected his thoughts and his emotions toward the necessary next step... and the next... and the next....

For only he could salvage this disaster. And salvage it he would.

In just minutes he had settled on the specifics. Within the broader fall-back framework of plans established earlier among those who were his most trusted confidants, Rademacher would execute a particular combination of those plans that would result in: first, death within the *Megiddo* underground for his immediate pursuer or pursuers; second, his escape from Israel with a half dozen carefully selected files of the Righteous; third, the immediate execution of those six Christians identified in those files; fourth, the execution, within hours of those six, of his newly understood nemesis, the handful of Christians who made up *Rebekka Yahalomin;* and, finally, asylum in one of two southern hemisphere nations that would not only welcome him and his men, but would provide a new and well financed platform for future endeavors.

Rademacher smiled to himself.

For not only were his alternative plans gratifying to contemplate, but implementation of the first element in those plans — the elimination of his pursuer or pursuers within the *Megiddo* underground — was near at hand. And that first step would almost certainly dovetail with the fourth, the elimination of those Christians comprising *Rebekka Yahalomin*.

*Very efficient,* he acknowledged to himself with satisfaction.

At that moment he heard for the third time the sound of a human being feeling his way through the darkness toward him.

In minutes, or perhaps in only seconds, he would wrestle the control valve's wheel in a counterclockwise direction and then climb the short ladder to the elevated platform that oversaw the intersection of water source, water control machinery, and both the primary and secondary horizontal connectors. After that, it was all quite simple.

He would cross under the fortress surface using several of his newly completed tunnel spurs to the eastern, or opposite, side of the fortress where at 0900 the van and his bodyguards would await him. He knew that Mossad and the Israeli Army, once they realized that he had eluded them at *Megiddo,* would hypothesize an escape to the north of Israel, across the Lebanese border and on to Beirut. That border, they would imagine, would be Rademacher's exit of choice because of its proximity, a mere thirty straight-line miles from *Megiddo.*

Accordingly, he would flee south and east, using the 505 to cross Israel in the direction of the Jordanian border. There he and his men would, as planned to the last detail, leave the van, board two off-road vehicles that would be waiting with expert drivers about thirty miles north of the Dead Sea, and follow the ancient trails to the banks of the Jordan River itself.

And there, just a few miles north of the place where Jesus Christ Himself was baptized by John, he and his men would ford the river, there to be met by his Jordanian contingent. That group would lead them up the steep bluffs on the east side of the river, thence to another set of vehicles, and then south and further east to Amman. By nightfall in Jordan he would be in the air again, on board yet another private jet, headed west and north over continental Europe.

He smiled once more. Then he turned deliberately, gripped the wheel with both hands, and forced it counterclockwise until it began gradually to turn in response to less and less force from his muscular arms and shoulders. He spun the wheel all the way to the stops, then clicked on his hooded flashlight and climbed the short flight of steps to the elevated platform.

There he stood briefly, listening to the mighty rush of water as it cascaded through the underground, overwhelming anything and everything in its path. Then, once more smiling to himself in the blackness, he turned toward the eastern-reaching passageways.

The new day, the Jewish Sabbath, was still young. By sunrise next morning — "the first day of the week" in the language of the New Testament's resurrection passages — Adolfus Rademacher fully expected the first four elements in his alternative plan to be completed, and he once more in the air, on his way to the far reaches of the southern hemisphere.

As time is measured among those who work the greatest Evil, he was still a very young man. There was yet much to be accomplished.

# Chapter Fifteen

Luke heard clearly through the blackness the metal-on-rubber squeak of the control valve's initial turn. He pivoted 180 degrees in that instant, shifted the M16 to the vertical in his left hand and, with his right, unsnapped the lightweight searchlight from his belt. Running hard in his third stride, he hit the searchlight's *on* switch with his thumb and tried to lift into a full sprint.

Sprinting proved difficult.

The unevenness of the tunnel's rocky, pocked surface forced him into a stumbling, staggering run that nevertheless propelled him rapidly away from the accelerating roar of the water. He understood from the nature of both sounds — the metal-against-rubber squeak and the splashing, roiling, liquid result — exactly what was about to happen. And he could tell from the escalating confusion of noise closing on him from behind that no more than ten seconds of free running remained before the torrent would overtake him.

While the searchlight's beam bounced erratically off the ceiling, floor and sides of the passageway, he set his hopes on reaching the narrow opening on the left that marked the only exit spur available within the modern excavation's elaborate network. That would be the rudimentary 150-foot horizontal, some of it mere crawl space, that led to the hidden, ground-level, shoulder-width exit at the base of the fortress's western wall. He had explored the exit spur fewer than twenty-five minutes earlier and had seen, via his NVD, the telltale evidence of recent egress: fresh, pebbly crumbles and, near the actual exit, smatterings of loose dirt from the surface.

That evidence had satisfied him that at least one of the terrorists had exited the cavern and its tunnel network that very morning. It had not in itself answered the question of whether or not any of the terrorists — Rademacher included — still remained in the underground.

He sensed that the onrushing water was upon him when he glimpsed the small opening on the left-hand side of the passageway, perhaps another ten running strides from him. He braked hard at the opening and lunged through, the M16 still held at the vertical in his left hand and extended well in front of him. His left foot and leg found purchase in the new corridor just as the wall of water smashed into his trailing right leg. The force of the impact spun him hard into the stony wall of the exit spur, but he fought his way clear and, right trousers leg and right boot soaked, resumed his careening sprint toward the distant exit.

Luke liked his chances. First, the aperture through which he had just exploded was more like a warship's hatch than a doorway, the base of the opening raised perhaps 18 inches from the surface of the main passage. Second, the spur angled away from the direction in which the water flowed, his lunging change of direction having been closer to 120 degrees than 90. Third, the force of the water combined with the hatch-like entry and the 120-degree angle would, for some time, send most of the torrent cascading through the major network, rather than into his spur. Fourth, he had found on his earlier reconnaissance that the spur sloped gradually upward toward the exit, an efficient engineering touch by Rademacher and his moles. Fifth, the crawl space upcoming would slow his flight but would also slow the onrush of water, the crawl space comprising a reduction in vertical space of about two feet both from the floor and from the ceiling.

Finally, on the other side of the crawl space, if the combination of barriers, angles and upward slope had sufficiently reduced the flow so that he could keep his feet in, say, waist- or chest-high water, he thought he could probably stride forward partially submerged until he reached the short vertical to the surface. He might even, in the end, be able to keep his weapon dry.

And so he pressed on, still running hard in his stumbling and now splashing gait, the weapon in one hand, the searchlight in the other, and the divine charge — *my life for yours* — foremost in his mind and heart.

The Army major in charge of the eight-man patrol assigned to comb the surface area to the immediate west of the fortress was by now satisfied that, if indeed any of the terrorists had escaped the cavern through a tunnel exit, they had disappeared in the early morning darkness, long before he had arrived. He spoke to his men in Hebrew.

"That's it, men!" he shouted across the width of the skirmish line that extended down the slope some seventy yards to the sergeant on extreme left cover. "Let's pack it up. Head back to the jeeps. Maintain ten-yard separation."

They turned into the fresh sunrise, guns up. The second and seventh men in the line walked backward, covering the rear of the slowly moving patrol, the third and sixth soldiers pacing within three feet of the two rear-guard members to warn them of roots or depressions in the irregular surface. Suddenly, the rear-guard corporal closest to the major pivoted to his right and swung his automatic rifle toward a rocky outcropping at the base of *Megiddo's* towering western wall.

"Gun!" he shouted in Hebrew.

Without command, the major, the sergeant at the far end of the skirmish line, and every member of the patrol in between dropped flat, rifles aimed up-ridge toward the fortress wall. The major, closest to the target, was the first to see what the corporal had seen. An Israeli Army M16, muzzle first, protruded from what appeared to be an aperture in the earth itself.

In the two seconds of elapsed time from the major's first glimpse of the weapon to his near-instantaneous judgment of the nature and extent of the danger to his men, the M16's barrel protruded still further from the earth.

But the major had seen that the M16 was not being aimed. It was being pushed.

He rose quickly to one knee, turned to his men, and raised his left palm to them, his own weapon held in his right hand. "Guns down! Guns down!" he shouted to them in Hebrew.

He then, still kneeling, turned back to face the fortress wall, and watched as the firearm was placed carefully in the thin, brown grass by someone who — most impressively to the soldiers — actually handled the full weight of the weapon with one hand placed low on the stock. That hand was followed by another, then by a pair of enormously muscular forearms, then biceps, then shoulders and a face.

Luke Manguson, struggling, extricated himself from the nearly invisible hole, rose carefully to his feet, and, hands held open and at his shoulders, said simply, "Major, do you speak English?"

The major nodded.

"I'm Lieutenant Manguson," he said slowly, enunciating carefully, "Royal Navy Reserve, on assignment with Mossad and your commanding officer. Would you be so kind as to inform the colonel by radiotelephone that the underground has been flooded and that I have emerged using the tunnel exit at the base of the fortress's western wall?"

He then looked down at himself, took note of his dripping wet clothing, and added, "And would you be kind enough, sir, to inform the colonel as well that I was able to keep the M16 and the Night Vision Device fully dry?"

The major stared. And then he smiled.

Mimicking Luke's Oxford dialect with a fine precision, the Israeli then added, *"Good show, Lieutenant!* The colonel will be delighted."

It was 1100.

The teacher held the child's hand and watched with Luke, Jaakov Adelman and the Israeli Army colonel, while the helicopter — not, in this case, a gun-laden Cobra, but a Black Hawk transport — settled onto the small plateau near the cavern's air vent. This was the newly developed medium-lift chopper designed and produced by Sikorsky for the U.S. Army, a fact that Kory van Dijk carried in her head along with so many others seemingly more pertinent to a veteran military analyst than to a junior-school teacher with but two years' active duty experience in the Royal Navy. Nonetheless, she not only recognized the helicopter and identified it to herself, but she knew as well, from scouring her reservist mailings, that the Israeli Army was freshly in possession of a dozen of these utility workhorses.

In the hours since the bloodless incursion into the terrorists' cavern, the nearly three hundred captives had been loaded into Army troop trucks for transport back to the Tel Aviv area. The files of the Righteous Among Nations, numbering just over 250 altogether, had been collected, organized, and boxed for immediate movement to *Yad Vashem* in Jerusalem, there to be compared with the master lists of the Righteous.

The quickly agreed-upon goal had been to develop, by midafternoon that very Sabbath day, a list of *Yad Vashem* names of the still living that, not having been matched to any of those in the terrorists' files, could be assumed to have been taken from the cavern by Adolfus Rademacher. Even now the soldiers were furiously loading the helicopter with the boxed files, and in moments the Black Hawk would be ready for liftoff and on its way south at flank speed.

Rademacher's whereabouts were not known. The Israelis and the *Yahalomin* assumed, however, that he would soon be in the air, whether with a single Righteous file or with dozens, moving in the direction of his newly intended victims. And they were aware that he could be on his murderous way even while they worked, he and his Nazi associates closer to their Righteous targets with every passing hour that the Israelis and the *Yahalomin* were forced to spend researching the missing files.

Kory circled behind the child and dropped to her knees. She drew the girl close with her heavily bandaged right hand, and shouted into her ear above the somber, distinctive threnody of the powerful Sikorsky engine.

"You see those two people just stepping down, Sari?" she said. "Those are our friends, Dr. Chapel and detective Belton. We'll all be going to Jerusalem together."

And in moments the engine's growling percussion was subordinated to the *whup-whup whup-whup whup-whup* of the rotor as the chopper lifted, turned, and, nosing down to gain more rapid acceleration, began to rise up and beyond the Mount Carmel ridgeline. On board were 268 boxed and alphabetized files of the Righteous Among Nations, three members of *Rebekka Yahalomin*, and a small Saudi child, still clutching the undamaged left hand of Kory van Dijk.

As one Black Hawk disappeared to the south, another sped in from the west. This one, hardly seeming to slow at all, arrowed in low over the same small plateau, but did not decelerate sufficiently to hover, to say nothing of initiating the time-consuming process of lowering itself onto the uneven surface of the ridge.

Instead, the pilot guided the craft across the small, open area at a thirty-foot altitude while his crew swung the pick-up wire-and-ladder device along the ground surface. Luke Manguson and Jaakov Adelman, with exquisite timing, adroitly stepped onto the moving ladder from opposite sides and clung expertly to the rescue device as the chopper's powerful winch rapidly pulled them up to and inside the rising and accelerating Black Hawk.

Israeli military personnel on the ground could see, as the two stepped forward, that the shorter and more muscular of the two wore an elaborate shoulder holster-and-belt that bulged with blades, tools, and accoutrement that they could not from a distance identify. And they saw that his tall, angular companion carried an Army M16A3 with a high-tech Night Vision Device and a 40mm under-barrel grenade launcher strapped tightly to his back.

It was obvious to the onlookers that the two were expecting a close-quarters engagement. It was equally obvious that they were in a great hurry to get there… wherever "there" might be.

And more than one of the observers found himself reflexively thanking God, on this Sabbath day, that he was not among those being sought by the two, each of them now but a tiny speck against the western sky.

# CHAPTER SIXTEEN

The international call was placed via a secure line — secure from the outside world, not from Mossad — from the agency's Tel Aviv airport "office," a space little more than a glorified storage closet in regard both to its size and its elegance. It was early afternoon in Israel, late morning in the UK.

"Yes?" said the mature contralto into the receiver.

"Mum?"

"Oh, Luke!" his mother exclaimed, "we have been *beside* ourselves! But wait… let me tell the others you're on the phone.…"

Luke waited, smiling to himself as he imagined the fact of his telephone presence spreading like wildfire through the house. He expected the next voice he heard to be the baritone of his father, but he was not surprised to hear a woman's voice– the other contralto — instead.

"Luke!" said Rebecca breathlessly, having raced up the stairs from the underground complex. "Tell me!" she demanded, eager to hear his voice and desperate for information.

He plunged in, providing his sister a concise summary of the events and outcomes of the night and morning. At the end of his narrative, he delivered three carefully measured warnings.

First, he noted that, in his mind and in that of the lead Mossad agent on the case, Adolfus Rademacher was a clear threat not just to those members of the Righteous Among Nations whose files he might — or might not — have taken from the cavern, but to the *Rebekka Yahalomin*, as well. Rademacher could plausibly, they agreed, have decided to travel directly from the Middle East to the Birmingham airport, thence to the lodge itself.

The primary goal of such an assault, they surmised, would be first to capture and then to murder Greta van Dijk, the member of the Righteous whom Rademacher had marked as first for extermination. Luke emphasized for his twin that, in New York, in then-Solomon Rosenthal's office, he had been forthcoming to Rosenthal about the security arrangements in England for the Dutch woman whom he had just rescued. He had even, he acknowledged shamefacedly, dropped into the conversation comments regarding the fact of the underground bomb shelter and the system of electronic sensors imbedded in the perimeter wall. All of this to make clear to Rosenthal that he, Rosenthal, did not need to be concerned further about the van Dijk woman's safety, but about all those other inductees into the Righteous Among Nations who were not thus so thoroughly protected from the Nazis who sought them.

Second, he explained to his sister that Rademacher would want more from a visit to the Birmingham compound than merely to retrieve and execute Greta van Dijk. He would, in fact, want to kill them all. Luke and his Mossad colleague had no doubt that Rademacher would hold Rebecca, Martha, and the entire group of visioners — the *Yahalomin* and anyone attached thereto — responsible for the destruction of his comprehensive plan to destroy the living population of the Righteous Among Nations.

And third, Luke continued, now relaying an urgent concern from Kory, it seemed plausible that Rademacher might also have an interest in Greta van Dijk's brother, Kory's father. And, by extension, Kory's mother, as well. Although neither Andruw nor Amelia van Dijk had been an inductee into the Righteous Among Nations, Rademacher knew that Andruw had been present in the van Dijk home at 9 *Hoofdstraadt* during the Nazi occupation. And Rademacher also knew that, while Andruw would not have been given chief responsibility for sheltering the young Jewess, he was certainly complicit.

Having now spoken nonstop for nearly fifteen minutes, Luke fell silent, mentally reviewing his statement for omissions. His sister waited, knowing exactly what he was doing. At length, he announced tentatively, "I think that's all, Rebecca. I don't think I've left out anything that could possibly matter."

"Luke," responded Rebecca immediately, "regarding Kory's parents... Greta had the same thought earlier this morning. She and Dad left straightaway. They're in London at this moment, picking up the van Dijks and Kory's little kitty. We expect them back here in about two hours."

"Excellent," he replied simply. "What else do I need to know?" he then added.

"I've had no more dreams, my dear," she said after a moment, "nor has Martha. So I've nothing to report from the Source."

A short pause ensued, at which point Rebecca decided to raise an issue familiar to them both. "Luke, do you feel that this is just the same as before, in regard to involvement from Scotland Yard… or the ordinary police… or even the intelligence agencies? I know we've always been certain that no law enforcement person could possibly take action on the basis of information gleaned from… well… from supernatural communication… but, this time, with Mossad already engaged and, from what you've told me, taking our work so seriously that they have even given us a name…."

"Yes," replied Luke immediately, "I admit I was incredulous — stunned, actually — when the agent told us in New York about the *"Yahalomin"* label they've given us. But I also saw, when we got to Israel, the rather thoroughgoing skepticism of most of Mr. Adelman's colleagues, at least until several of them came to understand that the air circulation vent near *Megiddo* was exactly where you portrayed it as being.

"But… still… the point is just this, Rebecca: agent Adelman is very much the exception, even within Mossad, regarding the validity of information garnered in this fashion. We simply cannot infer acceptance inside Mossad generally, to say nothing of MI6, CIA, Scotland Yard, or anyone else.

"No… I think we are quite on our own, as always."

"But," Rebecca replied quickly, "of course, 'on our own' simply means we have the Divine Source giving us His rather personal attention in the matter, while the law enforcement specialists look elsewhere."

Luke chuckled. "Yes. Nicely put, sister."

"In any case, Luke, I wanted to tell you that we've been hard at work," she continued, "in preparation for an attempt on the lodge. Without knowing anything for certain, we simply thought it prudent to inspect everything, especially the perimeter alarm and the remote camera systems, together with the master console's functions.

"Everything stands in readiness now. But, of course, we've always known we can be overpowered here if an enemy brings enough force to bear. We've no illusions about that. Enough numbers and enough weaponry can defeat us.

"And," she continued, "we've no illusions about the likelihood that Mr. Rademacher will infer a ventilation arrangement to our underground shelter similar to the one he installed — and I dreamed — near *Megiddo*. He'll know he can send something toxic through our surface vent just as readily as the Israelis did with his at Mount Carmel. We know better than to assume that we can simply close ourselves up as though the bomb shelter were impregnable.

"We can operate from there until the enemy is inside the perimeter and on the grounds in force, if that is what actually develops. At that point we'll need to be prepared to move the babies into the basement proper. And we'll need also to move into a highly proactive attack mode."

She paused, thinking. After a moment, Luke spoke.

"Yes. And speaking of 'highly proactive,' Rebecca," he said, "has Dad been working the dogs?"

"Yes," she replied, "they were out early today… worked for well over an hour, I'd say, before Dad drove out to London."

"Good," Luke responded simply.

There was another pause. Each twin could almost hear the other's concentrated thoughts as the two minds ran repeatedly through the permutations.

Finally, Luke brought the conversation to a close.

"Well, dear…" he said thoughtfully, "I'll be on my way soon, along with the agent I've spoken about. The Israelis are preparing one of the Mossad Lears right now for an early afternoon departure. I understand that we'll be refueling somewhere in northern Italy, and then heading straight for the Birmingham strip. We're projecting a 1930 arrival time, just at dusk in England. Then the two of us will be coming straight to the lodge by rental auto.

"We'll approach under the assumption that Rademacher and any number of gunmen will be doing exactly the same thing… conceivably at exactly the same time.

"I'll hope we're wrong about all this, but….

"Can you organize a prayer session this afternoon, Rebecca?"

"That's already on our schedule, Luke. That's the very last thing we'd leave out, you know. Mum has agreed to lead."

The group assembled slowly in the converted bomb shelter. The senior Mangusons, chairing, faced the rest from chairs placed near one end of the room.

Elisabeth began as soon as all — except Rebecca — were seated. Rebecca stood in the doorway, listening for the infants, freshly asleep in the room directly across the corridor.

"Welcome, all," Elisabeth said, smiling graciously.

"Before our opening prayer," she continued, "let me formally welcome our arrivals, Amelia and Andruw, and, of course, little Tiny."

Kory's diminutive tabby, curled into a tight ball in Amelia van Dijk's lap, responded on cue with a high-pitched meow. Her demeanor suggested that her comment had been directed more toward the German shepherd and the border collie than to Elisabeth.

Elisabeth smiled warmly at the threesome, then addressed herself to the group as a whole, which now numbered fourteen altogether: the senior Mangusons, the senior Clarks, Rebecca and Matt, Greta van Dijk, her brother and his wife, the two infants, and the three animals.

"This will be a prayer session, not a war counsel," said Elisabeth evenly, "but first… an update, so as to inform the details of our prayers: Luke has explained to Rebecca that Kory, Eleanor, and Sidney, along with the child, are in Jerusalem by now, comparing the files taken from the cavern with the central records at *Yad Vashem*. Once they have identified the discrepancies, if any, they will know which members of the Righteous are at risk, and on that basis Mossad, MI6, or CIA agents around the globe may be able to intervene, pulling the Righteous from their homes before they can be attacked. Luke and the Mossad agent whose case this has been from the first are on their way here.

"As, they suspect, may be Adolfus Rademacher.

"We know," she continued, looking now at the van Dijks, "that Greta, Andruw, and Amelia are not completely safe from him here, nor, in fact, would they be anywhere in the world. But we know that God has, in the end, always sheltered us from our enemies. We expect that each of you will be safer here, with us, than anywhere else you might be, and certainly safer than if you were to remain in your own homes."

Amelia and Andruw van Dijk each nodded solemnly, turned quietly to Greta, and whispered a brief summary translation to her. Then she nodded to Elisabeth as well.

Elisabeth bowed her head and the others followed her gesture. As her mother began, Rebecca immediately and gracefully knelt on the hard concrete floor at the room's entry door, folding her hands under her chin in her habitual attitude of prayer.

Elisabeth opened the prayer session with the familiar words of petition that each of them knew well:

> *... We make our address to thy Divine Majesty in this our necessity, that thou wouldest take the cause into thine own hand, and judge between us and our enemies. Stir up thy strength, O Lord, and come and help us; for thou givest not alway the battle to the strong, but canst save by many or by few…. Hear us thy poor servants begging mercy, and imploring thy help, and that thou wouldest be a defence unto us against the face of the enemy….*

In a small conference room within Jerusalem's *Yad Vashem* complex, the Chapel-Beltons and Kory van Dijk watched intently, fighting impatience, while four members of the Memorial's support staff worked to complete their painstaking comparison of the files collected from the cavern, one by one, with their own records. Both simplifying and complicating the process was the early decision, made jointly by Saul Coen and Sid Belton, to limit the comparison to those areas represented geographically by the 268 file folders: northern Africa, western Europe, and Scandinavia.

While the three *Yahalomin* watched the staff members, little Sari, who had refused any suggestion that she be separated, even for a moment, from her rescuer's side, watched Kory. She had already pulled her chair so close to Kory's that the chair arms actually touched, and now she wriggled still closer.

Kory looked down at the child and saw that she wished to speak. The youthful, but already highly skilled teacher of young girls leaned down reflexively in a practiced gesture that had so often meant the difference in a child's speaking her actual thoughts and in her not speaking at all.

Her ear now close to the girl's lips, she heard, in a small whisper, "Does your hand hurt very much?"

Kory smiled and cradled the child's head with her good hand. "It's going to be fine, Sari. Really. It's going to be just fine. The doctor is going to see me tomorrow. It will be as good as new. You'll see."

As she spoke the words, Kory became aware that three of the staff members had pulled their chairs close to each other, and the fourth had stood to lean over the others. They had finished the comparison count and were starting to combine their totals.

After no more than five more very long minutes, the English-speaking staff member looked up. "Two-hundred and seventy-four," she said simply.

The *Yahalomin* looked at each other. "Six, then," said Kory to the couple at her side.

The detective turned back to the staff member. "Does y'r count include Greta van Dijk?" he said in his brusque interrogative manner.

Hearing the name clearly, one of the Hebrew-only staff members flipped rapidly through the pages, ran her finger to a point on her fourth page, and moved her head aside so that her colleague, leaning over her, could see.

"Yes," said the English-speaker. "There is a discrepancy of six, and the discrepancy does not include Greta van Dijk. Her file — or a copy of her file — is here, among the 267 others from the cavern."

"Mr. Rosenthal — Mr. Rademacher, I mean — has taken six files with him, then?" asked Eleanor Chapel, wanting to be certain she understood.

"Yeah," said her husband, glowering at a spot on the table where he appeared to be imagining Adolfus Rademacher.

"Can you tell us — quickly, please — where the six Righteous members are shown as currently living?" asked Kory, anxiety rising in her voice.

"Yes," replied the English speaker. "It is easy to see the situation. All six appear to live in extreme northern Holland. Judging from the addresses — "rural routes" all — they seem to be Greta van Dijk's neighbors, dotted around the Ferwerd countryside, and perhaps all members of her Lutheran church. Their files indicate that they hid their Jewish persons in basements, attics, and barns, but all six presumably knew, and still know, each other... and Greta van Dijk, as well."

# Chapter Seventeen

Shortly after dusk on a June Saturday, two flat miles inland from the frigid waters of the North Sea, a Dutch octogenarian patiently reviewed her great-grandchildren's Sunday school lessons with them. The atmosphere in the cozy living room of the old farmhouse was warm with the love and respect continually exchanged among the four generations of family members who had resided there all their lives.

It had been 35 years since these Christians had harbored a Jewish family of four in their outbuildings for more than two full years, withstanding successfully the terrible scrutiny of the occupying Nazi forces, led by then-Major Adolfus Rademacher. The number of close calls had risen to the point at which no one in the family could remember how many there had been, or even cite them all. Often the Jewish family itself was unaware of a particular near-discovery until their host family later disclosed the circumstances.

Always the greatest fear had been that one of the two Jewish children — the younger a mere three-year-old at the start — would shout or laugh or cry or cough or sneeze at precisely the moment at which absolute silence was demanded. But in the providence of God they had all managed to avoid detection and the death camps that would have gladly offered their macabre welcome to them all, Jew and Christian, adult and child, man and woman alike.

To the matriarch, an inductee into the Righteous Among Nations nearly ten years earlier, and to her son and his wife, the memory of those years was at times dim and at times quite uncomfortably fresh. This was one of the latter times, for in nearby Ferwerd, just one week past, the children's elementary school teacher — who was their Sunday school teacher as well — had been taken from her home under circumstances that no one as yet fully understood.

Neighbors had heard terrible shouts, in German, that recalled the years of occupation to their minds. They had been too terrified to respond, and, thus, had neither seen anything nor been able to assist the town's four-man police force in any way. Greta van Dijk had simply disappeared.

Now, both in the town itself and in the farmlands throughout Friesland — "the cold land" — residents were on edge. Most of all those who, like Greta van Dijk herself, had sheltered Jewish families during the war, and had later been inducted into the Righteous Among Nations.

And suddenly the comfortable, prayerful ambience of the Sunday school lesson was shattered by the crash of impossibly loud hammering on the back door of the farmhouse. Instantly, the old woman, the children, and all others in the household rose and flew to the basement… all, that is, except for the great-grandmother's now sixty-year-old son.

He, a proud farmer and skilled hunter of small game, strode to the basement door, listened for the slide-and-snap of its interior dead bolt, and pulled his double-barrel shotgun from the top of the nearby dish cabinet. He had loaded the powerful firearm the previous Sunday, as soon as he had gotten news of Greta van Dijk's apparent abduction, had checked the mechanism daily, and knew it was ready to fire.

And he knew who he was. While he did not know his enemy in this case, he knew that anyone capable of shouting the infamous Nazi phrases reportedly delivered at the van Dijk home the previous Saturday night was capable of simple and ruthless murder, of him and of his family, for no reason other than their having sheltered a Jewish family from the Holocaust.

He walked to the kitchen, switched off the overhead light, and leveled the shotgun at the back door. He stood, waiting, his finger on the trigger.

But the voice he heard was not shouted, and it did not speak in German. It spoke in Dutch. It came from inside the house and it came from behind him.

He spun around, bringing the shotgun to bear on the figure of a man whom he did not know. The man held his palms open and at his own shoulders, indicating that he was not armed and posed no threat.

His words, though spoken in careful Dutch, were at first confusing.

The man said, speaking softly, "I come in the name of the God of the Hebrew and Christian people of the world. Your mother — a member of the Righteous Among Nations — will be threatened this night, along with all others who live here with her. I am authorized to take all of you to a place of safety for the night.

And, once you are all safe, we will come back and will face, capture, and imprison those who would do you harm.

"Please inspect my authorization."

With this, the stranger slowly reached to his breast pocket and removed a folded letter. He stepped carefully forward, extending the letter and opening it with the same hand as he did.

Both stood unmoving while the Dutchman read the missive.

The note was printed bold and large, and the householder could read its careful Dutch without stepping forward himself and without lowering the shotgun. The note read simply:

> By judicial authority of the State of Israel, and with the permission of the government of The Netherlands and the township of Ferwerd, the bearer is authorized by law and by local law enforcement to transport the members of the following families to the Ferwerd school cafeteria and auditorium which has been prepared to host all family members overnight.
>
> Please comply quickly, so that those who threaten the safety of our residents may be confronted, arrested, and extradited to the State of Israel for proper trial.

The document listed six local families by name, and, separately, the six members of the Righteous Among Nations. The letterhead was that of the Nation of Israel.

# Chapter Eighteen

While the Nation of Israel, with the blessing of The Netherlands government, proceeded with its round-up of the neo-Nazis in Holland, the adults, infants, and animals at the lodge in England prepared to face intruders with no such government intervention possible. In Holland, official action had been legitimized from the moment the six-file discrepancy was established by officials at *Yad Vashem*. Greta van Dijk's file, however, had been found to be intact, left untouched by Adolfus Rademacher as he fled the Mount Carmel underground.

And this meant that no preventive action could be authorized on behalf of Greta van Dijk, nor of her protectors, the *Rebekka Yahalomin:* not by Mossad, nor by MI6, nor by the CIA, nor by any branch of the governments of Israel, the United Kingdom, or the United States. There simply was no legally admissible documentation of the hypothesis that any of the occupants of the Birmingham lodge required protection.

And it was certainly a fact that the *Yahalomin* had grown accustomed to this degree of exposure during their annual crises. The detective had explained it all in the first instance, and had continued to explain it in crisis after crisis. In fact, the *Yahalomin* rarely gave the irony much thought: the peculiar fact that they were themselves always a target, yet never possessed a legitimate case for government protection. To them — the visioners — the circumstances were simply a consequence of their having been selected as divine instruments.

And so they accepted their godly obligations and willingly fulfilled those obligations, expecting nothing in return beyond the gratification inherent in attempting obedience. If, at times, divine obligations and divinely commissioned risks seemed to be proffered hand-in-hand with a touch, or at times much more than a touch, of divine protection, well, so much the better.

But such was neither assumed nor expected.

The fact that Jaakov Adelman accompanied Luke Manguson to what he expected to be a violent confrontation with Adolfus Rademacher in no sense implied either Mossad's or the State of Israel's endorsement of his decision. It was a personal action, decided upon by Jaakov Adelman alone, independent of both his colleagues and his superiors.

He understood that the consequences of his decision could include his termination as an intelligence agent. The mere fact of his authorization of the use of one of the agency's jet aircraft would likely be more than enough to warrant his dismissal from the agency. Criminal charges might even be brought against him.

On the other hand, some of those at his level and some of those above his level in the Israeli government knew of the existence and the work of the visioners, believed as fully as did Adelman himself in the divine validity of the *Yahalomin's* activities, and might in the end find themselves in full sympathy with Adelman's decision both to authorize the flight to England and personally to accompany Lieutenant Manguson on this high-risk intercept. That being the case, Adelman understood that the official outcome of the adventure, should he survive, might in fact be a formal government reprimand coupled with an informal and private commendation.

But Adelman was thinking not at all about his career. The motivation underlying his decision was the purest of any he had ever experienced: that is, he felt that he was being prompted to act truly and simply in service to God. And he found that that was all he cared about… a remarkably liberating experience, and one he was determined to experience repeatedly throughout the rest of his life, if there was, in fact, to be a rest of his life.

For he carried no illusions about the deadly strength of whatever force Rademacher had assembled. Adelman expected to be heavily outmanned, insofar as the number of actual combatants would be concerned, and thoroughly outgunned. He knew that their adversary would be as ruthless as any he had ever faced, and he knew, as well, that the consequences of capture would be considerably worse than the consequences of a quick death at the enemy's hands.

Nonetheless, he knew also that his choice had been right. Of that he had no doubt. And as the Mossad pilots lined up the Lear for its final approach to the Birmingham runway, he actually smiled to himself.

This, he knew, was the way to die... with absolute clarity in, and commitment to, the holiness of an endeavor.

An hour after the Saturday evening descent of full darkness on the Birmingham lodge, ten fully armed, dark-clad men hacked their way through the underbrush along the lower reaches of the substantial hill on which the lodge proper stood. Progress, to their leader, was maddeningly slow.

Although the moon had risen, clouds continued to shroud her bright beams, so that the climb from the staging area had been a continual stumble over rocks, roots, and outcroppings of stone and vegetation. All ten dedicated, violent-crime-hardened Nazis carried automatic rifles strapped to their backs, and half carried sidearms as well.

Two took turns shouldering a lightweight stepladder. Several carried battery-powered torches capable of spotlighting a victim at distances up to one hundred meters. None was equipped with night-vision scopes or goggles.

The point man for the long climb had been instructed to lead the group generally uphill, the premise being that, since the lodge stood on the point of highest elevation in the area, a gradient-based approach would yield success more readily than a direction-based approach under circumstances in which darkness would make use of the compass uncertain.

But the hill on which the resort stood was not in the least conical. The lodge itself and, indeed, the entire walled perimeter, stood, in fact, on a ridge line that ran generally northwest by southeast. That being the case, the line of men found itself snaking steadily uphill, but often in a direction parallel to the distant, not-yet-visible perimeter wall, and at other times in a direction that actually took them further from their goal.

After more than two hours of sweaty and confused hacking, stumbling, and climbing, clarity arrived in the form of a break in the cloud cover. The sudden appearance of bright moonlight provided the men with their first sense of the geological organization of the terrain they sought to negotiate.

The lodge's active defense force sat huddled in the kitchen. They numbered five: two women, a man, and two canine warriors. By name they were Rebecca, Greta, Jason, Margaret, and Max.

The others — a reserve force of nine — clustered in the basement. This group included the infants, their father, one of their grandfathers, both of their grandmothers, Kory van Dijk's parents, and her kitten. By name they were Joanna, Samuel, Matt, Paul, Martha, Elisabeth, Amelia, Andruw and Tiny.

They had chosen the basement rather than its adjacent bomb shelter because of the threat of gaseous toxins being pumped into the shelter by means of its ground-level air vent. The basement proper had no such vulnerability. Its weakness was its ordinary wooden doorway, a stark contrast to the bomb shelter's elaborate, vault-like sliding doors coupled with locking mechanisms that could be operated only by a set of coded electronic signals.

The host couple had retained the final say in the separation of personnel into an active defense force of five and a reserve force of nine, and they had reached their conclusions in husband-wife privacy. The outcome of this division into two groups was rationally defensible with one exception.

The exception was Greta van Dijk. Short of using physical force — binding her to a basement support structure — the others found that she could not and would not be restrained from joining the active defense unit. Amelia van Dijk, translating for her sister-in-law, said repeatedly in English on Greta's behalf, "This is personal. I am sorry. I will not passively wait for him in the basement. This is personal."

No one asked for clarification of her reference to "him."

As for the others in the active defense unit, the two dogs were considered essential and, thus, so was their handler, Jason Manguson. Rebecca was chosen to be the other *homo sapiens* defender for two reasons: first, she was the youngest and most athletic of the able-bodied adults — the qualifier pertaining to her husband whose three-years-previous automatic weapons injuries had permanently disabled his left shoulder, arm, and hand — and, second, Rebecca was the one most comfortable and skilled with the bomb shelter's master console and its electronic control systems. As for her status as new mother, Rebecca herself put the point succinctly: "When the enemy is inside the house, the mother protects her children by eliminating the enemy."

And then she added, "I am young… able-bodied… strong… fast…. I am the best that we have, unless and until Luke arrives.

"I should be chosen for this."

She made the assertion without a trace of *braggadocio*. It was a plain and unassailable statement of fact.

As darkness fell, the *Rebekka Yahalomin* and their associates had felt they were now as well prepared as they could be, but they also knew two imponderables remained, one small and one large. The small imponderable was Greta van Dijk's role. She had been assigned a role, but she was untested, save for her *brava* performance just outside the back door of her home the Saturday night previous. None could be certain in advance of the quality of her work under more demanding expectations. The planners' best realistic hope was that she would be but a minor encumbrance to Rebecca, her father, and the dogs.

The large imponderable was the arrival in time, or not, of Luke Manguson and Jaakov Adelman. With them in the battle there was a plausible chance, though small, of success and survival; without them, there was none except by purest miracle. But the *Yahalomin* were living exemplars of purest miracle.

Now, in the kitchen of the lodge, all was quiet. A small table lamp provided the only illumination, not only for the kitchen but for the entire house. Jason Manguson sat at the head of the table in his usual place. The two women occupied their usual spots as well: Greta to Jason's right and Rebecca to his left. Margaret lay on the cool floor between Jason and Rebecca; Max, between Jason and Greta. The kitchen had been as quiet as a tomb for perhaps ninety minutes.

Rebecca and her father were dressed for action. She wore one of her full-length tennis warm-up suits, black in color, and black running shoes with black laces, and, as well, a black ball cap with a small slit cut into the back to accept her long ponytail. Her glistening black hair was bound with a set of dark rubber bands. Her face and her hands were blackened with dark shoe polish.

Jason was attired similarly, but Greta, untamable, had refused all such precautions. She was dressed in one of Elisabeth Manguson's pastel house dresses, the one she had borrowed almost as soon as she had arrived at the lodge.

And now, cloaked in her school-teacherly dignity, Greta van Dijk appeared, in fact, to be perfectly ready to welcome her young Dutch pupils into her Friesland classroom. So it was that, while the superficial contrasts between the two women's appearances were stark, there was something quite similar about the two of them in regard to the Christian poise and confidence with which they awaited what might well be their final moments on earth.

The three adults prayed silently. The two dogs, after their fashion, did the same. Most assuredly, the two animals were not sleeping, nor were they even resting.

They were motionless, but their eyes were wide. Their ears twitched continually in response to the slightest sound, even that of the solitary cricket that hopped erratically across the back porch.

And then suddenly, and at the same instant, the collie's and the shepherd's heads jerked up sharply. Both pairs of ears were pricked and oriented in precisely the same direction. And from Max came the unmistakable growl of early warning.

Thus, they knew.

Rademacher.

# CHAPTER NINETEEN

Without another sound, Rebecca, Greta, Jason, Margaret, and Max rose and exited the kitchen. The two women strode down the main hallway, opened one of the two doors to the basement, and descended, closing the hallway door behind them. Jason, after switching off the kitchen lamp, took the dogs to tactically advantageous positions on the main floor.

Rebecca and Greta, feeling their way in the dark, reached the basement floor in an area removed by distance and by interior walls from the other group of defenders comprising adults, infants, and cat. Rebecca felt for the remote device, resting in its cabinet niche at the foot of the stairs, worked the device skillfully, and listened as the wall itself — sliding and folding simultaneously — become a doorway. Then, feeling with one hand and holding the older woman's hand with the other, she moved cautiously into the bomb shelter, a structure that lay entirely outside the foundation walls of the lodge. Rebecca allowed the sliding door to remain open, knowing that the two would retrace their steps in just moments.

Rebecca moved to her left, stepped into the control room itself and turned on the baseboard lighting system, one that provided just enough light for safe movement, but no more than that. She advanced to the master console and indicated an adjacent chair for her companion. Then she pulled up her own chair in front of the console.

Her first maneuver was simply to flip a master switch cutting off all electricity to the lodge itself. This would deprive the invaders of any use of the interior house lights in the unlikely event that they would wish to turn on overhead lights, stairway lighting, or floor and table lamps in the house proper. She did not cut the power to the bomb shelter and its electronic extensions, wanting the baseboard lighting and, of course, the master console, the remote cameras, and the perimeter wall detection system to continue in operation.

Next, manipulating levers skillfully, Rebecca swung the remote cameras so as to provide full visual coverage of the perimeter wall in the general area indicated by the two dogs' uniform response to sounds that only they could detect. The perimeter wall itself, though alarmed, could not provide directional information to the console: merely the fact of a breech. Only the dogs could determine the direction from which the assault would be coming. And they had.

Rebecca fixed her eyes on the monitors and waited. She knew the wait would be brief.

In the basement proper, the others made final preparations. Elisabeth Manguson and Amelia van Dijk held the infants close in their arms, in the corner farthest removed from the basement door and its wooden stairway. Tiny sat beside them inside her small carrying case. Her luminous feline eyes reflected the pinpoint of light generated by a slender taper placed on the floor under the stairway.

At the foot of the stairs, Matt, his parents and Andruw van Dijk waited quietly. Trip wires had been set up at four different levels on the staircase. At Matt's direction — he, unable to assist physically, having but one usable hand — Paul, Martha, and Andruw had done the work with two rolls of clothesline wire, assorted small pulleys, and more than a dozen substantial screw-hooks which had been set into the wooden beams by Jason Manguson years before.

Earlier that day, while her husband had worked the dogs, Elisabeth had brought Matt to the basement to explain the trip-wire systems and pre-arrangements to him. She knew she would be needed to care for the infants when the assault came. Her son-in-law's atrophied arm and hand left him impaired for many purposes, including that of cradling his own children under circumstances that might require actual flight, babies in arms. But Matt was a superb organizer and tactician. And Elisabeth saw immediately that he not only grasped the defensive concepts, but stood ready to improve them.

And he had.

The room had been eerily quiet before the short burst of ground-floor activity, and now was quiet once again. The six adults in the basement knew well that the flurry of footsteps, human and canine, had meant the intruders were at the perimeter.

The infants sighed contentedly from time to time. With each sigh, Tiny affirmed her existence — and theirs — in her squeaky, high-pitched voice. The adults prayed in silence.

When the Nazi force had reached the perimeter wall, the point man had paused, waiting with the others while Adolfus Rademacher advanced from his position near the rear of the file. He strode to the fore, directed the torches to illuminate the base of the old stone barrier, and indicated to the ladder carrier the spot at which to plant the ladder's base. A moment later, he wordlessly gestured to the point man to climb the sturdy, portable structure.

Rademacher had no concern about his enemy's detecting his force's incursion. He, in the guise of Solomon Rosenthal, had listened carefully in his Manhattan office to Luke Manguson's helpful description of the property and its defense systems, and so he understood clearly that the occupants of the lodge would know that his men were coming for them.

He relished the thought. He smiled to himself as he imagined Greta van Dijk and Rebecca Clark watching the bomb shelter's monitors as he and his squad of killers advanced upon them. Though he would have been surprised to have been informed that indeed those *were* the two who watched his men close on the lodge, it was always the two women — the Righteous honoree and the youthful visioner — whom he conceived as his victims. The others were merely casualties of chance.

One by one the ten intruders climbed the short ladder, placed both feet carefully on top of the stone wall, and dropped to the other side. In the control room, the women saw that each foot placement on top of the wall brought a series of flashing lights to the console. And as soon as each man appeared at the top of the wall, his image formed itself on all three monitors whose cameras were now angled toward this portion of the northwest sector. The tenth to drop to the grassy surface inside the perimeter was Adolfus Rademacher. Knowing he was now on camera, Rademacher strode to the point, indicated with a gesture for the others to fall in behind him, and moved confidently toward the lodge.

Within the bomb shelter, Rebecca stood.

Having now confirmed the dogs' directional analysis, and having, as well, determined the enemy force size of ten, she stepped to the cabinet adjacent the console. She stooped, opened the second drawer, and removed two boxes. She placed each on the long table used normally for the display of maps and charts.

Rebecca then reached back into the same drawer, lifted from it an empty cloth bag and, asking with her eyes for Greta to come to the table, placed the bag in the Dutch woman's hands. Spreading her hands to suggest opening the mouth of the cloth cavity, Rebecca watched with satisfaction as her signals were translated into movement by her companion. Rebecca then reached carefully into the boxes, removed a total of ten hand grenades from them, and placed them carefully into the bottom of the cloth bag Greta held tightly as its weight steadily increased with the addition of each of the explosive devices.

Seeing her colleague's eyes grow wide at the sight of the grenades, Rebecca paused in her work. She drew Greta's attention to her own hands, and, with repeated stabbing gestures in the direction of her own gray eyes, Rebecca gave her to understand that these were indeed weapons, but not conventional explosives. These were weapons designed to impair the vision of an enemy.

Rebecca considered trying to make plain that the impairment would come from impossibly bright flashes of light, rather than by a toxin, but quickly gave up the idea as too complex for her rudimentary signing efforts. When Greta nodded her understanding of the core idea, Rebecca returned the nod with satisfaction.

She then took the bag from her companion, tightened (but did not tie) its drawstring, and preceded the Dutch woman to the door of the control room. She looked back, her hand on the baseboard light switch, and then remembered something else. Handing the bag back to Greta, Rebecca returned to the cabinet, reached into its top drawer, and removed an object.

Greta cringed involuntarily at the sight of the wooden box.

Rebecca lifted the box carefully, returned to her colleague, and the two of them exchanged burdens. Thus, the two women prepared to retrace their steps out of the bomb shelter, into the basement of the lodge and up the stairs to the ground floor, one carrying the ten flash grenades and the other the wooden box containing the monstrous iron Swastika.

Again Rebecca looked back, her hand once more on the baseboard light switch. But again her hand was stayed, this time not by something she remembered, but by something she saw on the monitor that faced the doorway at which she stood. For on its screen she saw two other men emerging from the far side of the old stone wall, crouching briefly on its flat crest and then dropping onto the grass on the near side.

One of the men was tall and angular and carried some sort of weapon strapped to his back. She had never seen this man before.

But the other… ah!… the other.

Rebecca's most radiant smile flashed across her elegant face, moving the V-shaped scar on her right cheek. Greta inquired of her in silence, lifting her expressive eyebrows.

In reply, Rebecca spoke but a single syllable.

"Luke," she said softly.

Adolfus Rademacher, not pausing for reconnaissance, led his force rapidly and in single file directly up to the rear entrance of the lodge. There he stepped up and onto the porch, moved to the locked door to the working kitchen, and pointed to one of its small glass panes. The gunman second in line shrugged the automatic rifle from his shoulder and, in one motion, brought the stock of the weapon crashing into and through the pane. Rademacher himself then reached through, unbolted the door, turned the interior knob and pushed the door open.

He then stood aside while, according to his tactical plan, three men filed past him and into the kitchen. Four others, in response to his command, reversed direction, stepped down from the porch and turned right to circle the house from the east side. Rademacher, satisfied upon personal inspection that his tactical plan was correct, moved with the two remaining gunmen to circle the house from the west. He intended a pincer movement from which any escape — by anyone — would become quickly impossible.

In the blackness of the lodge's interior, the three-man frontal-attack unit moved confidently, automatic rifles at the ready. As they passed out of the working kitchen and into the main hallway, one turned into the first room on his left, the second wheeled into the stairway that led up to the lodge's guest-room floor and the third continued down the long hallway toward the front of the house. Their electric torches were switched off, Rademacher having made clear that he wanted the attack to go forward in darkness, both inside and outside the building.

Rebecca, lying flat on her stomach, extended one of her brother's 45-degree-angled mirrors along the floor from her position within one of the reading rooms near the front of the house. Moonlight filtering through the tall windows of all the main floor rooms provided just enough light for her to detect the dark presence moving toward her.

She not only could detect with her eyes, but also with her ears, the steady progress of the gunman as he moved along the main corridor, the old boards squeaking erratically under his footfall. At length, when her eyes and ears told her that he had advanced to within ten feet of her position, she brought one of the flash grenades to her mouth, placed her teeth on the pull-ring, and jerked sharply. She then rolled the oval device slowly down the hallway and, sitting up quickly, turned her face away from the impending flash.

The grenade exploded directly in front of the gunman. He emitted an involuntary roar of anguish, dropped his weapon, clattering, to the hallway floor and fell heavily to his knees, his hands covering his face. There he remained for perhaps two full seconds, swaying and moaning in anguish. Thus, he did not see — indeed, could not have seen — the heavy iron Swastika, wielded with a glad viciousness by Greta van Dijk, as it crashed into his skull.

The gunman fell sideways into a confused heap of oddly angled arms, legs, and torso, no longer conscious... no longer aware of his hate-filled and bigoted mission. He had scarcely hit the floor when the nearest of his two companions, the gunman who had turned left out of the kitchen, wheeled around the corner of the formal dining room and into the long hallway in response to the muted explosion of the flash grenade, the clattering noise of the rifle falling to the floor, and the unmistakable sound of a human being tumbling headlong and unconscious onto hardwood flooring.

He raced down the hallway, rifle up, looking for a target. Drawing abreast his fallen companion, he stopped. Hearing a small noise behind him, he turned just in time to absorb the second flash, Rebecca having moved to a doorway that placed her full in the rear of this secondary assault.

Unlike his companion, this gunman neither dropped his rifle nor fell forward to his knees. Blinded, but continuing to stand, he reflexively pulled the trigger of his automatic rifle, releasing a storm of medium-caliber rounds high into the hallway wall and ceiling. The rifle was still pouring forth a steady stream of fire when the iron Swastika, wielded once more with uninhibited exuberance, crashed down into the rear of his skull.

The Dutch school teacher scarcely had time once more to retreat from the hallway when the third intruder, having raced thudding down the stairwell from the guest-room floor, leaped into the hallway, his rifle aimed toward the front door and his finger on the trigger. Instantly stationary and stable in his shooting crouch, he made himself easy prey for the German shepherd's attack. Max, having just emerged from a storage closet near the kitchen, flew ten feet through the air toward his target. The hapless gunman, having heard, too late, the sound of Max's toenails against the hardwood, had time only to turn his head.

This movement brought his face and neck directly into the jaws of the animal, whose terrifying bite-and-hold turned the man's muscles into water and sent him to the floor with the full weight of the animal on top of him. No sooner had he hit the floor than Jason and the women were also on top of him, taping his mouth, wrists and ankles with heavy-duty strapping tape.

At the instant the second intruder reflexively unleashed his five-second burst of automatic rifle fire into the walls and ceiling of the lodge's main hallway, Jaakov Adelman, peering through his Night Vision Device at a range of fifty yards from the house, pulled the M16A3's secondary trigger. This action sent one under-barrel-mounted 40mm grenade rocketing toward the four-man assault unit moving along the east side of the house. The flash grenade, a much more powerful version of the small flash-explosives Rebecca had put to such effective use inside the house, actually struck the lead gunman in the shoulder, sending him careening into the side of the building, his head striking the upper edge of the foundation wall as he fell. He slumped, semi-conscious, to the ground.

Adelman averted his eyes to allow the flash to do its work, then immediately sited the weapon once more, this time with his finger on the primary trigger. Though his Mossad training and the Israeli blood coursing through his body told him to squeeze off four quick rounds and simply kill them all, the *Yahalomin* spirit with which he now fought led him to seek to incapacitate, not eliminate, his enemies. If he needed to fire the M16's rounds at these men, he would aim for their legs. At fifty yards, firing at stunned, motionless gunmen, he would certainly hit exactly what he aimed to hit.

But no further action was required from the agent, for he saw that the flash itself had rendered the other three sufficiently immobile that Luke, with a twenty-yard sprinting start on the grenade launcher, was upon the men in seconds.

Using the rudimentary German commands he knew, he ordered them to the ground, telling them they would otherwise be shot immediately.

Using the accoutrement — tape and small-diameter rope — from his shoulder belt and holster, he had the four gunmen trussed hand and foot by the time Adelman had risen to his feet and raced to his side.

They slapped tape over the mouths of the four, stood to survey their work critically, and, by prearrangement, separated immediately. Adelman moved along the east side of the structure toward the front of the house, the M16 in his left hand and his Mossad-issued Jericho 941 prototype automatic pistol in the other.

Luke circled to the rear and, after glancing through the kitchen and into the main hallway, continued quickly to the opposite side of the building.

# Chapter Twenty

Rebecca and Greta rose from the hallway floor, having helped Jason to bind the third intruder. The two women backed away from the hallway, Greta still clutching the iron weapon to her chest.

Jason took the shepherd swiftly back down the main hallway and ordered Max and Margaret — she, still in the sheep-herding "down" position, nose resting on front paws — back into the storage closet. He then turned and strode rapidly back toward the front of the house.

Suddenly he froze.

He found that Greta, facing the hallway, had been seized around the neck from behind. The gunman held her with his left hand. His right arm encircled her at the waist, and in his right hand he held an automatic rifle, muzzle pressed snugly up and under her chin.

He saw a split second later that Rebecca was also held from behind, in an identical manner, by a second gunman. This man was not simply stocky and muscular like his companion. This man was huge: at least six-feet-four-inches in height, and well over 250 pounds.

And finally, in another split second, he saw Adolfus Rademacher. His Luger was aimed at a spot squarely between Jason's eyes, at a distance of no more than ten feet.

All movement and all sounds had stopped.

Jason saw Rademacher now moving his eyes from his target long enough to assess the carnage in the hallway. Rademacher saw in one glance that three of his men were down: two, unconscious; one, conscious and struggling, but bound both by his ankles and his wrists. Duct tape covered his mouth.

Rademacher, now relaxing, permitted himself a smile. In English, he called out to the leader of his remaining troops, those whom he had sent around the east side of the house. "Karl! All clear! Bring your men inside!"

He paused for several moments, listening. Hearing no response, he repeated the invitation in a somewhat louder voice, adding, "Karl, I'll need you and your men to go down to the bomb shelter. The rest of the vermin will be cowering down there."

Silence.

Rademacher's demeanor suddenly changed.

"Karl!" he shouted loudly, now agitated, glancing first toward the front of the house and then toward the back.

Now turning his eyes to Rebecca for the first time, he appraised her coolly. "Ah… the visioner," he said simply.

But then he stepped threateningly toward her, moving the Luger away from the father and toward the daughter. He placed the muzzle of the weapon against Rebecca's temple and, leaning close to her face, hissed at her, "Where are the others, visioner? Where is your husband? Where is your mother?"

And then, like a cold wave of fresh understanding, he changed again. He stepped back from her and looked around wildly, appearing for the first time actually to be afraid. He spun around, waving the Luger in apparent terror.

Then he wheeled to face Rebecca again. "Your brother!" he screamed. "Where is your brother?"

He moved to her side again, and once more placed the muzzle against her temple. *"Where is your brother?"* he shouted at the top of his lungs.

Rebecca did not move… did not blink… did not flinch. She simply stared into the deranged face before her with a calm certainty in the Eternity that awaited her, a transparent confidence that drove her enemy to the edge.

Suddenly he pivoted, moved quickly around her, and placed the Luger against the cheek of Greta van Dijk. He then turned his face back to Rebecca and shouted, *"I'll kill her! I'll kill this miserable Jew-protector right now… right in front of your eyes.…"*

At this, Rebecca was moved to speak. Her voice was low and soft, belying the hardness in her gray eyes as she stared at her enemy.

"No," she said, "I think you want to do something with Greta and me that is more… ritualistic… than simply killing us in this room… in this hallway. You mean to do something more… elaborate… to the two of us.

"You have something *special* in store, Mr. Rademacher. Something more *worthy*… more genuinely *Nazi*.…

"Do you not?"

Rademacher did not reply to this, but, after a moment, he raised the pistol, took quick aim at Jason Manguson's right shoulder, and squeezed off a round. The bullet tore through the shoulder, driving its victim back into the hallway wall. He began slowly to slump toward the floor, left hand covering the wound. After a moment, he sat, silent, bleeding, his eyes on Rademacher, seeming to dare his adversary to fire again.

But Rademacher had already turned his head away. He now spoke in German to his two henchmen. "Take these women to the perimeter and place them on their knees in preparation for proper execution. I will join you there shortly. And I will execute them personally."

Both gunmen immediately spun their captives around to face the west-side entrance to the lodge, the entrance through which Rademacher and the gunmen had just come. Now with each automatic rifle pressed into the small of each woman's back, the gunmen herded the women through the two large sitting rooms and toward the side door onto the west lawn.

Meanwhile, Rademacher, after having begun to follow in the footsteps of the four, suddenly stopped and turned to face the fallen Jason Manguson. He raised the pistol, now from a distance of twenty feet, and once more squared the muzzle with the center of Jason's forehead. Rademacher spoke just loudly enough to be heard by his victim.

"Last chance, Manguson. Where are the others? Where is your son?"

Rebecca, Greta, and their captors were almost to the side door when the pistol's report rang out. Both women cried out and spun toward the sound. But their captors shifted their weapons in one swift, practiced movement to the port arms position and simply blocked the women away from the action. Only then did each man turn his head to ascertain the result of the single shot.

Rebecca could never quite reconstruct the events of the next twenty seconds to her complete satisfaction. But a kaleidoscope of individually clear images remained etched into her mind.

After spinning around to face the gunshot, she first saw a person that she knew instantly, from her brother's descriptions, and from having seen the man's grainy image on the bunker's monitor just moments earlier, to be Jaakov

Adelman. He was in a two-handed pistol-firing position, crouching in the room adjacent the larger sitting room, near the front entrance through which he must have entered.

Rebecca knew in the same flash of recognition that the Mossad agent had just shot Adolfus Rademacher. The enormous bulk of her captor prevented her seeing, as well, that Adelman's single round had torn through Rademacher's right bicep, rendering his right arm and hand useless, the Luger now clattering to the floor. Rademacher had, in fact, been driven to one knee by the impact, but was already beginning to reach for the Luger with his unimpaired left hand.

In the same instant, Rebecca heard Greta's captor open fire on the Mossad agent. And in the very same non-passage of time, Rebecca saw her brother flying through the air to strike that gunman from behind, while Jaakov Adelman crashed, spinning, to the floor.

Luke's rock-hard forearm had driven itself into the back of the gunman's skull, rendering him semi-conscious and sending him to the floor, Luke falling on top of him. Rebecca's own gunman, having released her to join in the assault on Adelman, now attempted to redirect the muzzle of his weapon toward Luke, who was just scrambling to his feet scarcely a rifle's length away.

As Luke reached for the barrel, the enormous gunman, seeing the range was too close to permit an unimpeded shot at Luke, rotated his rifle and swung the stock of the weapon toward Luke's head. But his target was too agile.

Luke ducked quickly, reducing the impact of the stock to a mere glancing blow off his shoulder. Luke then seized the gun barrel with one hand and the giant's trigger hand with the other, and began to grapple with him for control of the weapon.

Rebecca, seeking now to intervene after this near-simultaneous flurry of violent events, crouched quickly and directed a kick with her powerful right leg toward the back of the gargantuan's knee. The knee buckled, and Luke, thus assisted by his twin, bent his adversary backward, the two crashing to the floor at Rebecca's feet, still wrestling desperately for control of the weapon.

And at that instant, yet two more events transpired simultaneously. Luke's pressure on the gunman's trigger hand resulted in a stream of automatic-weapons fire erupting through the cacophony of shouts, groans, thuds, and breaking furniture, dozens of rounds splattering into the west wall of the room. But before Rebecca could move further to assist her brother, she felt the Luger against the back of her skull and heard Adolfus Rademacher, shouting in her ear over the gunfire, *"Move to the door! Move to the door! Do it now!"*

Rebecca, seeing from Greta's immediate movement that the command was given to both women, and wanting to detach Rademacher and his pistol from the presence of her brother, her father, and Jaakov Adelman, moved as ordered. The women found themselves quickly herded out the west-side entrance and onto the grassy apron, and not just by Rademacher.

For Greta's captor quickly joined them. The stocky gunman had almost immediately regained consciousness from Luke's blow to the back of his head, had scrambled to his feet, and now trailed the three out the side door. Already he had begun to level his automatic rifle at the women's backs.

The four, at Rademacher's insistence, then began to run, staggering through the darkness over the uneven ground. They moved erratically but steadily toward the perimeter tree line, Rademacher's right arm and hand dangling uselessly at his side, blood running down his arm and streaming from his fingertips, his left pointing the Luger in the general direction of the two women's backs.

Behind them, Luke and his massive opponent continued to grapple for control of the automatic rifle, rolling from side to side, crashing uncontrolled through and over small pieces of furniture, neither of them gaining sustainable advantage over the other. Near the two combatants lay Jaakov Adelman, hit by numerous rounds from the gunman's weapon, Jason Manguson, bleeding from his deep shoulder wound and fighting to retain consciousness, and, in the hallway with him, three gunmen, one of them conscious and beginning to try to work himself free of his bonds.

Crouched with the others in the basement, within easy earshot of the main-floor events, Matt Clark had tried to picture in his mind each stage of the unfolding events. He first had heard the deliberate, unhurried human and canine steps as the defenders moved out of the kitchen, having been alerted by the two dogs to the intruders' arrival at the perimeter. Soon after, he had heard the sound of breaking glass as the gunmen advanced from the back porch and into the kitchen. He had then heard the sharp concussions from the flash grenades, followed in the first instance by the immediate collapse of the lead gunman and, in the second, by the long, reflexive burst of gunfire before the second gunman also tumbled to the floor. Matt had even heard faintly the dull *thump* of the heavy iron Swastika against the men's skulls.

He had then heard the rushing footfall of the third gunman, thundering down the stairs from the upper floor and into the hallway, followed almost instantly by the scraping and clicking of Max's toenails as the shepherd dug into the hardwood floor, accelerating toward the gunman's back and driving him to the floor. He heard Max's ferocious snarls and the gunman's terrified screams and the defenders' scurrying movements to bind and silence their third victim. Then Matt had attended, tension mounting, to the lengthy silence that had ensued once the two dogs had been returned to their storage closet and Jason Manguson had walked back toward the front of thelodge.

Matt had correctly guessed the meaning of the silence.

Even so, he had been shocked into near-panic when Adolfus Rademacher's calm calls for assistance from one named "Karl" had turned quickly into shouted, agitated threats directed at Rebecca and then at Greta, followed shortly thereafter by a single shot — Matt had no way of knowing at whom it was directed — and then by terse commands from Rademacher to his men, these uttered in German.

In the brief seconds between first threat and first shot, Matt had snatched a long-handled axe from the stack of firewood piled neatly beside the basement stairs and had begun a circuitous sprint through the basement to the alternate set of stairs, those used by Rebecca and Greta earlier in their run to the bomb shelter and back. At length reaching those stairs, Matt had sprinted up to the main floor, taking the steps two at a time, the axe in his good hand.

But events had run well ahead of him.

In the time it had taken him to race through a maze of basement corridors to the alternate stairway and then to reach the ground floor, Matt had heard a second pistol shot, this followed by a burst of automatic-rifle fire. This was succeeded in the same fraction of a second by the sounds of strong men crashing into each other and then onto the floor, by a second lengthy burst of automatic-weapons fire, and by the continued sounds of men grappling, rolling, and fighting for their lives.

Matt's earnest promise to his wife that he would remain in the basement to protect the children, the parents, and the others had melted away in the instant he heard Adolfus Rademacher's screams and threats. He knew at whom those were directed and he feared that indeed his wife would have been the single most likely target for any of the uncountable bullets already fired.

His one desperate hope was that the other sounds he had heard while still crouched with the others in the basement — curious, indecipherable noises from *outside* the lodge, but near at hand, adjacent the building's foundation — had signaled the arrival of the contingent from Israel. Matt knew that Luke and his Mossad comrade were on their way. He had no way of knowing whether or not they could arrive in time.

He could only pray that they would, and that they had.

# Chapter Twenty-one

Emerging into the main-floor hallway, Matt's eyes fell first on Jason Manguson and the three prone gunmen lying haphazardly between Jason and the front door to the lodge. Jason's desperate gaze, Matt saw, was fixed on something in the rooms across the hall from where he sat, slumped, trying to staunch the flow of blood from his shoulder wound.

Matt sped past him and wheeled right into the complex of sitting rooms, the axe still clutched in his good hand. He glimpsed a man's prone body on the floor to his left, but his attention immediately shifted to the whirlwind of action directly in front of him. There, Luke and a man who, improbably, seemed twice Luke's size, fought hand-to-hand, rolling and spinning and twisting for advantage across the floor. Furniture casualties were everywhere.

In the brief seconds that passed while he raced across the floor toward the combatants, Matt saw that Luke's adversary had used his enormous size advantage to encompass his opponent in a bear hug, then to multiply the effects of the hold itself by pressing his full weight onto Luke's chest. Luke strained to loosen the giant's grip and to shift the crushing weight, but with little effect.

Neither man saw Matt approach and neither was prepared for the action he unhesitatingly took. From the instant he had snatched the axe and begun his sprint through the basement maze, thence up the stairwell and into the main hallway, Matt had moved on the assumption that Rebecca, certainly, and Greta and Jason, probably, were dead, wounded or in immediate and lethal danger. And when he had seen his father-in-law and the three gunmen in the hallway, then the bullet-riddled body in the sitting room near the front door, the terror that coursed through him stemmed not from what he saw, but from what he did not see: not his wife, not the Dutch woman, not Adolfus Rademacher.

Arriving at the spot where Luke fought for his life, Matt, without pausing or slowing, simply dipped his shoulder, turned the axe blade up, and drove the blunt head of the implement, lance-like, full into his enemy's massive skull. Matt's intent with the blow, knowing there was not a second to waste, was to render the huge man unconscious, assist Luke to his feet, and then sprint in whatever direction Rademacher had presumably gone with the women.

Matt was stunned at what actually occurred.

The axe head caved in the side of the behemoth's face, opened an enormous wound from which blood began instantly to pour, broke the crushing bear hug and successfully knocked him from his position astride Luke. But not only was the gunman not rendered unconscious, he seemed newly energized by Matt's assault.

He bellowed something in German, rolled one full revolution over and onto his stomach, sprang to his feet with jaw-dropping dexterity for one of such size, then turned and rushed Matt with the force of a high-speed locomotive. Matt, who had immediately dropped the axe to the floor in order to assist Luke to his feet, was unprepared for an impact that sent his 200-pound body flying through the air, tumbling and flailing, to the floor near the body of Jaakov Adelman. Matt, stunned, fought to regain his feet, but was still just beginning to rise when the monster rushed him again, now with the axe held high overhead in both hands.

Matt hurled himself to the side as the axe buried itself in the wall behind him. He tripped over Adelman's body, fell, rolled over, looked up from the floor and saw his adversary advancing again, blood streaming from the ruined left side of his face, the axe now ripped from the wall and once again raised high, already beginning its lethal descent toward Matt's upraised face.

Luke's carefully placed round, fired from Jaakov Adelman's Jericho 941, crashed into the giant's kneecap, collapsing his left leg and causing him to lose control of the axe. The implement tumbled harmlessly to the floor inches from Matt's head, while the colossus, clutching his knee with both hands, crashed to the floor, screaming imprecations in German.

Luke, switching the Jericho's safety switch to the "on" position, tucked the pistol into his belt, pulled Matt to his feet, and ran to his father.

"Dad! Okay?"

"Help me up," insisted Jason Manguson.

Luke and Matt quickly assisted him as he rose unsteadily. "Rebecca and Greta…" Jason said, speaking with difficulty, "Rademacher and another bloke took them out the west door."

Without needing to speak, all three, steeped in their common military understanding of the necessity to place reconnaissance above haste, moved immediately toward the rear of the lodge, the young men assisting Jason Manguson, the giant's screams gradually dissolving into prolonged groans behind them. In the darkened kitchen they moved to the west-facing window and studied the west lawn and tree line.

In the moonlight they saw a chilling sight. Rademacher stood holding the Luger on the two women, both of whom were kneeling, facing away from him and toward the lodge, clearly in position for formal execution. The other gunman stood at the ready, his automatic rifle leveled at the west entrance through which the women had been herded moments earlier.

"Dad," murmured Luke, "are you strong enough to send the dogs?"

"Yes," Jason replied softly.

Thirty seconds later, Jason Manguson, his shoulder wound staunched by a makeshift towel wrap, crept softly onto the darkened back porch with the two canine warriors. Crouching in the shrubbery with the dogs, he focused Margaret's attention on the scene across the west lawn. The border collie's bright eyes looked hard at the two men in the distance, both standing and holding firearms, and at the two women, kneeling, facing away from the men and toward the west door of the lodge.

Jason, satisfied that the automatic rifleman's attention was fixed on the west-side doorway and secondarily on the front entrance to the lodge, rather than the darkened rear of the building, whispered something into Margaret's quivering ears. Then he whispered the same instruction a second time.

Then he simply said to her, "Away!"

And she was gone in a blur of four-legged, black-and-white athleticism and intelligence, taking the sort of wide, circular route to her target that border collies have for generations understood in their very bones. In mere seconds she was visible to no one, even her master.

Adolfus Rademacher, oblivious to the threat to himself and his colleague now materializing from the darkened rear of the lodge, focused on his consuming desire: to achieve formal execution of the young woman who had, without leaving children or husband, orchestrated the destruction of his intricate and comprehensive plan… this young mother who had transformed the plan's graceful geometry into grotesque wreckage. Almost equally, he focused upon her Dutch companion, this wretched woman who had humiliated him as a young Nazi occupation officer.

Now that he had them both, he wanted formality. He wanted style. He wanted prolonged terror. He wanted these two women to contemplate the certainty of their deaths, and to do so at length.

But now, as he leveled the Luger at the backs of their heads, his left arm and hand only slightly unsteady from the pain and loss of blood in his damaged right bicep, he saw no terror whatever. He saw two women kneeling perfectly erect, shoulders back, heads bowed. And then he heard the low voice of the Englishwoman, praying. And as he began to attend to her words, he realized that she was praying not for herself but for him!

For him!

He heard only bits of her prayer before he snapped. The phrases that he heard were spoken with a calm and sure confidence that maddened him: "… and please forgive him and his men, Father, for they truly do not know what they do… they know not that 'Inasmuch as ye have done it unto the least of these….'"

And, hearing these words of the Christ — words from a parable that he, in fact, actually knew well from his boyhood Bible classes, now applied by his nemesis to himself — Rademacher broke completely. Until then icy clear in crisis, always and at all times, he was suddenly undone.

From the depths of his twisted being, he brought forth the primal scream of the savage that he had willed himself to become. He raised the Luger toward the Heavens in which he knew his Ultimate Adversary resided, and squeezed off three rounds in rapid, frenzied succession.

Then, after a brief pause during which the echo of the shots ricocheted endlessly through the woods, he lowered the handgun again with the intention of ending forever the earthly lives of these, his feminine bêtes noir. But as he leveled the Luger for the final time, he saw and felt something incomprehensible.

Canine fangs, seemingly materializing from nowhere, ripped into his left wrist, causing an involuntary twitch of his trigger finger which, in turn, launched a fourth round from the Luger's muzzle directly into the soft earth between the kneeling women.

Rademacher's henchman, ten feet away, was distracted first by his employer's scream, then by the three shots fired into the air, and now by the border collie's emergence from the woods behind them. He brought his weapon to bear on the twisting, growling animal, but saw immediately that he could not shoot the dog without hitting the man.

He froze, uncertain.

In that attitude he was slammed to the ground by more than one hundred pounds of hurtling German shepherd, the animal's powerful jaws fully encircling the victim's throat in his carefully taught bite-and-hold attack. The gunman was finished instantly, dropping his weapon as he fell screaming, utterly terrified of the teeth that held his neck, and thus, his life, at their mercy.

Adolfus Rademacher was, in one sense, more fortunate. His canine attacker, less than half the size and weight of her partner, had gashed his left wrist, ruined his aim and caused him to fumble the Luger into the grass. But Rademacher was still on his feet and still ready and able to fight.

He kicked viciously at Margaret, making glancing contact, and, as she darted around him, kicked again. And yet again.

As she backed away from him once more, growling, feinting left and right, he, in frustration, at length turned away from her to find the Luger, nestled somewhere, he knew, in the grass behind him. Now turning toward the spot where the gun lay, glancing nervously over his shoulder at the darting animal, he stooped and reached for his weapon with his freshly slashed left arm and hand.

The weapon was not there.

He looked up.

In the ample moonlight he saw that Rebecca Manguson stood facing him, holding the barrel of the Luger between her left-hand fingers and thumb as though it were something slimy that had just emerged from the mud.

Beside her stood Greta van Dijk, pastel dress undisturbed.

Flanking the two women were Luke Manguson and Matt Clark.

Rademacher stared for long moments, taking into his unwilling mind the fullness of the catastrophe.

And then slowly, at first almost imperceptibly, he sank to his knees on the soft ground. After pausing momentarily, he then fell yet more slowly forward to a hands-and-knees stance, his head drooping. He rested in that position for perhaps fifteen seconds. Then he lowered his forehead and chest gradually into the moist grass.

And then, his movements becoming steadily slower, he rolled carefully onto his side in a kind of slow-motion despair. He then covered his face with both hands.

And finally he curled into a compact ball of unmitigated self-loathing.

Luke accepted the Luger from his sister and kissed her tenderly on the forehead. Matt walked to the still-terrified and fully prone henchman, picked up the man's weapon with his good hand, and said something to Max. The shepherd then, and only then, relaxed his grip, rose, circled a short distance away from his prey, and sat down, eyes still on the hapless gunman.

Rebecca, relieved of the Luger, immediately dropped to her haunches and opened her arms to Margaret. The border collie flew to her, confident only then that she had done what had been wanted of her. Rebecca was conscious of the fact that Margaret's role in the fracas had comprised a substantial intellectual challenge. Once she had completed her great circle approach, she had been acting unnaturally, in accordance not with her genetic make-up, but with Jason's training regimen. That regimen had added a dimension to her repertoire quite unrelated to her impulse to circle widely dispersed creatures — sheep, children, other dogs — and to bring them together into a tightly packed group. Rebecca murmured reassurance and gratitude into Margaret's eager ears, and the border collie for the first time began to relax, burrowing her nose lovingly into Rebecca's rib cage.

Only then did Rebecca, still rubbing Margaret's ears with both hands, turn her head to assess the damage to her brother and her husband. She saw that

Luke's abrasions were numerous and impressive, but she also saw that he was not wounded in any substantial way.

And she saw that Matt was looking at her, smiling and unhurt.

"Dad?" she said, looking from husband to brother.

"One round in the shoulder, sis, but okay and in charge," said Luke.

"The agent?"

Luke shook his head. "No chance, I'm afraid, Rebecca. 'My life for yours.'"

Rebecca, still rubbing Margaret's ears, nodded and looked down, eyes closed, and for long seconds offered up her prayer for Jaakov Adelman.

At length she looked up at her brother and asked, "And Mum and the twins?"

"All safe," Luke replied. "I'm sure Dad has the other basement people — the Clarks and the van Dijks — helping him attend to the other prisoners."

Rebecca gave a long sigh. Then she smiled, gave Margaret a final, tender pat to the rib cage, rose to her feet and turned toward her enemy, who was still curled into himself, his face covered with both hands, in the fetal position. She moved three deliberate steps to Rademacher's pathetic form and kneeled beside it.

Greta and the men watched her, intrigued. Both animals lay down at the same moment as though they had been given the "down" command — they had not been addressed at all — seemingly as engrossed in Rebecca's gesture, in their canine fashion, as were Luke, Greta, and Matt.

Rademacher's henchman, curious, started to sit up. Max turned his head and fixed him with a baleful glare. The man returned to his prone position.

Rebecca resisted the impulse to place her hands on Rademacher's shoulders, fearful that both he and she might recoil in spontaneous disgust. Yet she remained near enough to do so if she chose, her knees just inches from her whimpering adversary, his face still covered with both hands.

She briefly composed herself and bowed her head once more as she approached the end of a long day filled with prayer. Her hands were now folded together in her lap.

Greta, Luke, and Matt — the men knowing that Max would not relax his vigilance toward the gunman — closed their eyes, as well. And in the night silence, they were able to hear Rebecca's low, measured voice.

They realized gratefully, from her first words, that she was including each of them in her prayer.

"Eternal Father, we give Thee thanks and praise that Thou hath brought us safe through the dangers that have compassed us this night. We give thanks for these two brave animals whose love, intelligence, and courage have helped us to prevail against the face of the enemy. And especially, Father, we ask Thy mercy upon this man who lies before us, destroyed. Please inspire him with Thy Holy Spirit. Consume him with Thy love. Give him yet another chance to choose Thy side, not that of the Enemy. Help him, Father, to understand that, as with Thy ancient servant Joshua, the time has come to choose. Now. We pray this in the name of Thy Son, our Savior, Jesus Christ. *Amen.*"

After a long moment, she opened her eyes and looked down at Adolfus Rademacher. He had removed his hands from his face.

His eyes met hers.

After a long moment, she leaned forward slightly and touched his shoulder. "Choose you this day," she said softly. Then she leaned closer to him.

And again, in a broad, urgent whisper, she said: *"Choose you this day."*

# Chapter Twenty-two

Now seventy-two hours, almost to the minute, had passed since Rebecca had prayed over the defeated figure of Adolfus Rademacher. And on this Tuesday evening in center-city Birmingham, a motley assortment filled the northwest corner of a waiting room just down the second-floor west corridor from Jaakov Adelman's hospital room.

They by now understood what had happened to the Mossad agent and, as well, how his life had been saved.

Luke's first impression that Saturday night — that Adelman could not have survived the fusillade he had faced during the melee — had turned out to be gloriously wrong. At least a dozen rounds had apparently been directed at Adelman from close range. Three had struck home. All three had missed vital organs.

Luke's quick judgment that his comrade had been killed stemmed equally from his assessment of the amount of blood that pooled immediately around Adelman's torso and from the obvious fact that Adelman was not conscious. Luke had had no time to examine the agent, and had simply assumed that the dozen or more shots he had heard, the amount of blood, and the inert posture meant death.

In fact, Jaakov Adelman was very much alive. He had struck his head in crashing to the floor and had been rendered unconscious by the fall itself. And one of the three rounds that had struck him had punctured an artery in his left arm, just above the elbow. His greatest danger lay in the possibility that he would simply bleed to death before anyone could attend to him. But help was coming.

Once Jason Manguson had sent the dogs on their way and had seen the outcome of the clash on the west lawn, he had — his own shoulder wound having been wrapped effectively by his son — moved swiftly to accomplish a host of needed actions.

First, he had called the others from the basement. Amelia van Dijk took the infants in her arms, and Andruw, Elisabeth, Martha, and Paul moved swiftly to Jason's side, awaiting orders. As they arrived, he assigned them to attend to, and truss where needed, Rademacher's downed men, both inside and outside the lodge. Next, he had run to the west entrance and shouted for assistance from Rebecca and Greta, while Luke, Matt, and the dogs remained with their two prisoners.

As the two women arrived in the lodge, he assigned Greta — with translation assistance from Andruw — to help Andruw and the other three with the downed prisoners in the house and on the east lawn, keeping Rebecca with him to attend to Jaakov Adelman, whether living or dead. Together they moved to Adelman's side and ascertained his actual condition.

Feeling a strong, regular pulse, they fashioned an effective tourniquet for Adelman's left arm, using the agent's own belt. The blood flow was staunched the moment Rebecca cinched the belt tight.

Father and daughter then looked into each other's eyes. And simultaneously they nodded their satisfaction at the decisiveness of the outcome.

The moment — a uniquely tender one under the circumstances — quickly passed, and they returned to the business at hand.

"Rebecca," said Jason, "run to the bunker and get on the emergency line. Contact Scotland Yard in London. When you get one of the officers, use Sid Belton's name. The officer will confirm the connection in seconds.

"Then fill them in. Put the situation in terms of 'armed intruders' at our lodge. Speak of automatic weapons, of gunfire, of wounded men. Tell them we need law enforcement and medical personnel equally... and several very large paddy wagons."

"No need then," replied Rebecca, "to try to explain anything about visions and Mossad agents and plots to murder the Righteous Among Nations...."

"Exactly," said her father, smiling. "Our enemies have conducted an armed assault on private citizens on private property. Their own methods have been turned on themselves.

"They have pulled down deep Heaven on their heads."

At this last, Rebecca beamed, recalling the familiar C. S. Lewis reference. Then she squeezed her father's hand, rose, and ran from the room.

And so it was on the Tuesday evening following that the mood was upbeat and expectant in the crowded northwest corner of the hospital's second-floor west waiting room. Four of those present had been there continuously since shortly after law enforcement and medical personnel had arrived at the lodge Saturday night and had taken ten prisoners into custody, and, in addition, had taken both Jaakov Adelman and Jason Manguson to the nearest well-staffed emergency room for gunshot surgery.

The four three-day veterans of hospital cafeteria food and hard-surface sleeping conditions — all four had brought sleeping bags and had slept on the waiting-room floor — included Elisabeth, Luke, and Martha and Paul Clark. By now, on Tuesday night, the foursome was tired but excited both by the fact that their ranks had been swelled by recent arrivals, and by their prospects for going back home that very evening.

They now numbered thirteen. Twenty-four hours after his admission for shoulder surgery to remove Adolfus Rademacher's bullet and to repair ligament damage, Jason Manguson had been released and had immediately joined the original foursome, sleeping on the waiting-room floor with them. Rebecca and Matt had adopted a complicated tag-team schedule that meant one of them was continuously at the lodge with the twins, while the van Dijks — Greta, Amelia, and Andruw — had taken Tiny back to her London home on Sunday afternoon.

But the van Dijks had not stayed there long, because the remaining four members of their small army had arrived in London Monday evening by air, and had motored to Birmingham immediately. And so it was that on this Tuesday evening the assemblage nearly overwhelmed the waiting room's seating capacity.

Not only was the original four-member contingent present, supplemented by Jason Manguson — right arm held in an elaborate sling — but, at that moment, also by eight others. The eight included Rebecca, Greta, Amelia and Andruw van Dijk, and, since late the previous night, Kory van Dijk — her right hand heavily bandaged — Eleanor Chapel, Sidney Belton, and, the focus of much of the group's attention from the moment of her arrival, young Sari.

The child continually clung to Kory, her small right hand nearly always in Kory's left.

At this particular moment, the group was on high alert in hopes that Jaakov Adelman would be released to them as soon as his physicians completed their twice daily review of his vital signs and his general progress toward full recovery. The chief physician had said that she viewed the chances as "about 60 percent" that she would be able to release Adelman that very night.

But when she appeared at the head of the corridor, her eyes searching for her contact-of-record — Luke Manguson — her expressive face made the verdict clear to everyone present before she had spoken a word. Jaakov Adelman would not be leaving the hospital with them that night.

Luke strode across the room to meet the physician.

She shook his hand, then turned and walked several steps back toward Adelman's room, beckoning for him to follow, thereby ensuring that their conversation would be private. Those in the waiting room could see the two of them thirty feet down the corridor, but could hear nothing of the ensuing conversation.

"Sorry, Lieutenant," she said truthfully, "but I need your colleague here for at least another twenty-four. He's still weak. And I want to see a little more progress on that left-arm wound. That's the really nasty one.

"The permanence of the damage to that nerve is still uncertain. And another twenty-four wouldn't hurt on his recovery from the concussion, either. Sorry to disappoint, but I think we'd better wait."

Luke thanked her for her professionalism and for her courtesy, and added, "Do you think several of us might actually visit him right now for a half hour or so, ma'am? I think it might do him good, and I *know* it would do *us* good."

She smiled and looked down as she considered the request. Finally she nodded. "Yes, all right. Let's say thirty minutes. You and two others. No more than a half hour. No more than three people…. And don't allow him to do most of the talking, even if he seems up to it. He's actually not."

She then looked down the corridor at the mass of humanity staring their way and asked with obvious bemusement, "How will you select only two from this throng, Lieutenant?"

Luke glanced back at his extended family.

The physician was surprised to see the color in Luke Manguson's face change perceptibly as he answered.

"Well, Jaakov will surely want to meet my twin sister, ma'am… and… ah… he'll… ah… want to renew his acquaintance with my… ah… with the young woman with whom he worked in Israel during the last few days."

The physician crossed her arms over her chest and adopted a severe demeanor.

"I see, Lieutenant. It is *Mr. Adelman* who will want to spend time with that young woman — the one with the bandaged hand — who is looking this way as if her world started and ended with you? Yes. Yes, I think I understand perfectly."

Luke Manguson looked down at his shoes and smiled.

Jaakov Adelman looked pale and drawn, but he was clearly energized to receive the three visitors. From his nearly prone position, he shook Luke Manguson's hand firmly, while Luke leaned down and into his comrade's chest, seeking the delicate balance between an embrace that would communicate deeply felt affection and gratitude, on the one hand, and respect for Adelman's damaged condition, on the other. They held this position for some time, and then Luke rose and stood back to allow Kory to come forward and to enfold Adelman in her own one-handed embrace.

As she stood, Adelman looked quizzically at the heavily bandaged right hand.

"It's going to be fine, Mr. Adelman," she said confidently. "No permanent damage… probably."

He gave her a look that said, "Probably?"

She laughed. "I might have difficulty writing for a while… maybe always. But I hardly ever handwrite anymore. I mostly type."

He gave her another look that said, "How is that any better?"

She laughed again. "Well, I might be forced into four-finger typing with my good hand and one-finger typing with my bad hand. That's not so terrible, it seems to me. Poor Matt has no use of his entire left arm and hand, and never will."

Then she turned very serious. "You know, Mr. Adelman, this little army does not often come out of its battles unscathed and unimpaired. Look at these twins' faces."

She stopped and looked at Rebecca's V-shaped scar on her right cheek and at Luke's shotgun-pocked left neck and lower jaw. "We are blessed just to accomplish our tasks and to survive, I think."

Adelman nodded, but seemed already to be tiring.

Seeing this, Luke turned quickly to Rebecca. "Rebecca Manguson Clark," he said with exaggerated formality, "may I present Mr. Jaakov Adelman, lately of Tel Aviv, Israel, who does *not* work for a secret intelligence agency, you understand…."

Adelman, momentarily enlivened by Luke's humor, shook his head and rolled his eyes in mock disgust at this, while Rebecca stepped forward and shook hands with the patient.

"It's so good to meet you, Mr. Adelman," she said, smiling. "Luke has told me a great deal about you… and about what you do *not* do for a living."

Then she turned serious. "Thank you, Jaakov, for fighting side-by-side with my brother throughout all this… for extricating Luke and Eleanor and the detective from their entrapment in New York… for saving their lives there and then for supporting them — and Kory — time and again in these recent days. I'm so grateful to you."

Adelman nodded weakly. "You are most welcome, Mrs. Clark. And let me express my gratitude to you for supplying us repeatedly with data which we could have obtained from no other source than you… you, personally.

"I… that is, we… have known of your…of your work… for some time now… but to be personally the recipient of your… your… 'special connections,' so to say… has been my privilege."

Rebecca started to respond, but stopped when she saw that he wished to continue.

"I just want to add, Mrs. Clark, that your repeated success at providing data that could only be from the Divine Source has meant a great deal to me personally… not just professionally. I have come to look at my own Hebrew history a little differently as a result of your interventions. I have become newly aware of the meaning of our long history and of my own life in the context of that history. And I think…."

Luke, smiling, interrupted him gently. "Jaakov, stop talking. I promised the doctor that we would concentrate on talking to you, not listening to you. So, stop. We understand what Rebecca does. We understand what she means… to all of us. We appreciate your feelings… and we can guess where all this has taken you… but you must stop talking."

Adelman smiled once more, a fleeting smile that in itself bespoke his physical weakness. He closed his eyes for a moment, then opened them again, and said softly, "Okay. I'm listening, Lieutenant."

Luke pulled a chair up to the side of Adelman's bed, sat, and leaned forward to provide details from the previous seventy-two hours, details that he knew the agent desperately wished to have. The women stepped to the other two chairs, pulled them nearer the bed, and prepared to listen and, where needed, to supplement Luke's account with their own perspectives.

Luke quickly covered the rapid-fire action that had transpired after Adelman had been shot, and Rebecca explained how her father had sent her to the bunker to contact Scotland Yard.

"As Dad told me," she explained, "when he sent me to the bunker after we had attended to you, Jaakov, Mr. Rademacher and his people had finally done something on which the law could act. Finally we could just say that ten heavily armed intruders had come onto our private property, and that they were wielding automatic weapons and handguns. And we could say that my father, the property owner, had been shot by one of the intruders inside his own home.

"The response was immediate and very impressive."

After a moment, Adelman nodded his understanding.

Then he spoke, sounding slightly stronger now, after having simply listened while Luke and Rebecca had given their complementary accounts of the action on Saturday evening.

"Scotland Yard, yes," he said quietly. "But what of MI6, CIA, Mossad?"

Though Adelman had directed the question to Luke, it was Kory who bounced up from her chair, stepped to the side of the bed, and answered.

"I was with the detective — and Dr. Chapel and Sari, of course — throughout the weekend, Mr. Adelman. Mr. Belton was on the phone continually with 'his buddies,' as he likes to say, at Scotland Yard and, less often, with all three of those agencies you mention. I eventually came to see that they all understand — at least the key players understand — exactly what you and your own colleagues in Tel Aviv have come to understand: that there are certain aspects in the analysis of these yearly events that cannot be meaningfully investigated beyond a certain point."

She paused for a moment, nodding thoughtfully to herself.

"It appears to me," she continued, "that most of the key players —  in Tel Aviv and within the other agencies, too — have even come to use your term, Mr. Adelman: the *Rebekka Yahalomin*… and to know exactly what it means."

A lengthy silence ensued.

The three hospital-room visitors spent these moments peering closely at the patient, trying to determine whether or not he had fallen into an exhausted sleep. Finally, exchanging glances, they prepared to leave quietly when they saw the agent's eyes open once more.

Jaakov Adelman frowned, looking at them accusingly.

"Trying to sneak out, eh?" he said, the corners of his mouth threatening a smile. "Don't even think about it."

Delighted at this indication both of Adelman's alertness and of his recovering energy levels, the threesome returned to his bedside and stood, smiling down at their comrade, waiting for his next request. And soon it came.

"Big picture?" he said cryptically.

"Say more," said Luke.

"Terrorists… Israel… Friesland…."

Luke nodded. "Got it," he said.

And so, still standing at bedside, the visitors provided their big-picture summary.

"The Megiddo three-hundred are all in custody in Israel," said Luke, "separated from each other, held in probably two dozen different prisons. Some will be extradited. Some will be held. Some will be tried. It's too soon to know much.

"The attack Saturday night in Greta's hometown was taken down beautifully. Your Israeli agents, with permission from the Dutch government, got to Ferwerd in time, collected all six of the Righteous and their families at dusk, and sequestered them about an hour before the first of what would have been six Nazi raids Saturday evening.

"There were eighteen Nazis involved there, altogether. We assume that Rademacher had most of that group standing by in Amsterdam, awaiting the files and a commanding officer. And we guess that Rademacher sent one Lear from Jordan to Holland with those six files and a commander — possibly one of the four henchmen he had with him at the fortress underground — and took a second Lear to Birmingham with another cadre that had been waiting for him in Jordan.

"One way or another, he ended up with a force strength of eighteen people in Holland and another ten, counting himself, at the lodge. When you think about it, Jaakov, eighteen in Friesland and ten at the lodge — armed to the teeth — should have been more than enough to wipe out everybody he had in mind. I mean, every single person. And yet, not one individual in Friesland was even injured, to say nothing of being killed, and here in the UK our father's shoulder wound represents the full extent of the damage. It's absolutely astonishing, when you think about it."

"Miraculous," corrected Adelman.

"Yes, miraculous," acknowledged Luke.

"And," Luke added, "they are all in custody. All of them. Extradition will be sought for each one."

Rebecca stepped closer to her brother. "Luke, our father's wound is not exactly the *full* list of damages. Jaakov's injuries...."

Luke laughed softly, as did Adelman. "Well... right... I meant that, considering Rademacher's actual targets...."

Adelman nodded. "Right. Luke wasn't counting me — the accidental cannon fodder from Tel Aviv."

Soft laughter all around.

Adelman thought for a moment. "Sari?" he said, addressing Kory.

She nodded, smiling. "That was the other thing that Detective Belton worked so hard on while we were still in Israel. He and Dr. Chapel together.

"They persuaded your friends in Tel Aviv to work directly with MI6 and MI5 in London, and then with other branches of both governments, to smooth out the legalities involved in bringing the child into a London-area household. I think it's actually going to work, Mr. Adelman. You and Mr. Belton are, it seems to me, much more influential than you want to take credit for."

"But... Sari is no ordinary child," noted Adelman thoughtfully. "How will she...?"

"You're absolutely right, sir," said Kory. "She's not really... socialized to live in what we regard as normal English conditions with a normal English family and in normal English schools. But already we have a family who wants very badly to take her in and attempt the job."

At this, all three looked at Kory in surprise.

"My parents and my aunt are already discussing details with the appropriate agencies," Kory continued. "Aunt Greta plans to move to the UK, to live with my parents, and to help raise this little girl. There's much to be done, but they're optimistic that it will work out to Sari's benefit. This child has much to offer."

At Kory's closing remark, Adelman's chief physician entered the room briskly and without knocking. The visitors stepped back away from the bed while she strode to the patient's side and began to check the monitors that traced and blinked and beeped near his head.

After several moments, she nodded in apparent satisfaction.

Then, still without speaking or acknowledging the presence of the three guests, she circled to the other side of the bed, moving Luke away with a touch of her hand. She lifted Adelman's wounded left arm and examined it. Then she took his left hand in her left in handshake position, and asked him to squeeze her hand.

He tried. Nothing happened.

She frowned and shook her head.

"I don't quite like how this arm and hand are progressing, Mr. Adelman," she said. "I should have thought we'd be able to get some response by now. I'm quite disappointed."

Adelman looked up at the doctor.

"You think the damage is permanent?" he said.

After a moment, she nodded her head.

"Yes," she said finally. "I do think it could be permanent."

Adelman continued to look the doctor in the eye, seeming to challenge her assessment.

"Oh, I'm not giving up, Mr. Adelman. Not at all. But I want you to know I'm surprised and disappointed. I don't like to keep things from my patients. And so I'm not. There should be a response by now."

Adelman nodded. "I appreciate your saying just what you think, ma'am."

The surgeon smiled. "Good," she said.

Then, after a moment, she added, turning to Luke, "That's it, Lieutenant. Interview over. Out. All three of you. Out."

Within seconds of his visitors' exit, Jaakov Adelman fell once more into a medication-assisted sleep. His physician made her final checks, entered her notes into his bedside log, turned down the lights in the small room, and left.

So it was that, moments later, the room was empty of visitors and of hospital personnel when a young girl glided noiselessly into the room. She wore a simple head scarf and a floor-length garment suggestive of her Middle Eastern origins. She smiled at the sight of the sleeping Mossad agent, now safe in this medical sanctuary after his life had so nearly been ended only a few nights before.

Young Sari was serene, her countenance untroubled, despite the fact that she had been uprooted from her native surroundings and transported swiftly, first to Jerusalem and then to England, all in the company of people about whose existence she had known nothing until the Saturday night whirlwind of action on the slopes of Mount Carmel. But under the placid façade there was a mounting turbulence in this child of a violent world in which her people's enemy had been identified and marked for her from the time of her birth. And that enemy, in the form of a man who was not only a Jew, but a Zionist and a Mossad agent, lay before her now, helpless.

As she drew near Jaakov Adelman's bed, her sweet, childish smile transformed itself into a primitive snarl, one that changed her countenance in a flash from that of innocent girl to single-minded murderess. It was the countenance no longer of a child but of a killer who appeared as a creature of no ascertainable age. She was the executioner, and, like all executioners, seemingly ageless.

She had become, quite simply, the avenger.

She slipped the knife from her garments, stepped so close to the bedside that her abdomen pressed against the starched sheets, and raised the knife high above her head to strike downward into the sleeping agent's jugular vein. Her furious eyes staring fixedly, trancelike, at the exposed jugular, she did not see Detective Sid Belton or his heavy wooden cane as it descended violently over her head and into her wrist, the sharp crack of wood on bone awakening Jaakov Adelman in time for him to glimpse the four-inch knife blade as it flew from the girl's hand and tumbled harmlessly onto his pillow, a scant two inches from his neck.

# CHAPTER TWENTY-THREE

On Friday of the week Jaakov Adelman found himself released from the hospital and subsequently enthroned, under Elisabeth Manguson's watchful eye, in the lodge's best guest room, Kory van Dijk and Luke Manguson sat down to finish the strawberries and cream they had begun in a center-city London inn two weeks earlier. Since they had, after some discussion, chosen to regard this occasion as a continuation of Kory's abbreviated birthday celebration, they had decided to dress as they had then: the freshly cleaned and pressed light yellow sundress for Kory, and the burgundy knit shirt and khaki trousers for Luke.

They sat facing each other at the same small table they had occupied two Fridays before. They found that they were no longer nervous with each other, but relaxed, confident, comfortable. They had emerged from the cauldron alive, and the shared experience had changed them, both as individuals and as a couple.

"Can you believe this, Luke?" said Kory incredulously. "Can you believe we were sitting here just two weeks ago? Can you believe what has happened since then?"

Luke smiled. "You know, I actually can. This is the way it has been every June for four years now, Kory. The visions have hit each year like clockwork: the cathedral visions that first year, the arena visions the second, the Amalfi visions last year, and now what we'll doubtless call the Jerusalem visions. And as soon as the visions hit, each time, there has been this incredible cyclone that has swept us along and then *wham!* It's over. And we always look back at what seemed like years while we lived it, and realize it's been just a few days.

"I think I'm getting accustomed to it," he added, only half jokingly.

"I can't imagine getting accustomed to this, Luke," Kory replied, thoughtfully licking a small dollop of cream from the spoon she held a little awkwardly in her left hand. "And I must admit," she added, her face suddenly serious, "I find that Sari's attack on Mr. Adelman has left me angry and a little sad… and a little…."

Luke reached across the small table and lightly covered her bandaged right hand with his left. "A little confused, Kory?" he said softly.

She smiled, embarrassed. "Yes. A little confused. I was so certain that Sari loved me. Loved us. Loved all of us. I just don't understand…."

Luke placed his spoon on the saucer's edge and sat back in his chair.

"It's okay," he said carefully, watching her intently, "to be confused by what she did, Kory. Really. It's okay."

She shook her head. "I don't think it is, Luke. Rebecca is never confused. You are never confused. Your parents are never confused. Eleanor and Sid are never confused. No one seemed truly confused by what she did, except me. Nobody in our whole family was confused by this at all… but me."

Luke lifted his spoon again and toyed thoughtfully with the berries before replying. He did not want simply to shrug this off. Kory was serious. She was obviously not just looking for attention, nor was she simply whining. She saw this 'family' — he noted that she had included Eleanor Chapel, Sid Belton, and herself in her list of family members, not just himself, his sister, and their parents — as essentially unaffected by what could only be termed an attempted murder.

"Well," he began at length, "you'd be wrong to think we were not surprised, Kory. If we'd had an inkling of what she was planning, we'd never have brought her to the hospital at all. I gave it no thought.

"It was only the detective who saw something in Sari's behavior while you four were still in Israel that made him wary. He told me that night, after the incident, that he noticed she was… well… different around Jewish people — especially Jewish men — during those several days you were in Jerusalem."

"He didn't say anything to me about that," she replied.

"No. He often sees things that put him on guard, and he often says nothing about those things unless they develop into something more pronounced. In this case, Tuesday night, when you and I and Rebecca got back to the waiting room and Sari excused herself to go to the ladies room, only he took any notice. That's when he picked up his cane and hobbled down the hall. He was behind Adelman's hospital room door when the child entered the room."

"But Luke…," she began again.

"Kory," he interrupted, "we were surprised, but we were not confused. She has been taught this murderous attitude toward the Jewish people from the time she could understand language. She is a loving child… but not to the people she has been taught to despise with all her heart."

Kory looked away. She shook her head. "How can she love me and hate him? I don't understand. I just don't."

After a moment, he leaned across the table again and covered Kory's good left hand with his right. "Have you talked with your parents and your aunt about their plan to take her into their home?"

She nodded. "Oh, yes. This morning, in fact. No change in those plans."

"Really?" said Luke in mild surprise.

"Really," she confirmed. "She *does* love us. She loves *us*. My parents and my aunt believe that they can teach her to love *all*."

Luke nodded somberly.

"See?" she said again, a small smile on her lips. "My parents and my aunt are not confused by this. Only me."

After a moment Luke, his hand still covering hers, spoke once more to her confusion. "Kory, thoroughly prudent people would not have formed the plan to take Sari into their home in the first place. And thoroughly prudent people would certainly not take her into their home after the incident in Jaakov's room.

"And thoroughly prudent people would not have taken all those Jewish people into their homes to save them from the Holocaust. Your Aunt Greta was not thoroughly prudent to take that young Jewish woman into her home in 1943.

"But prudence is not at the top of Our Lord's list, is it? *My life for yours* does not, in fact, leave a great deal of room for prudence as a top priority in life. This is a risk. Your parents and your aunt are taking that risk straight on."

Kory raised her left hand, lifting Luke's right hand as she did, and kissed his hand lightly. "So… I'm really not confused? I'm just forgetting that the blueprint of the universe does not include prudence as top priority?"

He smiled broadly. Then he nodded.

"And Kory," he said after a moment, "I think we all — all of us in our family, as you've so nicely labeled our whole group — just try to remember that… well… it's all just obedience."

He paused, looking at her closely.

She looked back just as closely.

"It's just daily obedience," he repeated. "Whatever it is you've seen in Rebecca and me and the rest of this family… it's just a group of people who are trying to be obedient to God.

"My sister is focused on obedience. So, she feeds her babies and attends to her husband and talks to her parents — our parents — and thinks about me, her brother… and now about you, her brother's… ah… friend… and, when the visions arrive… she does what is necessary to be obedient. And, whatever that entails, she does it fast, and she does it thoroughly, and she does it well.

"And notice how, in this instance, being obedient to God meant staying at home, in the lodge, with her babies. The thing became personally and physically dangerous for her only when the evil came to her… came seeking her… came to the lodge itself."

Kory looked down, thinking.

After a moment she looked up again and replied. "I think I see, Luke. I really do. And I think I'm not there yet. I still have to think very hard about how to look at things and what to do about… about *confusing* things. But I accept the possibility that I will get there and will be more like you and your sister and the others.

"And I *want* to."

At this, Luke lifted his right hand and cupped the side of her face gently.

"I'll be there with you, you know. We've been in our courtship for two whole weeks now. And it has been a most uncommon two weeks.

"But, going forward, every minute that you want me to be there with you, Kory van Dijk, I'll be right there. Right there at your side."

With his right hand still cradling the left side of her face, she beamed.

"I know, Luke," she said softly, turning her face slightly into his hand.

"I know."

~ End ~

# Acknowledgement and Tribute

Greta van Dijk's character, while wholly fictional in this novel, is based upon the life of an actual person. Sietske Postma was a twenty-eight-year-old school teacher — a Christian — living in her native Ferwerd, Holland, in 1943, when a twenty-two-year-old blonde Jewish woman, Noortje Hegt, knocked on her door. For two full years the Postma family hid Noortje "in the open," in the midst of the German occupying forces.

Sietske never allowed Noortje (who took the Christian name Franciska during her time with Sietske) to leave the house without her, risking her own life every day and every night in order to save this young woman — a complete stranger when she appeared on the Postmas' doorstep — from the death camps. At war's end, they learned that Noortje's mother and sister had been murdered at Auschwitz.

More than three decades later, in July of 1976, Sietske Postma was inducted into the Righteous Among Nations at *Yad Vashem* in Jerusalem. The two women, by then in their vigorous fifties (and Noortje the married mother of two children), happily turned over the earth for the planting of Sietske's carob tree along the Avenue of the Righteous.

The full account of this astonishing true story, along with five other similar stories, may be read in Peter Hellman's outstanding work titled *When Courage Was Stronger Than Fear* (Marlowe & Company; New York; 2004). The author, in each case, interviewed both the rescuers and the rescued at the time of writing his accounts.